SOLOMON'S DREAMS
POSSESSION

ERIC SUDDOTH

RISING SMOKE PUBLISHING

Unless otherwise indicated, Scripture quotations are from:
Holy Bible, New International Version®, NIV©
1973, 1978, 1984, 2011 by Biblica, Inc. ®
Used by permission. All rights reserved worldwide.

Rising Smoke Publishing
ISBN 978-1-949869-25-5

Then Solomon awoke –
and he realized it had been a dream.
1 Kings 3:15

SUNDAY

CHAPTER 1

Are you on your way? he texted as he squatted behind Mr. Lukin's detached one-car garage, which housed his collection of golden trophies from years of coaching high school sports. He waited for the response as he peeked once again at the many shiny plastic statues showcased on makeshift shelves of old cardboard boxes and plastic containers covered with a thick layer of dust.

Almost there, his phone lit up, breaking through the early dusk evening at a quarter to seven.

His smirk started to grow along with his heart rate. He leaned his back against the off-white aluminum siding, sliding his body down to the ground. The light from the moon wasn't powerful enough to spotlight his hiding spot if a neighbor peeked over Mr. Lukin's wooden fence. His eyes were slowly adjusting, allowing him to find his duffle bag on the ground beside him.

He gripped the metal latch slowly, unzipping his black Adidas bag. The unclasping of teeth broke the silence, causing him to wince at the deafening sound. He stopped and looked around, making sure no one was listening nearby. The only thing he heard was the cough of an old pickup truck muffler in the distance, allowing him to breathe a sigh of relief as he quickly finished unzipping.

As he felt around inside the bag for the tools for the evening, his growing smile enveloped his face as he felt the rough cotton fibers. He held the snakelike rope loosely in his hands, as if allowing it freedom to slither between his fingers. He slid the rope through his grip until he found the knotted end with its limp loop.

You should have been nicer to me in high school, Mr. Lukin, he thought as he lifted the noose, eyeing the quality and strength of the hangman's knot he'd perfected after watching a few how-to videos on the internet.

He closed his eyes and visualized his plan, a follow-through on the threat he'd uttered to himself after Mr. Lukin embarrassed him in the boy's locker room showers after gym class in the tenth grade. He'd always considered Mr. Lukin a pervert. The coach had converted an old janitor's closet situated beside the showers into his office. He had situated his desk directly in front of the showers so he could make sure there wasn't any rough housing, so he said. But the only wrongdoing was his intimidating comments while the boys would wash off dirt and sweat from their teenaged bodies.

"You need to get some sun on that pale skin of yours," he would say as he reclined in his squeaky, rolling chair. The squeak was louder than all the commotion from six showers jetting water against the moldy tile floor. "Do you not know how to do a pushup? Your arms look like a little girl's," he would laugh as the rest of the guys would start to chime in.

Well, not *all* the guys, he remembered.

"Ready?" asked his partner and leader as he walked up the driveway, dressed in black and unseen in the moonlight, awakening Mr. Lukin's public enemy number one from his memory.

"Just checking the knot," he commented, stuffing the rope back into his duffle bag and pulling out a few pieces of clothing before zipping it up.

"Are you sure about this?" the leader asked, reaching his hand down to help his partner to his feet.

He didn't utter a word. He just nodded his head with a wicked smile.

"Good," he grinned before putting on his ski mask and black leather gloves.

He mirrored the leader's motions to disguise himself before lifting the duffle bag.

The two walked through the darkened back yard to the back door, gripping the shabby screen door.

The leader turned the knob and found it locked. "Why so untrusting, Mr. Lukin?" he chuckled as he pulled out the lock-picking tool he'd purchased with cash from a hardware store in Philadelphia three months ago.

He fiddled with the unsophisticated lock for a few seconds, churning his face and gritting his teeth before he felt the latch inside pop. "That was easy," he said, putting the handy little tool away in his back pocket. He opened the door, and the two found themselves ready to initiate step two of their plan.

Mr. Lukin's worst enemy dropped the duffle bag at the leader's feet and walked through the kitchen to the hallway. He pulled out his phone and switched on the flashlight feature. A strange feeling of trespassing on his former teacher's residence coursed through him, but the strangeness subsided when he found his treasure sitting out on a desk in the spare bedroom.

He moved the mouse, and the computer instantly came to life, opening to the desktop screen. He smiled at Mr. Lukin's simple-minded ways. *Passwords are your friends*, he thought to himself, but quickly nixed that thought. Just as his friend said earlier: *That was easy*.

He opened a web browser and quickly conducted the same searches he had previously done on his own laptop. After typing in a few words, the how-to video of a hangman's knot was displayed. He opened a new tab and did another search, Suicide Prevention. He clicked on the first link and browsed the website, clicking here and there to make it look legitimate. He typed in a new search, and suddenly more images appeared of how to hang oneself.

He continued to navigate through the worldwide web, finding new websites and rabbit holes as the leader stepped into the spare bedroom and watched his friend fill Mr. Lukin's computer with several web pages that, from the outside, would look like a struggling man succumbing to his inner demons.

"When you're done, I have the rope rigged up."

"Okay." He opened a new document on the computer and started to type a suicide note.

"Don't you think it would be more personal to handwrite it?"

"I'm not going to print it," he said as he continued to write the fake letter. "I'm just leaving it for the cops to find when they search his computer. I'll just save it somewhere."

"Sneaky."

"Just trying to tie up all the loose ends." He smiled as he saved the document and closed the program.

"The only loose end now is him," the leader said coldly as he walked away.

He remained at the computer and clicked a few more websites that depressed people might look at before ending it all. He exited all the web browsers when a beautiful thought entered his mind.

Opening a web browser, he looked through his history. He found a familiar-looking site near the top and clicked it open. Once again, no passwords were needed.

He typed three words in the email.

I'm sorry. Ted

He found his email address book and selected everyone's name. Clicking into the options, he set the email to be sent at 6 a.m. the next morning. He hit save and closed everything on Mr. Lukin's computer once again. Leaning back, he heard a familiar sound triggering years of pent-up rage.

The chair squeaked.

He smiled, imagining the circle of life coming to fruition as he stood up and heard the metal squeak one last time.

Or maybe the circle of death.

CHAPTER 2

He walked out of the spare bedroom and found the leader standing by the front door, looking around the living room.

"So, let's practice what we're going to do to make sure it works," the leader said, holding the noose. "I rigged the rope around the baluster," he said, nodding up at the second floor. "So, when he comes in, you're going to slip on the noose from behind, push him forward, and then I'm going to pull," he said, acting out the pulling motion with his arms. "Then you'll run back and grab the rope with me, and we'll lift him until he's dangling."

"Is the wood not going to break?" he asked, looking up at the thick railings of the hundred-year-old staircase.

"I swung like Tarzan, and it didn't budge." The leader smiled, beating his chest. "That's the benefit of old homes," he said, patting the walls. "The bones of this structure are better than homes built today."

The young man stopped and looked around the room. "Then when we have him hung, where are we going to tie the rope?"

The leader smiled at the question. Walking over to the first step of the staircase, he wrapped the rope around the first newel. He leaned his body against the strong wooden beam. "It's solid. We quickly wrap the rope around this and tie. Then we can walk away and enjoy the show."

"Sure it will work?" he asked with a little doubt in his voice.

"I told you I tested it out," he said agitatedly. "Do you want to try it?" he asked, reaching out his hand to give his partner the rope. "We can test it around your neck if you like?"

He shook his head. "If you're certain this will work, I trust you."

"It will work," he snickered, patting his friend on the back. "I guarantee it."

"So now we wait?"

"Now we wait."

CHAPTER 3

"What's that look for?" I asked, scraping the uneaten macaroni and cheese from the dinner plates into the trash.

"Someone is about to be killed and there isn't anything I can do to stop it," Wint said, shaking his head as he took the dirty plate from my hands. "It's just..." He stopped and rinsed off the plate into the sink allowing the water to wash away the remnants of supper.

"I get it," I said, nodding my head. "The feeling of uselessness is sometimes more gut-wrenching."

Wint loaded the plates and utensils in the dishwasher before leaning against the sink, holding onto the counter as if clutching the marble for support.

I watched as my friend closed his eyes and shook his head at the truthful words I just spoke. Sometimes the dreams I dream don't make sense, but I've learned I can't wallow when they don't. Sadly, I don't always follow my own advice.

"What's wrong with him?" Elizabeth commented as she walked through the swinging kitchen door holding her half-drunk goblet of white wine.

"The realization that he can't stop tonight," I uttered softly. But my quietness didn't stop Elizabeth.

"Wint, you can't blame yourself for Solo's mistakes," she sucker-punched. "It's not your fault he couldn't figure out who is going to die tonight."

"Ouch," I said with a raised eyebrow. "I'm not sure your therapist is helping you with your empathy."

"Empathy?" she laughed. "Oh hon, I need an entire bottle of this knockoff chardonnay before I can empathize with you."

"Knockoff?" I scoffed. "I asked the cashier which bottle to get, and he said this is what his wife drinks."

"Solo, haven't you learned by now, you can't ask for help from the help if you are looking for something a little classier than Seven-Eleven wine?"

"I'll remember that for next time," I retorted sarcastically.

I turned my gaze away from her judgmental look to my friend standing by the sink, who now had a slight grin on his face.

We were an unlikely bunch of unsung heroes.

It all started a year ago when I had my first series of dreams that all came true the following day. It was a little confusing at first, trying to decipher between what was real and imaginary, when everything seemed like a work of fiction. Then, as the dreams continued and I saw the faces of the hurting, I knew I couldn't sit idly by and do nothing.

Elizabeth Hyde, who used to reside on the other side of the proverbial coin, had been having dreams since she was a young girl, yet did nothing but record them like a court stenographer. She would have a dream, write the details, and wait for the inevitable to happen. And it always happened. Her dreams always came true.

We had become quite a pair in the last year. We detested one another from the start, but we had grown to settle with each other's idiosyncrasies and shortcomings. Of course, she failed to see any shortcomings in the mirror, but she'd gladly point out a crippled man's hobble if it put her in a better light.

Or so she wanted people to think.

She may have had the persona of a trust-fund kid who looked down on anyone below her rank, but deep down in her icy core, she would sacrifice for the runts of the world.

Last October, we unofficially formed a partnership to try to stop the horrific events in our dreams if we could. It was a union that just seemed to happen without a word or a handshake. It was a bond that had intertwined into an inseparable tethered rope linking us together.

We still had our ups and downs. Our jabs and our slights. But we also had each other's back. And she reminded me of the times she saved my life as if keeping score for the MLB.

Four months ago, I let Wint in on our little secret club when a gunman was going to massacre innocent civilians at the Washington Mall on Independence Day. Elizabeth and I tried to solve the problem by calling the police, but it seemed like the police didn't believe us, even though we saw the gunman standing on top of the news van on the television like I had seen in my dreams.

So, I'd had to call Wint and give him a glimpse into our unbelievable world. But he believed it. Even as ludicrous as it sounded, he listened to my skeptical story and trusted me. From that moment, Wint became the third member of our little group. And it was nice to have him in our circle since he was a police officer for the DCPD. No more having to make 911 calls to the police from payphones so they couldn't track me down. Now I could call Wint and tell him about a robbery or a hit and run, and he could use his police skills to stop it.

But Elizabeth and I still stopped most of the dreams. We only got the police involved when it went beyond our comfort level.

"So, are we going to cut your cake or not?" Elizabeth smiled as she chugged the last bit of her wine. "I need something to cover the aftertaste of whatever this is."

"If it wasn't good, why have you had three glasses?" I pounced.

"Just being polite," she playfully grinned as she turned to head out of the kitchen.

"If drinking makes her polite, I need to keep a bottle in my car for emergencies," I said, following her to the door. I stopped and looked behind me.

Wint gave me a grin and pushed himself off the counter. He didn't need to say a word. I knew what he was thinking.

He patted me on the back as we walked into the adjourning dining room, finding Veronica lighting the candles on the cake as Jeremiah and Elizabeth sat holding hands.

Veronica started singing softly while Elizabeth and I tried to outdo one another, seeing who could sing the loudest. A year ago, Veronica would have scolded us and kicked us out of her home. But now, she even joined in, coming in a distant third as Jeremiah took in the spectacle.

"Make a wish," Veronica said as she squeezed Wint's hand.

Wint closed his eyes, inhaled a deep breath, and blew. When he opened them, all the flickering flames had vanished on his three-tier chocolate cake. He looked at me and Elizabeth as if telling us what his wish was.

We knew.

But sadly, not all wishes came true.

CHAPTER 4

The two men hid in the shadows beside Mr. Lukin's front door, standing like ninjas in their black attire, ready to attack the unsuspecting former teacher.

They each clung to their side of the rope. The helper held the noose while the leader held the other end, ready to heave and pull Mr. Lukin into a hangman's dangle.

"I think he's here," the accomplice said as he turned his head toward the sound of a nearby car door shutting.

They strained their ears until they heard a creaking board on the other side of the door.

They each took a deep breath and listened as their host for the evening fiddled with his house keys, jiggling the outdated lock until the deadbolt clicked and turned. The door slowly swung open and Mr. Lukin walked into his darkened home unarmed and unaware of the two killers within his reach.

He took another step into the darkness and reached his hand back to shut the front door.

Mr. Lukin didn't even see the two grown men pressed against the wall in their black ski masks and leather gloves. He was about to proceed to his living room when the first attacker jumped into action.

Swiftly, the young man moved away from the wall like a black leopard and flung the noose over Mr. Lukin's head, quickly tightening it around his neck.

"What the--?" Mr. Lukin quickly spit out as he tried to turn around with his arms swinging, but it was too late. The first attacker had already caught him off guard and pushed him toward the magic spot under the second-floor railing.

Mr. Lukin started to yell threats and warnings, but they were quickly silenced as the leader pulled with all his might, causing the teacher's feet to slide into place and his airflow to shrink.

Mr. Lukin was struggling with his hands around the noose, trying to squeeze one of his fingers between his skin and the rope. He was starting to gasp as he rose upon his toes like a scared ballerina. He could still barely touch the ground, but suddenly he felt weightless.

The first attacker moved to his place at the end of the rope, and the two began their game of tug of war. The two grown men grunted and strained, trying to lift their beer-bellied former P.E. teacher a foot higher off the ground.

Even though their eyes had adjusted to the darkness, they couldn't see Mr. Lukin dangling like a marionette, silently squirming for another precious breath to enter his hungry lungs.

They tightly wrapped the rope around the first and strongest newel post.

"Hold the rope," the leader croaked with a ragged breath.

The first attacker quickly jumped up a few steps and grabbed the trailing rope to allow his comrade enough slack to end the last bit of Mr. Lukin's hope with a strong knot at the end.

The leader inhaled a deep breath as he stepped away from his complicated knot and felt his ski mask dampening from the sweaty workout.

"Let go," the leader said as he watched in anticipation of whether his knot would work.

It did.

He quickly tightened the slack his friend was creating as the rope strained against the sturdy wood, but it wasn't moving. It was as solid as he had hoped and expected.

The leader pulled out his phone and turned on the flashlight and shined it on their former nemesis, who was still alert but losing his strength to fight.

The two stepped closer to the dying man as if getting a front-row seat to his execution. This moment was one they had been waiting for since high school.

Mr. Lukin reached one of his hands toward the two masked men as if begging for sympathy. His hands were trembling as if he knew his fate was in their heartless hands. He looked at them with tearful eyes, but his look of death didn't move them to act in remorse.

Their only movement was to remove their ski masks.

The two looked at their former teacher with disdain and hate. Mr. Lukin looked at his former students with fearful acknowledgement.

"Come on, lady," the first attacker said flatly. "You're not too sissy to climb that rope."

He had been waiting to say those words ever since Mr. Lukin had said them to him.

"Or are your girlie arms too small?" he continued.

He watched as Mr. Lukin continued to strain, reaching his hands up to hold on to the rope above his head, as if trying to climb to safety.

"Funny, isn't it?" he grinned. "Our girlie arms are the ones that are going to kill you," he said as he stepped forward. "Are you ticklish, Mr. Lukin?"

He looked up, hoping the former teacher had figured out why the two of them were doing this to him. He looked into his eyes, and they connected like it was their high school reunion. It was a look of pleading for forgiveness.

It was a look he had been waiting to see for years.

He raised his arms up and asked the question. "You didn't answer me, boy. Are you ticklish?"

After a few seconds, he found that Mr. Lukin, just like most people, was ticklish under his arms.

"I thought he told you to climb that rope," the leader sneered from behind. "Show us what a real man looks like. Isn't that what you always told us?"

The two stepped back and watched their former teacher start to twitch and flop like a fish out of water. They smiled. He didn't. After another minute, Mr. Lukin stopped moving.

The first attacker stepped closer to his foe and pushed his belly, causing Mr. Lukin to swing like a pendulum. The teacher didn't respond as his lifeless eyes looked down at his former students.

"How'd it feel?" the leader asked.

He looked up with a smile at the pair of frail eyes that were drained of life. "Time for round two."

CHAPTER 5

The two attackers walked freely around Mr. Lukin's home, staging the scene to look like a suicide and not a murder. The leader grabbed a chair from the dining room table and laid it on its side beside Mr. Lukin, making it look like he had kicked it away when he hung himself.

They flipped on the kitchen, hallway, and spare bedroom lights to make it look like he had been home for some time.

"Do you think I should print out the suicide letter?" he asked his friend. "I'm afraid the cops won't look too long for it or even find it now that I think about it."

"Do people type suicide notes?" the leader asked. "Don't they usually handwrite them?"

"You're probably right," he agreed.

"Guess you better find something with his handwriting and get to it then," he laughed. "You used to forge your father's signature all the time in school."

"That was different. And it took a long time to be able to do that." Suddenly a thought flooded his mind with a possibility. "I got it!"

"What?"

"You'll see." He started rifling through Mr. Lukin's drawers, trying to find anything that had his handwriting. An old checkbook, a grocery list, a to-do list. Anything that had several letters in the alphabet on it.

"Bingo," he said to himself as he found an old notebook with teaching notes on ping-pong. He scanned the notebook and realized Mr. Lukin didn't have very neat handwriting, which made it much easier.

Flipping through the notebook, he found a clean sheet of paper. He tore out the sheet and flipped the notebook upside-down. In his research, he had seen a video advising to look at the handwriting upside down to see it from a new angle and draw the letters instead of just writing. He slowly started to draw the suicide letter. He examined it and noticed a few letters seemed wrong. So he did it again. He examined it again and noticed a few more inconsistencies.

After his third try, he thought he got it.

"How's this look?" he asked as the leader walked into the bedroom, handing him the letter to compare it to Mr. Lukin's handwriting style.

"Pretty good," he nodded. "Not perfect, but decent."

"Pretty good?" he scoffed. "That is more than pretty good. And it's his suicide note. It shouldn't look perfect."

"I guess," he said, shrugging his shoulders as he grabbed the note. "Watch this." He led the way to the kitchen, grabbing a glass from the cabinet and filling it with crushed ice. He wetted his hands and splashed the counter, causing droplets to sprinkle. He laid the suicide note on the drops of water and watched as the paper quickly absorbed the liquid, bleeding the ink on the paper.

"That's creepy how quickly you thought of that," he laughed as he watched the straight lines of the handwriting ink start to slant and shift.

He placed his glass of ice on the paper. "It's a nice paper weight with some condensation to add."

"Nice touch," he smiled as they looked around the kitchen for anything else they needed to do.

They did one more walk-through to see if there was anything they were forgetting to make this look like a suicide and not a murder.

"The front door," the leader said. "It's unlocked. Don't you lock your front door when you come home?"

"Not always," he said. "But I have a security system that automatically locks all my doors and windows in the evenings."

"Some of us aren't as privileged as you," he kidded as he walked past the dangling Mr. Lukin. "Pardon me," he laughed as he continued to the door. "I'm locking it then."

CHAPTER 6

"Do you think he's going to make it?" Elizabeth asked outside Wint and Veronica's home as Jeremiah drove away.

I looked up at the sky and felt the chill in the October air. I took a deep breath and saw the warm air exiting my mouth, forming a cloud of condensation for a few seconds. "He'll make it," I nodded, shaking off the doubt in her tone.

"He's a great guy," she sighed. "I wouldn't want anyone else as my brother-in-law."

"Thanks," I said in a sarcastic, jilted tone.

"You know what I mean, man-child," she retorted.

"But it's just the way you said it," I laughed. "No 'present company excluded'. No 'you're a great guy'. Nothing but--" I started before she interrupted as she usually did.

"Don't make me shoot you in your bony butt, white boy, because I will, and Wint will probably help me dispose of your body."

"That wouldn't kill me," I laughed.

"My chamber holds six bullets," she laughed. "I'll use them all on you."

"Really?" I smiled. "I'm worth that much ammo? I'm touched."

"You're not right, kid," she said, shaking her head.

"Been told that a time or two in my life."

"Well, I've thought it a few times today, so put that into perspective."

"You've thought about me a few times today?" I gasped.

She went into spastic laughter. "You are so missing the point, bud," she said, reaching her hand out to smack the back of my head before I dodged it. "You're getting quicker."

"Fool me once," I smiled.

"Oh hon, I can't even keep track of the times I've fooled you. Like last week when you wanted me to go to the thrift store to stop the kid from shoplifting."

"You said you had a doctor's appointment," I said, shocked.

"No," she said, raising her hands up, showing her nails. "I said I had an appointment," she winked. "You're the one that put a doctor in it."

"I don't believe you," I stated defiantly. "You don't want people to see your true colors, but I see them."

"Oh brother, if you start singing Cyndi Lauper, I will definitely shoot one of us to end the misery," she said, reaching into her purse.

My eyes went wide. I knew she carried a gun, but I just wasn't that fond of seeing one waved in front of my face. Especially when she was the one waving it after drinking a half bottle of convenience store chardonnay.

"Oh, quit covering yourself. I'm not going to shoot you," she said snidely. "I definitely wouldn't shoot you there."

"Guns accidentally go off, you know," I added.

"Well, Sherlock, unless your fingers are bullet proof, I'm pretty sure your manhood isn't going to be protected very much."

"Why are we talking about this?" I asked, trying to find the start of this random conversation.

"Are you blushing, Solo?" she kidded. "I can't see your rosy cheeks."

"Wint," I said, changing the topic away from myself. "You wondered if Wint was going to make it."

"Yeah, but I'm past worrying about Wint tonight," she said slyly. "Let's go back to your typical man pose of guarding your junk. You can survive getting shot there, but if you get shot in the head, you are pretty much dead. You should be holding that."

"Yeah, but like you said, if I'm shot there, I will be dead. But if you shoot me *there*," I said, pointing down, "I will wish I was dead."

"Typical man, Solo."

"Is that a compliment?" I laughed. "Calling me a man. I thought you thought of me as a boy?"

"I gotta go," she said waving me off as she walked to her car, touching her nose with outstretched arms to check her sobriety. "I would hate to give you another backhanded remark and you twist it into a positive. What would people think if they knew I was such an encourager?"

"They wouldn't believe it," I said, shrugging my shoulders. "You're like Bigfoot."

"Bigfoot?" she stopped and turned around and headed back my way. "Never. Ever. Compare a woman to Bigfoot. Or I will shoot you where you will wish you were dead," she said, standing nose to nose with me. "Got that, big boy?"

"Got it, Ms. Hyde."

MONDAY

CHAPTER 7

The silence was broken as a cellphone chimed and lit up.

That was some night last night. The message then faded to black.

Clicking was heard in the darkness. *It sure was.* The message quickly flashed and disappeared.

Want to meet up again tonight? I'm free.

You don't like taking things slow, do you? The message once again quickly flashed and disappeared.

Life is too short for taking things slow.

It sure is.

So?

Sure. Why not? What do I have to lose?

That's an understatement if I read one.

The messages stopped as the cellphone was switched to silent mode as the screen faded to black.

A beam of light shined in the center, as if coming from a tunnel, filling the entire blackness with its warm glow.

Elizabeth sat shaking behind the wooden galley, holding onto the railing as if trying to control her uneasiness. Her eyes didn't dart around the room, but remained fixed, as if locked on something. Her lips started to move, as if spit-firing bulleted words. Her tirade didn't stop as she lifted her right hand from the wooden ledge and pointed forward.

"She's crazy all right! She got off scot-free from killing all those gray-headed tourists last year and then came immediately to kill us! If that's not crazy, I don't know what is!"

"So, you agree, she's mentally unstable?" a man asked in a calm voice.

"Oh, she's definitely not stable!" she erupted. "Want to see the scars she left on my friend?"

"So, just to reiterate, Jennifer Ascot was not in her right mind when she did this to you?"

"She hasn't been right for years, probably," Elizabeth huffed.

"Thank you, Miss Hyde," an unseen man said. "No further questions, Your Honor."

Elizabeth fumed as she started to rise from her seat. She stopped and quickly looked ahead of her to her right as her anger vanished in a second.

A handsome gentleman gave her a friendly wink and mouthed, thank you, before turning to his left and rubbing a young woman's shoulders.

Jennifer Ascot.

I awoke with the image of Jenny sitting timidly, like a fragile bird between two burly, able men. It was definitely an act. An act to showcase the insanity plea her attorneys were banking on.

Elizabeth had fallen into their scheming plan.

The master of said plan? Milo.

CHAPTER 8

The air in the faculty lounge was swirling with a mixture of Folgers coffee and copy machine toner as a few teachers sipped their hot beverages to gear up for their day. A couple looked like the walking dead from a late night of grading last minute papers. A few looked dead to the world from the late game that went into extra innings.

Twenty-five-year-old Ms. Calapernia was one of the few wide-eyed and gearing to go with her laptop open and her phone fully charged on the table. Her finger played with the mouse pad, letting the arrow circle around the desktop as the background programs were starting. She smiled happily as she tuned out the echoing yawns and murmurings. She loved being a teacher. This was her lifelong dream, and the rest of the staff at Woodward Wilson High School would not kill her determination or drive.

"Did you have a good weekend?" Ms. Calapernia asked a few of the teachers huddled around the same table.

Mr. Dalatino responded with a grunt, trying to hide his bloodshot eyes behind his knockoff Ralph Lauren Polo sunglasses. "Late night," he said, popping in a stick of gum to mask the alcohol on his breath from spending five hours at Stu's bar watching the game.

Ms. Calapernia looked to Mrs. Hasselburg, who ignored her question and kept her eyes glued to her cellphone.

Mrs. Daltson spoke up with a confusing tone. "Did you see the email from Ted?"

"What did the ol' man say?" Mr. Dalatino chuckled. "I'm surprised he knows how to use his email."

Ms. Calapernia shot Mr. Dalatino a judgmental look and then found the same email in her mailbox. "I'm sorry, Ted," she said in a heightened tone.

"Sorry?" Mr. Dalatino laughed as he took off his glasses to massage his temples. "What's he got to be sorry about?"

"I don't know," Ms. Calapernia responded. "I'm just reading the message."

"Has anyone heard or seen him this morning?" Mrs. Daltson asked as she looked around the room, although most of the faculty could not care less about the graying P.E. teacher. "I don't have his number, so could someone call him?"

A few of the teachers who were listening all shrugged their shoulders or shook their heads. No one had his number.

"Fine," Mrs. Daltson huffed as she scooted away from the table, quickly followed by Ms. Calapernia. "I'll do it myself."

"I'll come with you, Cheryl," Ms. Calapernia chimed in as the two started walking through the high school hallway past students hanging around their lockers.

"Go to the gym or the cafeteria," Mrs. Daltson shouted to the loitering students. "Now!"

"I'm just getting my algebra book," one student stated with angst.

"Whatever," Mrs. Daltson said under her breath. "I don't even know why we try anymore."

Ms. Calapernia just shrugged her shoulders and politely waved off the students with a cheery smile.

CHAPTER 9

The dismal gray sky this morning was not giving me hope of a beautiful autumn day. Or it may have been the dream I had last night of Elizabeth's downfall as a witness. I sat in the Vienna-Fairfax GMU Metro station parking lot staring at the foggy windshield, debating whether or not to grab an umbrella from the trunk of my car. I opened the door and felt a few sprinkles land on my forehead, causing me to end my debate and take the flimsy covering in case the rain came in opposition to the meteorologist's prediction.

The metro station was sparse as the early morning rush had ended about four trains ago. I scanned the surroundings to people watch and found the six people waiting were not as interested in watching me as I was in watching them. They were standing mannequins with their phones in their hands, either watching the latest episode on Hulu or catching up with the news.

Their lackluster entertainment caused me to pull out my own phone to entertain myself for the duration of my journey. I looked to see if I had any new texts from Elizabeth this morning, but after our uncivil exchange about my dream from last night, she was silent.

"How ignorant do you think I am, Solomon?" she'd protested.

I knew she was not happy with my stern warning when I heard my full name roll off her tongue and not my nickname. I quickly tried to come up with a cordial reply, but sadly, my thinking process was slower than my verbal response.

"Based upon my dream last night, you looked pretty ignorant." Right when I said those words, I wished I could have taken them back. "I'm just trying to keep you from making a big mistake."

But it was too late. She had already hung up before I could finish. I tried calling her a few more times as I was getting ready, throwing on a pair of khakis and a navy sweater, but each time she sent it straight to her voicemail. She didn't want to talk to me.

I tried to smooth out my demeaning end of the conversation, but she wasn't having it. Each text only said delivered, not read.

The subway doors parted and the seven of us entered the Orange Line Metro, heading to downtown D.C. I sat down and rested my umbrella on the seat beside me and started to text Elizabeth. But with each letter my thumb hit, it seemed like autocorrect was auto-wronging instead.

We proceeded through a few other stations on the route and eventually the train slinked its body underground. I reread the text I was about to send, offering a slight apology, while chastising her outburst, mixing in a few paternal words of guidance on how to handle her testimony without losing her cool, and sprinkling in a few gaslighting metaphors.

I was about to hit send when I lost reception. I looked around the train at the other passengers watching their shows or browsing the internet on their phones who appeared unscathed by the lack of reception.

I looked down at my text and reread it once again with a different viewpoint. My heart sank. I started to delete each letter. Elizabeth didn't need me to belittle her. She needed me to be my normal self.

My thumbs started moving once again to form a quick text. *You're going to do great today. I believe in you.*

Miraculously all my bars and data returned as if someone was watching over me and my prideful heart.

I hit send, and immediately the message was read.

I smiled at the three dots blinking signaling Elizabeth was texting.

See, that wasn't so hard to say, now was it?

I read the text and then reread it. The text literally left me speechless and annoyed. I didn't know how to respond. I knew what I wanted to say, but I was afraid the cellular reception would suddenly crash on me once again.

So I did the only thing I felt comfortable doing.

I didn't reply. I put my phone back in my pocket and started to people watch once again.

CHAPTER 10

"Can you believe the grand slam Reynolds hit in the eighth?" Jordan Lee asked, walking up to Stuart Weatherby's cubicle in the Department of Transportation Office.

"I thought the game was over in the sixth and went to the gym," Collin Diaz said, stretching his neck and pushing back his shoulders to expose his broadening chest. "I almost fell off the weight bench when I heard the bat snap."

"Really, Collin? Are you sure you weren't checking yourself out again in the mirrors?" Grant Harper laughed as he strutted up to his gang of friends.

"The bench was slippery from your butt sweat," Collin snapped defensively.

"I wipe down when I'm done," Grant rebutted with a toothy grin.

"Hold up," Stuart chimed in, looking up from his computer. "You did what?"

"Let's get back to the game," Collin rerouted.

"Oh, no, this is better than Game 3 of the World Series," Jordan concurred. "When was this?"

"Give it a break. Move on," Collin said agitatedly.

"Senior year," Grant snuck in.

"High school?" Stuart asked wide-eyed.

"College." Grant busted out laughing.

"Yeah, yeah, yeah. Have a good laugh," Collin said waving them off as he walked away.

"Oh, come on, Collin. We're just busting your chops," Grant said condescendingly as the three watched their clumsy friend flip them off with both hands.

"He's ticked," Jordan chuckled while shaking his head. "Typical."

"Yeah," Grant nodded in agreement. "But he slid right off the bench and landed on the ground because I swear he was checking himself out."

"I can see that," Stuart smiled. "Ever see him in the men's room after taking a leak? It's like he's primping himself for a photoshoot."

"Good ol' Collin," Grant grinned. "Once a playboy, always a playboy."

"Yeah, but he'd better find a woman soon because he's not getting any younger," Jordan said. "He doesn't make enough to keep the twenty-year-olds happy once his hair thins and wrinkles appear."

"Oh, he's got a plan," Grant smiled. "He'll move in with Stuart if he can't afford the hair plugs."

"Say what?" Stuart exclaimed in shock.

"Gotta get to work," Jordan said as he walked away.

"Me too," Grant said as he proceeded to the kitchen to grab a cup of coffee.

"You're kidding, right?" Stuart asked looking up at his two friends walking away. "Right?"

CHAPTER 11

"He's still not coming to the door," Marcus Doubleday, one of the school's guidance counselors said over the phone to the vice principal as he leaned back to scan the front of Ted Lukin's house.

"Well, is his car there?" Christine Jung asked as she continued to type a lengthy email to the parents concerning recent dress code violations.

"Yeah," Marcus replied, "it's here." He pounded on the door a few more times. "Wonder if he had a bender last night after the game?"

"Marcus," Christine said in shock.

"Oh, come on, don't play so coy," he said ringing the doorbell another six times.

"What about his neighbors? Maybe they would know something."

"Do you tell your neighbors everything?" he asked snidely.

"Well," she said quietly, "some people do."

Stepping off the front porch he walked towards one of Ted's neighbors when he stopped at a window with its blinds shut. Closing one of his eyes, he could see partially into the darkened living room.

"Doesn't look like he's awake," he said as he tried to see into the house. Something didn't look normal. He couldn't make out the image in the darkness on this gray morning. He started to squint his eyes to make sure of what he was seeing. "Call for help!" he spit out as he darted away from the window to get back to the door.

"Help?" Christine asked with alarm. "What's going on, Marcus?"

"Call 911 now!" he said as he opened the glass door. "I think he's dead," he said putting the phone on speaker and shoving it in his shirt pocket.

He wiggled the locked doorknob. He used to play football in high school and was used to taking a beating on his body, but that was over

31

a decade ago. He flexed the muscles in his torso and rammed his shoulder into the door.

It didn't budge.

He took a deep breath and tried it again. This time he heard some splintering of wood along with his own moan from the force he was taking.

He rotated his body to give it another go with a fresh arm. He closed his eyes, throwing his entire body weight into the door as he felt the wood break and the door swing wide. He caught himself before falling to the ground, but what he saw when he looked up almost caused his knees to buckle.

"Ted!" he shouted as he ran over to the dangling man with his eyes glazed over staring down at the ground. He wondered if there was any hope of saving Ted, but that thought quickly left when he felt Ted's cold, dead hand.

"The ambulance is on their way!" Christine came back through the speaker. "What's going on?"

"He's dead, Christine," Marcus said solemnly as he walked toward the front door to get some fresh air. "Looks like he hung himself."

"Oh no!"

CHAPTER 12

The courtroom was full of commotion as Miloslav Alexeev walked down the aisle to the defense table in his well-tailored Armani black suit. His gray hair was slicked back and matched his tie as if he'd had it made for this occasion. He was the epitome of past Soviet Union dominance, almost marching like he did when he was a soldier.

Jennifer Ascot sat emotionless and aloof. She was on trial for attempted murder of Elizabeth Hyde along with a list of associated crimes revolving around the intrusion last April.

Milo wasn't known for exhibiting warmth and compassion, so he wasn't going to start now. He looked over at his client and remembered they'd sat in this same position last April. He was actually the attorney who got her a not-guilty verdict with his theatrics and discrediting of evidence when she was on trial as one of the Carbon Monoxide killers.

Jennifer and her brother, Alexei Lechkov, were wickedly guilty. They caused havoc in the Washington D.C. area last October when they killed innocent tourists and one park ranger by attacking them in the metro station garages and then disposing of their bodies in nearby parks, making them look like suicides. It had looked like they were going to get away with it until Officer Winston Cooper shot and killed Alexei at the Huntington Station and apprehended Jennifer.

"It's all going as planned," Milo whispered into Jennifer's ear as her other attorney, Gavyn McKenzie, sat unfazed with his phone in his hand oblivious to Milo's appearance.

"Easy for you to say," she said unfazed, as if a professional ventriloquist. "You're not on trial."

"Well," he replied in his thick monotone Russian accent. "I'm just better than you at tying up all of my loose ends." He stopped and let those words sink into her mind. "I guess you took after your father in that way."

Straightening, he watched as she continued to stare placidly ahead. He knew his words stabbed at her icy heart, but that is what he did. He had no remorse for any actions he took, whether it meant taking a life, stealing from a partner, or stabbing someone in the back to keep himself safe. At the end of the day, he only cared about one thing. Himself.

Milo continued to watch his client sit rigidly, wondering if she was shaking on the inside in fury or if she was taking this as another lesson she needed to learn. Since he was the leader of their Russian mob circle in the D.C. area, he often wondered who would rise in power after he was gone. Would it be someone who would wait until he died of old age, or would it be someone who would try to take fate into their own hands and whack him when he least expected it.

He understood the risk he took being in charge. He often grinned to himself at the sick cycle they were in, because he had knocked off the leader before him. He knew he had a target on his back, but Jennifer had shown some potential a few months ago when she'd warned him of an assassination attempt on his life. That was the only reason he was sitting in the defense chair now. She had saved his life and he felt it was only fitting to help save hers.

Again.

He looked over at his client who continued to stare ahead, as if fixing her eyes on the plaque on the wall, E pluribus unum. Not for the first time, he wondered if she was really crazy or maybe something even more dangerous. What if she was a vindictive woman able to kill anyone with no remorse?

In a twisted way he hoped she was the latter. At least a vindictive woman would have made her father proud if he was still alive to see her.

But Milo made sure her father was never to leave the prison once he was sentenced.

And he had no remorse in that deadly decision.

And he had no remorse in keeping that knowledge away from little Jenika as her father used to call her when she was a little girl.

Just as he'd said earlier, he was better at tying up all of his loose ends.

And he wasn't lying.

CHAPTER 13

Gavyn McKenzie sat in the same courtroom with his mind in a different place as he scrolled through the messages on his phone. He was still reeling from the excitement of the night before, but he knew he had no one nearby he could talk to it about. He scanned his eyes to his left, noticing Milo had sat down at the table beside Jennifer Ascot. He knew he could probably entertain this pair with his details from the night, but he didn't care for them enough to allow them to live vicariously through him.

He knew each of them had a past with Milo's shady connections and Jennifer's previous murder trial. Even though his heart was racing with adrenaline, he knew it was just a molehill compared to the Russians' Everest-sized criminal escapades.

Gavyn started to relive the night. His breathing started to deepen and he moved around in his seat as if physically reenacting the night. He closed his eyes as a cunning grin spread over his face.

His phone vibrated, waking him up from his wicked thoughts.

That was some night last night.

He looked around the room and saw everyone was paying attention to someone other than him. His thumbs quickly replied.

It sure was.

He watched as his message quickly went from delivered to read. He watched anxiously as the three dots hypnotically lured him into a state of wanting more.

Want to meet up again tonight? I'm free.

He ran his fingers through his short crew cut blonde hair and quickly responded. *You don't like taking things slow, do you?*

The three dots blinked like a short string of Christmas lights. Suddenly, a new message landed on his screen.

Life is too short for taking things slow.

36

He nodded his head in agreement. *It sure is.*

So? The message appeared in a fraction of a second after his last message was sent. He contemplated his response. He started to mentally record a list of the reasons why or why not he should meet tonight. He awoke from the moral debate inside his head as the bailiff took command in the courtroom.

He frantically typed his message as the bailiff spoke, "All rise."

Sure. Why not? What do I have to lose? He hit send as he slowly stood up, readjusting his navy trousers and buttoning his suit jacket.

He was about to turn off his phone when a new message came in.

That's an understatement if I read one.

He powered off his phone and laid it on the table as a broad smile oozed confidence. The jury probably thought it was optimism for the case, but he had another reason to smile.

He already had the perfect idea for tonight.

CHAPTER 14

The lonely suburban home of a divorced man on a dead-end street quickly escalated to the epicenter of visitors in uniforms and badges. The first officers on the scene had to leave Ted Lukin's body hanging from the second-floor banister until everything was documented and photographed.

"Why is he still up there?" Detective Young shouted as he walked through the open front door making his arrogant presence known to everyone. "Don't you have any decency, Rickels?"

Officer Rickels inhaled a deep breath and counted to three before turning his attention from the crime scene videographer to the cocky detective. "Cameron's not done," he answered with as much respect as he could handle without losing his drive-thru breakfast burrito that was churning at the mere sound of Young's voice.

"Well, Cameron, get a move-on," Young ordered. "We have more important cases than a suicide." Young walked away with his shoulders back and his chest puffed up a little more than a minute ago hoping everyone in the room would notice how he took control of the situation.

"Jack--" Rickels started as Young turned around eying him like a jock in high school urging him to finish the phrase, "son, do you need anything?"

Cameron continued to walk around with his camera at chest level, watching the screen to make sure everything was being documented. "I'm almost done, Rickels," he said as he smiled knowing that Officer Rickels knew full well he didn't have Jackson anywhere in his name. But it had become a running joke at Young's expense that anytime someone was caught calling him a crude name, the person nearby would become the name.

Most people would realize and try to remember people's names after a few meetings, but not Young. Young felt he was too important to learn the names of those beneath him. They were to know his name, so he seldom learned the names of other officers.

Young turned again to proceed down the hall when he heard Dr. Raul Santiago's voice. Young's shoulders lost some of their posture and caved in. He hated Dr. Santiago and despised that everyone else loved him. He loathed that he was the brilliant chief medical examiner. He detested how handsome he was in his early 40s. But most of all he hated that he wanted to be just like him. And that caused his insides to revolt against themselves.

Young turned around and peeked his head around a doorframe to stay hidden and watched Dr. Santiago work his magic. He watched in envy as he called everyone he spoke to by their name with a friendly smile. He observed his charisma that balanced professionalism with politeness while doing his demanding job with ease.

A couple of officers untied the rope's knot and eased Ted Lukin down to the ground. Dr. Santiago reached into his medical bag and pulled out his tools and started scribbling some notes only he could read.

"I would say time of death based upon body temperature would be between 7 p.m. and 1 a.m."

Young walked into the action. "Would you say this is definitely a suicide?"

"I don't want to say just yet," Dr. Santiago said as he stopped and looked around the depressing room. He never liked to make claims without finding proof. His job was all about details, and assumptions didn't hold up in court.

"But you agree, it looks like a suicide," Young harped.

"As I said before," Dr. Santiago stopped and picked up his bag on the ground. "I don't want to say just yet. You can say it's a suicide all you want, but before I complete my paperwork and tests, you'd better not say *I* said it was a suicide." He stopped and looked Young in the eye like a disciplining father. "You understand me?"

"Yes, sir," Young nodded as Dr. Santiago turned to his assistants, ordering them to start the preliminary tests when they got back to the office.

Dr. Santiago turned back to Young. "I will let you know what I conclude once we've drafted our reports." He stopped and looked Young in the eyes. "Is that good enough for you?"

"Yes, yes, sir," he answered like a defenseless child.

"Good," Dr. Santiago replied as he followed his assistants out the door.

Young watched as Dr. Santiago left without ever saying his name. The only name in the room he usually got wrong.

CHAPTER 15

I walked three blocks from the metro station, thankfully between the rain showers, to the Superior Court of the District of Columbia. I wanted to be there for Elizabeth. I wanted her to know I had her back.

But mostly, I wanted to be there to remind her to keep calm and not go 'Elizabeth' on them.

"Hey man," I said picking up a call from Wint as I strolled on the sidewalk in front of Sips, the latest coffee establishment downtown.

"Well, they found him," he whispered.

I shook my head with the saddening fact that our dreams came true once again. And now there were going to be some hard telephone calls contacting the next of kin telling them he committed suicide, when he really didn't.

"Have they labeled it a suicide?" I asked, looking up at the graying sky, still clutching my umbrella.

"Not yet," he softly spoke. "But it's inevitable. They really made it look good."

"So is there anything you can do?" I asked, walking a few feet before stopping at a crosswalk.

"I don't know what I can do," Wint said in defeat. "I've been going over plausible ideas all morning and nothing sounds good."

"Want me to call in a report of two guys breaking into the guy's home?" I laughed. "I've done it plenty of times before."

"Yeah, but it still won't bring him back," Wint said with a huff. "At the end of the day he's still dead."

I listened to my friend wallow in the emotional toil of sitting on the sidelines of death and murder. I had often sat in that dugout, but Elizabeth always had a way of snapping me out of it.

Or slapping me out of it.

41

"Wint, this isn't your fault," I persuaded as I started to walk with a small group across the intersection. "I've learned sometimes we can stop it and sometimes we can't. But we can't stop living when we can't stop it."

"But I'm a cop, Solo. This is my job to keep people safe," he snapped back.

"You wouldn't have even known about this murder without us telling you, so if anyone failed, it's us," I reminded him, "not you."

I waited for those words to sink in. But I didn't want them to seep into myself so I quickly darted my attention to the cute blonde walking beside me. She had a slight smile as she, too, was talking on her phone. I started visualizing her watching her favorite television show in the evenings in her flannel pajamas with a pint of mint chocolate chip, which I detested but would pretend to like for her sake.

"Solo," Wint said, breaking the silence.

"Yeah," I said watching my unknown crush part ways, almost waving goodbye to her and wishing her a good day.

"Call in the tip," he said shortly. "I gotta go."

I stood at the metaphorical corner of uncomfortable situations and lost. I looked around my surroundings but couldn't find a pay telephone anywhere.

Sure, I thought with a humorous smile on my face as I realized I didn't even know the details to give the cops when I actually found a phone to use.

I felt a slight vibration in my hand as I looked at my phone. Wint had read my mind.

I had the address of the murdered man.

Now if he could have only found a payphone within a one-mile radius of me, we would have been set.

CHAPTER 16

I walked two blocks looking for a place to call the police and give an anonymous tip, passing by another coffee shop. The third since Wint had ended our call.

I peered in the window and noticed a few patrons sitting at a couple of tables working on their laptops with their cellphones nearby for easy access.

Would I let a stranger use my phone? I contemplated as I gawked awkwardly inside the coffee shop like a caffeine addict looking for a quick fix. *Yeah, I would,* I concluded and eased my way from the comfort behind the glass window and got the nerve to walk in.

I saw three likely prospects, one of which was a female. I glanced down and noted I looked presentable and approached my target, shaking on the inside like a seventh-grade boy at a school dance.

I tried to shake off the nerves. *Stop it, Solo,* I told myself as I started to uncomfortably walk towards the college-age woman in her vintage Beatles t-shirt.

"Excuse me," I said, catching her slightly off guard as she took out her earbuds. "My phone just died and I need to make a call. Can I borrow yours for two minutes?" I asked pointing down at her unused phone.

"Sure," she said shrugging her shoulders while handing me her sticker-covered device. I was amazed at the collection of musical artists arranged in a cacophony of mix-match styles. A miniature Bob Dylan was plastered beside Elvis, which was slightly covering Madonna, who was paying her respects to Bach.

I smiled politely as I stepped away from earshot, while remaining visible in case she cared to watch. But she didn't and returned to either a term paper or virtual date. These days, anything was possible.

I pressed 9-1-1 and waited.

"What's your emergency?" a nasally sounding woman answered as if it was her eightieth time uttering that phrase this morning.

"I'm not sure who I need to talk to, but I may have some information on a possible case," I said quietly, turning my back to the customers in the coffee shop for a little more privacy.

"What information do you have, sir?"

"Well, last night I saw two men walk into my neighbor's house, and I thought nothing of it. And now, there are cops all around and they just carried out a body bag."

"Sir, what is your address?"

I ignored the question and continued on with my information. "My neighbor's name is Ted Lukin, and I overhead one cop say suicide, but I'm telling you, it wasn't a suicide. He was murdered."

"Sir, I am going to transfer you to someone else," she said in a monotone.

"No, I'm about to go into a meeting and I don't have any more time."

"Sir, I have the information, but I need you to speak with--" she continued until I hung up.

I opened up recent calls on the borrowed phone and deleted my call. The less she knew, the better.

I walked back over to my music lover. "I think you need to add Smashing Pumpkins to your collage," I said with a smile before thanking her for the phone.

"Nah," she said unfazed. "Too commercialized."

I looked down at her in shock as if the music of Bruno Mars could have knocked me off my feet. Apparently, he wasn't too commercialized to be plastered beside The Who and Mumford and Sons.

I walked away stunned at her eclectic taste of music and my teenage guilty pleasure. I once again felt like the middle school boy being mocked by the cool kids in study hall.

I thought of how quickly unhealthy memories could resurface when my phone vibrated in my pocket. I waited until I was away from view before glancing down to see who was calling. It was as if the torrid memories vanished as I answered and heard her scathing tone.

"Solo! I thought you were coming!"

"Elizabeth, this day isn't all about you, you know," I laughed as I started picking up my pace toward the courthouse. "We do have other dreams than just your flub-up in court."

She hung up.

I knew that would get her.

CHAPTER 17

Elizabeth sat on a bench outside the courtroom, watching the spectators enter and find their seats before the main event of the three-ring circus – her testimony.

She had tried doing yoga this morning to clear her head, but it seemed like her warrior pose always flowed into a take-cover position. She wore the costume of being brave and confident daily, almost convincing herself of the charade of who she claimed to be as she put on her makeup.

But she knew the truth beneath the thin layer of foundation and lipstick. That truth had caused her hand to shake, almost poking herself in the eye with her mascara brush.

She'd looked in the mirror, falling deep into her eyes and seeing the same little terrified girl victimized years ago. Flashbacks of abandonment and loneliness flooded her memories. The paid-off silence. The coerced bargaining. The seasons of stalemate. All perpetuated by her career-driven, win-at-all-costs father. Once again, the soul-crushing realization was her father was somehow commingled in this mess. His firm was defending Jennifer Ascot once again.

It was going to be daughter against father.

Just like it had been their entire lives.

She'd dropped her mascara brush just as she'd dropped her guard. She had crumbled in front of the mirror, grabbing onto the counter for support. The only support she could find.

Then her phone had vibrated, and she'd looked over and saw it was a pillar much stronger and more stable than the marble she was clinging onto now. She found resilience in the name. She'd straightened up. Wiped her tears. Found the inner strength from an outside source.

She wasn't the lonely little girl anymore.

"Elizabeth," Solo had said with urgency, "I dreamed about you, last night."

"Don't most men?" she'd said in a sultry voice, putting on the theatrics of her persona.

"Gross," he replied.

"You sure know how to make a woman feel appreciated," she smiled as she picked up her mascara brush and finished her lashes with a steady hand.

"Anyways," he'd said with his typical change of subject, "you're going to mess up today if you don't focus."

"How ignorant do you think I am, Solomon?"

She opened her eyes after replaying her morning, seeing that she was physically alone. But she knew. No matter the quips and jabs and gut punching remarks, she wouldn't be alone for long. She looked down at the phone in her hand and reread the text message from her partner in heroic deeds.

You know I'll do anything for you.

She knew.

And she wasn't going to let her ego get the best of her during her cross-examination.

CHAPTER 18

Gavyn McKenzie took notes periodically during Finn Garrett's questioning of their star witness, Elizabeth Hyde. She answered all of the assistant district attorney's questions professionally and cordially, but he knew that their line of questioning had been rehearsed. Elizabeth knew what questions were going to be asked and when they were going to ask them.

She had been prepped, but it was his duty to try to dismantle that balance. When he started to see Elizabeth's demeanor ease with comfort, he started to object. But Milo must have seen the same thing and beat Gavyn to the proverbial punch.

"Objection, Your Honor," Milo stated unfazed, as if annoyed he was sitting in a courtroom this Monday morning.

The judge dismissed the objection, but Milo was doing his part in rocking the unflinching Elizabeth.

A few minutes had passed before the prosecution raised another questionable inquiry. Gavyn once again took notice and jumped. But once again, he was a second too late.

"Objection, Your Honor," Milo urged, this time with a little more persuasion in his tone and presentation.

The judge agreed with Milo and told Finn to move along. Unrattled, Finn stood before Elizabeth with his three-piece olive suit, giving her a friendly smile before stuffing his hands in his trouser pockets and moving onto his next question.

Gavyn looked over at Milo, who turned his head as if aware he was being watched.

"You'll get one eventually," Milo mouthed with a sympathetic nod which turned into a cunning smile.

Gavyn read between the lines and knew all the stories he had heard about Milo were true. He had realized on day one of the trial last week that this would not be a team effort to defend their client. He was just an attorney from Jennifer's employer to show the jury they were supporting their employee.

He knew he was being played. And he hated being played. He wasn't used to this type of belittlement. He'd graduated top of his class, passed the bar on the first try, and had countless firms offering him positions with sign-on bonuses. He'd believed Manfield & Hyde was the firm that would catapult him to fame and fortune.

Now he was playing second fiddle to a mob boss, defending a client he knew was guilty with only a small hope of getting the charges dropped with a Hail Mary insanity defense.

Things were not looking good for this once-shining star.

He wondered if this was why Veronica had high-tailed it and ran after they'd put her in this same predicament last spring. For a split second he wondered if he should do the same, but as quickly as it came, the thought left. He had other things on his mind like the events of last night and the possibility of events to come.

"So, Ms. Hyde, you were duct-taped to a chair by the defendant Jennifer Ascot with a knife in her hand before Solomon Davis entered the room. Is that correct?"

"Yes, he saved my life."

"So, Ms. Hyde, you are stating that if Solomon Davis hadn't entered the home of Officer Winston Cooper, who had previously arrested Jennifer Ascot on charges of being one of the Carbon Monoxide Killers, you would not be here today?"

"Objection!" Gavyn shouted as Milo softly applauded with his hands in his lap.

"He finally got one on his own," Milo whispered into Jennifer's ear, but loudly enough for Gavyn to hear as he sat down. "This is a big day for him."

CHAPTER 19

Elizabeth sat in the witness box beside the judge and answered the prosecution's questions like a pro. I sat watching her every move, nodding my head in reinforcement of a job well done.

"Let me rephrase," Finn answered, knowing full well that even though the judge told the jury to disregard the prosecution's last statement, they couldn't forget it. "So, Ms. Hyde, you are stating that if Solomon Davis hadn't stopped the defendant, Jennifer Ascot, you probably wouldn't be here today?"

Elizabeth looked directly at me and smiled, slightly nodding her head. "Yes, I cannot express how much gratitude I have for Solomon Davis saving my life," she said as she wiped a tear away.

We didn't talk much about that day. We both lived through the horrors of Jennifer's rampage, and we both had scars as proof of the incident. But I had never seen Elizabeth tear up from the after effects.

I nodded my head and mouthed, "You're welcome," as the memory of that day came flooding into my mind. I could still see Elizabeth taped to the chair, the look of fear in her eyes as the blade cut into her skin. I was so fueled with the rush of adrenaline coursing through my body that I never considered how close I came to losing her.

If I had hit a couple of traffic lights. If Wint hadn't talked to me about Elizabeth cooking supper. If I hadn't talked to Jeremiah earlier in the day. That witness stand could be empty right now.

I closed my eyes and said a quick prayer of thanks as the prosecution ended their questioning and the defense started their feat of unraveling Elizabeth's credibility. I shook my head and said another prayer, this one with much more urgency. "Please God, help her."

Gavyn walked across the courtroom so he was standing within an arm's reach of Elizabeth and started his questioning.

"I am sorry for your ordeal, Ms. Hyde. Truly." He stopped and waited for Elizabeth to respond, but she sat frozen, eyeing him with a look of judgment as if he wore snakeskin boots with leopard print pants.

"So Ms. Hyde, you stated you don't believe you would be here if Solomon Davis did not save you. Is that correct?"

"Yes," she answered without emotion.

"But you cannot absolutely be sure Ms. Ascot was going to kill you. Isn't that correct?"

"No," she answered shortly. "I'm pretty sure she was going to kill me."

"So you think you know what she was thinking when she came to the home?"

"You mean, when she broke into my sister's home and turned off the power?" She smiled sarcastically, glancing at the jury. "I'm pretty sure they know what she was thinking too."

"Your Honor," Milo interjected from his seat, "please direct Ms. Hyde to not speak to the jury." I watched as Gavyn gave a menacing stare in his direction. I sat dumbfounded at the tension between the two men that anyone in the room could have felt.

"She may speak to the jury," the judge corrected. "You may proceed, Mr. McKenzie, unless your co-counsel wishes to interrupt you again."

Milo waved Gavyn to continue. "Ms. Hyde, did you have a good relationship with Ms. Ascot growing up?"

"I wouldn't say it was bad," she said nonchalantly. "She was my sister's friend."

"So, you are aware of her troubling past?" he asked.

"At the time, no," she answered unfazed. "When she was younger, she was normal."

Watch it, Elizabeth, I thought to myself as I started to shake my head, warning her to watch her phrasing.

She noticed my movements which caused her to close her eyes and take a deep breath. "What I mean is, I didn't know of her family situation."

"But you just said 'when she was normal,'" Gavyn chimed in. "Does that imply she isn't normal now?"

"That is not what I mean," she said with her voice sounding strong and confident.

"What do you mean then, because you just said when she was normal, which makes it sound like you believe she isn't normal now?"

"What normal person wants to harm someone?" Elizabeth snapped.

"So, you agree then, that Ms. Ascot isn't in her right mind. Is that fair to say? The woman who barged into your sister's home, tied you up and threatened to harm you. Does that sound like something a sane woman would do? Do you think she's crazy?" Gavyn asked with a heightened tone as he slammed his fist down on the wood.

Please, Elizabeth. Please. Don't fall for it.

"I'm not a licensed professional to give that type of answer," she replied as she let out a breath, looking in my direction for support.

"But in your opinion, is she mentally unstable?" Gavyn asked, slightly changing his questioning from what was in my dream, which allowed me to take another breath.

"My opinion shouldn't matter," she answered. "As I stated before, I'm not licensed to make that type of judgment."

"Your Honor," Gavyn pleaded, "will you tell Ms. Hyde to answer the question?"

"Your Honor," Finn interrupted, "Ms. Hyde has answered the question. She's not qualified to provide that type of opinion."

"Your Honor," Elizabeth chimed in, "if you want to know my opinion, I will gladly give it."

The judge nodded for her to proceed.

Tread lightly.

"Mr. McKenzie, you want to know if I think someone is mentally unstable if they come to attack me, is that correct?"

"Yes, do you think Ms. Ascot was mentally unstable when she came to attack you?"

"There is more to that question than just Ms. Ascot. If all people who attack someone are mentally unstable, the mental hospitals would be full. There are many times when people attack for good reason. I do not think military soldiers are mentally unstable for attacking the enemy. They are following orders and attacking on command. Do you believe our soldiers are mentally unstable, Mr. McKenzie?"

"Ms. Hyde, you are twisting my words. I'm not asking about military personnel. I am asking if you think Ms. Ascot was in her right mind when she attacked you."

"And I'm telling you, Mr. McKenzie, that she knew what she was doing. She was planned and ready, just like a soldier. So if you think she was not in her right mind, you are basically saying anyone in the military isn't in their right mind. And I would never say that. I'm proud of the military that defends me and my freedoms."

I sat in awe of the way Elizabeth spun the questioning. And by the expression on Gavyn's face, he, too, was speechless.

"Excuse me," Milo said standing up and addressing his fumbling co-council. "Do you mind? I have a few questions to ask Ms. Hyde."

This is different, I thought. In my dream, Gavyn had sat down smiling beside Jenny. I watched the back of Jenny's head as Milo proceeded toward Elizabeth.

As if Jenny knew I was watching her, she turned her head to make eye contact with me. There was an eeriness in her gaze and a slight smirk, as if warning me something different was about to come.

As if she knew.

CHAPTER 20

"Ms. Hyde," Milo started with his deep bravado, oozing his Russian accent for the jury like an alluring perfume. "Jennifer Ascot works at your father's law firm, correct?"

"I'm not sure if she is still an employee since she has been in and out of jail for over a year," she answered with a tone of noncompliance.

"Well, let me confirm for you," he said with superiority. "She is still an employee." He took a step forward, breaching her personal space and asked, "Do you have a bad relationship with your father?"

"Objection, Your Honor," Finn shouted. "What does this have to do with anything? Elizabeth Hyde is not on trial."

"Agreed," the judge replied. "Get to your point, Mr. Alexeev."

"Yes, yes, Your Honor," Milo nodded, taking another step further. "You are taking out your issues with your father onto my client, wouldn't you say?"

Elizabeth looked at me as I gave her a smirk with an eye roll. *They are stretching,* I thought.

"My father and I don't have a perfect relationship, as probably many people here don't. But for you to imply I am taking out my issues on Jenny is idiotic," she said as Milo tried to interrupt. She continued speaking over him. "She tried to kill me. You want me to say she is crazy or mentally unstable, but to be honest, I think you are the crazy one for defending her because you know she did this to me and you're trying to trick the jurors into thinking she is this weak, troubled woman. But she isn't. She is a strong, calculating, barbaric murdering criminal who acts out her wildest inclinations with no remorse. She's not crazy, you are. But she needs to be locked up for the rest of her life."

"That colorful allegation makes it sound like you may have some issues, possibly from childhood, that you've been bottling up for some time," Milo stated as I sat in shock, watching the jaw-dropping expression on Elizabeth's face. I knew there were multiple ways she could react with that cunning, bullying remark about her childhood horrors. I just hoped my dream didn't come back to fruition.

"Objection!" Finn said, jumping up in Elizabeth's defense.

"Mr. Alexeev," Judge Otto scathed with the slamming of his gavel. "One more uncalled-for statement such as that, and I will put you in contempt."

"It's not just an allegation," Elizabeth smiled as I took a deep breath, waiting for the ax to fall. "It's proven by this scar right here," she said pointing to her right cheek and turning her head to let the entire jury see her battle scar.

She turned her head away from the jury and stared straight ahead to me as if telling me, *I've got this, Solo.*

Soon, it was going to be my turn in that stand.

Thankfully not today.

But tomorrow.

CHAPTER 21

Grant sat behind his desk in the D.C. Department of Transportation waiting for his wife, Whitney, to text back concerning her plans for the evening.

Whitney was a flight attendant who traveled around the world and came home for a few days here or there or for brief layovers. She had always wanted to tour the world and see the wonders such as the Taj Mahal, which was just a tourist trap; the Eiffel Tower, which was nothing more than an extremely large paperweight to her now; and the Pyramids in Egypt, which just left her feeling dirty and sandy.

Her outlook had changed from the 22-year-old wanting to see the world, to the 27-year-old wanting to make as much money as she could so she could flaunt her latest wardrobe on her Instagram feed and make her high school cronies green with envy.

I'm having supper with the girls again tonight, Whitney texted back.

Yeah, I just didn't know when you might be coming home. Didn't know if I should wait up for you.

You don't have to.

Grant read the text and wondered if there was something else going on. They were usually hot and heavy when she was home, but in the last month, it had mostly been lukewarm and separate sides of the bed.

Last night, she went out with a couple of her friends, and he was feeling like the third wheel in their marriage. He wasn't used to that feeling. He had done everything he could to better himself since high school. He'd gotten a good job with benefits. He worked out and tried to eat healthy. He saw the women in the office watch him as he walked down the hall when he wore his snug khakis.

He only wished his wife would look at him the same way.

Tomorrow night, let's go out. Just the two of us, he texted, catching his boyish grinning reflection in the glass picture frame sitting on his desk. He picked up the picture of their honeymoon trip to Tahiti and noted the happy couple with their arms around one another like intoxicated newlyweds.

He couldn't remember the last time she'd held on to him like that. It had been months.

Sure, she texted back with nothing else. No *I love you*. No *Can't wait*. No excited emoji like they used to send one another when she was on a red-eye flight to Zurich. Now it was just *Sure*, as if she were responding to a work text informing her of a flight change.

Can't wait. I love you, Whit, he texted as he waited for her to respond.

She never did.

CHAPTER 22

"Here you go," Officer Dakota Peterson said, handing Officer Winston Cooper his black coffee in a flimsy paper cup. "It's hot," she said with a sarcastic smile.

"What a new concept," he replied without looking away from the documents on his computer. "I wonder if that will take off."

Peterson walked behind him, looking over Cooper's shoulder to see the police report of a deceased man that was presumed to have hung himself. She skimmed the paperwork and it seemed like an open and shut case.

No forced entry.

A suicide note.

A farewell email to co-workers.

It radiated self-inflicted death with red neon letters.

"So someone said they saw something?" she asked, sipping her coffee while watching Cooper click open the video recording from the morning.

"Uh-huh," he murmured as his eyes fixated on the video, trying to zone in on something that would point to who the culprit was.

"So you believe the anonymous tip?" she asked quizzically.

Officer Peterson originally worked as a dispatch operator at the start of her police career. She had outshined most of the cadets during her training at the police academy, but she'd had her sights set more on catching a husband than catching a criminal. But after years of being overlooked or played by men like a toy, she'd had enough.

Her anniversary of being a police officer on the street was a month away. It seemed like everything had changed when Officer Cooper pushed her to look within herself and consider the possibility of making a change. She had jumped at the change of being his patrol partner, and it seemed like everything else started to fall into place.

Her relationship status had actually changed last April when she'd picked up a suspect for a case. A couple of weeks later they were out on their first date and they hadn't looked back since.

"Why would someone lie about this?" Wint asked as he studied the video, stopping and replaying each scene.

"I don't know," she shrugged, grabbing a nearby chair to rest her legs. "To bust our chops?"

Peterson watched as Cooper shook his head at the question. He was silent and engrossed with the footage. She knew Cooper was a good cop, maybe one of the best in their precinct, and if he had a feeling about this suicide, she needed to trust his instincts.

Because lately, his instincts had been on target.

CHAPTER 23

Come on! Come on! Cooper told himself as he walked away from the computer to go to the men's restroom. He walked down the hallway ignoring the other officers and workers in the precinct. With each step, he could hear his heartbeat pumping, drowning out any other sound in the often noisy hallway.

The men's restroom was lined with urinals, and a few partitioned toilets were empty. Standing in front of a mirror he splashed some water on his face, watching it stream down his cheeks until it was a light trickle. He closed his eyes and took a deep breath. And then another deep breath. And then another.

He felt the weight of an innocent man's death on his shoulders. A death he knew was going to happen, yet could do nothing to stop. He leaned over the sink, letting the last remaining droplets of water splash into the sink as he exhaled a hot breath of frustration.

Wiping his face with his damp hand, he looked once again in the mirror. He looked at the man who tried his best every day, but some days did not succeed. Being a cop demanded the best out of him every day because one little straw out of place could break the camel's back.

He was feeling like the broken camel.

He grabbed a few paper towels and dried his wet face. As he threw away the damp towels, he wondered what he was expecting out of this reprieve.

Did you really think a face of cold water was going to help?

He stood beside the trashcan and texted Solo.

I have nothing.

He watched his phone as a message quickly came back. *What?*

On Ted's murder. We have nothing.

Oh.

Cooper looked down at his phone and wanted to smack Solo with his quick response. He reread the two letters that oozed of little care.

Really? That's all you can say? A man died and all you can say is Oh?

Cooper looked down as his phone started ringing.

It was Solo.

CHAPTER 24

"Wint, what did you want me to say?" I snapped, slightly agitated by his heroic attitude. "Of course, they aren't going to find anything on their first look because it looked like a suicide, and you all don't want to waste your time on an open-and-shut case."

"What are you trying to say, Solo?" Wint asked with an undertone of controlled rage. "We don't take each crime seriously?"

"You know what I mean, Wint. Come on," I said trying to cool an already tense conversation. "If you were the first cop there and you didn't know what you already know, what would you have thought?"

Silence.

I stood in the quiet hall of the courthouse waiting for Elizabeth to come out of her meeting with Finn since Judge Otto called for lunch and for testimonies to resume afterwards. I paced the lonely corridor, feeling the defeat Wint was hanging onto.

"You still there?" I asked, looking out the window at the traffic creeping through the lunchtime hour. I felt like I was creeping by as well waiting for Elizabeth as her portion of the trial was complete, and my testimony was approaching tomorrow.

"So, what are you telling me?" Wint replied, "to let this go?"

"No. There are two killers out there and we have to find them. But you have to stop beating yourself up for not solving the case before it happened. All you had to go on was our dreams, and I agonized over every possible clue before I even let you know about it. And I didn't see anything."

"Then why have the dream?" Wint asked condescendingly. "Why even show you that someone was going to die if you weren't supposed to stop it?"

"I don't know," I stammered, ruffling my hair with my sweating palms as I had asked myself that same question hundreds of times in the last year. "Maybe to assure me He is still in control and it's not my purpose to fix it?"

"So, you're saying God just lets people die?" Wint asked with heaviness in his breath.

"People die every day," I said solemnly. "And sometimes, God uses us to save them."

"I have a hard time believing God is showing you a dream of someone's death just because," Wint replied.

I, too, had a hard time with that concept, but right now, that explanation was all I had to hold on to during these hard conversations and unsolved dreams.

"Oh, Wint," I said watching Elizabeth exit her meeting with a dazed look on her face. "I think they are going to kill again," I said in a quieter voice just in case someone walked by.

"You're just now telling me?" Wint asked. "When were you going to tell me? When it's too late?"

"After I talk to Elizabeth to see if she has anything," I said waving at her, even though she didn't wave back from down the hall. "I'll let you know. Got to go."

I put my phone up and started heading toward Elizabeth who didn't look amused or pleased after her compelling testimony.

"What's wrong?"

"The prosecution is considering accepting the insanity defense," she said in shock. "Finn spoke to his people a few minutes ago, and they agree she was insane during the time of the crime."

"You've got to be kidding me!"

Elizabeth started to shake and reached out her arms, digging her fingernails into my forearms trying to gain a little stability for the world that was just flipped from under her. "They're afraid of losing to Milo again. They have an election coming up and they don't want this to be the last thing the voters see before casting their vote." Her legs started

64

to go limp as I wrapped my arms around my shocked friend. "'She'll at least be locked up,' is all he would say to me."

"But for how long?" I asked as we hobbled to the bench overlooking the street. The traffic was crawling, but it was quicker than us as we sat frozen in disbelief.

After seeing Milo twist Jenny's murderous schemes into coincidental meetings and heart-wrenching tales of childhood tragedies during the last trial, I was afraid he was dementedly capable of proving her mentally insane.

I sat beside my friend who had bared her soul to a room full of strangers only for it to be rejected by the one person she was supposed to trust the most. I was wondering what would be the point of telling my story to the jury tomorrow.

But I was more afraid of what Milo might ask me. He had a way of knowing things no one else should know.

No one.

CHAPTER 25

We left the courthouse and walked to a nearby bistro, where the noisy atmosphere of clanking cups and scraping forks allowed us the freedom to speak openly.

"This can't be happening," Elizabeth said, shaking her head in disbelief as she ravished through her gluttonous hamburger like a woman coming off of a fast. She didn't care about appearances or caloric intake as she dipped her mozzarella sticks in marinara sauce while sipping on her triple chocolate shake.

"Maybe my testimony will sway them," I said optimistically as I found comfort in a fried chicken sandwich and garlic fries.

She rolled her eyes in annoyance.

I knew that look.

"Hon, your testimony isn't going to be any better than mine and they know that," she said without wavering. "That's why they chose me first, I guess to test the waters."

"You've heard the expression, save the best for last," I replied, stealing one of her mozzarella sticks as if proving my point.

"But you're not last, dear," she said condescendingly. "They have a few other people testifying after you," she smiled with a hearty laugh. "So you're basically just there to fill up time to make it look like the prosecution has a good case."

"But they do have a good case!" I exclaimed, slamming my fist and causing my last few fries to jump. "They have medical reports of what she did to us; they have our testimony," I said as she nodded in agreement.

"And I did splendidly," she chimed in theatrically.

"Sure," I said to get back to my point. "They have the paramedics' reports of her being in the house. They shouldn't lose."

"But," she stopped to take a sip of her milkshake. "Finn is afraid the jury is going to have a hard time finding her guilty for attempted murder when they think she is crazy."

"And if Finn gives her a deal, what does that mean?" I asked, shaking my head in disgust. "She will live in an insane asylum for no telling how long and then she will get out once she proves she isn't mentally unstable anymore?"

"He didn't go into all the details because once he started talking about not going after her for attempted murder, I went ballistic on him."

"You didn't threaten to shoot him, did you?"

"Solo, give me a little credit," she huffed, but then resigned to my look of judgment. "He's lucky they didn't let me bring my gun in, though." She picked up her last mozzarella stick and eyed it menacingly. "I may have said something about ways of making a man unable to have kids."

"You didn't," I scoffed, but knowing Elizabeth, she did.

"Well, he wasn't using the pair he had," she said as she started to chuckle.

"You didn't really say that!" I started to laugh, envisioning a strong, strapping man a head taller than Elizabeth cowering from her threats. But I shouldn't judge.

She's scared me a time or two with her threats, and I've been known to check myself after I woke up from a long nap to make sure everything was still in place.

Elizabeth said she knew people who would do things for her.

And I sometimes believed her.

"So Finn is on your blacklist now?" I asked.

"Do you really think I have a list?" she smiled playfully.

"You showed it to me with my name listed and scratched out multiple times from when you changed your mind about me," I billowed in laughter. "Now, will you actually do anything? That's what I'm not sure about."

"Oh, silly Solomon," she said pulling out her milkshake straw to lick off some of the whipped cream.

"What?"

She looked away and raised her hand to get the check as she spoke. "You think I scratched your name off because I changed my mind about you."

"Elizabeth."

The waitress walked over with the bill that Elizabeth gladly paid with a sizable tip as she continued to ignore my confusion.

"You never did anything to me," I commented as I tried to go through all my memories of us together. There were too many to remember. "Did you?"

She shrugged her shoulders as she stood up, tapping me on my shoulder as she walked by. She leaned down and whispered in my ear. "Time will tell."

"That's not funny," I said standing up to follow her. "Not funny at all."

CHAPTER 26

"Can he really do this?" Elizabeth asked for the tenth time as she paced around the newly furnished office of Cooper Law. Veronica sat behind her desk, redialing Finn's office, but still getting his voicemail.

"Finn, this is Veronica Cooper. Give me a call when you can," she said as she ended her call.

"Elizabeth, how many times do you have to keep asking the same question? The answers aren't going to change."

She stopped pacing the office and looked directly into my eyes with fiery rage. "Can he really do this?"

"Fine," I said standing up to leave the estrogen-filled office to get some fresh air. The coolness of the autumn air hit my lungs like an unwelcomed guest as I walked the sidewalk covered with fallen leaves.

I wanted to think of a solution to this problem, to ease Elizabeth's tension and help her in her resolution. But no matter what I thought, it kept coming back to the fallen leaves on the ground. My thoughts would circle with a possible scenario and a possible interaction, but it always culminated with me looking down at my feet kicking up some crispy leaves.

God, I said inaudibly as if starting a prayer as my thoughts circled back to the brown leaves crunching beneath my feet. *Am I like these leaves? Because I feel like them right now.*

I wanted to hear His voice. I wanted to feel something that reassured me He was with me. I wanted to see one of my stupid dreams foretelling me that everything was going to work itself out.

But all I heard was the crunching. All I felt was the rustling of feet through the shallow covering. All I saw were leaves that were once beautiful and full of life. But now they were nothing but dead fragments of something that used to cling onto a large, sturdy tree.

My eyes widened at what I saw. I was just like the leaf.

Dead, walking alone, feeling distant, when there was something bigger that I was a part of. There was something that we were all a part of, and I needed to get back that thrill of life. The last couple of months had been draining knowing this trial was coming. Elizabeth and I continued to work out our dreams and help as many people as we could, but we had lost the vigor.

It had become a job and not an opportunity. I had lost the awe and wonder in these dreams. The wonder I had a year ago when they were first being revealed. Six months ago, when a new band of killers were knocking off their old loves. Three months ago, when Elizabeth and I exposed our secret to Wint and welcomed him into our little circle of unbelievable encounters.

I had lost that excitement of making a difference. I had let the rush of saving someone's life float away like a leaf breaking away from its branch. I had forgotten that these dreams were a gift from God, and for some unknown reason He was inviting me to participate in this epic journey.

I glanced down at my unmoving feet and saw pieces of the last couple of months scattered among the leaves. I raised my head with a new outlook and perspective.

I wasn't going to let this be our demise. I knew in life I wasn't guaranteed success or easy roads, but I was always guaranteed to never be walking alone.

I closed my eyes and uttered *Amen*. A powerful gust of wind swirled around me as I stood still, allowing the breeze to toss my hair. I kept my eyes closed and felt at peace. Something was beckoning me to turn around. Demanding me to return to Elizabeth since we were a team. Reminding me that Wint's passion wasn't a character flaw, but a reason he was in my circle. I slowly turned around and opened my eyes.

I started to laugh as I looked at the sidewalk in the distance. It had been cleared of the dead leaves.

CHAPTER 27

Milo sat beside Jenny while the prosecution questioned their psychologist. Dr. Wallace Weaver answered each of Finn's questions with complete assurance and certainty. He explained the M'Naghten Rule and how Jennifer Ascot was not capable of knowing what she was doing at the time of the alleged attempted murders based upon her traumatic experience of hearing her brother was a part of the murderous Carbon Monoxide Killers.

The second part of the M'Naghten Rule stated she was not capable of recognizing how evil her crimes were.

Dr. Weaver went on and discussed another test, the Irresistible Impulse Test, where he stated Jenny was harboring so much mental anguish that forced her to chaotically go after Elizabeth Hyde.

Milo watched Dr. Weaver like a hunter scoping out a caged bear, savoring the beauty of what he was witnessing. Jenny looked over at Milo, shocked at Dr. Weaver's unwavering assessment of her mental state, adding another solidifying brick in her insanity defense.

"How'd you get him to say that?" Jenny whispered, leaning over to Milo.

Milo didn't respond. He just continued to watch the production he had concocted. He enjoyed the finer things in life, and this was just like one of his fine wines, his Russian arias, or the exquisite diamond Rolex on his wrist.

Jenny asked again, but he remained transfixed on Dr. Weaver, examining his movements and tone of voice as if working for security of the KGB. He knew how to sniff out a deceptive spy, as everyone has their own tells when lying. He had noticed Dr. Weaver's movement of adjusting his rimless glasses every time he was asked about Jenny's insanity claim. And every time he would recite verbatim what they'd paid him to say.

But not every payment was in cash or expenditures. They paid some people as forms of protection for themselves and family.

Milo's expressionless face morphed into somewhat intrigued with a hint of a smile when he caught onto Dr. Weaver's lying mechanism. He hadn't lost his touch.

He just hoped he wouldn't have to knock off Dr. Weaver if one of the jurors started to see through his fictitious reports and not allow Jenny her insanity defense. His smile faded to his usual placid gaze as he considered all the falling dominos he would have to have someone clean up once they had landed in their blood. He wasn't ready to waste that type of manpower.

And he never knew when he may need to use Dr. Weaver in the future. A good psychologist was hard to find.

"Milo," Jenny started before he stopped her with a turn of his head.

"Do you really want to know, Jenika?" he said cruelly, letting the words spill off his lips like venom. "Really?"

CHAPTER 28

I returned to Veronica's office to find Elizabeth in a slightly better state of mind and sitting down across from Veronica.

"Where have you been?" Elizabeth asked hastily, standing up and placing her purse straps over her shoulder. "We have something to do."

"Where are you two going?" Veronica asked, looking up from her laptop. But Elizabeth had already walked out of the room.

"I have no idea," I answered following the rushed Elizabeth to her car parked outside Cooper Law. "What was that about?"

"I forgot to tell you," she said stepping into her BMW and starting the engine. "I may have something about the murder tonight," she smiled as I buckled up.

"*Now* you tell me?" I laughed as I glanced down at my watch and saw that it was 3:34 in the afternoon. "You couldn't have told me that this morning?"

"Excuse me," she snapped, twisting her head to give me a look of annoyance. "You're the one who tore into me this morning about how I was going to mess up on the stand." But she didn't say *mess*.

I had learned in the last year it was easier to let her tire herself out on her rampage like a three-year-old throwing a tantrum. She continued to talk as I tuned her out. I had learned how to do that as well.

"Solo!" she shouted. "Solo!" she said again, snapping her fingers in front of my face.

"What?" I snapped back, waking from my quiet meditative state.

"You tuned me out again!" she billowed, rolling her eyes and shaking her head. "After I just apologized and thanked you!"

"I missed that?" I laughed as I straightened up and changed the radio station.

"Nah," she said in a more casual tone.

"You confuse me sometimes," I smiled, leaving the radio on an easy listening station. "So what do you know about the kill tonight?"

She smiled and nodded her head assuredly.

"Well?"

"Now you're listening?" she asked, letting the words hang in the air as if reciting the last lottery number. "What do you have to say?"

"Have to say?" I asked in shock, busting up in fits of laughter. "You are something else sometimes."

"And?"

I let that question linger for a few seconds before I succumbed to her childish inquisition. "And I'm sorry for tuning you out."

"Now, was that so hard to say?"

"It would be for you."

"Yeah," she answered nodding her head. "But you do it so much better than I ever could. So why look foolish?"

"Try it sometime," I smiled as I sunk back into the passenger seat. "So what do you have about tonight?"

She smiled and looked at me as if she was dangling a piece of candy out of reach of a child. "What would you say if I told you I have the next victim's license plate number?"

I understood her smile and started to match it with my own. After such a dismal day, I needed this bit of information.

The dead leaves were gone.

I was starting to feel alive.

CHAPTER 29

"Hey Wint," I said on speakerphone as Elizabeth continued to drive in the afternoon traffic. "Can you do a search on a license plate number?"

"Yeah, why?" he asked suspiciously. "Wait, do you know something?"

"Well, Solo is as informed as a cat with a stick up its--" Elizabeth started as I cut her off.

"Come on, just tell him the number."

I could hear Wint frantically typing on his computer, getting ready to take the numbers, getting one inch closer to saving the next victim's life and one second closer to ending this murderous duo.

Elizabeth grabbed her phone and started opening up an app.

"Excuse me," I said, grabbing the phone out of her hand. "You're driving," I protested. "I'll find it for you."

"Don't look in the photos," she smiled wickedly, and I shuddered at the thought of her sexual games with Jeremiah. "I'm kidding," she laughed.

"I still wouldn't test her, Solo," Wint chimed in over the phone. "There's no telling what you'll find."

"Winston!" she exploded as her cheeks started to redden.

"Oh, Wint, I wish you could see this," I jabbed when I realized he could. I picked up the phone and switched on FaceTime. "Look at those rosy cheeks."

"Are you blushing?" Wint chuckled.

"Get that phone out of my face or I won't tell you the number," she squawked. I continued to hold the device so her face was in view for Wint to witness. "I'm warning you," she urged.

"Fine," I relented, moving the camera shot to the license plate number I found in her notes CZ 4583. "Are you getting that, Wint?"

"Got it," he said, typing in the random numbers and letters.

I watched the phone screen as Wint clicked away on the keyboard, his eyes lighting up before they quickly darted away. "I got to go," he said, ending the call.

"Well that was short," Elizabeth said, slightly agitated.

"He probably isn't allowed to do things like this," I pointed out. "You know, give sensitive taxpayer information such as a name and address to us."

"It's a freakin' name," Elizabeth reiterated. "A name of someone we are going to save tonight. He shouldn't be mad that we got his personal information. He should be relieved when we stop the two from killing him tonight."

I understood her perspective, but I knew the rest of the police force probably wouldn't see it our way. I looked out the window as some of the gray clouds parted, allowing a sliver of light to stream down.

My phone vibrated. It was a text from Wint.

"Erwin Little," I said to Elizabeth who looked over at me with a beaming smile.

"Well, Mr. Little," she said encouragingly. "Your parents should have picked a better first name for you."

"Really?" I marveled. "That's all you have to say?"

"What?" she mused. "I bet he goes by his middle name."

I looked out the window as she continued to say his name in an awkward, demeaning tone.

"Erwin, it sounds so, so, so." She stopped and thought as she continued to drive. "So sterilized."

"It's just a name," I chuckled as she slammed on the brake and turned, almost hydroplaning on the narrow one-way road. "Elizabeth, what's wrong?"

"You know, we have more than one dream today," she replied nonchalantly.

"You never told me your dreams," I quipped as she slid into a parking spot and parked her car.

"Oh, did I forget to tell you?" she smiled cunningly. "A woman is going to go into labor in a few minutes, so you better run along and help her out."

"Help her out?" I exclaimed. "Help her out? Elizabeth, I don't know anything about that."

"Oh, Prissy, well you better get on YouTube then," she said as she pointed at the Vietnamese restaurant across the street. "Now get along. She's going to need you soon."

"Are you kidding me?" I asked in disbelief. "You have the equipment for this type of situation."

"Solo," she replied showing me her newly painted nails. "I have to keep these for two weeks because apparently Kim needed to go on a vacation and she didn't ask for my approval first. And Kim is the only one I will let touch my nails."

"You've got to be kidding me," I stammered.

"Go on, Solo, her water is going to be breaking soon, and no one else in there knows what to do," she said distantly as she picked up her phone and started scrolling through her missed texts.

"You're not lying to me, are you?" I questioned. "Not like last week?"

"I said I wouldn't do that to you again," she answered. "Didn't I?"

"Yeah, but you don't always keep your promises," I said as I looked over at the restaurant.

"You're going to do fine," she encouraged. "Just tell her to breathe and it will work out," she smiled. "Now go before it's too late!"

I ran across the street, praying with each step when it hit me, she hadn't gone into labor yet.

I pulled out my phone and dialed 9-1-1.

"What's your emergency?"

"A woman is going into labor at..." I looked at the red awning and tried my best with the pronunciation, "Cha Ca."

"Did you say Cha Ca?" the operator asked.

"Yes."

"Okay, just tell her to remain calm because someone else just called it in too. They should be there in a few minutes."

"Thank you," I said looking through the glass of the restaurant. I scratched my head since there didn't appear to be any commotion of a woman going into labor. Instead, there was actually a pregnant woman sitting comfortably eating her noodles.

I turned to see Elizabeth waving from the comfort of her driver's seat as a text appeared.

Oh, did I forget to tell you? I called for an ambulance already.

CHAPTER 30

I left Cha Ca's after the paramedics took Julie Inez to Howard University Hospital. Luckily, when Elizabeth called in the emergency, she warned the operator that there was road construction on Florida Avenue and for the driver to stay away from that road. That advice was the reason I could leave the restaurant without asking for towels or boiling water, which was everything I knew about birthing babies. And I only knew that much from the movies. I wouldn't think anyone would be interested in a cup of herbal tea during a labor, but I didn't know what other reason would call for boiling water.

Elizabeth dropped me off at Union Station where I hopped on the Red Line to meet Dr. Jeremiah Huffington for an early afternoon snack at a little coffee shop two blocks away from Ford's Theatre.

He ordered his black coffee with a couple of packets of sugar and a shot of hazelnut as I enjoyed a blueberry muffin and a strawberry iced tea.

We conversed in pleasantries as Jeremiah went on about an article in *The New Yorker* on the rise of cryptocurrencies, while I listened with a limited economic understanding of having $563.76 in my checking account. Elizabeth has asked me to start investing or using the money she gifted me, but I still felt weird about it.

"Solo, find a better place to live," she would nag as she would sit in her car in my parking lot on the mornings when she would pick me up, being too fearful to make the trek through the rough terrain of my parking lot.

Jeremiah continued to regale me on the intriguing and often misunderstood or commonly unknown investment strategies with this new tech currency as I just continued to politely nod along while enjoying my muffin.

"Oh, dear me, Solomon, I could go on and on. How are you doing?"

"I'm actually doing much better than I was this morning," I smiled.

"Elizabeth told me about the day," he grimaced as he stirred his coffee.

His frown was an understatement of the shambles of Jenny's case. He spoke of Elizabeth's attitude and I agreed with his assessment.

"It's a load of crock," I assured him. "Total bull."

Jeremiah took a sip and then put down his cup. "You mentioned in the text you had something you wanted my opinion on."

Yes. That text. I had almost forgotten, but I knew that if I could be open with anyone, it would be with Jeremiah. Even though Jeremiah was an atheist, he had an interesting way of seeing the world. I sometimes wished I could see everything how he saw it.

"Do you believe, hypothetically speaking in all of your research in all the cultures you write about, in possessions?"

"Hmm," he said as he sat back and pondered the question. "Are you asking if I believe in possessions or if other people believe in them?"

"Well, you probably don't believe in them, right?" I said gently. "I mean, how could you believe in something spiritually bad invading someone?"

"Solomon, there are many types of possessions. There are physical possessions," he said as he reached across the table and grabbed a crumb of my muffin. "I have now possessed your muffin. So, there are some possessions I have to agree with."

"You could have asked before reaching over with your grubby hands," I laughed as he shrugged his shoulders and popped the crumb into his mouth. "Fine," I resigned. "What about people being possessed by an outside force?"

"Just because I do not believe in it, doesn't mean that others don't," he said flatly. "But then again, just because I don't believe in it, I can't disagree with other people's findings in which they say possessions occurred. But did a possession really occur from an outside force, or did they just change their personality for a period, in essence possessing themselves? That is where the possession claim gets tricky."

I lowered my voice, sinking my head down as if two spies were speaking of their next move in this quiet coffee shop and asked, "Do people still claim possessions today?"

"Solo, now you are getting to what I can sink my teeth into," he relished as he leaned his elbows on the table. "People still claim possessions in many types of faiths and societies. You just don't hear about it much in America." He stopped and squinted his eyes. "But people still claim them here too."

"So what is your stance on possessions around the world?"

"Oh geez, Solomon, that is a big question. From an anthropology standpoint, I have to agree that many people believe they occur. In many societies in the world, possessions are a common occurrence. They are feared, dreaded, some are revered, and even honored."

"So you are telling me that there is scientific evidence that possessions still occur?"

"There is scientific evidence that some type of phenomena happens that some people call possessions."

"Really?"

"I would stake all my academia on it."

I sat there and looked down at my partially eaten muffin and lost the last bit of my appetite. I knew Jesus healed people who had been possessed, but that was 2,000 years ago. But in the far regions of my mind I knew that if it happened then, it was still possible today.

82

But when Jeremiah, with all of his anthropological studies, confirmed this phenomenon as something that still happened today, my insides churned.

Could Jenny be possessed?

Is that why she was so evil?

I was afraid to answer the question because on one side, if she wasn't possessed, maybe she was mentally crazy enough to come and hunt down Elizabeth.

Suddenly, my insides shifted as a chilling new thought invaded my safe space. Jenny wasn't coming to kill Elizabeth. She was coming to enact revenge on Veronica. But her hate erupted so much that Elizabeth was just a bystander.

Who would try to kill someone they originally didn't plan to kill just because they were there and she was ready to attack?

Someone crazy?

Someone possessed?

Or just someone incomprehensibly evil?

I picked up my tea with shaky hands and realized I didn't know how to truthfully testify tomorrow. I didn't know what Jenny was.

CHAPTER 31

Gavyn reclined on the weight bench and took a deep breath. Thoughts were swirling like an unwelcome guest around his head of the day in court and Milo's and Jenny's strange interactions. Reaching his arms, he gripped the bar and started his next set of presses.

He focused on the reflective bar, watching it come and go with each movement. His breathing was controlled and his muscles were contracting. He loved that feeling of a motion that caused a burn after ten presses, but the sensation was just too good to stop. He continued a few more reps, letting that tightness envelop his shoulders. He gritted his teeth as the tingling moved up to his triceps and biceps.

Come on, one more, he told himself as his workout jam blared in his ears. He watched the bar move up to its resting place and felt the rush of adrenaline of a job well done. He looked around the gym, packed as usual with the professional crowd of political aides and stockbrokers who had recently called it a day from their grind. He stood up and flexed in front of the mirrors, admiring the result of years of hard work, giving a few women on the ellipticals behind him a bit of eye candy to tide them over for another mile or two.

Wiping down his sweat from the bench, he reached down and grabbed his shaker bottle of water with some fruit punch protein powder swirled in and guzzled the sweetness. He posed like a Greek god, lifting the shaker as if he was Atlas keeping the world and heavens in place. This was another feeling he loved, knowing he was being watched and admired by women who wanted to be with him and men who wanted to be like him.

At least he was getting the limelight here since Milo had been stealing his spotlight in the courtroom during the last week. Gavyn knew he was arrogant and egotistical, but that was why he became an attorney, to let his arrogance shine and get paid doing it. And he was good at what he did.

His bottle ran empty and so did his insides as he had to admit that Milo was likely a better attorney.

It was a thought so disturbing and painful, he didn't want to think it anymore.

He went back to the locker room and checked his phone.

Still on for tonight? a text read.

He grinned wickedly as he took off his muscle tank and shorts that dripped of salty sweat, standing nude while allowing anyone who passed by to see his rippling physique. He held his phone and texted, letting the cool air collide with his surging body heat, feeling confident in his well-built skin and his plans for the night.

Sure.

CHAPTER 32

The three of us met at Napoli and each ordered our own traditional Italian pizza pie. Elizabeth tore apart her eggplant topping pizza a little more gently than her sandwich at lunch.

"So, what are you thinking about, Elizabeth?" I asked as I devoured my meat topping pizza.

"Well," she said wiping away the crumbs on her lips, "Erwin's clock radio showed 8:02 when he parked his car and got out. I saw nothing else, since my dream was fixed on the red Toyota. I remember hearing him open his house door and shut it. He walked through the house and then he was attacked after a couple of minutes." She cut away another slice of pizza. "So I think we should get to the house around 7:45 and wait until he arrives."

"And then stop him from going in his house somehow?" I asked.

"I was thinking about pretending to have car trouble or something, and then maybe he will let us into his home, and then Wint can do the cop thing and nab them," she said. "Pretend like you hear a sound and then maybe that will scare the thugs, and they will come running out and then we could get them."

"But," Wint interjected as he quickly swallowed his fully-loaded pizza. "But how will that connect them to the Lukin death?" He stopped and shook his head. "No, they could just say they were robbing the place and then Lukin would still be labeled a suicide."

"But I called and reported two people breaking into his house," I replied. "Wouldn't that be enough to tie the two?"

"Solo, if we go into the house without Elizabeth, *we* could look like the two killers," Wint explained as he took of sip of his water. "No, we have to wait until Little goes into his house and stop them before it's too late."

"So he's going to be like bait?" Elizabeth softly asked. "I mean, I'm fine with that. I use Solomon as bait often and he doesn't care."

"I do care," I burst out in shock, spitting a bite of my pizza across the table, landing beside Wint's phone. He casually flicked the half-chewed piece of sausage to the floor as I continued. "I care a lot, actually. You just never care to listen to me as I scold you."

"Tomato, potato," she sighed. "Everyone always has a side to their story." She stopped and took another bite of her eggplant pizza.

"And?" Wint asked as he looked at me confused.

"And what?" she asked unconcerned. "I don't care about anyone else's side." She smiled as she looked at Wint. "I only care about mine," she said with a wink.

"One day, I hope you know what it feels like to be bait," I laughed.

"Oh, honey," she responded as she tossed her hair for the single guy across the room. "I've been bait a time or two," she said as she waved flirtatiously. "But unlike you, I know how to slide off the hook." I watched as the young man strutted across the hardwood floor with confidence radiating from his bright white smile, but he walked back deflated as Elizabeth slid off her hook with no acknowledgement of his crushed spirit.

"Heartless," Wint uttered.

"Ruthless," I joined.

"Aww, guys," she chimed in like a peppy cheerleader. "I didn't know you knew my middle names. But you forgot Bitchy too."

"I didn't forget," Wint chimed in as he popped a piece of ice into his mouth. "Veronica reminds me of your name weekly."

"Why, because we're so alike?" Elizabeth quipped, tossing a piece of ice into her mouth.

I looked down at my watch with a smile trying to stay safely out of their conversation. Even after a year, I still never knew what she was going to say. We finished our meal and got a couple of to-go cups since it was a quarter till 7. We had a little more time to strategize a plan, get to Erwin's home, rescue him, and have the two killers in handcuffs before the seventh inning of the World Series.

CHAPTER 33

The two killers parked their cars at the baseball fields at Wheaton Regional Park. They wore their black attire to keep from being noticed, but they weren't afraid of being seen. They had planned their route that included a walk through the woods to the Arcola suburb. They looked at their watches knowing their next victim was attending an NA meeting, and they still had plenty of time before he would arrive home.

They walked through the woods openly discussing the kill from the night before.

"Any regrets?" the leader asked as he held his cellphone out like a flashlight, making sure not to twist his ankle on any protruding tree roots.

"None," the other one said as he readjusted his duffle bag filled with the tools for the night.

"Was it hard buying the stuff?" He watched straight ahead as his cellphone was the only light until the clearing of the trees.

"Easier than I thought," he laughed.

"That's what they always say." He nodded as he turned off his phone to remain invisible to the approaching homes in the distance.

They approached the edge of the tree line but continued walking in shadows until they came to their old teacher's home.

"Ready?" the leader asked.

"Oh yeah," he responded, pulling out their attire from his duffle bag. They each pulled down their ski masks and covered their hands with black leather gloves. They walked side-by-side through the grass to the back porch under the darkening sky.

The leader pulled out his tools to unlock the back door, when he gripped the knob and felt it turn. He looked back at this friend and smiled. "Stupid fool didn't even lock it."

"So, we're technically not breaking and entering," he laughed from behind as they slipped through the door.

"If not breaking into his house makes your conscience feel better, we need to talk," he responded detached.

"I was kidding. You know that."

"Just making sure," the leader answered as his accomplice laid his duffle bag on the floor and pulled out his plastic bags.

They both looked in awe at the black powder as if it was gun powder or sand as it shifted inside the little plastic bag.

"I thought heroin was white," the leader commented as he held the dark drug in his fingers.

"White is cleaner," he answered. "This is black tar heroin."

"Is it going to work?" he demanded, gripping the bag more forcefully, pressing it in his firm hands. "He has to die, not just OD."

"Don't worry." He pulled out a white bag of powder as well. "He'll be gone quick after shooting all this up."

The leader smiled and patted his friend on his shoulder. "I knew you could handle this." He brushed by him, walking through the kitchen into the living room. "I had no doubts about it."

"Sounded like you did," he murmured.

"Did you say something?" he asked as he examined the furniture and the contents in the room.

"Nope," he lied, opening the drawers looking for a tablespoon to get the powder liquefied. Rushing back to the table, he poured some of the black powder onto the spoon and then flicked his lighter. He watched in amazement like he was in his ninth-grade chemistry class. He chuckled to himself at the irony that he was about to kill his old chemistry teacher.

"How's it coming?" he asked, walking back into the kitchen, looking in bewilderment at his childhood friend getting a needle of heroin ready. "If only your parents knew what a bad influence I was on you." He stood with his hands resting on his head, taking in the sight. He could take a photo to make this memory last longer.

But he knew the memory would last for years to come. He wasn't the one about to overdose.

CHAPTER 34

Elizabeth insisted on driving her car to Erwin's house as I sat in the back seat laughing at Wint's white knuckles on the handle.

"I should've given you a couple of tickets on that ride," Wint scolded as he tore into Elizabeth's ignorance of speed limit signs and pedestrian crosswalks. "You could've killed that guy, Elizabeth!"

"But I didn't," she responded unfazed.

"What if you had hit him?" Wint interrogated, turning on the interior lights for theatrics.

"I guess I would take my car to the shop to get the dent out tomorrow," she answered coolly, causing Wint to become unhinged.

"Solo, you agree with me, don't you?" Wint pleaded, turning around in his seat, begging for me to agree.

"Me and Jesus get a little tighter every time I step into this car," I grinned as I laid my head back and looked out the passenger side window as they continued to bicker like siblings. For the first time in a few weeks I felt at peace. Even though they were breaking the silence, I felt like this was going to be a turning point for the week to come. We were going to stop these killers from doing any more harm, and even though Jenny's case was going in the crapper, this little ray of sunshine brought rejuvenation to my soul.

I glanced down at the Timex watch I'd had since middle school; it shone 7:54 in blue letters. Elizabeth continually ridiculed my time piece, so to be cautious, I had bought a replica on Amazon a few months back just in case she got the nerve to damage it in some way.

A pair of headlights shined behind me as a vehicle came down the street. I thought about closing my eyes since we still had a few minutes before the action was about to happen.

"As soon as Erwin goes into the house, I'm going to run into the house, and Solo, you are going to run to the back and block the back door with your body so they can't get out. Elizabeth you're going to--" Wint said before Elizabeth interrupted as the headlights slowed and turned into Little's driveway.

"Um, something's not right."

"What?" I asked, shaking my head alert.

"That's Erwin," Wint said as they watched a man in a business suit slam the door shut on his Ford F-250. "I pulled his driver's license and that's him."

"But that's not the car I saw in my dream," Elizabeth said, turning her face to me. I've only seen Elizabeth give that look a couple of times, and the few times she did, it wasn't good.

CHAPTER 35

The two heard the slam of the vehicle door as they stood in the shadows, one on each side of the door frame. The leader's heart was pounding because this was his night to enact revenge. Last night's victim had been his friend's hated PE coach, whom he'd also despised. But tonight was the man who he'd thought was a teacher who cared about him, but realized a little too late that he didn't.

He had asked him to write a letter of recommendation for a scholarship that would have paid for all his tuition and board. As a young kid he had wanted to make his parents proud and attend an Ivy League school. So he'd studied hard, harder than the rest of his friends. He'd made good grades and was involved in extracurricular activities that stood out on college applications. Most teachers even liked him. All he needed was a shining review detailing his exemplary character and ethics.

The day his application was to be sent off along with his transcripts and letter of recommendation, his beloved teacher was sick. Apparently, he had partied a little too much the night before and was too hung over to teach.

He mailed in his application to Brown University, but was denied scholarships because he didn't fully complete the application. Years later, he knew he hadn't been guaranteed a full-ride scholarship to Brown. He knew he could have possibly not been given any scholarship money, even with the glowing recommendation, but he would never know. The one thing he knew for certain was his chemistry teacher derailed that possibility with an early weekend bender.

He heard his once-beloved teacher slipping his house key into the lock and took a deep breath. He heard the lock unclasp as the door squeaked open, letting a trail from the streetlights cascade onto the beige shag carpet.

He pressed his body closer into the wall, almost becoming a part of the wood paneling, camouflaging into the darkness like a puma ready to attack.

CHAPTER 36

"Mr. Little!" I yelled, as Elizabeth, Wint, and I rushed through his front yard, hurdling over the dead flowers that lost their blooms at the first autumn frost.

He turned startled, standing with his front door open on his dark front porch.

"Yes? Who are you?" he asked gruffly.

"I'm Solo, and this is Officer Cooper," I answered when I reached his porch. "Sorry to startle you, but we're looking for someone we thought lived here."

"Yeah?" he asked questioningly. "It's just me and my wife here."

Wint showed Mr. Little his badge as he asked, "Where is your red Toyota?"

"My red Toyota?" Mr. Little responded confused. "I sold that car a couple of weeks ago."

My mouth dropped at the realization that Elizabeth was definitely right. We were at the wrong house.

"Who?" Elizabeth charged in from behind. "Who bought your car?"

"I don't remember his name," he sighed, looking down at his watch.

"Sir," Wint stepped forward with his police stance. "Can you please find the man's name? This is an urgent police matter, and we need to find him quickly."

Mr. Little pulled out his telephone and clicked on an app. He typed a few words and started scrolling through his phone with his thick fingers. I watched in agonizing wait.

Come on, I pleaded silently. *Hurry up.*

Elizabeth felt the same internal struggle, but she vocalized hers. "Do you want me to find what you are looking for? Because as Officer

Cooper didn't say, this is a life or death matter. So if you could speed it up a little, I think he would appreciate it."

"I'm trying," Mr. Little hissed as he continued to squint at his phone, removing his glasses to see the little screen easier. "I should have a check on here with his name and address from where he bought my car."

"That would be great," Wint grinned as he commanded me and Elizabeth to step back.

"Finally," he said as he enlarged the picture on his phone. "Jake Hill on Hermitage Avenue," he said, flipping it around for Wint to see the check. Wint pulled his phone out like he was at a gun fight, taking a picture of the check image.

"Thank you, sir. Thank you," he said as we ran back to the car.

"Where in the world is that?" Elizabeth shouted as she started her engine, squealed her tires, and bulleted down the road.

"It's 35 minutes from here," I stuttered, staring at the directions on my phone as Wint dialed a number on his.

"Shelia, Officer Cooper. There is an emergency at 437 Hermitage Avenue in Silver Springs. Get an ambulance and some officers down there now!"

I glanced down at my watch, and the sometimes comforting blue light of my watch gave off an eeric glow.

8:03.

CHAPTER 37

Mr. Hill stepped into his darkened home unaware that two former students from a time in his life when he wasn't so dependable were lurking in the shadows. He kicked the door closed and stuffed his keys back into his pants pocket. He took two steps away from the door as the leader eased from the shadow. His vision had adjusted to the darkness, but he hoped that Mr. Hill's hadn't yet.

The leader hurled forward, knocking the wind out of Jake's lungs, who quickly spread his arms to get in a defensive stance. However, the leader saw the opportunity to slide both his arms under Jake's. Jake's eyes widened as he felt his attacker's fingers interlock behind his neck. He was caught in a Nelson hold.

The second attacker held his 60-inch black zip tie firmly and dropped to his knees wrapping the plastic tie around Mr. Hill's thighs. He knew that was the easiest spot to start hog tying him because kicking feet could go in many different directions. He threaded the loose cable tie through the lock and pulled as if playing a game of tug-of-war. Mr. Hill's thighs couldn't fight against the sudden tightness, locking them like a tree trunk.

Still kneeling, he pulled out a second zip tie, placing it below Mr. Hill's knees to keep his legs from kicking anymore. He grabbed one more, circled his ankles, and tightly pulled. In thirty seconds, Mr. Hill easily turned from a once-sturdy man into an unbalanced one-legged creature.

During this time, the young man was so focused on doing his job he hadn't even paid attention to Mr. Hill's screams.

"Ready?" he asked his leader as he stood up and got behind him.

"Get off me!" Jake shouted, but he quickly realized he was standing prey with his legs bound. He tried to fight, moving his arms, but with each swing of his fist, he became more off balance.

"One, two," the leader started, but didn't finish. He let go of his Nelson hold grabbing one of Mr. Hill's wrists as his friend grabbed his other wrist. They each pulled until Mr. Hill's arms were behind his back.

"You got it?" the leader asked as his friend grabbed both wrists.

"Got it," he answered with stolen breath.

The leader grabbed one of the long zip ties out of his pocket and encircled Mr. Hill's right bicep and then wove it around his left. He threaded the cord through the lock and started to pull.

"Don't pull too tight," his friend answered. "We don't want to leave any marks on his arm."

The leader nodded his head as he continued to tighten the cord enough to immobilize Mr. Hill. He followed his friend's orders and thought he had done enough as he stepped back.

"Let go," he said as his friend stepped back.

"Why are you doing this?" Mr. Hill screamed, his legs and arms immovable. "Take whatever you want."

The two started to laugh as Jake looked at each one of them when they walked in front of him dressed from head to toe in black, unrecognizable.

"Mr. Hill, we are only here to take one thing," the leader said wickedly. "Your last breath."

CHAPTER 38

Jake's eyes widened with nervousness when the attacker said his name as if they knew one another.

"How'd you know my name?" he asked.

"We don't have time for reunions, Mr. Hill," the other one spoke up. "We are here to give you one last good time," he said with an evil laugh.

"Go get the bottle and the needle," the leader commanded as he watched his friend follow his orders.

"Bottle? Needle?" Jake trembled in fear. "You don't have to do this. You can just walk away."

The leader walked closer until their eyes were inches apart. "But I don't want to, Mr. Hill. I really don't want to."

His friend walked back in with a bottle of Jack Daniel's in one hand and a filled needle in the other.

"You've stayed clean way too long, Mr. Hill. I think it's time to reward your dedication with a little fun," the leader said as he started to clap his hand in applause. "What do you want to do first?"

"Please no," Jake pleaded.

"Don't people usually get down on their knees when they plead?" the leader asked his friend standing next to him. "Let's help him out."

Mr. Hill tried to jump away, but he didn't get too far before his lack of balance took over.

"Hold up, Mr. Hill," the leader laughed. "You can't leave your own party. What kind of host are you?"

They each took an arm and lowered Jake to the ground on his back.

"Since you're on your back, I think you need a little Jack," the friend said grabbing the bottle on the coffee table and handing it to the leader.

"Good idea," he noted as he straddled Jake's chest, resting all his weight on his knees on the floor. "A very good idea, don't you think, Mr. Hill?"

"Please no," Jake answered, shaking his head, sealing his mouth shut as he looked up into the attacker's eyes.

"Come on, open up," he smiled opening the bottle. "It's going to taste so good to you. Just like old times, remember?" the leader asked. "Hold his head still."

His friend knelt down, clasping Mr. Hill's head between his knees. Mr. Hill was unable to move as he tried to squirm, but the weight on his chest left him with no option.

The leader squeezed Mr. Hill's cheeks together, forcing his lips to form a circle. "There you go, Mr. Hill. Be a good boy and drink all you want," he said with a fatherly tone as he turned the bottle over and placed it in his mouth. "Drink up," he said soothingly, but none of the liquid was going down.

"He said to drink up, Mr. Hill," his friend reiterated.

Still Jake wouldn't take the bottle. His lips enclosed around the opening, causing none of the alcohol to escape.

"You leave us no choice," the leader said as he started to tickle Mr. Hill under his armpits and around his chest. Mr. Hill held firm, keeping his mouth from snickering so that not even a drop passed through his lips.

The friend looked up and shook his head at the ridiculous attempt. "Really?"

"You have a better idea? It worked last night."

Mr. Hill's eyes widened as he moaned.

"Watch and learn," he said as he pinched Mr. Hill's nostrils, closing off his airways. "Just wait, because he will eventually have to take a breath."

Mr. Hill's face started to turn red as he held his breath, but he couldn't hold out long enough for them to release his nose. His sealed mouth opened causing the torrent of Jack Daniel's to flood his taste buds. He started to cough, but they didn't relent as they watched the air bubbles make their way to the top of the emptying bottle.

The leader looked down and lifted the bottle away from Mr. Hill's wet lips. "Now, didn't that taste good? Want some more? Or are you ready for round two?" he asked gingerly. "Now, don't worry. If you want more to drink later, I will happily give it to you."

"Help!"

CHAPTER 39

I sat in the backseat watching the time pass under the nighttime sky as Elizabeth drove through red lights and stop signs. This time Wint didn't have a problem with ignoring the rules.

"How did I get this so wrong?" she muttered to herself as she skidded through a right turn.

"Elizabeth, he's not dead yet," I said grabbing the overhead handle.

"Come on, Solo," she said with haste and a roll of her eyes. "He's dead and you know it."

"Just because they attacked him at eight doesn't mean they immediately killed him," I refuted as Wint looked back at me with an unappreciative look. "You two can believe he's dead, but I'm hoping we still have time." I leaned my head back and closed my eyes, saying a few quick prayers that Mr. Hill would be okay, that the cops would get there fast and save him, or a neighbor would possibly rescue him. My mind was fluttering with the endless miracles that could happen, because today was going to be a turning point to make up for the last few weeks.

"Keep hoping for the three of us," Wint said as he looked down at his phone.

Elizabeth cocked her head over at Wint. "I don't need any help with my pessimistic attitude," she announced. "So you better jump off that 'there's nothing we can do' mentality and be more like Solo for a change."

I opened my eyes, wondering if my ears had deceived me. I knew Elizabeth had a wickedly sarcastic sense of humor, but her tone wasn't demeaning. It was appreciative. I raised my head and looked ahead. Even in the darkened car I could see Elizabeth's eyes in her rearview mirror watching me, as if telling me she was on my side even if it didn't sound like she was.

I thought about coming up with a comical response, but she didn't need a laugh. She needed something bigger.

She needed a miracle.

CHAPTER 40

"Hey, bring the socks when you come back," the leader said as he poured another few ounces of Jack into Jake's screaming mouth. He looked at the mostly empty bottle in his hand, smelling the aroma of the hard liquor as it filled the small living room. He pulled the bottle away from Jake's mouth, slamming it on the coffee table behind him.

His friend returned with the socks, and he stuffed them in Jake's mouth to stifle the cries for help.

"Much better," he smiled. "So how are you going to do the heroin?"

Jake's head started shaking as his groans erupted. They couldn't make out the words, but they could see the displeasure in his red eyes.

"Come on," the leader said, "cry a little more. That will make this look even more realistic." He looked at the needle on the coffee table and knew it was time. "Flip him."

The two stood up, one taking the head and the other the feet, and eased him to his belly. Mr. Hill started wiggling like a disabled snake.

"Where do you think you're going?" the leader asked bending down so their eyes could connect. "I said we have round two now. And I remember how much you liked heroin."

His friend grabbed a smaller zip tie and tightened it around Mr. Hill's biceps to cut off the blood flow and make his veins pop. He handed the needle to the leader as they both stooped down to watch Mr. Hill's arm start to look like a street map.

"Now, which vein should I use?" the leader playfully asked as he gripped the needle and straddled Mr. Hill's back to keep him from moving. "Mr. Hill, I have never actually done this, so try to be patient with me."

Jake moaned, pleading for his captors to stop. But they couldn't stop. They had a debt to collect.

The leader flicked the needle and then Mr. Hill's arm. "Oh, that's a nice one," he said stroking a beautiful thick vein as if finding a piece of treasure. He pressed the needle into Mr. Hill's arm. Jake screamed at the top of his lungs, but the sock muffled his cries.

The leader slowly pressed the contents from the needle until he had reached the end. He pulled out the needle and admired his new skill.

"Not bad for your first time," his friend commented, handing him a pair of scissors to cut the zip tie.

"Who knows," he shrugged cutting the tight cord around Mr. Hill's bicep and then standing up. "Maybe I should return to school and become a doctor?"

"Don't forget to get his fingerprints on the needle," his friend directed, passing him the lighter and spoon to do the same.

"Good thinking," he smiled as he stooped down and planted Mr. Hill's fingerprints. He laid all the pieces beside the Jack Daniel's bottle on the coffee table. "Now to watch and wait."

The two once again grabbed Mr. Hill, flipping him over onto his back so they could watch his facial expressions run wild as the liquor and heroin coursed through his drought ridden veins.

"How long before he feels it?" the leader asked as he bent down to get a closer look at Mr. Hill.

"Oh, he feels it already," he answered as he knelt down and pulled out the sock from his mouth. "He drank almost the entire bottle and then we shot him up with enough drugs to kill a few people."

"Let's move him to the couch," the leader said. "It will look better for the cops than finding him lying in the middle of the floor."

"I was thinking the same thing."

They each grabbed an arm and pulled up the deadening weight, maneuvering his limp body around the coffee table. They pushed the body back and let him fall on the couch. He looked like a zombie with his eyes slightly open and his mouth ajar.

"And you're sure this will kill him?" the leader asked as he looked at his old teacher and waved his hand in front of Jake's empty eyes.

"If you want to shoot him up some more, I have a little more, but this should do the trick," he explained. "His body has had nothing like this for years. It's going to go into shock. Just wait."

The friend grabbed the pair of scissors and started cutting the zip ties that bound Mr. Hill's legs and arms.

"I thought he was going to die quickly," the leader said, shocked. "I thought overdoses happen fast."

"It's not like hanging someone where you cut off their air supply," he responded as he raised up his ski mask. "Damn. We forgot to show him who we were."

"Is it too late now?" the leader asked taking off his mask and leaning into Mr. Hill's face. "Do you recognize us, Mr. Hill? You said I was your favorite student, but look at me now."

Mr. Hill didn't respond. He sat dazed as his eyes fluttered like robin wings taking flight as sweat dripped down his discoloring face.

"You hear that?" the friend asked as his ears perked at a distant sound.

"What?" the leader asked still watching Mr. Hill closely as his breathing had become more shallow and strained.

"Sirens."

CHAPTER 41

"Maybe it'll pass by and not stop here," the leader softly hoped as his friend slinked over to the window.

Peering his eyes through the window blinds he eagerly watched as the sirens neared. His heart started to pound as he turned his head and noticed that Jake was still slightly breathing. His mind jolted to the negative regions of his psyche where every moment since they'd entered Mr. Hill's home was scrutinized.

His friend got up from the couch, forgetting about his most hated science teacher and approached the window with slight reservation. "I hear them now."

He nodded his head as his friend waited beside him, breathing his hot air down his already sweaty neck. The sirens blared as if coming down the street. They stepped away from the window when they saw flashes of light hitting the aluminum siding three houses away.

They crouched down in the middle of the floor in the darkness away from the window, still able to see out but unable to be seen from the outside. He looked at the one in charge of the night as the police car's lights flashed over him. He had never seen that look of fear on his friend's face. That expression sent ice through his veins.

They stood up ready to flee as they watched the police car pass their home.

They breathed out in relief.

"That was clo—" the leader started as tires screeched.

The accomplice felt his heart hit the wall of his chest as the police cruiser revved in reverse.

"Move!" the leader commanded as they grabbed the evidence from the night scattered in the living room. He picked up the socks, and his friend picked up the zip ties scattered on the floor.

"We don't have time!" the friend gasped as the police car pulled into Jake's drive way, parking behind a red Toyota sedan.

The leader looked down at Mr. Hill who looked lifeless. He lifted his eyelids, but they just gave a blank stare.

"Come on!" the friend motioned when they heard a car door slam shut. "Now!"

They didn't look back. They ran through the living room to the kitchen, not giving that room a second glance. They heard a knock on the front door as they closed the back door, jumped off the porch, and fled the scene under the darkened night.

They never said a word. They sprinted like Mr. Lukin used to make them in gym class for missing a pop-up ball in softball.

He watched as his friend passed him; after all these years, he was still the fastest and fittest one. He ran, fearing that at any second he would hear the back door open and someone would yell "freeze" right before they fired a shot into his back. He could see the tree line along the edge of Mr. Hill's back yard. He was so close when the terrible thought came to him. He couldn't believe it, but he kept running. He wasn't going to stop now. It was too late for that.

He looked ahead as the leader ran into the trees but didn't stop. He kept running at his faster pace as if his life depended on it.

But sadly, he knew that running wasn't going to save him. He finally entered the cover of the trees but continued to run. He still couldn't believe what had happened. Jumping behind the safety of a tree, he looked back at Mr. Hill's house. No cops were outside looking for anyone yet.

He coughed as he tried to take a deep breath. He felt his insides churning as if his supper was going to shoot up his throat. He looked down as his vision started to blur, unable to make out the details of his sneakers.

He heard the snap of a branch causing him to rise from his state of confusion.

"Come on, we have to get out of here," the leader said walking up to him. "You can't be that tired, man," he said shocked.

He didn't know how to tell him what he'd realized or if he even needed to. But deep down, he knew he had to tell him. It affected him too.

He raised up and leaned against the tree.

"We may have a problem," he said shaking his head in disbelief.

"Problem?" the leader asked belligerently. "What kind of problem?" He stopped and looked down at his friend's side. He lifted his eyes so they stared into his friend's. "Where's your bag?"

He inhaled, but didn't answer. He already knew where it was. Still by the back door in Mr. Hill's kitchen.

"Did you have anything in there that could lead the cops to you?" the leader asked. When his follower didn't answer, he repeated the question slower and more forcefully.

"I don't think so," he finally answered. "It was just an old duffle bag."

"Okay," he said motioning for his friend to follow him through the woods. "I mean, if anything, I'm still safe."

Those words cut at his heart. The leader had already thought of his way out of this situation and would leave his friend to hang.

The leader stopped and turned around, poking him in his chest. "But if they connect you to this crime, you better keep your mouth shut. Because they have nothing back there on me other than your word. So I would suggest using your words very carefully if that time comes."

CHAPTER 42

"Police!" Office Dobson shouted as he knocked on the front door of Mr. Hill's residence. He turned to his partner, Officer Spellman, who gave him the go-ahead as they each had their guns ready with their fingers on the triggers in case of a sudden attack. "We're coming in!"

The house was dark with only segments of foggy light coming from the windows and door. Officer Dobson had been on the force for six years, but it seemed like every day he put his life on the line to help someone else.

He walked into the living room shining his flashlight around, finding Mr. Hill sitting upright on the couch, but not moving.

"Sir!" he shouted rushing over to take his pulse as Officer Spellman started investigating the other rooms in the house for intruders. "I've got a pulse!"

"Clear!" Officer Spellman shouted in the first bedroom he entered after opening the closet doors and checking under the bed.

"I have a 10-50 and 11-41. Repeat, I need an ambulance fast!" Officer Dobson shouted into his two-way radio. "Spellman! We've got a problem!" Dobson pushed Mr. Hill down onto the couch, pulling his unconscious rigid arms so he could fit his entire body on the couch. He placed Mr. Hill on his side to keep his airwaves open.

He looked at the coffee table noticing an almost empty liter bottle of Jack Daniel's and drug paraphernalia and knew that wasn't a good sign. He didn't know how much he had drunk or used, but he hoped the unconscious man hadn't drunk the entire bottle tonight. He had seen too many drunk people to know the average person can usually only have three or four shots before becoming intoxicated.

Looking closely at the remnants on the spoon, he saw traces of dirty looking heroin. Pure heroin was bad, but dirty heroin was worse since no one knew exactly what they were putting in their bodies. But when someone wanted a fix, asking the purity levels was not a priority.

Dobson walked into the living room after checking the rest of the house. "He's foaming!"

"Oh crap!" he turned, readjusting Mr. Hill's neck to open his mouth trying to give him some more air. "Where's the ambulance? This guy is foaming!"

"An ambulance is on its way," the dispatch operator responded professionally. "They should be there in about five more minutes."

"I'm not sure the guy has five minutes," Spellman commented as he walked into the kitchen looking out the back door. "Did someone say this guy was attacked, because it just looks like an OD to me."

Dobson listened to Mr. Hill's fragile breathing when it quietly faded away. "Spellman! He needs CPR!"

Spellman rushed into the living room helping to move Mr. Hill down to the floor. Dobson started the chest compressions as Spellman ran out the door, coming back with their pulmonary resuscitator. He placed it over Mr. Hill's nose and mouth and squeezed on cue.

The two didn't speak. They had been in this position multiple times, but their success rate was only about half with no fault on themselves. They didn't choose the crisis circumstances they were placed in. They only did their best in each one.

Dobson continued the chest compressions as Spellman squeezed the plastic tube trying to force some oxygen into Mr. Hill's defunct lungs.

Come on, paramedics, Dobson thought. *Before it's too late.*

CHAPTER 43

We pulled down Hermitage Avenue stopping in front of Mr. Jake Hill's house where two police cars remained.

"Stay here," Wint said eyeing Elizabeth suspiciously.

"What?" Elizabeth responded raising her hands in surrender.

We watched Wint walk up to the house and show his badge to the standing officer at the door. They spoke for a couple of minutes before the officer allowed Wint to enter the crime scene, if they even called it a crime scene.

"Do you think we saved the guy?" I asked. "I don't see the coroner van here."

"Unless they already came and left," Elizabeth sighed.

"They wouldn't have taken him that fast," I replied. "There is too much paperwork to complete."

"How do you know?" she asked unconvinced.

"Elizabeth, we've been doing this for a year," I answered shaking my head. "And we haven't stopped all of the deaths."

"What, do you keep a time log or something?"

"There are some things you just remember," I replied looking out the window, hoping that we did some good today.

The interior car light flicked on as her car door opened. "Where are you going? Wint said to stay here."

"I never agreed to it, though," she grinned leaning down to look in the back seat. "Well, are you coming or not?" she asked before closing her door.

I knew Wint wanted us to let him do his thing, but I was pretty sure he would rather me stick with Elizabeth than let her wander aimlessly alone.

"Wait up," I said opening the back door and chasing Elizabeth up the porch to the officer that let Wint through.

"So, what happened here?" she asked quizzically.

"Please step away, ma'am," the young officer commanded with a hint of peach fuzz above his lip.

"Just tell me, did something happen to Jake?"

"Ma'am, are you related to the man who lived here?"

Elizabeth looked at me as I opened my mouth. "I'm not, but *he* is," she added, nodding at me.

"You're a relative?" the officer asked me as I looked at him wide-eyed and then back to Elizabeth. I lowered my head wondering how she always got me in these types of situations.

"I'm sorry, officer," she chimed in. "He's mute. Been mute since birth."

I once again opened my mouth, but she interrupted. "They're brothers," she added as my eyes went wider in shock at the snowball of lies she was forming. "He was texting Jake this evening, and when he didn't respond he reached out to me to bring him here to check on him."

"I'm sorry," the officer responded. "They have taken him to Holy Cross Hospital."

"So, he's alive?" Elizabeth asked in shock as I, too, started to feel some relief.

The officer shook his head, shrugging his shoulders with a downcast look. "I don't know."

"Thanks for your help," Elizabeth said as we turned to leave, stepping off Mr. Hill's front porch.

"Sir, since you are his brother, can you answer a few questions before you leave?" the young officer asked.

I now wished I was pretend deaf too.

Elizabeth jumped into action. "Can this wait? He really wants to see his brother," she said patting my shoulder sympathetically. "You know, before it's too late."

The young officer looked around noticing no one saw we were there. "Go on," he said nodding his head. "If they have any questions, I guess they can find you there."

"Thank you, sir. He will be there," Elizabeth replied waving to the kind officer. We started walking towards the car as she locked her elbows with mine.

"You little liar," she whispered in my ear with laughter in her tone.

"I didn't say a word."

"Exactly," she said, "because you knew this was a better way."

"No," I said walking with my back to the officer. "I was afraid he would have cuffed you for lying to him."

"Oh, Solo," she laughed as we approached her door. "If I went to jail every time I lied, I would be doing a life sentence from just the times we're together."

"What are you trying to say?" I asked in shock. "You lied to me? When?"

"When I compliment your clothes, or your apartment, or your cooking," she stated as if she had a mental list.

"But you never complimented me on those things," I disagreed. "You tell me I look like a hobo, I live like a hobo, and I eat like a hobo."

"See, I was lying to you," she smiled.

I let those words sink in as I got into her car, but shook my head in confusion.

"Yeah, because a hobo is a compliment compared to what I'm usually thinking."

"Really?" I asked in amazement as I buckled up.

"Why are you buckling up?" she asked confused.

"You're supposed to be taking me to the hospital to see my brother," I answered snidely. "Remember?"

She started her car and proceeded down the street, stopping near the end.

"Should we tell Wint where we are?" I asked with a grin.

"I say let's see how good his detective skills are," she laughed as I felt my phone vibrate.

"It's Wint."

Why'd you leave?

To go visit my brother, I texted back.

Do what? Wint replied.

Elizabeth. Do I need to say anything else?

Gotcha.

"Rude," she said looking over my shoulder to read my texts.

CHAPTER 44

The hospital room was dishearteningly quiet as Nurse Whitmore started bagging all of Jake Hill's belongings. She looked over at the man lying on the bed and felt saddened by his need to fill a void caused by whatever inner demons he was battling with such a toxic combination of whiskey and heroin.

She had been in this type of situation too many times during her twenty-one-year career as an emergency room nurse at Holy Cross Hospital. Sometimes the families were aware of their patient or decedent's battle with narcotics or alcohol. Those conversations seemed to her like they would be easier to have. She felt as if the parents should know the prospect of having this conversation one day so the shock should not be so debilitating. But there were some cases when the parents were completely blindsided by their child's double life.

She held Mr. Hill's phone in her hands and wondered if he called someone. Did he reach out? Did he seek help?

The hospital had suicide prevention posters with help telephone numbers placed on various walls through the building, but she had never seen anyone write down the number or take a picture of it. She looked down at his phone once again and knew that things had changed so much in the last decade; but even though the world was so easily connected to one another, it had also become more disconnected.

She dropped the phone in a Ziploc bag and sealed it shut. She found a few items loose in his pants pocket. She flipped open his wallet and saw a teacher's ID for Montgomery Blair High School. She shook her head wondering what his students would think tomorrow.

Did they see the signs? she asked herself. *What about the staff?* In an environment where they look out for their students' well-being, did he fall through the proverbial crack?

She sealed up his wallet in another bag and moved on. She found his keychain with various sized keys and cherished tokens. She held them in her hands and noted several colored poker chips, but she knew they weren't for playing cards.

She flipped through the colors reading each inscription. 30 Days. 60 Days. 90 Days. 6 Months. 9 Months. 1 Year. She continued to look at the colorful chips until she came to the last one. 7 Years.

Her heart sunk. He had been clean and sober for seven years and then this happened. She wanted to shed a few tears, but she knew someone else would be wheeled in here soon, and she couldn't cry for everyone who passed through these doors. She dropped the rest of his belongings in a sealable bag and laid it with the rest of his things.

She looked over at Mr. Hill who looked different from his teacher ID. In his school photo he was smiling and full of life and vigor. He looked as if he knew this was his calling, his passion, his will for life. A single tear started to fall down her cheek before she brushed it aside.

Now he was just another man who died too young.

CHAPTER 45

The stars were not shining bright, but they never did because of the city lights of Washington, D.C. We drove to drop Wint off at the precinct to get his car, but we never said a word. We each just sat staring out the window as if the last three hours had never happened.

I replayed the afternoon wondering if we could have contacted Mr. Little to warn him. Could we have reached out to him about his red Toyota? Would he have told us he no longer had it, or would he have hung up on us? How would we have known about the vehicle sale unless we were told?

There was no way of knowing.

"A man is dead because of me," Elizabeth said as the two of us drove through the city passing by familiar landmarks and iconic museums.

"Elizabeth, this is not your fault," I reiterated turning my head from my window to look at her trembling lip.

"Why didn't we do more research? We had Wint at the station. He could have done something." She stopped and let a single tear fall.

"He could have found out nothing that would have changed tonight."

"But we'll never know," she said wiping her tear away.

I couldn't disagree. That sentiment was genuine. We would never know. But we would never know a lot of things that happened or didn't happen. All we could do was try.

"Pull over," I said eyeing a blue and white logo.

"Solo," she said annoyed.

"Come on, Elizabeth. You need this. I need this. We both need this," I begged, seeing a little piece of heaven on earth so close.

"I'm not even hungry," she said as she pulled over and parked.

"But its Ice Cream Jubilee," I said as if those three words would change everything. She looked at me as if that was supposed to mean something. "Jubilee," I said with a smile. "Ju-bi-lee."

"I hear you, but I don't get it," she said turning off her car but staying seated. "You go on and I'll stay here."

"Elizabeth, if you don't come in with me, I'll just have to surprise you."

"Don't you dare," she replied.

"But you need it," I said, holding her hand that still gripped her gear shift. She looked over at me and another tear fell. "You need this. Tears and ice cream are a perfect combination."

"Whatever, Solo." She hit me as she wiped away a few more tears.

"Really. Have you ever wondered how they came up with sea salted caramel ice cream?" I asked while giving her a coy smile.

She rolled her eyes and opened her door. Small victories, I thought.

I locked elbows with her as we strolled up to the door front. "Well, there is a story that goes Old Mr. Hubbard broke his wife's favorite gravy boat. She loved that gravy boat. Her grandmother had bought that gravy boat from someone whose ancestors sailed on the Mayflower. I mean, the gravy boat didn't sail over, so I'm not sure why that is important to the story, but still."

"Oh, Solo," she smirked as we entered the ice cream parlor.

"Well, Old Mr. Cubbard was carrying the gravy boat that--" I started as she interrupted.

"I thought his name was Hubbard," she eyed suspiciously.

"Well, it used to be Hubbard, but then the Geppetto found out about him and he had to go into witness protection and he changed his name."

"Geppetto? Do you mean the Gestapo?" She rolled her eyes.

"No, the Geppetto was a ruthless mob who--" I stopped as she once again interrupted.

"Let me guess, tortured people who lied to them."

"So you have heard about them." I smiled. "Well, Old Mrs. Hubbard."

"I thought her name was changed to Cubbard," she snickered.

"No, that's the point of the story. That the witness protection didn't bring her, so she was left to fend against the Geppetto herself. And one evening when she was crying over some spilt milk, she had a thought. And she dipped her finger in it and tasted it and thought salty ice cream, isn't that good?"

I stopped and looked at the different flavors of ice cream, asking for two scoops of rocky road in a dipped waffle cone.

Elizabeth looked at me quizzically with her mouth slightly opened, as if confused.

"What? Can't decide what flavor you want?"

"Aren't you going to finish your idiotic story?" she groaned, throwing her arms in the air.

"That was the end," I said casually as I paid for my ice cream and took a lick of the sweet chocolate and marshmallow.

"But you didn't finish," she pointed out. "You didn't even get to the sea salted caramel part."

"Oh, the Hubbard/Cubbard family didn't invent that," I said taking another lick. "I don't know who invented that."

"But," she stammered looking at me more confused as she ordered her scoop of ice cream. "Then what was the point of that story?"

"I don't know," I said shrugging my shoulders. "I just wanted some ice cream." I stopped and took another lick as the lady behind the counter handed her a cup with a single scoop. "And now you did too."

"I just ordered this to be nice," she scathed, taking a small bite of her ball of ice cream.

"What flavor did you get?" I asked, already knowing. She looked down at her cup and ignored the question. "Sea salted caramel is quite appealing, even if Old Mrs. Hubbard didn't really invent it."

Elizabeth glanced up from her cup with a slight smile.

"I told you," I said looking into her eyes with our ice cream between us. "We both needed this. Both of us."

TUESDAY
CHAPTER 46

Judge Otto banged his gavel as I walked up to the stand, raising my right hand and looking at the bailiff. I sat down and looked out into the courtroom seeing Jenny sitting stoically between her two attorneys.

I closed my eyes and took a deep breath as the prosecution stood up and proceeded to talk. As he spoke, he walked toward me. His mouth quit moving as he nodded his head.

I scanned the room, looking at the jury watching me. A few were scribbling notes, and one appeared to be falling asleep with his eyes closed. I turned my head to give the prosecution my attention as his mouth started to move once again.

The attorney started moving faster, as if in fast-forward. Talking and then stopping. Walking and then stopping. Talking again and then stopping. My focus went in all directions as if spinning down into a whirlpool.

Suddenly the fast-forward stopped as Milo stood and walked toward me.

"So you and Jenny dated?" he asked.

He watched me with his piercing eyes.

"What a pity, you two could have been a fine pair. She is so beautiful and you are very handsome. Do you have any regrets?"

He once again stood, folding his arms and watching my movements.

"Why did you go to the Coopers' home that day when Jennifer Ascot had her breakdown?" he questioned, stepping closer. He touched his face as if listening to a fascinating story.

"How did you know to go there?" he asked taking a small step forward, moving closer with each question.

"You don't know?" he gasped in shock. "Do you routinely just show up at someone's house for no reason?" He took a step forward.

"Do you believe my client is crazy?" he asked, moving closer as he reached out his hands to grip the railing that separated us. "Don't you believe you have dreams that tell you what's going to happen, and that is how you knew to rescue Elizabeth?"

I felt like I was falling into another whirlpool. I started spinning as the prosecution jumped up from their table. The jury started whispering, pointing, and laughing in my direction. The judge looked down at me with sympathetic eyes while banging his gavel.

"To me, *you're* the crazy one," Milo muttered as he sauntered back to the defense table, taking his seat beside the grinning Jennifer Ascot.

My vision tunneled until darkness encompassed everything.

I gasped as I rose out of bed. I reached my hand up and felt my throbbing head that was soaked with sweat. My stomach churned as if still in the whirlpool as I jumped out of bed and ran to the toilet. I fell to my knees and hugged the porcelain as my insides felt like they were ripping apart and coming out. I lost all my strength and my grip, toppling over onto the bathroom floor. I laid there curled with my knees to my chest, rocking myself to a state of delirium. I tried to think, but it was too painful. I just wanted to lie there in silence. I didn't want to replay my dreams like I always did. I just wanted to pretend like it didn't happen. My heart started to beat faster, pounding into my chest as if begging for me to stop the madness and end it all. But I couldn't stop it. I didn't know how.

My worst nightmare was happening.

I was going to be exposed.

CHAPTER 47

"Solomon," Elizabeth answered groggily. "Do you know what time it is?"

"He knows," I answered shaking my head, trying to hold my phone with my shaky hands.

"Who knows what?" she asked sleepily.

I heard her, but my mouth couldn't speak. I opened it, but no words were coming out. I tried again, but all I could get out was a shallow breath straining to speak.

"Sol, you're scaring me," she said waking up with alertness in her tone. "Who knows what?"

"Milo," I whispered, finally getting it out as if it was using up all my strength and energy.

"What does Milo know?" she asked. "What happened in your dream?"

"He knows about me." The words came out in trembles, falling off my lips like someone else pushed them.

"Solomon, that doesn't make any sense," she replied tenderly. "What does he know about you?"

That question sent me into a tailspin, reliving the nightmare of what was going to happen later that day. I couldn't get the images out of my head. It wasn't the question that stung, but the looks on everyone's faces in the courtroom. Some stared at me like I was a liar. Others pointed at me like I was a freak show booth entertainer. A few nodded their heads sympathetically like I was the crazy one in the room.

"The dreams, Elizabeth. He knows about the dreams," I finally answered as I felt a little piece of me slip away.

"How?"

"I don't know, but he's going to ask me about them when I'm on the stand today," I manically said. I waited. I didn't know how she was going to respond. She could give me some encouraging words, which wasn't always in her nature. Or she could tell me to man up and lie. Or she could say she would shoot him before he had the chance to ask that question.

But she didn't do any of those. She just went into a cursing spree, saying every bad word I knew a couple of times. She even started saying a few in French, or I presume they were cuss words, because those were the only words that made sense.

I felt the same way. We sat in silence for a minute after she finished her vocabulary lesson.

"So what happened when he exposed your abilities?" she finally asked after refocusing.

"Remember how people looked at the freaks in high school?" I asked. "Well, I was the freak and all eyes were on me."

Elizabeth started talking of possible situations. She was spitballing a few scenarios or ways out, but none of them seemed possible.

"What are you going to do, Solo?" she asked with as much compassion as I had ever heard.

"I…" I started as I closed my eyes and thought. "I don't know."

CHAPTER 48

I got up out of bed, since going back to sleep was useless, and changed into my fall running gear of black Nike compression pants and a green hoodie. I didn't look at the time when I put my shoes on and headed out the door. The day was still a long way off as the moon was still shining overhead.

"God," I started as I ran along the sidewalk on the deserted street. I didn't know what I wanted or needed to say. I didn't have a clue. I felt as though my prayer was like this jog, wandering aimlessly, passing under random streetlights, hoping for some direction.

I approached a crosswalk but didn't stop. There weren't any cars around so I kept running even though the street sign said to stop. I felt like my life was this crosswalk. I had always followed the rules, but something about running through the red light seemed like I was doing something bad. There weren't any cars in sight, but I still felt like it was wrong even though no one else knew or cared.

I continued to jog further down the sidewalk, passing homes with front porch lights on, but nothing else. They were probably filled with people sleeping soundly behind the locked front door in the comfort of their bed with no nagging dreams.

I counted these dreams as a blessing most of the time. I was a vessel being used to help change the lives of those I came in contact with for the better. Some days I was better at achieving the goals I set out to accomplish. But if I was truly honest with myself, there were moments when I didn't see these dreams as a blessing. They were a hassle that hounded on me even when I slept. And I hated that attitude. I hated it with a passion even as I would think those defeated thoughts.

I continued to jog and my mind was blank. There were a million places my brain could have traveled, but it didn't move. It didn't continue to run down the rabbit hole of grave decisions and errors. It didn't journey through the forest of ifs and regrets. It was just there, in the quiet. As if it were telling me to chill in this state of darkness.

The good thing about the darkness is one can't see the trouble lurking on the horizon. I knew the opposite could be said, but I wasn't ready for my mind to leave this place of ignorance.

I closed my eyes and jogged down the empty sidewalk, trying to leave all my troubles behind me. I was trying to run further into the darkness.

"Please help," I prayed. I kept repeating the words in my mind as I heard the same two words coming from the voice of a child.

"Please help."

CHAPTER 49

A little boy around seven years old sat on the steps of a front porch in his Superman pajama pants and t-shirt, rocking himself in place.

I immediately stopped running, shocked that a child would be outside this time of night, wearing only a thin layer of clothing.

"Hey, buddy," I said, walking over to the shivering child sitting on the darkened stoop. "What are you doing out here?"

He looked up at me with his gray eyes but then darted his attention to the door behind him. His mouth parted slightly as if startled from a monster behind the door.

"It's okay, buddy," I said bending down and seeing his chattering teeth ricocheting off one another. "It's chilly out here," I said, pulling off my hoodie and putting it over him. He tucked his knees to his chest, turning my over-sized sweatshirt into a cozy blanket.

The house was dark with no light shining through any of the windows. He started to close his eyes, warming himself and feeling safe as sleepiness started to wash over him like a summertime breeze.

"Why are you out here, buddy?" I asked once again, looking down at the sleepy child. His eyes opened as he became startled, frantically looking around. Large tears started to form.

He cried softly, scanning his surroundings as if it were a new place.

"Hey bud, do you live here?" I asked, bending down to one knee, so we were eye to eye. "Is this your home?"

He turned around as his lips started to quiver. He shook his head as the tears started to fall. He grunted soft and low as my heart started to break at the emptiness he was feeling.

"It's okay, buddy," I said pulling him into my arms, rubbing his shoulder and back. "It's okay. What's your name?"

129

He didn't answer as he looked up at me. I pulled away to look around at the surrounding homes. His nose started to run as he continued to rock.

"My name is Solomon Davis, but you can call me Solo." I stood up and walked away from the porch down the walkway, causing him to groan and squirm.

"I'm not leaving, buddy," I said turning with a smile. "I'm just looking up and down this street. I bet your mom is worried." I looked at the house behind him once again. I didn't know what else to do, so I walked back to the porch and rang the doorbell.

He stood up shaking, standing behind me for protection. I saw a light come on inside the house as I held my breath. And then another light turned on. I looked down at the boy and patted his shoulder encouragingly. "It's going to be okay," I said as the front porch light turned on.

"Who's out there?" an old man asked without opening the door.

"Sorry to bother you, sir, but I was hoping you could help me."

"It's late," he gruffed still behind the locked door. "Go away."

"I'm sorry, but--" I started.

"Just leave."

"There is a little boy on your front porch," I said, finishing my sentence. "Come on," I said sheltering the child with my body, guiding him down the stairs to leave this man's property.

"Boy?"

CHAPTER 50

The door unlocked and the screen door opened as we were stepping off the porch.

"Son, is that you?" the old man asked as he stepped onto his front porch.

The child and I turned to see a man in a dingy orange robe and striped blue pajama pants stepping off his front porch. My heart leapt when the man offered his arms stretched out. I couldn't believe my luck. I looked down, but the child didn't have the same relieved expression on his face.

"Come here, boy," the older man said coming closer.

The child cowered behind me, burying his face into my back with a disheartening groan.

Something didn't feel right.

"Hi, I'm Solomon," I said, reaching out my hand in greeting. "And who are you?"

"I'm his grandpa," he said grinning down at the child, ignoring my presence.

I stepped between the two, protecting the shaking boy with my body.

"What's his name?" I asked, standing my ground to defend this petrified boy.

The gray-haired man stood up and looked me in the eye with a gentle smile. "Harold Brooks, Jr.," he answered. "Just like me."

The child moaned as loudly as he could, still hiding behind me, wrapping his arms around my midsection as if I were a life preserver.

Suddenly, the image of the boy's face filled my vision. "What color are his eyes?"

"Brown," he answered confidently.

"Sir," I said taking a step back. "I think you are confused."

"Blue. They are blue."

I broadened my shoulders as the small child continued to latch onto my back.

"I know my own grandson," he snapped, reaching his hand out to touch the child's blonde curls.

I caught his hand before he could get any closer. "I think it's best if we leave," I said taking another step back.

"I don't think so," he grinned wickedly looking down at the boy and then up at me. The man grabbed my shirt as the child continued to moan into my back without opening his mouth. I felt pinned between the two.

I readjusted my stance as I fought off the older man who ripped my shirt at the neck. I quickly turned to push the boy out of the way as the man grabbed at my neck, trying to put me into a chokehold. I watched as the child stood frozen, rocking near the sidewalk. I didn't want to take my eyes off of him, but I needed to focus on the man attacking me.

I balled my fist and started punching at his side, trying to get a few good licks in so he would lessen his hold. I looked down at his shoeless feet and stomped on his toes. He groaned and released my neck.

I spun, watching the hobbling man, but I wasn't going to let him go. I raised my fists and threw a couple of punches, smashing his cheeks as he spit out some blood.

"Stay away!" I shouted with my fists raised, ready to throw another punch as the old man turned away, trudging up the steps of his porch to slink back into his home.

He turned behind his screen door and stared eerily at the child.

"It's okay, buddy," I said rushing to the boy's side to check on him. "It's okay."

The child buried his head into my chest moaning as he continued to rock.

"I'm going to find your parents," I said patting his back. "We are going to find them."

CHAPTER 51

We stood on the sidewalk looking at the surrounding homes, but finding none with any lights on inside. I looked down at the child who stuck beside me like my shadow, clenching my t-shirt like it was his security blanket.

I led us to the middle of the quiet street to get a better perspective, but the only light was coming from the streetlights along the sidewalks.

"Does any of this look familiar?" I asked, but he didn't answer. He just looked up at me with a tired expression.

I wondered about going door-to-door, hoping that one of these homes had his parents tucked away in their bed, but after the last experience, I nixed that idea. Things always look bleaker at night. People look less trusting. Hope seems more distant. Faith seems dead.

I called the police and reported a lost child. The call seemed like a last resort, but I hoped that with the police sirens and commotion, his parents would wake up. The two of us waited at a bus stop, while I wrapped my arms around his small frame, trying to keep both of us warm.

"It's going to be okay," I kept repeating to him as he started to sink further into my arms closing his heavy eyes. I swayed on the bench as if we were gliding over the waves in a lifeboat. My eyes also started to feel the weight of a restless night without sleep.

My ears perked to attention as the sound of sirens became audible in the distance. I located the direction they were coming from and waited to see the red and blue lights ignite the bland, gloomy street.

The officer pulled up as I rose to greet him, waking the sleeping child who moaned in protest. I picked him up and carried him, laying his head on my shoulder.

I started to see nearby homes slowly come alive with lights and front doors opening. I waited to see a parent come running toward us, noticing the familiar pajama pants. But no one came.

The police asked a few questions, but I couldn't answer them.

"Does anyone know this boy?" I shouted to the neighbors watching from behind their screen doors, but no one came forward.

Officer Keystone asked for dispatch to look through the records for a missing person, a seven-year-old autistic boy with blond curly hair weighing around 50 pounds. But there were not any missing persons fitting that description.

Officer Ritter started going door-to-door asking questions to anyone who would answer, but once again the search came back empty.

No one knew this little boy or why he was out in the cold.

I continued to hold the boy in my arms with his legs wrapped around my waist, pacing the sidewalk and hoping for some good news. But soon everyone had been questioned and there were still no answers.

"And you found him on that porch?" Officer Keystone asked, pointing at the house behind us as the old man watched through his blinds.

"Yes," I nodded seeing the stranger's eyes. "And you may want to do something about him," I said pointing in his direction. "He was pretending to be the kid's grandfather in order to get him."

"Are you sure he's not?" Officer Keystone asked.

"I'm pretty sure he's just a creepy old man that needs to be watched."

"Noted," Officer Keystone commented as he took down the address of the stranger's home. "I'll look into him later."

"What's going to happen to the boy?" I asked as Officer Ritter came walking back from the last house he questioned.

135

"We'll take him down to the station and put out a bulletin for him. Hopefully someone will come and claim him," he answered pessimistically.

"And what if no one does?"

"Let's not think that way," he answered. "We will contact the schools in a couple of hours and see if anyone recognizes his picture."

"Even though this sounds bad," Officer Ritter added, "I would rather have a missing parent than a missing child any day."

Officer Keystone reached out his arms to take him from my neck, but as he pulled him away, the little boy continued to cling to my shirt. His eyes remained shut as he moaned in fear.

"Do you mind if I come with you?" I asked, pulling him back into my arms as his moans hushed. "Just until he feels a little safer."

The four of us got into the police car and drove away. I looked out the window, noticing all the homes were dark again. I rocked the child in the backseat as he continued to snore lightly in my ear as his hand gripped onto my t-shirt.

"It's going to be okay," I whispered into his ear. I wanted to believe those words. I wanted to hope he had wandered away from his home in a sleepwalking episode, but that didn't seem plausible since no one recognized him.

He continued to sit in my lap as I rubbed his little legs to try to keep him warm when my hand felt something in his pocket. I reached in and pulled out an orange prescription bottle and a letter.

"I think I know who this boy is," I said reading his name on the pill bottle. "William Stinnett."

I passed the bottle up to the police as I unfolded the letter. My heart broke into a million pieces at the handwritten words.

Please take care of him. I can't anymore.

136

"What's going to happen to him?" I asked Wint over the telephone as I waited in the subway station. I couldn't get the image out of my head of William's outstretched arms grabbing at me as the police asked me to leave. I didn't want to leave. He had already been through so much, and for some reason he felt safe with me by his side.

"We will try and find a relative to be his guardian, but until then DCS will take him and put him with someone temporarily," he answered groggily since it was still before 7 A.M.

"What about me?" I asked quickly. "Would they let me take him?"

"Solo, you know nothing about kids. Especially a kid with autism."

"I'll learn," I refuted.

"Solo, they just don't give kids to people. You have to go through classes and trainings." Wint started going through the logistics of the DCS system. "You're not even in the system, so for all they know, you could be a drug dealer or a psycho."

I listened to his words and understood the rules and guidelines they must follow, but it still didn't make this situation any easier. We ended our call as I got onto the train and headed toward the station near my apartment.

As I sat in the empty subway car, my mind started to spin with the possibilities. Should I start this process to help a child in need? Could I even do it if they gave me the green light? Would they even allow me to raise a child with my past stint in the mental institution after my wife was murdered?

I started to weigh the pros and cons, quickly listing them off in my head, playing devil's advocate with my strengths and weaknesses. I came to my stop and found myself in the same place I was when I entered the train car. Unsure of anything anymore.

I pulled out my phone and texted another friend, a friend who I needed to see for no other reason than to check up on him.

Good morning, Eugene. Feel like a donut this morning?

Make it a blueberry fritter.

See you around 8.

CHAPTER 53

After returning home I quickly showered and got dressed in a navy suit and white button-down shirt. I threw my golden tie in my pocket to put on later.

Elizabeth called and left a voicemail while I drove to Eugene's, but I didn't feel like talking to her yet. I knew I would see her at the courthouse later, and my focus was on my questions for Eugene. *Is it okay to lie under oath?*

I picked up our breakfast and headed to Dr. Eugene Wright's home in the Kenwood district. Eugene was a theology professor at Wesley Theological Seminary whom I met last fall during one of my lectures. I soon came to find out that Eugene and Jeremiah, though on different sides of the religious spectrum, had been best friends since their youth. Through my interactions with Jeremiah, we soon became a trio that would meet periodically.

However, last spring, Eugene was diagnosed with an inoperable brain tumor. He still was part of the faculty at Wesley, but he was taking a leave of absence.

I knocked on the door as Eugene greeted me warmly with a hug, one that I desperately needed after the emotionally grueling morning. But after looking at my sick friend, I wondered if the hug was really what he needed.

I wrapped my arms around his torso that had been strong and full of vigor last fall, but now seemed very frail. He stood with a smile I couldn't help but reciprocate.

"How are your classes going?" he asked as we walked through his living room towering with columns of books beside his recliner. I scanned the stack from Chesterton to Lewis, including different religious works of the Koran and L. Ron Hubbard, until I found myself in his kitchen. He pulled out a couple of mugs and poured a cup of black coffee for him and milk for me.

"They are going pretty well," I said nodding my head in thanks as he handed me my beverage and I gave him his blueberry fritter.

"Pretty well is pretty good," he grinned. He closed his eyes and breathed in deeply, filling his nostrils with the sugary icing laced with blueberries.

"How was your night?" I asked, taking a bite of my cinnamon twist.

"Very good," he smiled with a mouth full of fritter, a portion of the icing sticking to his upper lip.

I smiled across the table at my friend and just enjoyed being in his company. We chatted about a few random things, including his assortment of books, but nothing striking, just a dialogue between friends over breakfast.

"So, what brought about this meeting?" he asked as he eyed me suspiciously.

I looked at my friend who was battling for his life and saw the smile on his face. A slanted smile that radiated openness and honesty for anyone who was sitting in this chair. His question was more than a simple 'how are you'; it dug deeper into the dirt as if wanting to get in the trenches with me. Jeremiah had a way of seeing the world differently; whereas, Eugene had a way of seeing the person differently.

I posed the question in my head, but as I sat and pondered the words, I knew this wasn't the time and place to discuss my minute problems. In the grand scheme of time and my place in this world, if Milo asked about my abilities today, I knew how I needed to answer him. And nothing would change that.

"I just wanted to see you," I smiled, taking my first sip of milk. I quickly spit it back into the cup and saw a chunk floating on the top. "When was the last time you bought milk?"

He laughed heartily causing my own heart to warm a little more.

CHAPTER 54

"How much longer is Whitney going to be home this time?" Jordan asked as Grant, Collin, and Stewart walked into the Department of Transportation building together.

"She hasn't told me yet," Grant responded as he held the door open for the three men. "I usually don't know when she is flying out or coming home until the day of because her shifts change so much. People trade flights to earn more money, so she could be gone tonight or next week."

"Making her work for your toys," Stewart chimed in, patting Grant on his back in congratulations. "Everyone needs a sugar momma."

"Just one?" Collin commented with a devilish smile as he strutted down the hall. "I look too good for only one woman to pamper me."

"Please," Jordan said choking on his laughter. "You can't even keep one."

Collin eyed Jordan playfully. "I don't want to keep a serious relationship going, but I want to keep multiple flings going. Those are more fun."

"Seriously," Stewart remarked. "I feel like sanitizing myself every time I'm around you, because there's no telling what you have going on."

"I'm always safe," Collin responded winking at Stewart.

"Sure," Stewart replied.

Collin looked around, noticing no one was around. "When are we going to start Round Two?" he asked in a lower tone.

The three other men froze in place, looking at one another as if a rule had been broken.

Grant grabbed Collin's neck, causing Jordan to wince in discomfort. Grant directed Collin's head close to his mouth. "Never mention that here," he hissed.

"Okay. Okay," Collin said pulling away from Grant's firm grip.

"We'll discuss it later," Jordan responded as he looked at Grant who nodded. "So want to go out tonight?"

"I need to check with Whitney," Grant answered.

"Me too," Stewart said as Grant eyed him suspiciously. "You know what I mean."

CHAPTER 55

Elizabeth called Solomon again, leaving another voicemail about the dreams she had last night as she drove toward the courthouse sipping on her latte. She hoped today was going to be better than yesterday, but she wasn't sure.

"Call Wint," she said in her car as her cellphone started dialing her brother-in-law.

"One second," Wint answered. Elizabeth could hear him talking to Dakota. "Okay, I can talk now."

"What did they say about Jake's death?" she asked with a jitteriness in her voice. "Are they looking for the killers?"

"They are calling it an OD," he said solemnly.

"But we called and told them. We told them two people were breaking in," she pointed out, gripping her steering wheel as if it were her last thread.

"No, I called and said there was an emergency and to go there," he stated coldly. "An OD is an emergency," he said shortly. "I never said anything about someone killing him."

"So tell them now," she demanded.

"Tell them what, Elizabeth?" he snapped. "Tell them that my friends have dreams about the future and they told me about this crime?"

"No," she answered in an agitated tone.

"Then tell me what to say to them," he whispered angrily. "Because you know there is nothing I can tell them without having them ask questions that we can't answer."

"So what are you going to do?" she asked deflated, slamming on her brakes to stop for the school bus ahead of her.

"I have to go," he said ending his call before she could say anything else.

She screamed and pounded her fist on the steering wheel, hitting the horn unintentionally. A few of the students on the back of the bus flipped her off. She did the mature thing in her opinion and returned the gesture with both hands.

"Call Solomon."

CHAPTER 56

Gavyn sat in the lobby of the courthouse scrolling through his messages. He thought he should look over his notes for the case, but he didn't see any need in it since Milo was taking over.

What are you thinking about? A message appeared on his phone.

Last night. He smiled as the events of the night returned. He replayed every moment and didn't have any regrets.

Well, I was wondering what you had planned for tonight.

What are you trying to do? He laughed to himself. *I need to rest sometime.*

Fine. Rest up tonight.

So are we on for tomorrow then?

I'll be in top form.

You'd better.

He finished his text as his phone started to ring.

"Mr. Hyde," he answered. "What can I do for you?"

"I had a very interesting conversation with Milo last night on how you are handling Jennifer Ascot's case," he said smugly.

"Oh, you did," he responded with distaste in his mouth. It was one thing to railroad someone in court, but it was another thing to tattle.

"Yes," he said slowly, as if carefully picking his words. "He was giving you some high praise, and coming from Milo, that is something he doesn't always give."

"Well, thank you, sir," he stammered in shock at the unexpectedness of the conversation. "Is that all you were calling me about?"

"That was all, Mr. McKenzie," Luther said. "Well, there is one other thing."

"Yes, sir."

"If Milo asks you to do something," he stopped and took a breath. "You do it. Do you understand me?"

"I think so, sir. Yes, I understand," Gavyn answered as he looked around the lobby in confusion.

"Good, because he isn't someone you want on your bad side," Luther said ending the call.

Gavyn held the phone in his hand and noted the time as he quickly analyzed the call. After replaying the conversation in his mind a second time, he was even more confused. He seriously doubted Milo's affirmations were truthful after he had repeatedly made snide remarks about his skills. He even wondered if Milo and Luther actually spoke yesterday about the case.

The more he thought, the more certain he was that something else was going on and he was caught in the middle.

At the beginning of this case he was hopeful this was going to seal his reputation and move him further up in the firm, possibly getting him on a faster track to become partner. Another person might have some reservations after the last telephone conversation and worry about watching out for himself.

But luckily, he wasn't the kind of person who lived in fear. That was one thing that Luther and Milo did not know about him. He didn't run away from conflict, he thrived in it.

And he wasn't going to start running now.

CHAPTER 57

I left Eugene's house with a full stomach and an empty heart. As I drove to the courthouse I couldn't get him or William out of my head. Eugene was facing a monumental medical hurdle with only prayer and a God-sized miracle in his back pocket, and little William was abandoned.

My little worries and problems, even though leaving me petrified in anxiety, seemed so insignificant compared to these life-altering events of a medical death sentence and a heart-wrenching realization that everyone was not loved as much as they should be.

"Please God," I started praying, hoping God was listening to my broken and contrite heart. "Please help the police find William's parents. Or guardians. Or someone who will love him as much as he deserves. Oh, God, please make the parents realize they made a mistake. Please let them see that. Please God. Please."

I changed my ramble to address my beloved friend. "Oh God, heal Eugene. Make the cancer disappear. Make the brain tumor vanish. I know you can. I know you can, God. I know you can do it. So please." I stopped and looked out the window at the blue sky and radiant sunlight. "Do this for me."

I continued to drive and pray, stopping at every light that seemed to suddenly turn red when I approached. I wasn't frustrated by the delay since I had plenty of time to make it to the courthouse for my appearance, but it just started to become too much. I looked out the windshield at pedestrians walking by. Some of them were smiling, but many were not. Most were walking without an expression on their face other than the look of trying to get to their next destination on time.

I watched a middle-aged man in his business suit and tie, holding onto his briefcase in one hand and a cup of coffee in the other. I watched as he walked. His strides were short and slow, and his head was looking down, as if defeated. I noticed another woman walking the same way, but with a slightly quicker pace. I watched the intersection and wondered what baggage each of these people was carrying.

I craned my neck and watched the man with the briefcase continue to walk with his shoulders hunched, knowing it wasn't the lightweight papers inside causing his drag. There was something else causing his tiredness. Maybe it was the late game last night, I thought. I hoped there would be a happy reason for the dismal look on his face. But the more I watched him walk alone down the busy sidewalk, the sooner that optimistic thought crashed.

A car horn blared behind me causing me to quickly look ahead at the green light before me. I proceeded forward until I hit another red light.

Once again my attention rested with the pedestrians. They looked tired as they walked across the street with its morning traffic. It seemed that wherever I looked, I saw the same expression on most of their faces.

I felt my heart crumble as I looked at so many blank stares. A gaze that I knew I would see on my own face if I looked in my rearview mirror. The red light changed to green and I moved behind a car covered in bumper stickers. We went a couple of blocks before stopping at the next red light.

I started reading the collection of decals. I chuckled at the political ones as I noted they had voted mostly for candidates that lost their elections. The driver was obviously a music lover with the edges of the back glass plastered with 90s rock bands.

I read further and a couple stuck out. *I have an opinion about everything!* and *"My mind was changed by a bumper sticker" said no one ever.*

The car pulled away, but the bumper sticker messages remained in my memory. I reflected back to the start of the car ride with my prayer, which wasn't really a prayer, but suggestions for how God should handle a few problems. Suddenly, my state of mind shifted and the second bumper sticker was now a lie.

"God, just be God," I said driving as I saw yet another red light ahead of me. "I trust you on that. I know you have everything figured out even though I don't."

I was about to brake when the light changed to green.

"And that is okay with me," I said with a smile. "Just keep being God."

CHAPTER 58

"Solomon!" Elizabeth raged when he finally answered his phone. "Why have you been ignoring my calls? I've called I don't know how many times."

"It's been a morning," Solomon sighed.

"Don't you sigh at me, boy," she remarked as she circled around a block, looking for the entrance to the parking garage near the courthouse.

"Won't happen again," he said with a louder sigh.

"Good thing I can't see you, or I would smack you right now."

"Close your eyes and picture me," he laughed. "I went to the police station this morning," he said casually.

"Why?" she asked shocked. "About the killers? Do you know something new?" She skidded to a stop as she slammed on her brakes when the flower delivery van in front of her suddenly stopped without pulling to the side. "A little warning would be good!"

"What did I do?"

"Not you," she said shaking her head and watching the delivery man jump out with an arm full of roses. "I hope one of them has a thorn."

"Huh?" Solomon asked in a confused tone.

"Not you!" she barked.

"Then why did you call me?"

"Do I always have to give you my undivided attention? You're like a lost puppy. So needy." She smiled as she enjoyed giving her partner in dreams a hard time, especially when he hadn't answered her five phone calls.

"Why do I put up with you?"

"Because you love me," she grinned. "So why did you go to the cops this morning?"

"I found a little boy this morning who was apparently dropped off on someone's front porch. And it was a good thing that I found him because the guy who owned that house was probably a pervert or something."

"So Solo saved the day like always?" she bubbled sarcastically, eyeing the delivery man walking back to his van. He waved and apologized, but Elizabeth wasn't as forgiving and took a picture of the van to call and complain to his supervisor later if she still cared by then.

"Not exactly," he said in a downtrodden tone. "The cops are looking for his parents, but whoever dropped him off left a note saying they couldn't do it any longer."

She said a few choice words she knew Solomon would never say, but she was certain by his silence he didn't disagree. "Some people don't deserve to have kids. I say, spay and neuter the whole bunch of 'em."

"I called Wint and asked if I could do something," he said timidly, "but he quickly nixed that idea."

"Solo," Elizabeth chimed in as she continued around the block. "I know you want to save the world, but you can't save everyone."

"But--"

"I know, Solo. As much as I hate to compliment you, you would be great at it," she said encouragingly. "But you have to let the rest of the world help too."

"I know, but what if no one is there to help?"

"But what if the right person is?" she said intuitively, allowing Solo to let those words sink in when he didn't respond right away. "Are you still there?"

"Yeah, I'm here," he said. "Thanks for the compliment, though. Wint said I couldn't do it."

"What does Wint know?" she erupted. "He's probably still sulking over last night. Yes, it's tragic the guy overdosed, but we tried our best." She saw the parking garage entrance and slowed down to enter. "Back to the point of my call," she started as she pulled in and rolled down her window to get her ticket. "I had a couple of dreams last night and one was about you."

"What happened?"

"Well, I saw you testifying. I can't remember everything that was asked or said by both sides, but something didn't make sense," she started as Solo interrupted.

"Eliza...bre...up."

"Solo, I can barely hear you."

"We...ing...so...."

"Solo, listen to me!" she said frantically driving in the parking garage, rounding the curves with squealing tires. "Listen to my voicemails. I already explained everything. Milo is going to ask--" she started before her call ended as all her reception on her cellphone disappeared in the depths of the parking structure. She hoped Solo heard enough to figure out what she wanted to say, but knowing Solo, she was fearful he was going to go on the stand without knowing her side of the story.

She looked at the metaphorical angel on her shoulder and felt sorry for Solomon and the inner turmoil he was enduring. Then she looked at her other shoulder, the one she was used to siding with most of the time, and laughed.

CHAPTER 59

Take a deep breath, I told myself as I walked up to the witness stand. Memories came hurling toward me as if a hundred fists were hitting me in the stomach. I stepped up into the stand, shaking and wounded, turning around to see every eye on me. I squeezed my eyes shut, trying to forget the last time I stood in the stand. But I couldn't shake that memory. I could vividly remember the voice of the defense attorney that day.

"First, let me start off, Mr. Davis, in giving my condolences for the loss of your wife," the defense attorney started.

I didn't say anything as I nodded. I would not let the weasel of the man who was defending my wife's killer get any satisfaction or sympathy from the jury.

Lance Wright. I would never forget that name. He was the defense attorney who was trying to get a lesser charge for his client. I remember looking across the room staring at the man who shot my wife and wondering which man was worse. Was it the man who killed my wife in a drive-by shooting, or the man knowingly trying to get him off with a lesser charge?

At the end of the day, they were both scum in my book.

"I do," I said waking up from my daydream and replying to the bailiff. I sat down and watched as Finn Garrett stood up and approached the witness stand. He started asking the questions we had practiced the week before with me retelling the events that led up to shooting Jennifer Ascot in self-defense.

I turned my head to the people in the courtroom as an image of my mother and father clutching onto one another hit me like a cold sweat. They came to the trial of my wife's killer with me every day because they knew I wasn't able to handle the emotional toll. They picked me up from my stay in the psychiatric hospital, which was more like a peaceful retreat, a couple of weeks before the trial started. I wasn't going to let the trial pass me by. I couldn't let Chelsea's memory be overlooked. I made it my mission to remind the court of her beautiful life that had been taken too soon.

I blinked and my parents were gone, but in the room with me now was my new rock. Elizabeth sat unblinking, watching and nodding at everything that I said. I fixed my eyes on her, and she could tell I needed it.

You're doing great, she mouthed.

I relaxed a bit as a feeling of warmth started to invade the cold sweat, forcing it to leave.

Finn asked a few more questions, and my level of bravery increased. I looked over at the jury as I detailed my injuries and the number of stitches I received in my leg. My mind almost went back to Chelsea's murder trial again, but I glanced at Elizabeth. For her sake and mine, I didn't need to lose my focus. She was depending on me to not make a mistake with a misspoken word.

And I wasn't going to let her down.

It had taken me a few years to fully convince myself that I hadn't let Chelsea down. For years I had replayed her death. I had contemplated whether if I had noticed the car a few seconds beforehand, I might have saved her. If I had told her the lighting for the photograph was better on the other side of the road. If I had told her the story was too dangerous to tackle. I still had my moments of second-guessing, but Elizabeth was always there to shake me out of my self-pitying rabbit hole. Well, smack me out of it was probably a more accurate statement.

My heart rate started to rise as I heard Finn's last question. He turned and walked back to his table as Gavyn McKenzie stood up, buttoned up his suit, and walked over to me.

"Mr. Davis, first let me offer my condolences for the horrific trauma you experienced when you were fighting for your life against my client, Jennifer Ascot when she was off her medication and not in her right mind."

"But she was in her right mind," I interrupted. "She definitely was."

I wasn't going to let his flattering words move the jury. In an instant, my confidence doubled, my feeble attitude vanished, and I squashed my fear of Milo's questions.

I wasn't going to play defense anymore. I was done being attacked. I was finished playing the wounded victim. Jenny didn't kill me, and I wasn't going to let my quiet nature allow her to get off thinking she did.

I was alive and she was going to hear about it.

Take a deep breath, I thought as I let a smirk slip through my lips. *She's going to regret not killing me.*

CHAPTER 60

"So what's wrong?" Officer Peterson bluntly asked her partner Officer Cooper, who was staring off into the distance as she drove them on patrol.

"Huh? What?" he asked waking up from his thought.

"What's going on with you?" she asked again. "You've been acting strange lately. Is it Veronica?"

Cooper shook his head as he stopped looking out the passenger window and took a sip of his lukewarm coffee. "Veronica's fine."

"So?"

"So what?" he responded in a jaded tone.

"Cooper, we've been partners for almost a year, so I tend to know when something's wrong with you. And I'm a pretty good cop, so I can tell when people are lying to me."

He sat there and sipped his coffee, taking a moment to collect his thoughts. Yes, there was something wrong, but he didn't know how to tell her.

"You don't have to tell me, but I've been told I'm a pretty good listener." She smiled as she merged onto 295 heading south. "Is this about your friend's case?"

"Friend's case?" he asked befuddled.

"Yeah, the Ascot case. How's Veronica dealing with all that again?"

"She's past it," he said stretching his arms back. "I think we all are."

"I can't imagine being best friends with a killer," she started as she weaved between traffic. "To think, when they were thirteen and at a sleepover, she could have rolled over and saw her friend sleeping and had no idea she was capable of killing all those people. It's just unreal."

"That it is," he nodded, agreeing more with the unreal part. It was unreal that Solomon had tracked down Jennifer at the Huntington Station to help take down the Carbon Monoxide killers. It was unreal that he'd saved Elizabeth's life when Jennifer broke into his house to kill them all. It was unreal how many cases had been solved by their random tips and how many cases hadn't come to fruition because of their selfless actions.

Unreal was definitely an understatement for the last year.

"Oh, crap," he said looking down at his phone and noticing the time.

"What?" Dakota asked, startled from her driving.

"Solo's in court today," he said connecting the dots in his head.

"He'll do fine," she said optimistically.

"You don't understand, it's the first time he's had to testify since his wife died."

"And?" she asked, not seeing the significance.

Cooper quickly sent a text to Solomon, followed by a brief text to Elizabeth. "His wife was murdered."

"Oh," she said comprehending the magnitude. "Hopefully this won't bring back those memories."

Cooper turned and cocked his head at Dakota. "Have you never met Solomon?"

CHAPTER 61

Gavyn asked questions similar to those he asked Elizabeth, and I answered each one of them calmly. My hands were resting in my lap as if this was any other day and I wasn't being grilled in front of strangers on Jenny's state of mind.

"So you agree she wasn't in a good mental state when she was attacking you?" Gavyn asked.

"I don't know anyone who would be in a good mental state when trying to kill someone, but I wouldn't say everyone who attempted to kill someone was insane," I answered.

"But we are discussing Ms. Ascot, not everyone else," he stopped. "I mean, how many other killers do you know to give that type of statement?"

I looked at Elizabeth who smirked with the secret knowledge of the number of murderers we had been in contact with over the last year.

"I know the man who killed my wife wasn't insane," I quipped, watching Gavyn's head spin as he realized he had stepped where he should not have.

I looked back at Elizabeth who mouthed, *Good one.*

I felt proud of myself with that response. Gavyn paced around the floor, stumbling over his words, when Milo stood up and motioned for Gavyn to walk back to his seat.

"Yes, Mr. Davis, you have given your opinion, but were all the other people you encountered at Whispering Hills visibly unstable?" Milo asked, poking into my past stay in the mental institution.

"Well..." I started, not knowing how to answer the question. Because some of the patients seemed clinically sane during parts of the day, but then they would have a tantrum or spiral out of control.

159

"Well, what?" Milo asked walking closer to me. "Did some patients appear mentally stable even though they were not?"

I looked over at Finn who laid down his pen and watched. He didn't object because there wasn't anything out of line with the question.

"But--" I started, but Milo didn't let me finish.

"Don't look at Mr. Garrett for an answer," he said stepping in front of my view. "Did everyone at the mental institution you were in five years ago appear insane all the time?"

I was caught and he knew it.

"No, but..." I answered, wringing my hands together to calm myself.

"Very truthful answer, Mr. Davis," Milo nodded. "I just have a few more questions," he said with a slight smile.

My insides churned as if my stomach was being peddled like a bicycle.

"When you went to Whispering Hills, did you know you were mentally unwell, or did you have someone to tell you?" Milo asked, leaning against the railing as if engrossed by my haunting story.

I rolled my eyes and wondered why he was focusing so much on my stay when I wasn't the one on trial.

"Your Honor," Finn said standing up. "Mr. Davis isn't on trial and neither is his past."

"No, Mr. Garrett," Judge Otto said as he waved him off. "I will allow this."

"Thank you, Your Honor," Milo said standing to attention. "Once again, Mr. Davis, did you have someone to show you that you needed help?"

I didn't want to answer, but I knew I had to. I hated answering the question, but I couldn't lie. I just wouldn't lie.

I nodded my head. "Yes."

"So you had support from friends and family who saw that you were in trouble and assisted you in getting the medical help you needed. Is that correct?"

I nodded my head again. "Yes."

"What if all of your friends had turned against you and you didn't have any family to turn to? Do you think you would still have gone to Whispering Hills?"

"I…" I started as I looked down at my hands, trembling not from anger, but from emotionally fueled stress reliving the lowest moment of my life. "I don't know."

"Once again, a very truthful answer, Mr. Davis," he said as he took a step back. "You appear very mentally stable, Mr. Davis. Do you consider yourself stable, or would you say you are crazy?"

My eyes widened at that question. My heart started to race at the word *crazy*. I closed my eyes and took a deep breath. His line of questioning had changed from my dream, but this seemed somewhat familiar.

"Stable," I said, choking on the word as my mouth quickly dried, causing my tongue to stick to the roof of my mouth.

"So you consider yourself stable even though you have…" He stopped and turned around finishing his sentence, but I didn't hear anything as my vision tunneled.

Then it all went black.

CHAPTER 62

The four friends from the Department of Transportation walked to a nearby bistro for lunch. Grant ordered a tuna salad on a croissant; Stewart got his hot ham and cheese panini; Collin was dieting, so he only got a side salad with grilled chicken; and Jordan pigged out on a double cheeseburger.

"So can we talk here?" Collin asked softly as he stabbed his spring greens sprinkled with vinaigrette dressing.

Jordan shook his head while rolling his eyes. "We don't want to rush it, Collin."

"I know, you don't, but I never got to kill anyone," he answered as he dropped his head so only his friends could hear him.

"If you didn't mess up the first time," Grant said before he stopped and shook his head. "Forget that," he commented as he took a bite of his sandwich.

"Is that what you all think?" Collin asked. "That it's all my fault?"

"Well," Stewart said softly looking at the other two. "You were the one who screwed it up for me."

"I couldn't help it," Collin sulked. "It could have happened to any one of you, and I wouldn't be blaming you."

The other three had their mouths full as they furrowed their brows in unison not believing his sentiment.

"What?" Collin demanded, raising his voice.

"When I struck out last summer, you kept reminding me for two weeks how I lost us the game," Stewart remarked.

"It's softball!" Collin erupted. "How do you strike out at softball?" he asked condescendingly. "I thought you played cricket in England!"

"Cricket and softball are two different throws," Stewart explained. "And that was over ten years ago."

"And his strikeout didn't almost land us in jail," Grant pointed out. "Your error could have."

Jordan took a bite of his hamburger as he stared out the window. Awkward silence invaded the lunch as the four of them continued to eat their meals. Collin opened his mouth, but then stopped. He could tell no one wanted to talk at this moment, but he really didn't care.

"Well, maybe it's time I prove myself to you all once and for all," Collin said, taking one last bite before grabbing his plate.

"What does that mean?" Grant asked, looking up at Collin who had stood up to throw away his trash.

"Just what it sounded like," Collin answered as he walked away.

"You don't think he's really going to do it?" Jordan asked in a state of shock.

"No," Grant said flatly. "He probably doesn't even have a plan."

The three continued to eat as Stewart's eyes widened. "But knowing Collin, he probably won't have a plan."

"Well," Grant said smugly, "that'll be his own fault."

"But," Stewart started feebly as he looked to Jordan for support. "What if he gets caught and rats us out?"

"He wouldn't," Jordan chimed in defiantly.

"Really?" Grant said annoyed by the ignorance in Jordan's remark. "If you think he won't turn on us to save his own skin, you are one stupid son of a bitch."

"Grant," Stewart defended.

"What, Stewart?" Grant asked rudely as he took another bite of his tuna sandwich. "We better hope he gets himself killed, or we all may be in a shit storm."

Jordan looked up at Stewart who stared back with fear in his eyes. Jordan had never seen Grant so ruthless before, but he knew he shouldn't be surprised. It was Grant's idea to kill their exes last spring.

It was Grant's plan of how to do it. It was Grant who got them all to join in with this revengeful plot.

Jordan pushed away the remaining few bites of his burger as he suddenly realized he was going to be tethered to the three men for the rest of his life. It was one thing to be friends with them, but it was another thing to know each other's deepest darkest secret. He looked over at Stewart who continued to eat his hot ham and cheese and envied him. He was the only one who wasn't connected with any of the crimes. He was the only one who would walk away free and clear if anything did happen. He was the only one who had nothing to lose.

"I'm going to go check on Collin," Jordan said dumping his plate and heading out the door.

He started walking down the sidewalk and looked back into the bistro's window. Grant continued to eat his sandwich as if nothing was wrong, but Stewart, on the other hand, watched him from the other side of the glass with no expression.

Just like a blinking mannequin.

CHAPTER 63

"Give him some air," I heard someone say while I slowly opened my eyes. I blinked a few times, allowing my eyes to focus as I felt my hands touch the hard, cold floor. I looked around and saw bodies huddled around me as if they were devising a plan.

I tried to raise myself up, but someone stopped me.

"Just lie still for a minute," a woman said as she held my wrist. "You had a nasty fall when you passed out."

"Passed out?" I asked in shock. I couldn't remember a time I had ever lost consciousness. I'd heard about people falling over when their blood sugar got low, but for me, this wasn't common.

"I think I'm okay," I said looking up at the woman taking my pulse. "I'm not sure what happened."

I looked around the circle and saw Elizabeth's watchful eyes. I waited for her to have a snappy comment about my fainting spell, but she didn't say a word. She just looked at me with concern.

The bailiff handed me a cup of water as a juror helped me to my feet. I didn't know what was more embarrassing, talking about my stay at Whispering Hills or fainting in a courtroom while being questioned about it.

"Let's have a recess so Mr. Davis can get something to eat and then we can finish this up," Judge Otto said. "Is that fine with you?"

"Yes. Yes, Your Honor," I said as the courtroom started to file out. Elizabeth stood back and hooked her elbow with mine.

"You didn't listen to my voicemails, did you?" she whispered in my ear as we walked down the aisle.

"No, why?" I asked, realizing immediately it was a stupid question. "You knew this was going to happen."

"Yes, I knew," she said raising her hand to smack me before she stopped herself. "Remind me to smack you next week."

"Noted," I smiled.

We proceeded out of the courtroom, dodging the congestion in the noisy hallway as she continued to walk by my side.

"My dream was wrong," I said surprised. "It's never wrong. I've never been wrong." I looked at her for an answer, but all she gave me was a shrug.

"Well, mine was right."

"But why?" I asked once again.

"Sounds like you just had a normal nightmare," she consoled. "You've been worrying about this for a few weeks, and it finally got to you."

I nodded in agreement. I had been worrying too much about this day. My mind was full of stupid fears of questions that would never be asked, and I let my fear run wild until my body just collapsed.

"Maybe God was trying to show you something different," she added.

"With a fake dream?" I remarked. "He could have just shown me everything was going to be okay, and then I wouldn't have fallen on my face in there."

"I wish I had my camera ready," she said in regret. "Well, what do you know," she smirked as she pulled out her phone and played the video.

"You didn't!" I scolded.

"Oh, I did," she laughed. "I couldn't let this pass by without recording it."

"You really could have, though."

She thought for a second as she replayed the video. "Nah."

"Yeah," I grinned. "I would have done it to you too."

CHAPTER 64

I curled up on my worn-out couch with its loose springs and throw afghan that Chelsea had crocheted, and channel surfed, flipping through the various stations, hoping something would be boring enough to help me fall asleep. I looked down at my phone and saw it was only three in the afternoon.

What a day, I thought.

I laid down the remote when I stopped on a 24-hour weather channel. I knew this wouldn't keep me glued to the television, but I wasn't ready for complete silence either. My mind started running circles around itself.

I started to wonder about William, hoping the police had found someone who would take good care of him tonight and for the rest of his life. Everyone needs love and support. My eyelids started to get heavy as I started hearing Milo's voice in my head. I breathed easier knowing he didn't ask questions about my dreams.

The mind is an interesting tool. It can help when one needs helping, or it can be one's worst detriment when peace of mind seems unattainable.

I felt my phone vibrate, signaling a text, but I was too tired to look. If it was really important, whoever it was would call eventually.

The weatherman spoke of a cold front entering Washington, DC next week as I fell deeper into a state of relaxation. I let myself fall into the Zen state until the falling felt more like floating.

It had a purpose. It had a purpose. It had a purpose.

I awoke with a weatherwoman forecasting a snowstorm that would dump up to a foot of snow in some areas of Wyoming. I looked down at my phone that had fallen to the floor and saw I had seven missed calls in the one hour I slept.

I rubbed my eyes to make sure I saw my phone correctly. I started listening to the voicemails from various friends who were calling to see how I did in court. I sat up feeling refreshed but also confused by the voice in my dream.

What had a purpose?

I continued to play the voicemails until I got to one from an unfamiliar phone number.

"Hello, Mr. Davis, this is Officer Keystone from this morning. I was calling to let you know DCS has William Stinnett. This is not customary, but seeing how he latched onto you, I was wondering if you could go visit him this evening. He ate nothing at lunch, and he isn't eating again for supper. I wouldn't be calling you, but you mentioned this morning that if we needed anything to let you know. Give me a call when you can."

I called Officer Keystone as I threw off the blanket I was under and rushed to slide on my shoes. I got the address where William was being kept and was out the door in less than a minute.

I didn't know what I could do, but I knew I had to try something. Something was better than sitting at home watching the meteorologist talking about the storm fronts invading the central plains.

CHAPTER 65

Gavyn sat on the couch with his laptop, reviewing his notes for the day and the witnesses for tomorrow. He tried to carefully read the text, but his mind kept bouncing between his telephone conversation with Mr. Hyde, his co-counsel Milo, and his guilty client. He massaged the bridge of his nose and hoped the tension was just from stress and not seasonal allergies. Stress could be dealt with, but allergies needed medication.

"I brought home some pizza," his roommate Collin Diaz said, holding up a cardboard box. The aroma tickled Gavyn's nostrils with the tangy marinara sauce and robust peppers.

"You got gluten-free crust, right?"

"I got it," he groaned laying down the pizza box on the kitchen counter and grabbing a couple of plates.

"You'll thank me later." Gavyn got up and walked into the kitchen, patting Collin's love handles. "Those aren't going to disappear on their own."

"A brother can't starve himself." He smiled as he pulled a couple of slices of grilled chicken and veggie pizza onto his plate.

"Wouldn't hurt you," Gavyn laughed raising up his shirt to show off all his hard work with his defined abs.

Collin didn't respond but grabbed a bottle of water before he sauntered to the living room.

"What time does the game start?" Gavyn asked as he filled up his water bottle and added a couple of lemon slices.

Collin glanced down at his watch as he took a bite. "In about an hour," he replied with his mouth full.

Gavyn walked in, handing Collin a napkin before sitting down in his leather recliner. "That'll give me a little time to go over my notes one more time."

"This case has really been keeping you busy, huh?" Collin asked, turning on the television to watch the sportscasters discuss preliminary analysis on the upcoming game.

"Yeah," he grunted, taking a bite of his pizza. He looked over at Collin and wondered if he could trust him with his secret. They had been roommates for the last two years after Jordan had moved out to move in with his girlfriend. Collin wasn't the brightest bulb, but he was a pretty good wingman when he needed one.

He just hadn't needed one lately.

"So she did it, right?"

"Yeah," Gavyn agreed. "We're trying to keep her out of prison with the insanity defense."

"Did she kill all those people last year with her brother?" Collin asked, watching the television as if he was following a doctor's light.

He shrugged his shoulders.

"So, just hypothetically, how likely are you to be caught and found guilty for killing someone if you plan it out?"

"Depends," Gavyn said coolly as he, too, sat engrossed with the game highlights from the night before. "There are probably hundreds of cold cases in just D.C. So if you plan it well enough, there's a chance they won't catch you."

"But then if they do, I always have you have as a Plan B," he smiled with a wink.

"Collin," he laughed. "You couldn't afford me."

"What about a friends-and-family discount?"

"We don't do coupons," he answered as he returned his attention to the unbelievable diving catch from the eighth inning.

"Guess I better come up with a good Plan A then."

CHAPTER 66

Jenny stared at the chip in her brick wall, the same chip she had been staring at since she was released from the hospital after surviving multiple gunshot wounds to the chest and being arrested for the attempted murders of Elizabeth Hyde and Solomon Davis. She had heard stories of prisoners breaking out of cells by chiseling through the layers of cement and escaping through sewer tunnels. It was a thought that kept her up some evenings.

Not because she was considering breaking out of this temporary jail, but for whenever she was transferred to her final destination of either a women's penitentiary or a mental hospital. She had wondered how many handcrafted shivs she would need to accomplish such a feat. When time was all she had, three years of working in the dark evenings wasn't that much if it allowed her to escape.

In those calculating thoughts of escapes, she would recall Milo's voice at the start of the trial. His words were cryptic and his message unclear, yet she clung to the conversation like a life preserver.

"Trust me, Jenika," Milo had whispered on the first day as they were seated at the defense table in the courtroom while Judge Otto was situating himself and his laptop on the bench.

"Trust you how?" She leaned over and said the breathy words coated in a mixture of apprehension and confusion.

"I have a way." His voice, usually rough like gravel and cold as winter, actually had a hint of paternal guardianship.

"What is it?"

He never answered. Not then, and not the two other times she'd asked. He looked through Jenika as if she were a ghost from his past. A past filled with many other specters and skeletons, so he was used to ignoring anything that conjured such a trepidation of fear.

She stood up and felt the chilled wall, pressing her face against the smoothness of the brick, dreaming of the day when her freedom would come. She scratched at the chip with her fingertip, but the only thing that flaked was a piece of her own nail.

She looked down at the chipped nail and wondered if she was like that broken piece in Milo's eyes. She turned her head and felt the chip in the wall. She knew what she was made of, even if Milo didn't see it.

But he would one day.

One day he would see.

CHAPTER 67

I walked up the driveway to the Nelsons' home with a bag in my hand and a prayer in my heart. Phineas Nelson opened the door and introduced me to his wife, Katrina. They stared at my bag as they welcomed me into their warm home and briefly told me their story of spending the last few decades helping the foster care system.

I walked through the living room, glancing at the pictures of different children hanging on the walls and seeing the hairdos and clothing style fads come and go through the photographs. I wanted to stop and look closely, examine the dozens of smiling kids' faces opening Christmas presents in July, vacation pictures with Mickey Mouse, and the plethora of poolside snow cones or popsicles.

"William," Katrina said knocking on the bedroom door. "Someone is here to see you."

I didn't know what to expect when I looked down at the child playing with a mountain of Legos. He didn't turn around but continued to build a lopsided tower.

"Hey, buddy," I said walking into the room.

He stopped building and raised his head at the sound of my voice. He didn't turn his head to look but sat still.

"Hey, William, it's me, Solomon," I said stepping further into the room. I walked around him until I was standing on the other side of the colorful, plastic mountain. "Can I join you?"

He didn't look up at me but went back to building his tower.

I sat down across from him, watching his every move while the Nelsons watched me like they were conducting an experiment and I was the lab rat. I just didn't know if I was the control or the variable.

I set my bag down beside me and waited.

"That's a nice tower," I said. He still didn't respond. I looked up at the Nelsons and gave them a half-smile when William pushed his hand through the pile of Legos in my direction, as if offering them to me.

"Thank you, buddy," I said grabbing a handful and starting my own construction. "I used to play with Legos with my best friend, Winston, but we all called him Wint. Do you like to be called William?" I stopped and watched as he continued to press the pieces together. "What about Willie?" Once again, he didn't look up. "How about Will?"

He raised his head and looked me in the eye. We connected.

"So, Will, are you hungry?" I asked, opening the brown paper bag I brought. "I know it's not healthy," I smiled as I looked up at the Nelsons, "but it's a guilty pleasure of mine, and I thought you would like some too."

I pulled out a chicken strip and some fries and a biscuit that coated my fingertips in buttery goodness. I offered him a strip as I took one for myself, dipping it in the barbecue sauce. "Want to eat supper with me?" I asked taking a bite of the lukewarm chicken. "I hate eating alone."

He grabbed a blue Lego with his right hand and a chicken strip with his left. I watched and waited. He held tight to the chicken strip as if holding the string of a balloon. He placed the blue Lego onto his tower and grabbed another piece. And then another. He continued to hold on to the unbitten strip.

He placed three more Legos onto his tower before he looked up at me and took a bite of his chicken, chewing with his mouth open. He looked down at my sauce and shoved his strip into the plastic container, causing half the contents to ooze out the sides. He popped the strip into his mouth, licking the barbecue sauce off his lips.

"You like it, Will?"

He grabbed a spicy fry and dipped it in the sauce as well.

I grabbed a few fries and scraped up the sauce dripping down the side. "Thanks for eating with me, buddy."

I wiped my hands on the napkin and stood up.

Will's eyes shot up as he groaned.

"I'm not leaving," I said, dropping down to one knee. "We need something to drink. I'll be right back."

He looked into my eyes as I nodded, reassuring him. He grabbed another fry and a Lego.

I walked toward the Nelsons who stepped out into the hall. "I hope I didn't intrude or break any house rules by asking him to eat in there."

They shook their head no and waved off any apprehension. "I'm just glad he's finally eating," Katrina beamed as we headed to the kitchen. She filled a couple of glasses with water.

"I have plenty of chicken if you want to come and eat with us."

Phineas got two more cups out of the cabinet and filled them with ice water as he kissed his wife's forehead. He looked into her eyes and gave Katrina a nod as if he knew everything was going to be okay.

CHAPTER 68

Grant sat on the loveseat in his living room as he watched Whitney across the room play on her cellphone. He had mentioned going out to dinner, but she wasn't feeling it, she said. He then mentioned going out to a movie, but she didn't know what was being shown at the cinema. He'd brought up the idea of going for a nighttime walk around their neighborhood, but she was tired. Everything he suggested, she struck down with little reasoning.

He sat stewing, watching the wife he loved ignore him. "What are you looking at?"

"Oh, nothing much," she said as she continued to type and scroll through her phone.

"It must be something since you've been on it all night."

"It's nothing." She looked away from her phone and gave her husband a few seconds of her time as her eyes scanned the room. "Yeah, this is much better."

"What's going on here?" Grant asked, throwing the television remote down.

"What do you mean?"

"This!"

"I don't know what you mean," she snapped as she waved her arms and bobbed her head.

"You've been home for a while, and you haven't once wanted to have dinner with me."

"I'm sorry, but I didn't know you were so needy."

Grant shook his head as his wife slipped back to the screen on her cellphone rather than talk to him. His heart was pounding in anger, yet he felt an icy chill in the room.

"Why is it *needy* to want to spend time with you, Whitney?"

She didn't respond. She didn't look up or even acknowledge the words he said. She continued to sit on the couch eight feet away texting someone else.

"We haven't had sex in over two months!"

"Oh, is that what this is about? I'm just your toy for when you want me?" She laid her phone down and started taking off her shirt.

"What are you doing?"

She rose up, unzipped her pants and let them fall to the ground. She stood before Grant in nothing but her lacy bra and panties. "I thought this is what you wanted, Grant!"

"Whit! Why are you acting like this?" He stood up and stomped towards her, grabbing her arms with his hands. His grip wrapped around her thin wrists like shackles. He looked into her eyes, but she wasn't looking back. Even though he was holding her, she was somewhere else.

"You want this, don't you?" she said moving her hand down to his belt.

Grant stepped away, throwing her arms down.

"What?" she huffed. "Not in the mood anymore?"

Grant didn't answer. He grabbed his phone from the arm of the loveseat and stomped down the hall.

"Good talking to you!" she shouted from the living room as he walked into their bedroom, slamming the door behind him.

CHAPTER 69

I spent the evening getting to know the Nelsons as the three of us tried to understand Will a little more. He never said a word, but his eyes would light up at the mention of superheroes.

I stuck around for a couple of hours playing Legos and eating the rest of our supper. We ended the night watching an episode of the original *Superman* television series in black and white. Will sat between me and Katrina, resting his head on my chest.

I looked down at the precious child and then over at Katrina while thoughts and emotions I hadn't dealt with sucker-punched me. Will started to doze off to sleep, and Phineas came over and picked him up. Will readjusted himself in his arms, wrapping his skinny arms around Mr. Nelson's neck as he smiled at the hug. Mr. Nelson walked out of the room with Will in his arms to put him to bed.

I sat on the couch and looked around the room, seeing what could have been my life if tragedy hadn't struck. I stared at the array of framed photographs on the entertainment center, and I knew I needed to leave before falling deeper into my heartache.

"If either of you need anything," I said standing up as Mr. Nelson walked back into the room, "call me. Day or night."

"I think we may be seeing you again, Solomon," Phineas smiled as Katrina rose up and stood beside her husband. He clutched at his wife's waist, pulling her into his side.

"Please, call me Solo." We said our goodbyes, and I left the quiet home with a loving couple caring over a fragile, scared little boy. I got into my car and pulled away. But the more I drove, the more I wanted to stop. I wanted to stop everything. I didn't want to leave that setting that wrapped me with love. I didn't want to walk away from a child that desperately needed a father to look after him. I didn't want to lose the feeling of being married to Chelsea with our child sitting between us as we watched an old black and white show.

My eyes started to swell with tears as the memory of Chelsea hit me with full force. Even though she died about six years ago, I still missed her.

I missed the smell of her shampoo after she washed her hair. I longed to hear her contagious laugh as she messed up while retelling a joke. I looked at both my hands on the steering wheel and the empty passenger seat. I used to never drive with two hands, because she would usually hold my right one.

I took my right hand off the steering wheel and stared at the lonely appendage sitting on the console where she used to lace her fingers into mine. A tear rolled down my cheek as I imagined her being in the passenger seat once again.

I looked over and I could almost see my lovely wife looking over at me. She turned her head to the backseat, and I didn't want to look, but I had to. I peeked into the review mirror and saw a two-year-old little boy sleeping in his car seat with his sippy cup laying sideways as his feet dangled in his white Nike Velcro shoes.

I looked back over at Chelsea who lifted my hand up to her lips.

"Watch where you're going!" a man screamed as he honked his horn.

I woke up from my hypnotized drive to find myself alone in my car. I turned right at the next intersection and parked on the quiet street of closed shops.

I wanted to get the illusion of Chelsea back, but she was gone. All the untapped dreams I had with Chelsea disappeared as well. We had talked about having a couple of kids when we were in college and full of innocent hope.

"Let's name our first son, William," she had said as we sat in the library studying for our chemistry final.

"Where'd that come from?" I laughed, looking up from the periodic table in the back of my book.

"I don't know," she said shrugging her shoulders as she went back to studying. She reached out and held my hand.

I remembered looking up at her and knowing she was the one. I had many other times before when I thought she was perfect for me, but at that moment I knew beyond a shadow of doubt she was the one for me. She was the one I would grow old with. The one I would go on adventures with and tell all my secrets to. The one I would die for.

But sadly, not all things happen as we dream.

"I like it," I had said back to her as she looked up from her chemistry book and raised her eyebrows in question. "Will," I smiled.

"Will," she said back. "I like it too."

I remembered shaking my head as I walked around the table. I clung onto her hand as I needed her strength to finish. My hands shook, but hers were still. My heart was pounding so hard that I felt like I would faint. I dropped down to one knee and looked up into her eyes. "Will you marry me?"

Now I looked over at the empty passenger seat and started to cry. I cried for the woman I loved and lost and the child I never got to know.

"Was this the purpose?" I screamed hatefully through wet eyes and a runny nose.

WEDNESDAY
CHAPTER 70

A notepad with Hit List written at the top of the page appeared in the darkness. A list emerged beneath in two different handwritings.

Ted Lukin

Jake Hill

Timothy Easton

Kelsey Slanders

Jessie Kingston

Michael Neely

Clint Browning

Suddenly a red pen appeared and crossed out the name Ted Lukin with a thick red line. The ink bled down as if blood. Then the pen crossed out the name Jake Hill. It hovered in space above the list before moving down to an empty line below Clint Browning. It slowly started to print each letter.

Collin Diaz glowed as if lit like a neon sign.

The pen fell to the pad, forming a puddle of ink in the openness at the bottom. The scene focused on the puddle as it zoomed in. Quickly the red ink covered the view, and the notepad in the black background was gone.

The red image remained as a voice broke the silence.

"Breaking news. Two people were found dead at a residential home in the Manor Park neighborhood. As of yet, no names have been released."

Two rapid gunshots echoed followed by a scream and the sound of running feet disappearing into the void. A slam of a trunk followed as the sound of multiple pairs of feet walking drifted away into silence. The red scene started to pan out. The redness started to reflect fragments of light. It continued to zoom out until the smooth rounded edge of red hit a dark stained wood. The scene quickly zoomed out showing the red was a large growing puddle.

A man's head laid in the red as blood poured out of his wound. The scene froze.

"This has not been confirmed, but from what we have been told from neighbors, it appears to be a gruesome murder suicide. We will keep you posted on this breaking story as more information comes our way. Back to you, Brock."

"Back to you, Brock," the female news reporter kept repeating, lowering in volume each time until it faded out.

The scene zoomed out at warp speed showing the full body of the man lying in the middle of floor with another smaller body with long blond hair lying on the other side of the room.

Elizabeth woke up from her dream and quickly started typing the details into her phone. She typed all the names and then moved to the two deaths. She underlined and bolded Brock's name. She quickly searched the internet for "Brock news Washington, D.C." The two-second wait seemed like two hours. Elizabeth's eyes lit up as she read Brock Michaels was an evening news anchor for Channel 9. She wished she had a more definite address and time, but breaking news with a nighttime news anchor would signify sometime in the evening.

Even though she didn't know all the details of the murder-suicide, she smiled as she looked at the list of names and recognized the first two. Timothy Easton would be the next Hit List attempt, but he wouldn't be the next victim.

Tim, you're not going to die tomorrow.

CHAPTER 71

The alarm from Grant's cellphone chimed waking him up earlier than normal from his anxious sleep. He rolled out of bed stiff and unrested from his nonstop tossing and turning while his thoughts ran marathons through his brain.

He started to truthfully question his relationship with Whitney. He had occasionally wondered if their marriage would last through the cycles of their lives. If it would survive a health crisis, raising children, or a financial ruin. He would casually dismiss his thoughts when he would look at his wife smile back at him or when she was on a flight and would send a heartfelt response to his loving texts.

But now, he was looking at everything through a different lens. It was a lens that cast a gray silhouette on the years of playful jokes, tender touches, and romantic getaways. He now questioned the sincerity of all the moments he had previously cherished.

The last two months had been hard, and he was tired of the nagging doubt in his mind. He was ready to find the answer, whether it was good or bad.

He stood in his boxers before his open closet door and pulled out a pair of khakis and the baby blue sweater that Whitney had often said brought out the color of his eyes. He hoped the sweater would bring some good luck as well.

He quietly got dressed and ready for work before the sun was even up. He looked at his watch and yawned at the time: 6:02 A.M. The door squeaked like a mouse as he poked his head out into the dark hallway. Slowly he walked down the stairs leading him to the ground floor. He gripped the handrail, watching his step on the moaning boards on the third and seventh step from the top.

He turned and walked into the living room, finding his wife sleeping soundly under a quilt his grandmother had given them on their first anniversary. He walked more comfortably on the carpeted floor towards Whitney. Six months ago, he would have tiptoed quietly as to not wake her so he could pick her up and take her to bed after a late-night movie on the couch together. But not now.

He was within three steps of her when she let out a breath. He froze in place, looking down at her as she readjusted her arms behind her head with her palms facing up.

He took the final three steps and picked up her phone from the coffee table. He punched in the passcode she had used for years and waited for the phone to unlock.

It didn't.

He looked at the screen and tapped the four digits again with a surgeon's precision.

It still didn't unlock.

He looked down at his wife as his blood started to pump.

What are you hiding?

He stared at the phone and thought of the endless combinations. Birthdates, years, locker numbers, ATM passwords. The combination seemed impossible to crack. He tilted the phone to check for fingerprints like they did in the movies, but he couldn't see any.

He bent down to put it back on the coffee table when he saw her fingertips. He looked at the sensor button and wondered for a second. He lowered the phone's button onto her pointer finger.

He held his breath.

He heard a click.

He turned it around and saw the beautiful image. Her unlocked phone. Free to look through. He walked cautiously away from her and went into her settings and changed the auto lock from two minutes to never.

He tucked her phone into his pocket and left to uncover any secrets she had been hiding. He didn't know if he should be nervous as he stepped out the front door, but either way, he had to know the truth.

Good or bad. But he knew that whatever he found would not be bad for him. He had learned to deal with bad news with no emotional strings attached.

It may only be bad news for her.

CHAPTER 72

I woke up and met Jeremiah at a little coffee shop near American University where he taught anthropology and where I was studying at Wesley Theological Seminary. He was already sipping his latte and eating his strawberry scone as I sat down with my chocolate milk and double chocolate muffin.

"Healthy start," he commented eyeing my sweet tooth choices with a dubious smile.

"I see you're about to do a triathlon yourself, Dr. Huffington."

We laughed and enjoyed our breakfast together as we normally did a couple times a week. He discussed the latest findings in a test drug as I sat and listened like an oblivious child. Yet, he never looked down on my ignorance. He would politely school me on the areas that fascinated him, and I would listen intently.

"The other day you asked me about possessions," Jeremiah started as he set his latte down on the saucer. "It really got me thinking."

"It did?"

"Yes, it really did." He smiled as his eyes lit up. "I was talking to a colleague of mine and she also found the discussion interesting. She is going to look at possessions in various cultures, especially to look at them through the vantage point of cultures with and without mental health professionals."

"So are you two thinking many professed *possessions* are a form of mental illness?"

"I am not concluding anything yet," Jeremiah corrected. "But we are toying around with plausible hypotheses."

"And what are some of them?" I questioned.

"Well, we are all in agreement that people believe other people are possessed. So one hypothesis could be religious teachings affect the number of possessions, raising the question if sects with no spiritual affiliation claim possessions. Will certain religions unbalance the scales of claimed possessions?"

"Interesting. Because I've never heard of Muslims or Buddhists claiming a possession."

"Yes, but how many people of differing faiths do you really know, Solo?" he asked inquisitively. "It's like the statement, 'I'm the best scone baker I know,'" he said pointing down at his crumbs. "But if you don't know of any other scone bakers, that statement is both true and corruptible at the same time compared to the population of scone bakers around the globe. You could be the best one you know, but you could also be the worst one in the world."

"I see your point."

"There are many different directions we can take this study, but after our discussion yesterday, we both agree that this could be a paper that could be published if we really want to research it. So I want to thank you, Solo, for bringing up the question."

"No problem," I smirked, waving off the acknowledgement.

"No, really, your question is a good one. Could people be possessed from a spirit? I'm not sure. Could people be possessed by other influences such as violent video games? Or what about the media or Hollywood propaganda? We know people can be easily brainwashed through acts of obedience like in Stanley Milgram's shock test."

"Is that the," I started squinching my face, searching through my memory. "Oh, the test to show how the German soldiers followed Hitler with the concentration camps and killing millions of innocent lives?" I asked, shaking my head in disgust.

"Yes. Milgram showed that normal, everyday people will do things they don't agree with when someone in authority tells them to. So if people can be brainwashed in that way, they can be brainwashed in other ways. The human mind is a very delicate organ that can be both stubborn and easily swayed."

"Do *you* believe in possession?" I asked, waiting for his answer.

"I wouldn't say I believe in possession, as belief seems like a choice. But I would say I find there is proof that possessions can occur. But the basis of the possession is where we diverge."

"But who knows?" I smiled as I broke off a piece of his scone. "I may be the best scone baker in the world."

"Oh, Solo," he laughed. "I've seen how you cook your grilled cheese sandwiches. And I can guarantee you are not the best scone baker in the world. You're probably not even the best in your apartment building."

"Touché, Dr. Huffington. Touché."

CHAPTER 73

Gavyn and Collin returned home from their early morning five-mile jog through their neighborhood. Collin grabbed a protein bar for breakfast, eating it in three bites as Gavyn pulled out his phone.

"I'm hitting the shower," Collin said, taking off his compression shirt and leaving Gavyn in the kitchen.

"Don't use all the hot water!" Gavyn yelled as he scrolled through his messages.

Did you get some rest last night? he texted.

Some. Did you?

I did. Just stayed at home and relaxed. Prepping for tonight.

Tonight?

Yeah, tonight. You didn't forget, did you? He grinned grabbing a banana from the counter and peeling it as he waited for a response.

No. Just playing with you. How about we meet at your place tonight?

My place? What about Collin?

I don't care about Collin.

He stopped and looked around the place. He felt uneasy with the possibility of getting caught. Even though he was an attorney, he hated lying to a friend. He was about to respond when a new message appeared.

And if all else fails, if he's there, he may want to join in on the fun.

I'm not sure that's a good idea, Gavyn replied, knowing that if someone else was added it would mean more secrets and possible fallout if caught.

Yeah, I'm not sure how he would handle it. He may be a little surprised and would probably need to think it over before jumping into it.

Good thing we don't, Gavyn added as he took a bite of the ripe fruit, leaning against the counter. He closed his eyes and imagined the thrill of what would come that evening.

"It's all yours," Collin said, walking into the kitchen with one towel wrapped around his tan waist and drying his thick black hair with another.

"I have someone coming over tonight, so…" He paused, allowing Collin to chime in.

"You dog. Yeah, I'll stay away. Just text me when she's gone. I would hate for her to dump you after seeing me."

"In that case, you don't have to stay away. I don't think I have to worry about that," Gavyn laughed as he headed to the bathroom to wash away the workout sweat.

CHAPTER 74

Good thing we don't, Grant read as he started brainstorming for the kill for the night. He wanted tonight's to be special. Not that his past kills weren't, but tonight's was going to be different. He had never killed two people in one night, but there was always a first time for everything.

He pulled out a folded sheet of notepad paper he kept in his wallet. Hit List was written on the top with former teachers, professors, co-workers, and bosses that had made one or all of the group members' lives a living hell.

He smiled at his own craftiness, remembering the exact moment in early July when he'd started daydreaming of possible murders that would look like suicides. He had been lying in his empty bed since Whitney was flying somewhere in Washington when the idea of hanging Mr. Lukin had entered his mind. He smiled at the irony of hanging an old P.E. coach that used to make them climb ropes.

Grant mentally moved on to their next victim, Mr. Hill. He thought the drug overdose was very apropos since his teacher had never completed his scholarship recommendation letter because of his old partying lifestyle. Grant wondered if Mr. Hill saw his life come full circle, but sadly, he never got to see who killed him. He had already started to lose consciousness before Grant could remove his mask for his once favorite teacher.

But tonight was going to be spectacular.

A murder-suicide seemed both fitting and doable.

He reached under his driver's seat and felt around. He stretched his arm letting his head lean against the steering wheel as he felt the cold, hard barrel of his pistol. He didn't keep bullets in it on the off-chance of it accidentally firing while he drove. But they were safely stored in the glove compartment, ready to be loaded.

He gripped the handle and sat up, admiring the sleek, black handgun. He looked around the empty parking lot and lifted the gun and aimed, pretending to shoot the aluminum Pepsi can six parking spots away.

Bang. Bang. You'll both be dead tonight.

CHAPTER 75

Elizabeth stood looking out her living room window holding a hot cup of coffee and basking in the early morning sunshine. She held the cup with both hands allowing the warmth to melt her frigid fingers. She closed her eyes and breathed in deeply, letting the robust caffeinated smell sink deep into her soul. A soft smile started to grow as she meditated on the events of last night's dream.

She had already texted Wint and Solo about meeting up for lunch to discuss their plans for the evening. Wint was going to track down the address of Timothy Easton; hopefully, by knowing he lived in Manor Park, they could easily save his life and apprehend the killers.

She stood preparing herself to seize the day. She hoped this day was going to be the turning point of a blah week with Jenny's case going down the toilet as well as the deaths they weren't able to stop earlier in the week. She needed this hump day to actually bring some relief.

She heard a knock on the door as it opened. "Elizabeth?"

"In here," she said as she continued to stare out the window, enjoying the early morning rays of the sun.

Solo walked through the living room into the kitchen.

"Just make yourself at home," Elizabeth kidded as she stepped away from the sunlight and followed him. She turned and suddenly felt the chill of an early autumn morning.

"I just needed to wash my hands," Solo responded, wiping his hands dry on his thighs since the paper towel holder was empty.

"Did your mother not teach you to never dry your hands on your pants?"

"Did you mother not teach you to never leave an empty paper towel roll on the counter?"

They were both in top form this morning as Elizabeth huffed and opened the pantry door to unwrap the plastic from around a new paper towel roll. "Better?" she asked, throwing the empty one in the trash.

"You don't recycle?"

"Don't start," she laughed. "One freakin' cardboard roll isn't going to be the end all of civilization."

"Fine," he said as he raised his hands in surrender. "Just ask the paralyzed camel what he thinks."

She rolled her eyes, shaking her head at the absurdity. "Just because you talk to animals like they're your relatives, doesn't mean the rest of the world does. Some of us aren't crazy."

Solo eyed her suspiciously, cocking his head to the side to take in the statement. "I've seen you talking to a new pair of shoes like you gave birth to them. So who's crazy?"

"Oh, you're definitely still the crazy one." She refilled her cup and stirred in a few ounces of caramel creamer, causing the black coffee to morph into a dark tan.

"Really?"

"Ask any woman," she started before Solomon could interrupt. "Let me finish. Ask any woman with manicured nails, waxed legs, and who still has all her teeth, and she will say the same thing."

"All her teeth?"

"Solo, don't play coy because you know the demographic I'm pandering to. And your eastern Tennessee bloodline doesn't fit in my circle of opinions that matter."

"Fine, but Aunt Jolene may surprise you. She almost wet herself seven Christmases ago when Chelsea and I bought her a new pair of steel-toed boots she'd commented about on Facebook. So remember, even some toothless women will do anything for a nice pair of shoes."

Elizabeth blinked a few times, staring at Solo as if wishing she could forget what he just said. But she knew that the image of a squirming Appalachian woman holding up a pair of work boots and running to the bathroom was going to be an image seared into her brain for many sleepless nights to come.

"What are you even doing here? Don't you have school or something like that?" she asked, sipping her coffee like it was a morphine drip.

"I'm playing hooky."

She smiled devilishly looking at him with a little more respect than a minute ago. "Men who are almost thirty don't play hooky."

"Really? Then what would you call it?"

"I don't care. Call it whatever you want, but just don't say hooky." She shivered squishing her face as if smelling some rotten fish. "It sounds creepy hearing you say it."

CHAPTER 76

"Whatever, Elizabeth. But now that I'm here I guess I can tell you what I dreamed about last night," I started as I pulled out my phone with the notes I jotted down when I woke up. "Oglethorpe Street." I smiled and nodded my head as if the word evoked some intoxicating memory.

"And?"

"Well," I began as I strutted to her showing her a zoomed-in map on my phone. "Oglethorpe Street."

She blinked her eyes in a blank expression.

"Here, let me do this," I said zooming out to show a six-block radius of Oglethorpe Street. "See it now?"

She watched as the map stopped moving and words and locations popped onto the screen. "Manor Park!"

"Bingo."

She stared at the map and counted out loud. "Six! There are only six blocks of homes on Oglethorpe."

I smiled as she saw the same thing I did. "We can park our car on the street the middle of the six blocks and watch and wait."

She smiled while shaking her head. "Solo, I have the name of the next victim. Wint is probably going to call soon and tell me the address and any other information he has on Tim Easton." Her phone on the kitchen counter started to ring as she looked down at it. "Speak of the handsome devil. Hey, Wint, what have you found out?"

"Well, there are two Tim Eastons in Washington, DC," he answered on speakerphone as Elizabeth and I huddled near the counter.

"So which one lives in Manor Park?" Elizabeth asked.

"Which one lives on Oglethorpe?" I corrected.

"Neither," Wint answered, and I felt the air leave my lungs like a popped balloon.

"You must be wrong," Elizabeth snapped. "I saw the name Timothy Easton in my dream with a news report of the murders in Manor Park. And then Solo had a dream that showed Oglethorpe, which is a street in the same neighborhood. So, I don't know what to tell you Winston, but you better do your search again."

"I did, Elizabeth," he huffed. "I did it a couple of times with different spellings. I tried Timothy. I tried Tim. I even tried Timmy. And each time I only found two guys and neither one of them has ever lived in Manor Park."

I tried to calm the rising tempers on both sides of the phone call. "What if they are skipping Tim and moving down to the next name on the list?"

"Maybe," she softly said, resigning the fact that Timothy Easton was the next target.

"Do you remember all the names on the list?" I asked as she had already started to open the notes app on her phone. She copied the names and texted the list to both me and Wint.

"I just sent you the list."

"Okay, I'll check out the names as I have time this morning."

"Call us if you find anything," I said as I saw Elizabeth's shoulders sink lower as if the weight of the world was on them.

"Will do."

The call ended as Elizabeth closed her eyes and screamed. I watched and felt the same way, but we handled our stress and disappointment in different ways. "I just don't get it!" she erupted, donkey kicking the cabinet behind her. "I just don't get it. How are we messing this up? I thought the license plate was good two days ago. And then last night, I thought we were golden with the name and neighborhood."

I listened to her as something clicked inside me. "But we still have the street. We know it's going to happen on Oglethorpe sometime today."

She looked over at me as though wanting to hold on to her rage with her clenched jaw and tapping foot.

"You know I'm right," I said pouring some more coffee into her mug. "Do you want me to stir in a muscle relaxer to calm you down?"

She smiled at the comment, and her entire body started to shake as if knocking off the remnants of the last few minutes.

"Feel better?"

"I will," she said picking up her cup of coffee. "And I don't need a muscle relaxer," she said with a smile as she opened a drawer and pulled out a Ziploc baggie and waving the dried green contents in front of my face.

"Elizabeth!"

"It will relax you," she said opening the plastic baggie and taking a deep breath. "Jeremiah was the one that recommended it."

"I don't care who recommended it. It's illegal!"

She heaved with full body laughter, folding her body forward and then quickly rising back up. She wiped tears from her eyes while I stood mesmerized. "It's chamomile, you moron. Chamomile."

I grabbed the bag and inspected the dried contents, seeing and smelling that it wasn't pot. I threw the bag back at her as she continued to laugh at my expense.

"But you know, if you ever want to try it, all you have to do is ask Wint," she grinned. "Cops always get the good stuff."

"No!" I said in shock, but then it made sense. When they have drug deals, they have to keep it and dispose of it in some way. "Really?"

"Where do you think it goes?

"I don't know. I've never really thought about it."

"They have to burn it, Solo."

"They don't smoke it, Elizabeth!"

She grinned. "All I'm saying is when he got picked to burn the drugs in a 55-gallon barrel in an open field with a couple of other police officers, they didn't move their lawn chairs when the wind blew in their direction."

"I don't believe you!"

"Veronica said he was so mellow that evening."

"I'm not listening," I said stomping out of the kitchen.

"Just think about it, Solo! Just consider your boy Wint as high as a kite pigging out on a bag of Oreos and Chex Mix."

"I'm not listening," I said trying to tune her out by turning on the television. But even though I wouldn't admit it to her, it did make sense.

CHAPTER 77

"What are you up to?" Officer Peterson asked as she tapped her fingernails on Officer Cooper's desk. He sat staring at the screen, jotting down tidbits of information while ignoring Dakota's appearance since he didn't have much time before their shift started.

"Anyway, Stu and I had a great night last night," she rambled. "We haven't gone out to dinner in about a week, so he surprised me and took me to Julio's."

"Uh-huh." Cooper only had two more names on the list, and so far, no one lived in the Manor Park neighborhood. He typed Clint Browning in the search box, and a few names appeared on the screen. His heart got excited and also frustrated because he had to click on each name to get their personal information stated on their driver's license.

"It was amazing! Have you been there? It's a little Italian place on the north end of town. I got their lasagna and Stu got the largest plate of spaghetti and meatballs I have ever seen. It may not be Veronica's type of place, but you'd love it."

"Uh-huh."

Dakota walked around his desk and stood behind Wint peering over his shoulder to see what was so important for him to ignore her.

"Who's Clint Browning?"

Cooper didn't respond but scribbled down the addresses of each resident of Washington, D.C. along with their demographics that may be pertinent. He looked down at the list, but so far no one lived in the area Elizabeth mentioned. "Maybe she's wrong," he whispered.

"Who's wrong?" Dakota asked, leaning down so her eyes were at Cooper's level. She looked down at the list of the various names, reading them silently.

"It's nothing," Cooper answered as he started typing in the last name.

"Collin Diaz? Why are you looking him up?"

His eyes widened as an address appeared. "Oglethorpe," he whispered. A smiled appeared on his face as he wrote all the information. His heart started to pound as he started to think about the possibilities. He thought he'd reached this edge two nights ago, but it suddenly avalanched tossing him into the raging sea below. He hoped this feeling wasn't going to end in a sudden crash of missed opportunities. He jumped up from the computer and dashed toward the door as he quickly called Elizabeth.

"What did you find out about Collin?" Dakota asked, but Cooper was already gone.

CHAPTER 78

Grant walked through the halls of the Department of Transportation and found his friends standing around Stewart's cubicle. The three were laughing as Grant entered the little circle.

"Did you see the hit in the sixth last night?" Jordan asked eating a bagel covered in cream cheese and sliced strawberries.

"I didn't," Stewart said a little jilted. "I told you I went out."

"Oh, that's right," Jordan replied.

"I saw it," Collin beamed with his cellphone in hand. "That ball flew out of the park."

Grant looked over at Collin, watching his movements as if stalking his prey. He looked him up and down as if seeing him for the first time.

"What about you, Grant?" Jordan asked with a few bagel crumbs falling out of his mouth.

"I didn't see it," he said looking at Collin, inching closer in the circle.

"Your loss." Collin turned his head looking away from Grant.

"Yeah, I guess it is."

Stewart and Jordan felt the tension between the other two as they acknowledged it with their raised eyebrows and casual nods.

"Want to meet for drinks tonight?" Jordan asked.

"I can't," Grant answered as he continued to stare at Collin.

"I don't think I can either." Stewart shook his head looking up at Grant who didn't take his eyes off of Collin.

"Depends on the time for me," Collin said shrugging his shoulders and looking into his hands as he typed on his phone.

"Got plans tonight?" Grant asked menacingly.

"Nothing definite yet," Collin replied, once again shrugging his shoulders and moving his eyes between Stewart and Jordan. "But you never know."

"Yeah," Grant said. "Being single has its benefits sometimes. You're able to do as you please." Grant looked at his watch and turned and walked away, pulling out a phone from his pocket.

"What's up with him?" Collin asked the remaining two. "Still upset from yesterday?"

"Who knows?" Stewart added as the three watched Grant walk away checking the message on his phone.

CHAPTER 79

Grant woke his computer and typed in his security passwords for all his programs to open for another day of work. But he didn't feel like working. He felt betrayed. He felt scorned. He felt rage. He was a swirling tornado with the heat and cold of his insides colliding.

He looked down at Whitney's cellphone and reread the text messages from her lover over the last two months. He felt sick at the pornographic images they sent one another, exposing their nakedness. He looked at the images Whitney had sent and the time stamps on them. His heart sank when he noticed the date on one of them was a day he used to cherish, their anniversary.

He read the flirtatious texts and sickly envied the man she was cheating on him with. He used to get these types of texts from his wife a year ago, but not anymore. Now it was generic texts of *Will you get some milk?* or *I got another flight, be home in a few days.* He couldn't remember the last time he received a sexual text from Whitney.

He went back to the beginning of the text messages and noticed they started two months ago, but thinking back, he'd felt the chasm begin months earlier. His mind started to form new questions. Was this her first affair? Or had there been others? Should he get tested for an STD? How many flings had she had?

He scrolled through the images in the texts and saw her beautiful body in risqué poses. He started feeling aroused as he looked at his wife. The thrill caused his rage to intensify. Suddenly the sexual tension passed and his revengeful instinct was rising. He scrolled down a couple of images and saw her lover's picture in her phone. He wanted to reach out and strangle the man sleeping with his wife. But he knew strangulation wouldn't look like a suicide.

"We need to talk," Collin said walking behind Grant.

Grant turned around to see his former friend standing behind him and felt the urge to just kill him for keeping this secret from him for two months.

CHAPTER 80

Jenny Ascot sat across from her two attorneys and wondered if she was trusting them too much. "You have to look medicated," Gavyn had said before the start of the trial. "If we want this defense to work, you have to look like you are on the medicine they are supposedly giving you."

"Yes, Jenika," Milo reiterated during one of their meetings in the jail late July. "You are guilty. There is no denying your intentions, but in order for us to play the insanity defense card, you must play it too."

"But I'm not insane."

Now she looked at the two men across the table from her, thinking of the times they'd visited her since her arrest. Gavyn visited her the most, but he was only doing his job. Milo had only come to visit her because she coerced him.

"Gavyn," Milo said softly, "will you please give me a minute with Jenika?"

"Whatever you want to say, you can say it in front of me." Gavyn stayed seated, trying to look confident and strong against these two.

"Do what he says, pretty boy." Jenny started to laugh looking at Gavyn like he was a child. She had only worked with Gavyn periodically before her first arrest, but he had the reputation of being a playboy, a playboy who never gave her any attention. If there was only one benefit of these weekly visits, it was seeing that piece of fine eye candy.

Gavyn looked at Jenny with fierceness in his eyes and a cocky smile. "I'm more than just that."

"Are you?" Jenny stood up and paced behind the table, watching Gavyn's eyes track her movements. "The only reason you're here is because I requested you. And the only reason I did that is because I'm in a jail full of women and I wanted something to look at a couple of times a week. So if you would please leave me and Milo for a few minutes, I would appreciate it." She stopped and stood seductively with her finger in her mouth. "And when you get back, we can have Milo leave if you're man enough."

Gavyn stood up with a sexy grin. "Don't flatter yourself, Jennifer. You weren't my type last year, and you're definitely not my type now."

Gavyn walked toward the door before Jenny stopped him. "Science has confirmed that women can rape men. So, why don't you do some push-ups while you wait. I like men with firm bodies."

Gavyn turned around and sarcastically winked at Jenny before leaving the unrecorded room. "Jenika," Milo started.

"I don't mean it," she hissed. "I'm just bored."

"Well, maybe you should keep your mental games away from your defense attorney. Your life depends on it."

Jenny started to laugh as she took a seat, straddling the chair between her legs. "We both know he's not going to do anything but sit and look pretty for the female jurors."

Milo nodded with a sinister smile. "And I thought that was my job."

She imagined herself placing her hand on Gavyn's knee, moving it higher up his thigh until she had her hand on his groin. Her expression must have betrayed her thoughts to her other attorney.

"Quit toying with him, Jenika."

"Yes, Milo."

CHAPTER 81

Grant silently followed Collin to the men's restroom as his mind was churning with questions he wanted to ask. The two went to the urinals along the wall as Mickey from IT was washing up. Collin turned his head as he zipped up and saw Mickey leave.

"What's your problem, Grant? How long are you going to sulk like this?"

"Sulk?" Grant mocked as he flushed.

"Yeah, you didn't talk to me at all yesterday after lunch and again just now. Everyone saw it."

"Saw what?"

"Man, come on."

"What do you want me to say?" Grant shouted. "Yes, you screwed up! And sometimes I can't even look at you because you screw everything up that is around you!"

"Really?"

"Yeah."

"Well, what else do you think? Just let it out and tell me what a failure I am. At least I don't have a wife who only comes home and sleeps with me a few times a year."

Grant shook his head, clenching his fists as the soapy water ran over them.

"What? No response, Grant?"

"At least I have a woman who chose me. You don't have anyone but a roommate that lives with you."

"At least I get rent from Gavyn. What's the last thing Whitney's given you other than a cold shower?"

Grant turned around with his hands in a fist as he threw the first punch. Collin didn't expect the hit from the expression on his face, but it only took a second for him to regroup and throw his first punch.

The two took their stance, looking in each other's eyes as if they had been enemies for a lifetime and not just a day.

"You can't handle me, Collin."

"You always think you're the leader of this group and you can talk down to Stewart and Jordan, but you can't talk that way to me." Collin launched forward with years of oppression bubbling to the surface as his fist collided with Grant's face. Collin grabbed Grant and pushed his back into the bathroom stalls.

Grant wrapped his arms around Collin's neck, but Collin easily maneuvered himself out of his grip. Collin jumped behind Grant's back, grabbing his arm and twisting it behind his back as he wrapped his free arm around Grant's neck.

Grant looked in the mirror and saw himself in a submissive pose. A pose similar to the one he had placed Mr. Hill in two nights before.

"I don't know what I did to you, Grant, to make you hate me, but I'm done with it."

The bathroom door swung open as Jim from maintenance walked in. Collin immediately released Grant, pushing him away. The two looked in the mirror straightening their clothes, but they didn't look at themselves. They were watching each other in the reflection.

"I'm done too," Grant added as he grabbed a tissue to wipe the blood from his nose. Collin followed him out of the bathroom, his stride confident.

"None of my business," Jim said as he lathered his hands at the sink.

CHAPTER 82

"I'm not sure about meeting for lunch," Wint whispered on his phone in the men's bathroom. "But Dakota and I will patrol Manor Park this afternoon so we can try and stop this before anything happens."

"I still don't know what the plan is," I said on speakerphone as Elizabeth scooted closer on the couch.

"Well, you two have all day to come up with one. I'm about to start my shift and I'll try to think of something."

"What about calling the police and letting them deal with it?" Elizabeth laughed. "Oh, wait, that won't work because you *are* the police."

"Funny," Wint mocked.

"I mean, seriously, what can we do? Call this Collin guy and give him an anonymous tip to be careful that someone is going to want to kill him?" Elizabeth said. "That sounds very believable."

"Well, you two have some time to come up with a plan."

"Gee, thanks." I looked over at Elizabeth who looked as clueless as I felt with the task of saving two people's lives today.

"Can you send us Collin's picture and anything else you have on him?"

"Will do," Wint said as someone else entered the bathroom. "I'll text it to you soon. Got to go."

"Well, any suggestions?" I asked looking at Elizabeth without a clue as to where to start. "Was the news reporter standing in front of a house in your dream?"

"Yeah, but I don't remember what it looked like."

"Okay, I was just thinking if we went there, maybe something would jog your memory. Just to make sure that Oglethorpe Street is the one with the two murders," I said frowning. "I just don't want to make the same mistake twice."

"We have time to kill. So I guess it wouldn't hurt."

I winced at her choice of words.

I had already started a Facebook search for the only Collin Diaz that showed up in the D.C. area. I clicked on the name and saw the profile picture of a man in his mid-twenties. "Do you think this is him?" I asked, showing Elizabeth his picture as she was sliding on her shoes.

"He's cute," she said.

"Yeah, he's a good-looking guy," I said scrolling through his information of work and school history. Nothing screamed future victim. I went to his wall and scrolled through his posts of workout pictures, laughing friends, and family gatherings.

I read through a few of his posts that tagged the same group of friends as an uneasy feeling hit me.

"Elizabeth," I feebly said handing her my phone again. "Look."

"Yeah," she joshed, examining his muscle poses more closely.

"Not those." I scrolled through the posts pointing out the ones with the same group of friends. "Those."

She looked down at the post as her eyes widened. The coloring in her face changed as her tan complexion drained a few shades.

"Those...those..." she stammered as she looked into my eyes.

Immediately I remembered why those names sounded familiar. It all came back like a haunting memory from six months ago.

Her color quickly recovered as her expressionless face changed to a bright smile six months in the making. "We got 'em."

211

Finn stood behind the prosecution table as his surprise expert witness, Dr. Hansel Burgg, swore to tell the truth. He watched Dr. Burgg raise his right hand as he looked over at the defense table huddling together as if planning their next legal move. He smiled as he saw the fire in Gavyn's eyes when he remembered the voice of his colleague, Jill Stapleton, during a conversation they'd had two nights ago. "Jenny is not mentally insane. She's pure evil, but not unstable in the realm of a defense."

Jill had tried to convict Jenny in April on multiple counts of murder, but Milo's theatrics didn't just punch a hole of doubt into the minds of the jurors, he knitted one perfectly. "Don't let Milo take control of the room," she advised.

"But how can I stop that?" Finn had asked in Jill's office the night before.

"Pray?" She smiled. "I don't know, Finn. I've read over the case and nothing in there screams mentally insane."

"But they want a closed case with her locked up somewhere," he said, speaking of his superiors and politicians.

"You know what is interesting?" She stopped, tilted her head and looked up at him from behind her desk. "Why is Milo asking for an insane defense?"

"Because he believes she's crazy?"

Jill shook her head no. "He doesn't think he can win without it. What did your psychologist say before he suddenly changed his mind?"

"Dr. Weaver was siding with me and then he just changed."

Jill pulled out her phone and searched for a contact. "Call Dr. Hansel Burgg."

"Who's that?"

She looked at him playfully. "A psychologist...who I am dating."

"I didn't know you were dating anyone."

"And no one needs to know. He's getting a divorce and we are trying to keep it hidden until it's finalized." She straightened the papers on her desk. "Just give him a call. Tell him you know me. You have the medical records from Dr. Weaver, so send those to him. I would go back to getting her found guilty on attempted murder," she smiled. "Stick it to Milo and Jenny."

"You think?"

She nodded her head. "So, are we done here?" He nodded his head as she yelled into the hall. "Veronica, we're done now."

Veronica walked back into the room empty-handed and sat behind her laptop. "I hope you get her," Veronica said politely as Finn started to leave the office.

"Aren't you supposed to be for your client?" Finn laughed as he walked out the door.

"Former client!" Veronica shouted. "Former!"

Finn walked down the hall pulling out his phone as he received a text from Jill. He opened the contact and called in mid-stride.

"Dr. Burgg," he said clearing his throat. "I need a favor. Jill Stapleton said to call you."

CHAPTER 84

"Dr. Hansel Burgg," Finn started as he walked across the courtroom to stand near the jury. "Please tell us your credentials."

"I received my doctorate at Cornell University specializing in social and personality psychology. After receiving my PhD, I worked under Dr. Joseph Gatz who specializes in dissociative identity disorder, more commonly known as multiple personality disorder." Dr. Burgg sat in his gray fitted suit accenting his 6'2" slender build with an emerald tie to match his eyes. He spoke to the jury through his rectangular framed glasses, smiling to show his sparkling and straight teeth.

"Objection, Your Honor." Gavyn jumped up causing the jury to turn their attention from the handsome doctor to a handsome attorney. "Dr. Burgg never interviewed or met with Ms. Ascot, and I don't see how he can give expert testimony without such an interaction."

"Mr. Garrett, is this correct?" Judge Otto questioned with an off-balanced look in his eyes.

"I was going to get to that, Your Honor. If you will allow me to continue."

"I will allow it, but tread carefully."

"Thank you, Your Honor. As I was about to ask, Dr. Burgg, you did not speak with the defendant, Jennifer Ascot, correct?"

"Yes, that is correct."

"So how do you feel you can give expert testimony on her condition and well-being at the time of the crime?"

"I have read through her medical files and watched many hours of her interviews. I feel through my years of research and analysis in this precise area of psychology, I can still give my assessment, even though I didn't interview her. It is like watching a baseball game. You didn't have to be in the grandstands in person to watch Babe Ruth hit his home runs. You can see him through the many hours of video footage that has survived through the ages. The same can be said with psychology. Many times during our scientific research, we are not the ones administering the tests, but are the ones watching. I used the same standard in this scenario."

"Your Honor!" Gavyn once again erupted. "This is preposterous!"

"I will allow it," Judge Otto sided. "Let's see what Dr. Burgg has to say before any more objections."

"Thank you, Your Honor," Finn nodded as he went back to the witness. "So, Dr. Burgg, you are highly respected in your field with years of research and other trials. Please give us your opinion on Ms. Ascot."

"Yes, I watched the footage of Ms. Ascot's interviews with Dr. Wallace Weaver. And there were some things that he missed since he probably didn't rewatch his own video. This often happens when interviewing patients, or in this case defendants, in person. Even if he did rewatch the footage of the interview, he had already come up with his assumption of her mental state, and it is very hard to change your own mind after you have made up a decision."

"Very true, Dr. Burgg. I think we all can say we agree with that statement."

"Yes. For example, you make a judgment of someone within the first seven seconds of meeting them. Therefore, since I have been on the stand for about four minutes now, the jury has already subconsciously decided to trust me or not, over three minutes ago." He smiled politely to the jury. "It's okay, we all do it."

"So, you believe that Dr. Weaver fell into the trap of this type of judgment?"

"I wouldn't say trap, but he missed a few crucial subliminal body language characteristics that reveal the mental status of Ms. Ascot."

"And what did he miss?" Finn asked, leaning forward as if asking the jury to lean in as well.

"Based upon the tests he conducted, he never asked what Ms. Ascot's name was."

"And how is that important?" Finn asked, tilting his head.

"Because I am pretty sure, if he'd asked what her name was, she wouldn't have answered Jennifer Ascot."

The silent courtroom suddenly stirred with a flurry of commotion at the twist Finn, himself, didn't see coming.

"Uh...um..." Finn looked breathlessly at Dr. Burgg with rage in his eyes as his precisely calculated questions were thrown off kilter with the unforeseen stab in the back. Finn didn't know what to ask, but he knew he needed to ask something. He had already told the jury this man was an expert, so he couldn't try to dismantle his testimony. He couldn't try to tear down the man he just raised up with all his laurels. He couldn't undercut him like he had just been. "Dr. Burgg are you certain of this diagnosis?"

"I am fairly certain since her medical professional is prescribing her a combination of selective serotonin reuptake inhibitors, or SSRIs, which can be an effective treatment with dissociative disorders."

"Uh, no further questions, Your Honor."

Finn walked back to his chair in a daze. A million questions smashed around in his brain. He sat down and looked to his co-counsel who lowered his head in disbelief at what just occurred. Finn closed his eyes and took a few deep breaths, but it wasn't working. He wanted to bend over and put his head between his legs because he felt like he might pass out from the rug being pulled not only from under him, but the whole judicial system.

He looked up through his watery eyes as he watched Dr. Burgg turn his head to face the defense table and give them a subtle nod. Finn turned his head as Gavyn and Jenny were looking away, looking toward the man Dr. Burgg was eyeing.

Milo.

CHAPTER 85

Milo didn't acknowledge Dr. Burgg's gaze but stared at the judge with the utmost respect and admiration.

"What just happened?" Gavyn asked as Milo shook his head.

Milo slowly stood and walked toward the psychologist still seated in the witness stand. His shoes clapped against the hardwood floor, echoing through the silent room. He never said a word as he walked, but continued to stride across the courtroom until he was face to face with the expert witness.

Dr. Burgg looked at Milo, giving him a weak smile that the attorney didn't reciprocate. Milo paused, eyeing the witness with his squinting eyes allowing the rest of the room to remember this moment. He wanted the jury to have dreams tonight of this moment when Dr. Burgg announced that Jennifer Ascot was insane.

"I have just one question for you, Dr. Burgg," Milo breathed out slowly.

The man sat frozen in his chair, except for his blond wavy hair moving from Milo's breathy enunciation of his name.

Milo turned around, his back to Dr. Burgg as he looked at the jury with expressionless eyes. "Based upon your years of education and experience, do you whole-heartedly believe that my client, Jennifer Ascot, should be found not guilty by reason of insanity?"

Dr. Burgg looked through Milo staring into the unknown distance and nodded his head. "Yes. Not guilty by reason of insanity."

Milo looked at the jury and extended his arm toward the witness as if presenting them with a new car behind the curtain. But just like in game shows, many things in life are staged.

"No further questions, Your Honor," Milo said as he slowly returned across the courtroom towards his table. He looked at the dumbfounded Gavyn and the apparently drugged Jenika as he glided by Judge Otto.

He sat slowly, his twisted smile barely showing, wondering what kind of bonus he would present to Pyotr after the trial. Pyotr was a loyal member of their organization. And loyalty and dedication deserved a nice reward. Without Pyotr, Milo wouldn't have known about this surprise expert witness with his blackmail-worthy secret.

Without Pyotr, Dr. Burgg would have told the truth.

Without Pyotr, Dr. Burgg might have caused the jury to lean to a guilty verdict for his client.

He looked over at Jenika and realized Pyotr didn't owe her anything else now. She'd saved his life four months ago, and now he'd saved hers.

CHAPTER 86

We drove through the quiet neighborhood where newly cemented sidewalks and tall elm trees lined Oglethorpe Street. I looked out the window like a dog admiring the two-story homes and curbside parking, imagining myself living in such a quaint section of town.

"Does any of this look familiar?"

"You dreamed it too," Elizabeth snarled. She drove the desolate street at a snail's pace, looking at all different styles of homes with their different color bricks and aluminum siding.

"All my dream showed was a street sign with the sound of a few gunshots and feet running away," I answered as I smiled at the green shutters on the two-story bungalow styled home. "Isn't this street charming?"

"Charming?" she coughed in shock. "Two people are going to die here today."

"Well, besides the double deaths. This is a nice street. Look at that metal fence. It's a perfect place for a dog."

"You getting a dog?" she asked in disdain as she inched forward, turning her head back and forth to see both sides of the street.

"Why don't we just park the car and walk?"

"Did you bring your leash?" She pulled over and parked beside the curb in front of a newly planted tree that had only a dozen leaves remaining.

"Funny. I promise I won't run off this time."

Elizabeth parked near the corner of Fifth and Oglethorpe and we headed east. We strolled the leaf-littered sidewalk as she tried her best to remember her dream while I pulled out my phone to get Collin Diaz's address. "I think Collin's home is one block further up."

"Solo! Why didn't you tell me Wint had already sent you the address? I'm looking like a dementia patient trying to remember where I parked my car while you knew all along."

"I didn't know if the news reporter was standing in front of the house. Sometimes they keep the reporters away during the investigation."

"Mm-hmm." Elizabeth picked up her tortoise walk as we crossed the street to the next block. "This street really isn't that bad."

"Would you live here?"

"God no!" she said as if the thought involved eating a bug. "But this area could suit you."

"You say that like my standards are beneath yours."

She stopped and turned to me, looking in my eyes. "You live in a trash heap that the city should demolish because even the rats have moved out to find a better place."

"It's not that bad."

"How many meth addicts live in your building?"

"Exactly. Meth isn't the cheapest drug. You can buy heroin or marijuana cheaper than you can buy meth."

"Wow! That should be on their renter's pamphlet. *The classiest apartment to get high on the south side. Because here, we have standards.*"

I didn't say a word. I understood her concern, but there were many good things about the apartment. It was mine and Chelsea's first place after we got married. We were poor newspaper employees trying to make ends meet. When we moved in we didn't know about the shady renters two apartments down from us. It was just a place to live until we could save enough money to buy our own place.

"I'm sorry."

I stopped at the sound of her voice since it sounded like an apology. I wasn't used to hearing her say those words out loud. I

221

cocked my head and looked at her. She didn't say it again, but I saw the look in her eyes as she turned to look away from me.

"I know you hold some sentimental value to your home," she started as we continued to walk. "But she would want you to better yourself. And live in a safer place where you don't have to sleep with a baseball bat beside your bed."

"I've never had to use it."

"But the point still remains, you have it in case someone breaks in."

"Why are you judging me? You carry a gun at all times." I laughed at the slightly off-balanced scales.

"I carry a gun because I'm a single woman who lives alone in a nice subdivision. You have a bat because you've watched too many zombie movies, and when someone is high on meth, they're like a zombie. That's a big difference."

"We're here," I said noticing the number on the house. "Collin Diaz's home."

She turned around and shrugged her shoulders. I could see the disappointment on her face as she closed her eyes. "It doesn't look familiar to me. It just looks like any other house on this street."

I didn't want to say anything, but my mind went back to two nights before when we were so close to saving Jake Hill, but at the same time we were miles and almost an hour away.

CHAPTER 87

Finn stormed out of the courtroom tracking down Dr. Burgg who had turned out of view heading down the stairs.

"Dr. Burgg!" Finn shouted, but he either ignored him or couldn't hear over the loud acoustics in the courthouse's openness. "Dr. Burgg!"

Finn chased after his expert witness reaching the stairs as the man looked behind him halfway down. The two caught each other's sight. "Dr. Burgg!"

He didn't stop. Instead, he picked up his pace, sidestepping a couple of people to exit the stairs as quickly as possible. Finn saw a clearing in the stairs and ran down the middle, taking two steps at a time. His elbows hit a man in his back, but he didn't stop to check on him. He kept his eyes locked on the speed-walking psychologist.

Dr. Burgg headed toward the exit as Finn jumped from the last step, dashing across the marble floor. His slick bottom dress shoes didn't give him any traction, but he wasn't going to stop. He didn't want to call him. He didn't want a text. He wanted his answer face to face.

Finn skated around two other attorneys, missing them by only inches as his body bent and maneuvered around the oblivious lawyers. His heart was racing as his arms were beginning to sweat under his layers of clothing. He pushed open the exit and started making up ground. His sprint was catching up to the doctor's walking pace.

He dashed forward, reaching out his arm as if passing a baton. He grabbed a hold of Dr. Burgg's arm, twirling him around on his heels. "Get your hands off me!" Dr. Burgg stopped walking and shook off Finn's grip, smoothing out his clothes and combing back his hair.

"What happened in there?"

The doctor shook his head. "This isn't the place."

Finn looked around the front of the courthouse with pedestrians passing by without a second thought of their commotion.

"Trust me," Dr. Burgg said softly with firmness in his tone. "They are probably watching us."

"Who's watching us?"

He cocked his head at the dimwittedness in Finn's question. "You know who."

"Did they coerce you?" His voice started to rise before he quickly lowered it, hoping the passing traffic drowned out his question. "Did Milo threaten you?"

"I stick by my testimony, Finn. And you should just allow the insanity defense." He looked Finn in the eyes as if he had something else to say. His eyes moved looking behind Finn, and he held his breath as a look of fear glazed over his emerald eyes. "Just let it go, Finn. I've got to go."

He turned to walk away leaving Finn standing confused as he watched his only legal hope get lost among the crowd in the crosswalk. Finn turned around and spotted a black Lincoln Continental a block away, parked in a towing zone. The vehicle immediately turned on its ignition and slid into the traffic, driving away.

Finn looked across the street and found Dr. Burgg standing on the other side of the street, pulling his cellphone out of his pocket. He looked down at the phone as his hands started to tremble. Finn squinted his eyes and could see the relief on the doctor's face as he mouthed, "So, she's safe? She's with you?"

Finn watched the lying man across the street and wondered what he would have done if he was put in the same predicament as Dr. Burgg. Would his morals outweigh his heart? He didn't know who the psychologist was speaking to, but with the relief on his face and the wiping of a couple of tears, somehow he knew beyond a shadow of doubt that his testimony this morning had been purchased.

Not with money, but a life for a life, apparently.

Finn picked up his cellphone and was relieved when Jill answered his call. "How'd it go?"

"Good. You're safe. Does Hansel have a kid?"

"Yeah, a daughter. Why?"

Finn looked across the street as Dr. Burgg ended his call and continued to walk down the sidewalk. He didn't walk with any more pep in his step than before, but occasionally he would turn his head to look in all directions, as if making sure he was safe.

"I gotta go, Jill. Thanks."

"Finn! What happened?" she asked as Finn ended the call. He watched until his witness blended in with the other pedestrians. Despite how many times he had pleaded and begged for people to testify against killer gang members, he had often felt grateful for never being the one having to decide whether to do what was right or do what was safe.

Even though it sickened him, he couldn't be upset with Dr. Burgg's choice. If given a life or death ultimatum in a court case that could still swing either way, he would have done the same thing if someone had threatened his son. No matter how fair the judicial system was supposed to be, many times it was the things that seemed the most perfect that were actually the most corrupt.

CHAPTER 88

"Coming to lunch?" Stewart asked as he and Jordan stood at Grant's cubicle.

"Not today," he said, grabbing both cellphones and stuffing them in his pocket. "I have a doctor's appointment so I'll probably be late coming back."

"Everything okay?" Jordan asked as Grant stood up and walked between his two friends without an answer. "This doesn't look good."

"Nope."

The two walked over to Collin's computer and found him still nursing his hand with an icepack. "He said no?" Collin asked spinning his chair around hearing Stewart's and Jordan's chitchat. "So now you can ask me for lunch?"

"It's not like that," Stewart replied, his deflated tone signaling his lie.

"It's okay," Collin said as he flicked off his desk lamp. "We've always known you and Grant were best friends and I get that. Jordan and I are closer because we roomed together for a couple of years. It's just how the cards fell. And I'm really okay with it."

"So are you in?" Jordan asked, annoyed by the feeling of being pulled to two sides like they were still in high school.

"Sure, why not?"

The three walked to a nearby pizza joint, Wiseguy Pizza in Canal Park, their conversation centering on Grant's sudden mood change.

"Do you know what's going on?" Jordan asked as they waited for the crosswalk sign to change.

"I don't know, but he's changed," Stewart commented. "The other night, he said..." he started before he caught himself and stopped talking.

"What did he say?" Collin pressed.

"He was just," Stewart started as he looked at his two friends. "He was just different."

"How so?" Jordan looked over at Stewart as Collin started walking ahead of them.

"He was just snarky," Stewart answered as he looked at Jordan. "I don't know, but it just rubbed me the wrong way."

"He's always snarky to me," Collin interjected. "Always mocking me because I'm single. Or if I gain a few pounds, he's always the first one to rip me a new one. Or at work when I don't do something exactly the way he wants, he sends a demeaning email and copies my boss on it. It's like he has it out for me for some reason."

"I've always thought he was somewhat jealous of you," Jordan pointed out as they walked into the restaurant.

"Sure," Collin uttered unconvinced.

"I bet he's jealous of all of us," Jordan reiterated as they slid into a booth. "Stewart has his new hot thing. You're always going out with a different woman each week."

"So what does he have to be jealous of *you* about?" Collin laughed.

"My fiancé loves me for me, love handles and all," he laughed. "It gives her something to hold on to. Can you imagine what Whitney would do if Grant gained a few pounds? Whitney is too…you know," he started as the others nodded.

"Mrs. Thing," Stewart chimed in with a sassy attitude, "would drop him faster than he could try to run it off."

The waitress came and they ordered their drinks and pizza. The three talked sports until their food came and Collin shifted the topic.

"Do you think of me the same way Grant does?" Collin asked, revealing his insecurity.

Jordan felt the vulnerability as he looked over at Stewart who stopped chewing his food. The two stared at one another as if playing a mental game of rock, paper, scissors.

Stewart was about to answer but had to swallow his large bite of pizza first, allowing Jordan to jump in.

"Well, I'm definitely not jealous of you, man," he sarcastically bolstered as Collin and Stewart joined in with the friendly laughter.

"You would tell me, right?" Collin laughed.

"Yes, we would tell you," Stewart responded as he looked over at Jordan wondering if that was a lie or the deep-hearted truth.

CHAPTER 89

Grant revved the engine of his sedan at every red light. His road rage was getting the better of him as he weaved in and out of traffic, not caring if he cut someone off or even almost caused a wreck. He only had one thing on his mind.

Good thing I'm not going to a doctor's appointment because my heart rate would be hospital-worthy, he thought as he smiled at the wickedness.

He pulled into his subdivision and sped down the street. His tires skidded, leaving black marks on the street as he turned in his driveway hopping the hump of the curb. He grabbed his wife's phone from the passenger seat, reading the new texts from her boy toy on the side. He screamed at the top of his lungs, slamming his fist into the roof of his car.

He opened the car door and held her phone in his left hand as he felt it vibrate once again with a new message. It was another from him.

He looked down the driveway and wondered if anyone saw him pull into his home. He glanced down at his watch and knew kids were still in school and most people on the street were either at work or sleeping from their midnight shift. There were not very many stay-at-home housewives in this section of town.

He walked up to his house's back door and opened it. He took a deep breath and walked into what once had been a happy home. A home he had wanted to raise children in. A home he'd thought about renovating and selling for a profit so they could purchase a larger place with some land. A home he'd thought was full of love and a future.

"Grant, what are you doing home?" Whitney asked confused, looking down at her phone in his hand. She looked up at him with anger in her eyes. "Why do you have my phone? I've been looking for it all morning!"

"Were you ever going to tell me?" He shut the door behind him as they stood in the kitchen staring at one another with no love between them.

"Did you take my phone this morning?" She stomped over to Grant trying to pull it free from his grip, but her frail hands were nothing compared to his testosterone-fueled clutch.

"I asked you a question. Were you ever going to tell me about him?"

She didn't answer but continued to pull at her phone. She reached back and smacked Grant on his face, causing his right hand to react in kind.

His large open hand slapped across Whitney's face, causing her head to twist. Her long blond strands flung around, covering her eyes with her own locks. She reached up and felt her stinging cheek as an angry, fearful tear started to fall.

"I'm going to ask you one more time. Were you ever going to tell me about him?" He slammed her phone down on the counter, showing the conversation he had fraudulently been having all morning.

"Why would I tell you?" she shrieked, grabbing it and reading the messages as all the air left her lungs.

"Do you know how stupid I look?" he asked as he clenched his fists.

She didn't respond but gasped in horror at the morning's messages between her unknowing lover and her husband.

"Answer me, Whitney!"

"Fine! You want answers? I've been cheating on you for years!"

"Years?" Grant's insides flipped as the gnawing questions from the morning were painfully answered with no remorse or resentment. "Are you proud of yourself?"

"I'd be prouder if you didn't find out," she snapped back.

"Is that how you really feel?" He looked at his wife and wondered if their entire marriage had been a lie. Had she ever truly loved him, or was she just using him for her own enjoyment?

She didn't answer as she continued to rub her reddening cheek.

"Did you ever love me?"

She refused to answer. She looked down at the phone in her hand as a message came in. She started to type a reply before Grant swung his arms down, pushing her cellphone away from her hand. They watched as it flipped in the air as if in slow motion until it collided with the ground.

"Grant!" she screamed bending down to get her phone. But before she could reach it, she felt his hands around her throat, stealing her breath. She tried to speak, but she couldn't get anything out.

CHAPTER 90

Grant looked down at the whore he'd once called his wife as she stooped down to pick up her phone. She was more concerned with her text messages than this argument.

Suddenly, his arms reached down and his hands wrapped around her slender neck. She looked up petrified and off balance as her center of gravity had suddenly shifted.

She tried to straighten her body and stand up, but her thin frame couldn't compete against Grant's muscular one. She was straining to get her legs underneath her, but he was pressing down too much. She used to run periodically to keep her waistline trim, but she never lifted any weights. She now realized that was a deadly mistake since fighting off Grant was going to be like bench pressing two hundred pounds.

She reached her arms to grab at his face, but they were too short. She thought if she could reach for his eyes she could gouge them, but attack scenes in movies were well-rehearsed and choreographed. And the character was usually ready for the attack. She wasn't.

She pounded her fist at his firm chest, but he wasn't flinching at the weak punches. She looked into his eyes, begging him to let go through her straining teeth and tear-stained cheeks. But he didn't ease up. As he looked into her eyes, his strength seemed to intensify.

Her lungs were hurting, starving for oxygen. Her hands reached up at her throat, clawing at his hands. He grinned as she felt her strength dwindling.

Her legs had little leverage as he had pushed her to the ground. She was sitting, yet she felt her body rise. She tried to get her feet underneath her to gain some momentum, but as soon as her feet touched the ground, he lifted them up off the kitchen tile floor.

His bending back was now upright as he lifted her by her neck. Her legs dangled underneath her torso as the two limbs started to move. She thought she got a good kick in as she saw him wince, but he didn't let up. He lifted her head higher until she was less than a foot away from the ceiling. She looked down into his eyes as he was gritting his teeth, straining for her to die.

She continued to kick and scrape her nails on his hands when she noticed his eyes were closer than they were a minute ago. She let go of his hands and reached out with her trembling hands toward his face.

He closed his eyes as she felt around. She started throwing her fists at his head, hoping he would loosen his grip so she could get one breath of air.

She reached further down as she saw the room move around her. She lifted her hand, but it was too late. She felt the back of her head collide with the wall behind.

She raised her hands up to protect the back of her head, but all it did was cause her fingers to break when he slammed her head into the wall again.

And again.

She knew she couldn't do anything. Her lungs were empty and her strength was gone. She was tired of fighting. She was tired of being married to Grant.

Her eyes started to flutter as she had a morbid but fitting thought.

'Til death do us part.

CHAPTER 91

Grant looked up at his lifeless wife as he slammed her head into the wall. Her arms swayed beside her limp body like willow branches in the wind. He wondered if she was dead, but he wanted to make sure.

He lowered her body onto the white-tiled floor, giving his shaky arms a little relief from the murderous workout. His biceps released their tension as he took a deep breath, but he continued to grip his hands around her throat. He straddled her body, resting his body weight on his knees as his numbing hands circled her throat. Her telephone pinged, breaking the deathly silence, signaling a new text.

Sweat started to drip off his nose onto her t-shirt. He looked down at the woman he said he would die for and shook his sweaty head. He never thought they would be in this position. He never thought she would cheat on him. He never thought he could be so hurt that her death was the only thing that would bring him a little solace.

He looked up at the wall where he had slammed her head and noticed an indention in the drywall and a smear of blood. He looked down at his wife with her discolored face as shock hit him.

"What did I do? What did I do?" he moaned as he looked down at his once-beloved as a surge of regret hit him full force.

With all the murders he had committed, he had never once felt regret. But he'd never killed anyone in the spur of the moment. He was always planned and prepared.

This was different. This was like an out-of-body experience. This wasn't like Sabrina Latener last April who had also cheated on him. He had years to dream of killing her. Then this week with Ted Lukin and Jake Hill; once again, he had years of anticipation of those kills.

His mind started racing. He hadn't come up with all the pieces of this kill yet. In the past he always had an easy getaway either by driving or running away.

But not here. Here was his life. This was his home. This was the dead body of his wife. He considered the possibility of leaving and coming home later tonight and "finding" her. Coroner reports would show she was murdered long before he would return.

But he didn't have an alibi. No doctor's appointment. No lunch with friends. No working through lunch at work with security cameras. He was screwed.

He jumped up and looked out the living room window. He turned and looked at Whitney lying on the floor.

"Don't react. Think!" he told himself as he took a few deep breaths. "You can do this."

He walked away from the living room and stepped over his dead wife. He looked out the back window. His back yard had a privacy fence that separated his neighbor's property from his own. He looked and could see part of the Dennises back yard.

Can you see mine? he wondered. *Are you even home?*

He pulled out his phone and started to call the Dennises but only had their cellphone numbers. Most people didn't have home lines. He looked down at his phone and wondered what he would say. "Hello, are you home? Oh, you are, never mind. I was just going to get rid of my dead wife."

He looked back at his lying wife on the floor and shouted, "Why did you have to cheat on me? Do you see the problems you've caused?"

He looked at the time on his phone and knew he needed to get back to work soon. He considered leaving her body and disposing of it this evening when a different thought flashed in his head.

He let the idea swirl as he tried to look at the situation from different angles. And from every angle he looked, he saw the definite possibility of this ludicrous idea working.

He grabbed his car keys and headed out the door. He started the ignition and put the vehicle in reverse. Slowly he backed out of the driveway looking in all directions for nosey neighbors.

He didn't see any of their vehicles at home. He started to smile as his idea started to seem very possible. He just hoped the rest of the sporadic elaborate plan would work.

He pulled out his phone and quickly texted Stewart.

Appointment ran later than I thought it would. I'll be back soon.

CHAPTER 92

Dr. Hansel Burgg returned to his office and locked the door with the deadbolt. He stood at the window, peering through the blinds wondering if anyone was following him. He had a couple of appointments later in the afternoon, but he needed some time to decompress after the heart-pounding drama of the morning.

He stood still by the door as his cellphone rang. He slowly pulled out the phone and looked at the unknown number. He clicked to ignore the call. He didn't want to have another phone call like he did last night.

He could still remember the chilling feeling he got when he'd answered.

"Dr. Burgg?" a husky voice asked in a thick eastern European accent.

"Yes, this is he. Who may I ask is calling?"

"Who is calling doesn't matter," the man replied. "You need to say Jennifer Ascot is mentally unstable tomorrow when you testify."

"Who is this?" Hansel demanded walking into his study for some privacy while his nine-year-old daughter practiced the latest TikTok dance.

"Once again, Dr. Burgg, you don't need to worry about who I am, but you do need to worry about what you're going to say tomorrow. Or else."

"Or else what? Are you threatening me?"

"I wouldn't call it a threat yet," he snickered. "But if you want a threat, I can give you one."

"I have your number and I'm going to call the police."

"Dr. Burgg, you don't have my number," he said calmly. "And even if you did, I would suggest you not call the police. Or else."

Hansel looked down at his phone and realized the man was right, he didn't have a number. It just said Unknown. "Or else what? What are you going to do?"

"Your daughter, Liv, how old is she? About eight or nine?"

"Stay away from my daughter!"

"Dr. Burgg, in order for your daughter to stay safe, we need you to keep Jennifer safe."

Hansel gripped the knob of the door he was leaning against, steadying his wobbly legs. He stood in the darkened room, feeling his world tightening around him.

"I don't want to hurt Liv, but I will sleep well no matter what I am told to do. And I always follow my orders. So I hope you will follow my instructions for the sake of your daughter's life."

"Please don't hurt her," Hansel groaned.

"I promise I will not hurt your daughter if you just convince the jury that Jennifer is clinically insane," he said gently like talking to a friend.

"But I'll be under oath."

"Would you rather live with the memory of lying under oath and seeing your daughter grow up, or live with the torment of telling the truth knowing your words killed her?"

"You wouldn't kill an innocent child!"

"Dr. Burgg, don't tell me what I won't do. Because you don't know what I'm capable of. We can ruin your life. We can tell your wife about your relationship with the assistant district attorney, Jill Stapleton."

Hansel gasped.

"Yes, Dr. Burgg, we know about her as well. So, tomorrow you can do us one little favor or we can quickly make you wish you were dead."

"Please no," he stammered as he felt pinned up against the wall. "I'll do it. I'll say whatever you want. Just don't hurt them."

"That's a good answer, Dr. Burgg. So, tomorrow when you leave for the courthouse leave your daughter at home. You can have someone stay with her until you are finished tomorrow. But if you try anything funny, we will find out."

"I promise. I won't do anything."

"That's good. Then you won't mind us watching you tonight."

Hansel stepped away from the door and raised the blinds in the study, letting the light from the streetlight in.

"Good evening, Dr. Burgg," the man said cunningly. "That's a nice sweater you are wearing. Very appropriate for autumn."

Hansel looked down and felt his orange cashmere sweater. His eyes darted towards the street at the various parked cars lining the dimly lit road.

"I wouldn't waste your time looking for me, Dr. Burgg. Because even though you cannot see me, I can definitely see you."

Hansel stood in front of the window as he heard a knocking on the door behind him.

"Looks like Liv wants to show you her new dance, Dr. Burgg. But before I go, I just want to make myself perfectly clear. Do not call the cops. Do not try to run. Do not do anything out of the ordinary. When you leave tomorrow for the courthouse, your daughter will stay back. Make up an excuse. Then when you are finished on the stand, you can let Liv go to school. But once again, if you say anything contradictory tomorrow or do anything that I said not to do, it's not me that will kill your daughter. It will be your actions that will kill her."

The call ended as Hansel heard Liv knocking on the door.

"One minute, hon," he shouted through the door as he tried to get his bearings.

Still shaking from the memory, Hansel looked at his phone as it signaled a voicemail. He lifted the phone as the message started in a familiar voice.

"You did a fine job today, Dr. Burgg. Very fine. But we will still be watching you for some time to make sure you don't do anything that could harm this trial. We may even need another favor from you in the future. So once again, do not call the cops or try to be a hero. Because even heroes die when they least expect it."

CHAPTER 93

We walked four blocks north of Oglethorpe Street and ate some chicken and waffles at Janess Backstage. I fell more in love with this neighborhood because of this restaurant.

"You're such a man. You would walk to Hell if they offered you something deep fried."

"I wouldn't go that far," I said cutting a piece of my waffle as Elizabeth tried to figure out how to eat it. "It's not that hard."

"It doesn't even make sense why people would eat this," she said as she looked around the crowded restaurant and then down at her plate.

"Take a piece of chicken and a piece of waffle and dip it in the syrup." I demonstrated the process where the sweet and salty mixed perfectly on my taste buds.

She sunk her head down, hiding herself from anyone watching as she put the unusual concoction in her mouth. I watched as she started chewing apprehensively. She suddenly stopped and looked up at me. I stared at her in silence as I saw her start to swallow. A bashful smile broke through her prejudicial lips.

"That's actually not bad."

"Told ya."

I watched as she timidly ate her lunch, looking over her shoulder periodically as if someone from her country club was going to see her and report to the review board. I just laughed to myself and enjoyed the rest of my lunch.

"So do you feel confident yet?" I asked.

"Uh…uh," she stuttered as she looked down at her half-eaten plate.

"Not the food. Your dream."

"Oh," she sighed as if having to admit her lunch was bearable was the worst thing that would happen today. "I'm hopeful."

"Hopeful is good."

"Hopeful is hopeful, Solo," she said pessimistically taking a big bite of her waffle.

"I have a feeling about today," I said with an opportune grin.

"That could be good or bad."

I looked at her, confused at the statement.

She wiped her hands and explained. "Pissing your pants is a feeling and I wouldn't say that it's a good feeling to have. But it's a feeling."

"You know what I meant."

"Solo, your intuitive meter isn't the most reliable," she said taking a gulp of water. "Maybe fifty-fifty."

"I'd say I'm more than fifty-fifty," I remarked. "Maybe eighty-twenty."

"Eighty-twenty!" She shot out a laugh causing the entire room to turn our direction. A few minutes ago she would have been in agony, but now she was back to her old self. "What? Can't a woman laugh?" she asked the crowd, her head bobbing with attitude.

She waited until everyone in the restaurant went back to eating before she turned back to me.

I looked across the table and saw something I didn't see a minute ago.

"You have something on your chin," I said reaching over the table with a napkin.

"Solo!" she grunted as she dipped her napkin in her water to wash her face. "I told you I would not like this place."

"It's not the restaurant's fault you eat like a three-year-old."

She stared at me with wickedness in her eyes.

"What? Do I have something on my face?"

She picked up her dirty napkin and started to reach her arms toward me. "No, I can't do it," she said shaking her head.

"Elizabeth got a conscience?" My eyes widened as if in shock of the new discovery.

"I need some more syrup," she said standing up and holding her little container of syrup. "Looks like you need some too," she said walking beside the table.

"Well, aren't you sweet?" I smiled.

"You know it." She got a couple of containers from the counter and opened them as she walked back to her seat. "Here you go," she said holding out her hand.

I reached out to get it from her but she quickly lifted her hand to my face, pressing the open container to my cheek. She let go as the syrup dripped down my cheek to my chin. I sat in shock, mesmerized as her socialite reputation quickly morphed into a teenage boy's persona while she returned to her seat.

"Looks like you have something on your face."

I slowly smiled as everyone in the restaurant once again turned their attention to our little two-seater table. "Oh, I do?" I asked sarcastically, pulling off a piece of waffle and dabbing it on my face. "Did I get it all?"

"Perfect. You got it," she beamed as I continued to drip the remaining syrup onto my plate pretending to be oblivious.

"I still don't know why you say my intuition isn't good."

CHAPTER 94

Jenny sat in the courtroom and looked medicated as she had pretended to all week. She watched astonished as Milo started calling the defense witnesses who testified to her insanity. The courtroom cycled through medical professionals she had never met as they lied about their tests and procedures.

She looked at Gavyn sitting beside her and wondered what he was thinking. She had been an attorney who once held her professional ethics in high regard, but that was before her reunion with her brother, Alexei. After that, all ethics and high morals went out the window like the hoses they used to kill their victims. She wondered if Gavyn was a straight-laced rule-following lawyer, or if he didn't mind bending the law for the sake of his client.

"So to confirm what you are saying, Dr. Greenleaf, my defendant Jennifer Ascot," Milo announced as he pointed in her direction, "was suffering from a mental breakdown and wasn't aware of what she was doing when she attacked Elizabeth Hyde and Solomon Davis. Is that correct?"

"It is," Dr. Greenleaf nodded as he kept his eyes glued to the ground.

"No further questions, Your Honor."

"Your witness, Mr. Garrett," Judge Otto motioned.

Finn stood up and buttoned his suit jacket. "I have just two questions for you, Dr. Greenleaf." He stepped away from the prosecution table and headed toward the witness stand. "Dr. Greenleaf, can you lift your head and look toward the jury?"

Dr. Greenleaf slowly raised his head and looked at Finn inquisitively.

"I asked if you could please lift your head and look toward the jury."

"Yes," he answered with an expressionless gaze.

"I haven't seen you look toward the jury yet, Dr. Greenleaf. Will you please demonstrate?"

Dr. Greenleaf's eyes shone resentment and annoyance as he turned his head away from Finn and looked over at the jury.

"Thank you, Dr. Greenleaf. Will you please state once again, looking at the jury, what you just recited, I mean, *truthfully testified* about Jennifer Ascot's mental state at the time of the crime?"

Finn walked back to the defense table and picked up his notepad as Dr. Greenleaf spoke to the jury. Finn listened to Dr. Greenleaf's repeated testimony as he looked down at his notepad while he walked towards the witness stand.

As Dr. Greenleaf was speaking, Finn started reading aloud from his notepad the testimony he'd scribbled down just a moment ago. Finn spoke along with Dr. Greenleaf as if the two were in unison.

Dr. Greenleaf stopped talking as his head snapped back to Finn.

"No, go on, Dr. Greenleaf. You still had a few more statements to make about Ms. Ascot's mental blindness to the crimes she was committing."

"Objection, Your Honor!" Gavyn stood up. "This is ridiculous and proves nothing. Many testimonies are rehearsed since witnesses are not allowed to bring anything to aid them."

"Move on, Mr. Garrett," Judge Otto demanded siding with the defense.

"My apologies, but I was wrong. I have three questions for Dr. Greenleaf."

Dr. Greenleaf stared at Finn with a deadened glare in his eyes.

"How did they coerce you today?" Finn asked with defiance as he looked into Dr. Greenleaf's soul-purchased eyes. "Did they pay you? Did they threat--"

He stopped as Gavyn erupted from his chair and Judge Otto pounded his gavel.

"Mr. Garrett, do you have any proof of these allegations you are making toward Dr. Greenleaf and the defense?" Judge Otto asked looking down from his bench and pointing the gavel at Finn as if about to strike him.

"No, Your Honor," Finn resigned as he stood in front of the judge waiting for his condemnation. "I don't have any proof. I just have a hunch."

"Well, keep your hunches silent. My courtroom isn't about hunches. It's about finding the truth."

"Yes, Your Honor. No further questions," he added as he walked back to his seat.

Jenny wanted to smile, but she knew she couldn't. She continued to sit silently as she bowed her head looking at her hands in her lap. A little drop of blood started to drip from her clenched hands. She had learned to suppress her emotions by digging her fingernails into the palms of her hands. She opened her fist and turned up her palms, keeping them hidden from anyone else's view.

She didn't have a problem with seeing her hands covered in blood. She just preferred it to be someone else's.

CHAPTER 95

"Everything okay?" Stewart asked walking up to Grant's cubicle catching his friend staring at his hands.

"Oh, yeah." Grant nodded his head and placed his hands face down on his desk.

"Are you sure? Because you don't look too good."

Grant combed his fingers through his hair and gave Stewart a conniving smile.

Stewart looked at Grant and knew something wasn't right. He didn't know what was wrong, but in the last twenty-four hours, something had shifted and things were not as aligned as they had been a few days earlier. Grant put his hands on his keyboard and started working on the proposal he was given the week before.

"Wasn't that due already?"

"I don't know," Grant answered not looking at Stewart as his eyes darted around everywhere but at the computer screen. "And I don't really care."

"Okay." Stewart backed away from Grant's cubicle and took a few steps before stopping. He turned around and saw Grant grab an ink pen from his desk drawer and start writing on a scrap sheet of paper. He watched for a few seconds before finally deciding to move along.

His mind kept going through possible circumstances that could have caused the sudden mood change in Grant; unfortunately, many of them involved a health crisis.

"Do you think Grant has a brain tumor?" Stewart whispered bending down beside Collin's desk.

"Brain tumor?"

"Yeah, that would make sense with the change in his attitude lately."

"In that case, he's always had a brain tumor when I'm around." Collin shook his head as he sighed at Stewart's naivety. "Grant is just being Grant, and you are finally seeing it."

"Maybe." Stewart stood up, feeling his group of friends falling apart. Grant was fighting with Collin. Jordan was engaged. He finally had a serious girlfriend. He hated that he was awakening to the realization that their brotherly bond to always have each other's back was fracturing like the San Andreas fault. "What if it's something else?"

"Like what?"

"I don't know." Stewart's voice sounded frazzled, his body language exhibiting his anxiety. He tapped his finger on Collin's desk as he tried to think of something that would appease Collin.

"We could follow him after work," Collin said unfazed.

"Follow him where?"

"I don't know. That's the whole point of following someone, you moron."

"I meant," Stewart started, "never mind. So when he leaves we will follow him."

"Sounds like that's the plan," Collin remarked as he spun around in his chair to return to his work.

Stewart walked away feeling even more confused. Collin was being helpful as Grant was being distant. It was as if the world had flipped and Stewart wondered if it had turned in a good way. *Only time will tell,* he thought.

CHAPTER 96

Elizabeth and I walked around the Manor Park neighborhood, killing time until the showdown on Oglethorpe Street.

"I wonder what happened today at the trial?" I asked as we walked down Peabody Street enjoying the warm sunshine on this late October day. I was once again admiring the homes of the neighborhood as she pointed out their flaws.

"If you asked me a few days ago I would probably give you a different answer. But right now, I really couldn't care less." She walked with her head held high in her Versace sunglasses as the wind tossed her hair around her shoulders, but I could see the brokenness she was hiding.

"What if she really is crazy?"

She stopped and looked at me through her black lenses. "Jesus, Solo, they even convinced you? You saw her when she was trying to kill us."

"That wasn't the Jenny I was set up with."

"Exactly. So why are you asking those idiotic questions?"

"But she was totally different. What if she has a split personality?"

"Solo! Do you hear yourself?" Elizabeth lowered her glasses to the tip of her nose to let me see her shocked eyes. "Jenny doesn't have any split personality. She didn't speak in another voice or say she was Becky," she shouted flaring her arms in the air. "God, Solo, she called me sis like Jenny would always do," she said in a heartbreaking tone to her voice.

"All I'm saying--"

"I seriously can't be having this conversation with you right now." She raised her glasses back and stepped away, walking ahead of me on the sidewalk. After a few steps she stopped and turned around. "Seriously, Solo? Are you freakin' serious?"

"I don't know," I said walking towards her kicking a stick out of my way like it was a soccer ball. "I've just been thinking about it lately."

She stared at me. I could imagine her eyes rolling behind her black lenses. "That is one of my least favorite traits of yours. You know that?"

"What?"

She huffed as she started to walk as I followed, picking up my pace so we were walking side by side. "You always try to see the best in people, even if it means coming up with excuses about their mental state."

"That's what I do for you." I smiled and she cocked her head at me with a crooked grin. "So that's your least favorite trait of mine?" I smiled, trying to ease the tension with some humor.

"I said *one* of my least favorite."

"How many do you have?" I asked in shock.

"There aren't enough hours in the day, Solo."

She hooked her elbow with mine as we walked down Peabody Street. That was the thing with Elizabeth. She would tell me what she thought without holding back, but she would also let me know that despite everything, we were an unlikely team to the very end.

She stopped and pulled me back a step. We were standing in front of a two-story home with a For Sale sign in the yard. "Want to take a look?" she asked with a shrug. "We have time."

"I thought you said--" I started.

"I said *I* wouldn't live here," she said taking off her glasses. "But your standards are much lower than mine. And this community is much better than your apartment."

"Much better?" I smiled.

"Solo, a homeless shelter is better than your apartment building."

"Really? It's not that bad, Elizabeth."

She pulled my arm with a groan as I followed her up the walkway lined with dead flowers from the autumn cold. We took the stairs up the front porch that had a swing bolted to the wooden ceilings. She knocked on the door as I looked behind the white painted banister into the front yard that seemed made for warmth and a pitcher of lemonade in the summer evenings.

An older woman opened her front door and greeted us with a kind smile. "Hello."

"I know this is presumptuous, but we were just walking by your home and wondered if we could take a look at it?" Elizabeth asked as I looked around the surroundings, already imagining myself rocking on the front porch with a good book in my hand.

"Well," she feebly answered turning around to look behind her. "My living room is a mess and my realtor usually handles visitors."

"I understand," I said turning around. "If you would feel safer we can come back later. But a messy house isn't what I'm going to be looking at."

"And we have cash, so why pay a realtor their commission when we were just walking by?" Elizabeth asked with a wink.

That piqued the woman's interest as she nodded her head. "My daughter wanted me to use a realtor because she was afraid I would get taken advantage of." She stopped and looked at me and Elizabeth as she patted her cheek. "But I have a good feeling about you two." She opened the door to allow us both in.

"Do you want to call someone before we come in since you don't know us?" I asked standing on the front porch as Elizabeth walked into her home and shot me a dirty look.

"I have a security system," she smiled showing us a necklace with a button. "If you try something, the police will be here in a few minutes."

"That's good to know. Seems like a safe neighborhood," I commented as I stepped into her home and took off my shoes. Elizabeth looked back and rolled her eyes.

"If it's so safe why have a security system?" Elizabeth mouthed as I shook off her question.

I admired the stained hardwood floors in the entryway that flowed into the adjoining living room and a flight of stairs a few steps forward.

"This is a beautiful home," I said feeling the wood paneling on the walls that looked to be custom made when the house was built.

"My husband's father built this home in 1927. He carved that wood with his own two hands."

"Exquisite," I said, tracing my fingers along the wood. I turned my head and the messy living room was anything but as the woman folded her blanket and turned off the television show she was watching. "I'm sorry, I didn't introduce myself. My name is Solomon Davis, and this is my friend Elizabeth Hyde."

"Solomon?" she asked with a grin. "That is an uncommon name anymore."

"Yeah, it's a family name."

"Nice to meet you two. My name is Ruth Edsel, and my late husband's name was David."

I smiled as I saw the correlation. "That's funny. Ruth, David, and Solomon."

"What's funny about that?" Elizabeth asked as she examined the brick fireplace.

"King David from the Bible had a son name Solomon, and Ruth was David's grandmother, I believe," I explained as I grinned at Ruth.

"Great-grandmother," she nodded. "See, I knew I had a feeling about you two."

"Well, a feeling about one of us," Elizabeth politely corrected. "He's the theology student. I'm just…" She stopped and looked at me. "I'm just here."

"So you two aren't together?" Ruth asked before immediately waving off the question as if afraid of intruding.

"Oh, it's fine," I smiled. "We're just friends."

"Definitely just friends," Elizabeth agreed from across the room examining the front window.

"Oh, I'm sorry. I just saw you two through my window and thought you were such a lovely young couple."

"No, I'm dating someone else and he's a widower who needs to move on finally."

"Widower? You're so young," Ruth said shaking her head in condolence.

I didn't know how to respond so I just nodded my head and continued to walk around the room. Ruth allowed us to roam freely through the two stories as she followed. The two women continued to chit-chat, and I was shocked by how polite Elizabeth was acting by laughing at Ruth's stories and actually telling a few herself.

"What did you think?" Ruth asked as we were standing back at the front door.

I turned around and could picture Chelsea coming down the stairs holding onto the wooden banister. I was afraid of losing Chelsea by leaving the apartment we lived in, but I realized I would never leave Chelsea there. Her memory was going to follow me wherever I lived.

"I think I have some serious thinking to do, Mrs. Edsel," I said shaking her hand. "I will be in contact. Promise."

She reached her arms out and gave me a big hug. I could have let her hug me for hours as her warmth seemed to cause some of my uneasiness from the last few days to drift away with the autumn breeze.

"Don't look past your friend here," she whispered in my ear. "Some of the best romances start as friendship."

I pulled away and thanked her for her hospitality. Elizabeth and I went out on the front porch as I once again looked around, imagining myself sitting on the green steps resting after a morning jog. We walked down the walkway, and I hooked my elbow into hers.

"What did she say to you?" Elizabeth asked as we walked down Peabody Street.

"She basically wants me to woo you," I smiled as we walked in stride turning down Fourth Street toward Oglethorpe.

"That little old minx."

CHAPTER 97

Gavyn left the courthouse and went back to his office at Manfield & Hyde to pick up a few things and check in on a couple of other clients' issues.

He was sitting behind his laptop about to pack up for the early evening to do some things at home later when Luther Hyde entered and shut the door.

"How did it go today?" Luther stood across the office with his arms folded catching Gavyn off guard with the intrusion.

"It went as well as was expected," he answered. If he was truly honest, he would have confided in his belief that Milo was doctoring the witnesses' testimonies. But based upon his telephone conversation yesterday morning, he believed his opinion would be quickly sidestepped or even misconstrued as not being a team player on this case.

"Is it what you were expecting?" Luther asked in a degrading tone as he continued to stand still like a menacing statue.

"I wasn't aware of half the witnesses Milo called this afternoon," he answered, a little too quickly judging from Luther's flinch.

"Wasn't aware? I don't pay you to sit idly by and let another firm do all the heavy lifting while you take all the credit."

Gavyn sat stunned at the demeaning speech. He had seen a new side of Luther during this court case with Jennifer Ascot. It was a side he wasn't too fond of.

"Milo doesn't tell me what he is thinking of doing," he started, but Luther shut down the excuse as the cement statue broke free with a stomped foot.

"Milo doesn't need to tell you what he is thinking. You need to think of ways to serve your client. And then do them."

"But--" Gavyn started before Luther snapped his fingers as if commanding his dog to sit.

"I don't want to hear your *buts*!"

Gavyn tried to sit with his chest out and shoulders back to put on a show of vigorous defense, but on the inside, he was breaking. He didn't respond to the shouting. He just sat like a child taking in the verbal assault and making a vow to never be in this predicament again.

"You have until the end of this case to show me your worth," Luther charged as he turned his neck to examine the diplomas hanging on the wall. "If you can't prove it to me, then you'll need another wall on which to hang those useless, overpriced pieces of paper."

Gavyn stared aloofly. He had never been threatened with a demotion, let alone a termination based upon his performance. He didn't know how to respond. "Yes, sir." He choked out the words as if someone was strangling him from behind, like a surprise attack.

Luther turned and opened the door, leaving the room like a dwindling tornado fading into a small storm cloud sprinkling a few drops of rain.

Gavyn grabbed his belongings, sliding his messenger bag over his shoulder with his laptop safely inside. He turned out his lights and looked back into the darkness wondering how many more cases he could handle working for Mr. Hyde. A few of the paralegals working in their cubicles told him to have a good evening, and he politely nodded with the same sentiment.

He pressed the elevator button while pulling out his phone and watching the floor numbers steadily increase.

Can I give you a call? I need to talk to you, he texted.

He watched the three blinking dots and waited for a response.

You'll be blacklisted if they find out.

I don't care. I'm already there.

He stepped into the empty elevator and waited for the door to close before he dialed the number.

"Hello, Veronica. I'm screwed."

CHAPTER 98

"Screwed?" she asked as she saved the contract she was working on for a business merger.

"Luther. Since I started on this case, I see a totally different side of him."

"I've been following the case. How can you live with trying to get a not guilty by reason of insanity?" she berated, tossing her glasses aside and fluffing her hair to ease the stress of the last two hours from rereading the same document.

"You pleaded not guilty when she murdered all those people," he quickly rebutted. "So I think it's safe to say we were both pushed into corners without our choosing."

"But I was forced to take the case. My hands were tied," she corrected.

"And you think I chose this? You know Luther. When he assigns cases, you don't say no. You just ask when."

"Gavyn, what's Milo doing this time?" She heard a dinging in the background when Gavyn didn't answer.

"One second."

She stood up and stretched her back, doing a few toe touches and side bends while she waited for Gavyn to return.

"Sorry. I didn't know if someone was standing outside the elevator and I couldn't take any chances."

"Elevator? At the courthouse?"

"No, at work."

"Gavyn! Dad has the entire office bugged. He knows everything that is going on there. Do you seriously think anywhere is safe in that prison? You can't imagine how many hidden cameras he has in the bathrooms, let alone in an elevator."

Gavyn didn't respond.

"Oh Veronica, I'm royally screwed now."

"Just breathe. He doesn't watch the tapes unless he suspects something."

"How about threatening to fire me? Would that warrant a reason to watch me and listen to everything I say?"

"Jeez." She was glad Gavyn couldn't see her expression because she knew he was approaching some very thin ice.

"That's the reason I'm calling. Do you know of any firms that are looking to hire anyone? You talk to a lot of different people. Have you heard anything?"

"Gavyn, are you sure about this?" she asked, remembering the backlash she went through when she left. "He's not very forgiving when you walk away."

"He basically told me I was fired five minutes ago," he said as he walked toward his car in the parking garage. "I'm just trying to beat him to the punch."

"There are a few places that are hiring, but they probably can't compete with the pay or benefits."

Gavyn laughed at the comment. "Some pay is better than none."

"That's true."

"How's your place going? Looking for another attorney?"

"Are you wanting to get us both killed?" Veronica laughed. "Dad wouldn't have a second thought about getting Milo to whack us."

"I'm serious. You're a good attorney. And I am too. We could do this."

"Gavyn, slow down."

"Seriously, think about it. What kind of law have you been specializing in since you left?"

"I've basically been handling business clients, trying to stay away from criminal trials. I'm finished with defending murderers and repeat offenders just because they can pay."

259

"Sounds like you could use someone to handle estate planning."

"Gavyn, really. You need to slow down. This is a big decision you are considering."

"Veronica, I've been thinking about this most of the week when I'm trying to fall asleep. We could do it. I can swoon the older ladies with my charm and you could get the men. I'm not opposed to using my good looks to draw up business. And I'm pretty sure you have a way of getting the men to give you a second glance. And then. Pow! We show them we have the knowledge to back it up."

Veronica looked in the mirror in her office. "I don't play that card, Gavyn."

"You don't, but you should," he laughed. "We both should."

She went back to her computer and quickly did an internet search for firms in the D.C. area who specialize in estate law. There were many firms who had it listed.

"What are you doing?" he asked.

"I'm looking up something," she said clicking on a few of the links and checking out the profile pictures and bios of the attorneys that handled estate law.

"There aren't any attorneys handling estate law in D.C. that are as hot as we are. I told you, I've been thinking about this."

"I don't want to be known for using my looks to get clients."

"Veronica, people judge on appearances. There have been studies done where people were shown multiple photos and they were asked who would they trust the most. And guess what? They usually chose the attractive ones. So why not use what we've got going for us? At least for a little while. I'm not always going to look like this. I might as well use it while I can."

She clicked around at some of the firms and noticed the bulk of the attorneys handling estate law were older. She wasn't saying they weren't good attorneys, but Gavyn had a point.

"Let me think about this for a couple of days, okay?" she said as she continued to look at a few other firms' employee directories.

"Okay, but if you're not interested, it's your loss."

"Good talking with you, Gavyn. I hope you lose your case for my sister's sake."

"Oh," he groaned. "That's right. I keep forgetting how tangled you and your family are with this case."

"Yeah. I wish I could forget. I'm fine with letting the strings knot and strangle her. But knowing Milo, he has some magic pair of scissors that will save her from a horrendous death. Have I told you how much I hate him?"

"See, another reason we should partner because I hate him too. We already have something to bond over. Our number one enemy."

"Don't forget Luther," she added. "He's my number one."

"Your family is definitely not normal," he sighed.

"Sure you want to get closer to the drama? Because it can kinda suck you in if you don't watch out."

"I'm used to watching my back."

CHAPTER 99

Collin's ears perked at the sound of walking feet coming from behind. He casually turned his head to see Barbara in payroll carrying her water bottle as she left for the night. He smiled as she passed by and then proceeded to stare at his emails on his computer.

Have you seen him? he messaged to Stewart.

Nope.

Collin rested his elbows on his desk as he sat and waited, hoping Grant would walk by soon. A few minutes passed as various other co-workers walked by, fleeing their unread emails for the night. He looked at his watch and wondered what point following Grant would solve. He placed his fingers on the keyboard and started to type a message to Stewart, when he heard another pair of feet. He didn't turn around, but waited for the person to say something. But he didn't. Collin held his breath and looked up as the person passed.

"Night," Collin casually said, but Grant didn't respond.

He's leaving! Collin quickly closed his email and started walking behind Grant from a distance, trying to be undetectable.

"See ya, Grant," Stewart said in the distance as Collin poked his head around the corner and watched Grant silently wave to Stewart as he continued to walk down the hall.

Grant turned down another hall as Collin sprinted towards Stewart's cubicle. Stewart was ready, and they both started walking quickly, stopping at the next hall and peering around the corner in case Grant turned around.

"This is like *Mission: Impossible*," Collin whispered with a grin.

The two proceeded to the stairs as they watched Grant enter the elevator. Collin ran down the two flights of stairs like a professional athlete as Stewart started to huff near the bottom.

"Come on, man!" Collin encouraged as he peered his head out the door to see Grant walking through the lobby. "He's about to exit."

"Okay, okay," Stewart said wiping his hair out of his eyes.

"You really need to work on your cardio," Collin commented as the two exited the stairwell. They waited until Grant was walking down the sidewalk, heading to the parking garage before leaving the building. "Okay, how about you go and get your car? If Grant sees you, he won't think of anything. Then I will stay outside and watch for which direction he heads. Then you can pick me up."

"That's really not a bad idea."

"I'm not as stupid as you all think I am."

"I've never said you were stupid."

Collin looked over at Stewart with an unbelieving expression on his face. "You never said I wasn't. Now, go get your car."

Collin watched Stewart run down the sidewalk to the parking garage, laughing to himself at his friend's uncoordinated stride. "That boy really needs to learn how to run."

He walked up the sidewalk to the exit of the parking garage and waited. He leaned against the wall with his back to the exit and listened for outgoing cars. He looked down at his watch and realized they had been out of sight for five minutes and wondered if something happened. What if Grant had caught Stewart following him and beat him up as well?

He started pacing the sidewalk as his fears began to get the better of him. Suddenly he heard a vehicle and a beep signaling the security gate rising to let the vehicle leave. He bent down and pretended to tie his shoes as Grant's vehicle exited the parking garage. He continued to kneel watching Grant's car proceed down the street, stopping at the red light ahead.

"Come on, Stewart!" Collin mouthed to himself as he walked in front of the exit so he could run up and jump in his car when he saw it

263

approach. He saw a pair of headlights coming around the parking garage curve before he looked back at Grant's car, still stopped at the light with a couple of cars pulled behind him. Collin turned his head and saw Stewart swipe his card. As the gate lifted, he jumped into the car.

"He's at the light! Go! Go! Go!"

"Chill, Collin."

"This is so exciting!" Collin bubbled as Grant's red light turned green. "See, there he is!"

"You don't have to shout. I'm right here beside you."

"Sorry. I just can't help it."

Collin buckled his seatbelt as Stewart followed Grant at a comfortable distance while the sun was setting in the west.

"Make sure he doesn't see you."

"Thanks for the tip."

"I just mean, keep a couple of cars in between us. That's what they do in the movies."

"Yeah," Stewart nodded. "But this isn't a movie."

"I know," Collin squealed. "It's so much better."

We returned to Elizabeth's car in the mid-afternoon and discussed the house at length, citing the pros and cons. I knew I shouldn't be in love with a home after not looking at any others, but I was. I was fully enamored with the outside aesthetics from the green-colored porch to the matching wooden shutters. Even the quaint porch swing was swaying me to actually consider purchasing the home.

"It's actually a cute house," Elizabeth said as we were watching dusk approach as the sun was disappearing behind the tree line of Manor Park.

"I can see myself jogging these streets in the evening. Did you notice there really wasn't very much traffic this afternoon?"

"Most people work. That's why there wasn't traffic."

"Fine, but did you see the old-fashioned tub?"

"Do you take baths? Because you look more like a shower guy to me."

"How often do you think of me in the shower?"

"Only this one time," she said chuckling. "And it wasn't a turn-on. It was actually a sad picture."

"Anyway." I looked over at Collin Diaz's home two houses away and waited for the excitement to start.

"I really liked the fireplace," Elizabeth commented. "In my next house I want one."

"I don't see you making a fire."

"Solo, they make electric ones, you know. All I would do is flip a switch and voila. Instant fire."

"Just like God intended," I nodded encouragingly.

"Look at these hands," she said showing me her manicured nails. "I don't want to get splinters, so electric fireplaces are the way to go."

"But that one was real, right?"

"Yeah."

I stopped and a strange thought entered my brain. "Where would I get the wood?"

"Why are you asking me? Am I wearing flannel?"

"It's got to be sold somewhere. It's gotta be," I said confidently. We continued to talk about the home as I looked out the window and watched the streetlights start to flicker on. "When do you think it's going to happen?"

"Soon."

"Is that just an optimistic guess or your keen insight intuition telling you this?"

"Why don't I just let you guess," she sneered as a vehicle's headlights shone behind us.

We both sunk down into our seats watching the vehicle slowly pass by us. I held my breath as the car pulled over to the curb, parking under a streetlight that shone perfectly overhead onto the black BMW sports coupe. I looked at my watch: 5:18 p.m. shone in blue neon light.

"Is that him?" I leaned towards Elizabeth, stretching my neck to see the man getting out of his car. My heart fell into my stomach as he turned his head looking in our direction. "That's not Collin."

Elizabeth didn't answer but continued to stare at the stranger five cars away. "No, that's not Collin. But it's someone else we know."

"Who?" I asked straining once again to see.

"Gavyn McKenzie."

"Who?"

"You know, Jenny's defense attorney," she said gripping her steering wheel. "How is he connected with this?"

"Are you sure this is where it's going to happen?" I asked.

"Solo! You're the one who dreamed about Oglethorpe! And Collin was the only one on the list that lived on Oglethorpe."

"But why is he here?"

"If I knew that, I wouldn't be talking to you right now." She groaned as she opened up Collin's Facebook account. "Look up Gavyn's Facebook and see if Collin is tagged in it."

We both scurried through the Facebook accounts looking for anything that tied these two people together, but we found nothing. "All his posts are hidden!" I shouted. "The last post I can see was Christmas when his family tagged him in a picture."

"Why are people so secretive? It's not like we're trying to steal his identity. We're just trying to save his freakin' life."

"You got anything?"

"Nothing," she huffed. "Why do I even care about him? He's defending the woman who tried to kill us. We should just drive away and let him get what's coming to him."

"Elizabeth! You don't mean that!"

"Oh, I could have said something much more colorful, but I was trying to be polite."

CHAPTER 101

"Where do you think he is going?" Collin asked from the passenger seat of Stewart's Honda Accord.

"I have no clue. He's definitely not going home, though."

"Yeah, maybe he's just driving around to cool down or the gym, possibly."

"Some of us don't live at the gym like you do," Stewart commented.

Stewart continued to drive keeping his distance and hiding behind a couple of cars so Grant couldn't easily see them. He wondered what Grant was up to because something didn't feel right. Stewart may have grown up sheltered with a military father, but in the last year he had changed. He wasn't sure if all his friends had noticed the change, but he was pretty sure Grant saw it. But he had seen a new side of Grant in the last few weeks as well.

"It's funny, this is how I usually drive home. Maybe we should have taken my car instead of yours."

"But you would then still have to go take me to get my car."

"Yeah, I guess you're right," Collin said watching the car ahead of them. "So, after this, you wanna grab some supper?"

"Possibly." Stewart couldn't give a definite yes just yet. His stomach was churning anxiously. "I have an idea." He held down his call assist button on his steering wheel. "Call Grant."

The phone started to ring. "Hey, this is Grant, leave a message."

"Why did--" Collin was saying before Stewart shut him up.

"Grant, it's Stewart. Call me when you can. Thanks." He ended the message as he looked at Collin. "Sorry, I didn't want him to hear us together."

Collin agreed and continued to watch Grant's car three vehicles ahead as he weaved in and out of traffic. "Don't lose him."

"I won't."

"I mean, if we lose him, we won't know where he's going."

"I understand that, but there is a fine line between being sneaky and being seen. And I definitely don't want to be seen yet."

"I gotcha. So if we go out, what do you feel like? I haven't had Chinese in a while. How does that sound?"

"I can do with some Chinese," Stewart grinned. This was the first time in a few months that he and Collin had spent some time alone. He wondered if Collin ever felt left out since the rest of them were all either married, engaged, or seriously dating someone. He looked over at Collin who was smiling and flipping the radio stations just like they would on a Friday night when they were sixteen years old. They used to be good friends back when Collin would sit behind him and cheat off Stewart in algebra, and Collin would try to help Stewart with his lack of love life. "Sorry about yesterday."

"It's all good, man. It's all good."

That was the good thing about Collin. He seldom held grudges unless he was truly hurt.

"This is really uncanny," Collin started to laugh. "He's going my exact route home. Weird."

"Do you think he's going there to get you?"

"But he left before me. Why would he be going to my house unless he knew I was there?"

"What if he's planning to surprise you?"

"Man, he's got to do a better job than that to surprise me. He doesn't know we are following him. So if anyone is going to be surprised, it's going to be him."

"I'm not sure about this," Stewart said shaking his head. "I'm really not sure."

"Oh, you worry too much. He's not coming after me. I pretty much beat him up today. I think he knows not to come after me."

269

"You know Grant is a hothead sometimes. And he likes to get revenge. He has all those lists of people he wants to get, and some of them are from a decade ago."

"We all added names to the list, Stewart. Even you. So it sounds like we are all just like Grant."

"Possibly."

CHAPTER 102

"Excuse me, do you know how fast you were going?" Officer Cooper asked leaning down to the driver who had been going thirty over the speed limit.

"Forty?" the young woman asked looking up at the cop with petrified eyes.

"Sixty. That's reckless endangerment. I could take you in for such a stunt."

The nineteen-year-old woman's nose started to run as her eyes began to water. "My dad is going to kill me. Please. Please, Officer. Please, I promise I won't do this again. I was running late and--"

"Let me see your license and registration," Cooper coldly demanded. She reached for her glove compartment as her shaky hands fumbled around the paperwork.

"Here, here, here you go." Her voice stuttered in fright as she wiped her cheek dry. She lowered her head as her tears flowed more freely.

Cooper had seen all the theatrics. He had heard almost every excuse in the book, and he couldn't let her go with just a warning since her speed was double the actual limit.

"I'll be right back." He walked back to his car and found Dakota sitting in the passenger seat already starting the paperwork for a speed violation.

"She cried, didn't she?"

"She cried."

Dakota shook her head in disgust. "Why do women think they can get off with shedding a few tears?"

"Are you telling me you've never cried to get out of a ticket?"

Dakota gave a half grin seeing she was caught. "Well, that was different. I was young and immature."

"So is she." Cooper handed Dakota the college age student's driver's license so she could look at the downfall of feminism.

"Did the tears work? Are you going to give her a warning?"

"She doubled the limit," he gasped. "That surely deserves something."

"You're a real bully sometimes," Dakota laughed as she continued to complete the ticket, writing the date and time of the violation as 5:34 p.m.

Cooper felt his phone vibrate as someone was calling him. He looked at the screen. "I need to take this." He got out of the vehicle as he answered the call. "Hello."

"Wint, where are you?"

CHAPTER 103

"Wint, where are you?" Elizabeth asked in a softer tone than usual. I leaned over to listen to the conversation since Elizabeth didn't put it on speaker.

"I'm giving someone a ticket. Are you two there?"

"Well, we're here, but something doesn't make sense. We saw Gavyn walk into Collin's home and we haven't seen Collin show up yet." If it was any different time, I could almost laugh picturing Elizabeth with curlers and a floral nightgown peeping through the window blinds watching her neighbors and telling her drowsy husband about the scandals going on across the street. But this wasn't any laughing matter tonight.

"Gavyn who?" he asked as we could hear his shoes pacing on the concrete between the passing cars.

"Gavyn McKenzie. The attorney handling Jenny's case."

"How is he tied up in this?"

"We don't know. And after this week, I'm quickly losing confidence that the double murder is going to happen here tonight. What if it's somewhere else in Manor Park? This neighborhood is pretty large so it could be happening anywhere." Elizabeth's voice started to shrill, and I shared in her anxiety wondering if we were once again in the wrong place at the right time. I moved like a nervous animal looking in all directions for any sign of life.

"Just stay calm and I will be on my way. I'm actually only a few minutes way. Dakota is finishing the ticket."

"There's another car coming," I said smacking Elizabeth on her shoulder pointing at the blinding headlights coming down the street. "There's another car."

"What was that?" Cooper asked.

"It's stopping, Wint!" Elizabeth shouted as I started to bounce in my seat. "Another car just stopped."

"Well, what's going on?"

"The person in the car is just sitting," Elizabeth stated as she squinted her eyes. I watched the parked visitor wondering what he was up to. On one side I wanted this person to be going to another home, but the more I thought about it, I nixed that idea. I hoped this person was going to see Gavyn. I didn't want to be at the wrong address again.

"Oh wait, now he's getting out," I said gripping Elizabeth's arm.

"Well, where is he going?"

"He's walking toward Collin's home. Or I mean, Gavyn's home," I answered feeling flustered. "I don't know whose home, but it's the home we are watching."

"Wint, you need to get here." Elizabeth's frantic voice dropped to a timid whisper as we watched in eagerness. "He's knocking on the door." She narrated the events like a PGA announcer, solemn and crisp. The front porch light turned on, illuminating the strange man's dark silhouette.

"Gavyn's opening it," Elizabeth said in a hushed tone.

My heart stopped beating as I saw the look on Gavyn's face when he opened the door and saw the man on his front step. His smile that was beaming suddenly morphed into a look of discomfort and confusion.

"He looks surprised to see him, Wint. You need to get here now!"

"Elizabeth, what's happening?" Wint asked.

A pair of headlights shone behind us and I immediately spun around. "Another car!" I whispered excitedly. "They're pulling up!" I watched as the car drove by us. "And it looks like two people are in there."

"The stranger just went into the home, Wint! He just went in! And it didn't look like Gavyn wanted him inside. It looked like he forced himself in," Elizabeth said biting her nails.

I turned my neck to quit watching the vehicle and saw the front door of the house start to close.

"Do you hear that?" I asked closing my eyes to focus on the sound. "I hear shouting."

Grant wasn't in the best frame of mind as he texted and drove from work to Oglethorpe Street. He was texting the same person he had been the entire afternoon from Whitney's cellphone. He drove down Oglethorpe Street looking for Collin and Gavyn's home as everything always looked different in the dark. He remembered theirs was one house past the home with the year-round Christmas lights in their tree.

He pulled to the curb and sat behind the wheel for a few seconds responding to a few texts.

That's not what I meant.

He took a few deep breaths as he looked over at his loaded gun in the passenger seat. He slid the weapon into his pants and untucked his shirt to hide the grip sticking out. He looked into the rearview mirror but couldn't see much in the darkness. He actually thought it was better to not look at himself in that moment.

He looked up and down the street, seeing only one car coming down the street a couple of blocks away. He got out and walked across the street to their home. He had been there a few times in the last year, but never like this.

He walked up the walkway and climbed the two steps of the porch. He rang the doorbell in the darkness and waited. His heart started to pound as the front porch light turned on and he heard the door open.

"Come on--" Gavyn started to say behind the glass door before his smile quickly vanished into a look of despair. "Grant, what are you doing here?"

"Who were you expecting?" Grant asked with heated breath. "Whitney?"

"I…uh," Gavyn stammered behind the glass as if it were a wall of protection and not a flimsy see-through barrier.

"Yeah, Whitney will not be coming to see you tonight, stud. Just me."

"I don't know what you mean."

Grant pulled out Whitney's phone from his back pocket and started reading the texts through the day. "I guess I should have told ya. You've been texting me all day."

"Listen, Grant," Gavyn began, but Grant stopped him.

"I think it's time for the two of us to have a little conversation. Man-to-man." Grant opened the glass door and found himself face to face with the man who had been sleeping with his wife for the last few months.

Gavyn didn't take a step back, but stood his ground.

"Don't be brave, Gavyn," Grant smiled as he pulled out his gun.

Gavyn jumped back as Grant took a couple of steps into the house closing the door behind him.

"Put that down!"

"What? This?" Grant laughed raising the gun up to his head, twirling it around on his finger. "It's safe. I have the safety on."

"Grant, come on! Just put that away."

Grant looked at the petrified Gavyn as he took another step into the house. "The way I see it. I have the gun and you have…" He stopped and looked him up and down. "Nothing. So I don't think you should be telling me what I should do." Grant stopped spinning the gun as he moved further into the living room, gripping the gun firmly and pointing it to the ground.

Gavyn took a couple of small steps back towards the hallway, looking around the room for something to use as a weapon. "Fine. What do you want?"

"What do I want?" Grant laughed as his volume started to increase. "Now you want to know what I want? What do you think I want?"

Gavyn didn't answer the rhetorical question but kept his eyes fixed on the gun dangling beside Grant's thigh.

"I said, 'What do you think I want?'"

"I, I don't know," Gavyn answered with a tremble in his voice.

"But I think you do!" Grant yelled. He stared at Gavyn's handsome features seeing what Whitney saw in him as he heard the door creak open behind him.

He turned his neck to see a wide-eyed Stewart enter the room.

"Stewart!" Gavyn screamed from the across the room as he started to flee the living room.

Grant caught sight of Gavyn darting away from the corner of his eye. He raised the gun and fired.

"Gavyn!"

CHAPTER 105
5:25 p.m.

Gavyn walked out of the bathroom smelling masculine with a few squirts of cologne. He considered stripping down to something more comfortable for the evening, but then thought Whitney may enjoy the sight of a man in a suit. He strutted down the hallway as he felt vibrations of a text in his pocket.

He grinned at the provocative message sent by Whitney.

You are one dirty girl. His mind started to brainstorm the possibilities of the evening. This was the first time she had been to his home under these circumstances. In the past she had always come as Grant's wife. But tonight, she was coming as his lover.

Am I to die for?

Definitely. I can't wait to see you. He walked into the kitchen putting water into a pot to boil for some pasta. *It's good for marathons,* he thought.

I can't wait to see you breathless.

Oh, you always leave me breathless. He opened the cabinet and grabbed a box of whole grain wheat bow tie pasta.

That's not what I meant.

See you soon.

Gavyn scooped up the dirty dishes in the sink, placing them haphazardly in the dishwasher, not caring about the spacing of Collin's crusty dishes. He walked past the microwave, checking his hair in the reflection as he heard the doorbell ring.

He walked to the door and unlocked the latch opening it with a seductive pose. "Come on--" He couldn't finish his sentence as his heart stopped and his throat clenched. His pent-up sexual tension from an afternoon of dirty texts vanished when he looked into Grant's eyes. "Grant, what are you doing here?" He tried to remain cool releasing his body from his flexed position, but he felt sweat starting to form underneath his clothes.

"Who were you expecting?" Grant asked. The question seized Gavyn like a punch in the gut. "Whitney?"

Gavyn's insides flipped at the sound of her name on Grant's lips. He knew he was caught. But how? he asked himself. They were careful. So very careful.

Gavyn didn't know how to respond. On one side he wanted to flee because he was pretty sure he could outrun Grant, but on the other side he wanted to stand up and fight. Not because he was in love with Whitney or anything that romantic, but because he never liked to lose.

"I...uh." Gavyn stood motionless with only a thin layer of glass between the two strong, handsome men. He looked out the door past Grant to see if Whitney was in the car.

"Yeah, Whitney will not be coming to see you tonight, stud. Just me."

"I don't know what you mean."

Gavyn watched as Grant reached into his back pocket pulling out a phone that appeared to be Whitney's.

"Care if I read a few of these to you, Gavyn?" Grant looked into Gavyn's eyes without waiting for an answer. "I can't wait to taste your lips tonight. They are sweeter than cherries. So plump and juicy. I'm ready for all of you tonight. I'm not sure you can handle all of me. You're going to make me blush. I can't wait till your smooth hands touch me. I need to feel your touch. No one touches me like you, Gavyn. No one." Grant lifted his eyes from the phone and grinned. "Do you want me to continue?"

Gavyn shook his head as he tried to stand straight, looking into the eyes of the man whose wife he'd been sleeping with for a month.

"I guess I should have told ya. You've been texting me all day." Grant smiled as he scrolled through all the messages they had texted one another. All the illicit descriptions of what they were going to do to one another's starving bodies.

"Listen, Grant."

"I think it's time for the two of us to have a little conversation. Man-to-man." Gavyn watched defenseless as Grant opened the door without an invitation. He stepped inside with a menacing smile until their noses were an inch apart. Gavyn tried to remain calm, but he could feel Grant's hot air on his chin.

"Don't be brave, Gavyn."

Gavyn's eyes widened as he watched Grant pull out a gun from his waistband and close the door behind him. He jumped in shock trying to keep some distance from the barrel of the gun. Suddenly all the trainings at work about disgruntled clients vanished from his memory, but he knew this was not a good situation. And angry, revenge-seeking men with weapons usually don't end well for the other party. He had seen too many domestic abuse cases in the last two years to realize he didn't have the upper hand in this scenario.

"Put that down!"

Gavyn's body started to quake from the insurgence of fear escalating exponentially by the second.

"What? This? It's safe. I have the safety on."

Gavyn sunk his shoulders down, trying to keep his head out of the spinning gun's trajectory.

"Grant, come on! Just put that away."

Gavyn knew he was a few steps away from the hallway. He started to come up with a plan to dart into his bedroom and climb out the window. But he started seeing the consequences of that action. *Collin's room is closer. Does Collin leave his window unlocked?* He had never opened Collin's window, but he hoped it wasn't sealed shut. He looked over his shoulder to see if there was anything he could throw from the bookcase, but nothing looked defense worthy.

"The way I see it. I have the gun and you have," He stopped, looking Gavyn over with a twisted smile. "Nothing. So I don't think you should be telling me what I should do."

Grant gripped the gun's handle and lowered it to his thigh, pointing the barrel to the floor.

"Fine. What do you want?"

"What do I want? Now you want to know what I want? What do you think I want?"

Gavyn stared at the gun pointing at the ground. He could have kicked himself for stepping away so far back in the last two minutes, because if he was within reach he could have jumped Grant and taken the gun. He knew Grant used to be fit from what Whitney said, but in the last couple of years he had let himself go. Gavyn considered the possibility of running toward Grant now, but he knew even if he got to Grant before he raised his arm up, he could still be shot in his midsection or leg. He thought he was quick, but he knew he would not be quicker than a trigger-happy finger.

"I said, 'What do you think I want?'"

"I, I don't know." Gavyn's voice cracked like a boy going through puberty. He hoped there was a way out of this situation, but his strong biceps were no competition for a gun. He knew assassins in action movies could walk away from situations like these, but those were movies. Not real life.

"But I think you do!" Grant shouted.

Gavyn continued to watch the gun as if he were watching the pendulum of his biological clock come to a stop. He heard the turn of the doorknob and saw the door swing open.

"Stewart!" Gavyn screamed at the top of his lungs as he saw Grant turn his head away. This was his chance. This could be his only chance. He turned and darted toward the hallway as he heard a gunshot fire.

"Gavyn!" Collin screamed from behind as Grant fired off another round.

Gavyn felt the second shot.

"Why is Grant driving toward my house?" Collin asked. He eyed Stewart watching his every movement down to his facial tics as they drove down Oglethorpe Street.

"I don't know."

"Stewart, don't you lie to me!" Collin's anger was getting the best of him as he clenched his fists. But he knew hitting Stewart as he drove wasn't the smartest idea.

"I'm not. I didn't know," Stewart answered raising his quivering voice in return with uncertainty. He looked over at Collin as they watched Grant's car park in front of Collin's home. "I promise. I didn't know."

"Did you two plan this?" Collin continued to watch the shaky Stewart for any tells or signs of lies.

"Plan this?" Stewart barked back. "You're the one who said we should follow him."

"Yeah, but," he stopped and shook his head replaying the afternoon when Stewart approached him. He couldn't put his finger on it, but something wasn't adding up.

"Collin, I didn't know." Stewart slowed the vehicle as they watched Grant get out of his car and head to Collin and Gavyn's home.

Collin watched as Grant walked up to his front door remembering Gavyn saying he had someone coming over this evening. He thought it was a woman, since he knew Gavyn was seeing someone, but he had never divulged any details.

"Gavyn said someone was coming over this evening."

Stewart turned his head, looking at Collin quizzically. "Gavyn? I didn't know they were close." Stewart slid in behind Grant's car as they watched the two men talking.

"I didn't either," Collin said. "Can you see what's going on? All I can see is Grant's back."

Stewart shook his head as he stretched his neck to get a better view. "Me neither."

Collin watched Grant walk into the house as Gavyn didn't back up. "They are standing really close to one another. You don't think…?"

Stewart's head whipped around. "Grant's married."

"I'm just saying that could explain why he's been acting so weird lately."

"Has Gavyn been acting strange?"

Collin didn't respond. Gavyn had been acting a little different, but he assumed it was stress from the court case.

"They closed the door," Stewart commented. "Ready to go in?"

"Dude, I don't want to see that!"

"We don't know anything," Stewart reminded him. "Except something strange is going on." Stewart looked at Collin motioning him to get out of the car with him.

"Fine," Collin said unconvinced. Both men suddenly looked at the house.

"Did you hear that?"

"Yeah, I heard that," Collin perked up, jumping out of the car as the two ran across the street and through the grass.

"What do I want? Now you want to know what I want? What do you think I want?" Grant shouted from behind the door.

Stewart and Collin looked at one another awkwardly. Collin didn't know what to think. He turned around at his neighbors across the street, but it appeared the street was void of life.

"I said, 'What do you think I want?'" Grant shouted again as they stood by the front door, eavesdropping onto the heated conversation.

"I, I don't know."

"Gavyn sounds scared," Stewart commented as Collin nodded in agreement. "We have to go in," he whispered putting his hand on the door handle. "Are you ready?"

"But I think you do!" Grant shouted.

"I'm ready," Collin agreed, but deep down he wasn't. He didn't know what he was getting himself into. He hoped Stewart was telling him the truth and not leading him blindly into a cage fight. He hoped he could still trust Stewart, but deep down he knew his friend would do anything for Grant. Even befriending him if Grant asked him to.

Stewart opened the glass door and then the front door and walked into the living room.

"Stewart!" Gavyn shouted.

Collin poked his head into the house as his stomach leapt into his throat. Grant winked at Collin entering the house before turning his head. Collin didn't see the gun until the first bullet was fired hitting the wall, leaving a hole like a hammer and nail incident gone wrong.

"Gavyn!" Collin yelled as his world started to spin like a whirlpool. He wanted to close his eyes and pretend this wasn't happening. He wanted to pinch himself and wake up from this horrid dream. After all the scenarios he had discussed, this wasn't in any of his wildest dreams what he expected to see. He looked at Gavyn as he moved in slow motion. He wanted to run into the house and deck Grant in order to save Gavyn. He caught sight of Stewart frozen to his left and wondered if this was planned.

His mind spun as Grant fired another bullet. The single piece of shiny metal floated through the air like a child's bubble until it popped into Gavyn's skull. He now knew what blood splatter actually looked like.

"Gavyn!" Collin screamed as his friend's body fell lifeless onto the hardwood floor, his blood pumping from his wound. His body twitched until it moved no more.

Grant turned around to smile at Stewart. "Hey partner, nice of you to show up."

"Partner?" Collin asked feebly as he reached his hand back for the door handle.

Stewart didn't respond but looked at Collin with apologetic eyes.

"Yeah, partner," Grant answered. "We killed Mr. Lukin on Sunday evening and Mr. Hill on Monday." Grant stopped and looked at Stewart with a wicked grin. "And Mr. McKenzie tonight."

"But," Stewart started as he looked to Collin.

"Get him, Stewart," Grant softly commanded with a tyrannical tone. "What's a third dead body today?"

"Third?" Stewart asked in disbelief.

Collin stepped back into the glass door, blindly grasping for the handle.

"Where do you think you're going?" Grant asked, sinisterly raising his gun.

But Collin wasn't going to be the third victim. He jumped back as the glass door swung open, breaking the hinges.

"Stewart!" Grant yelled as Stewart continued to stand frozen by the front door. Collin jumped off the front porch and darted into a row of bushes in front of the house. He lowered his head, keeping it below the hedges, but he never looked back. He scurried into the shadows of the neighbor's yard before running through their property to get to the next neighbor's house.

He never looked back. He just continued to run, hoping Grant wasn't aiming his gun at him like he had aimed it at Gavyn. He didn't have time to mourn his friend; he only had time to run.

He ran to the last house on the block and ducked behind a tree. He looked behind and saw two figures standing in the road in front of his home. He exploded from the safety behind the tree to run across the road as a faint siren started to sound in the distance.

"Please, God!"

CHAPTER 107

"Wint!" Elizabeth screamed at the sound of the gunshot. "Shots fired! Shots fired!"

I stared at the front glass door, seeing the backside of Collin and the new guy, which Elizabeth and I both thought looked like he could be Stewart from the Facebook pictures. "Where's your gun?" I shouted. Elizabeth began to frantically dig into her purse pulling out her small pistol and handing it to me as the sound of another gun shot went off.

"Solomon! Stay in the car!" Wint shouted. "We are on our way."

"That's what you said a few minutes ago!" Elizabeth griped.

"We can't just stay in the car! Someone needs us in there," I said to Elizabeth, covering the phone so Wint couldn't hear.

"What do you want to do? It's four against two!" she frantically whispered back.

"I don't know, but this wasn't how it was supposed to go down! Not again!"

I looked at the door as Collin darted out. "Collin's running away!"

"He's running?" Wint asked.

"Yes!" Elizabeth screamed as we watched him fade into the shadows of the trees. "He's running." She looked to me for help. "Which direction is he running?"

"West! He's going west!"

"We may see him. Was he the one who fired the gun?" Wint asked as I looked to Elizabeth.

"I can't stay here," I said getting out of the car.

"I'm pretty sure he wasn't the one," Elizabeth answered as she, too, got out of the car. I circled around to her side as we stood in the middle of the street. I looked down the street to try to see Collin, but I couldn't find him anymore. Then I quickly looked back at Collin's home and saw Stewart still standing through the glass door.

"And I don't think Stewart was in on it either."

"Stewart?" Dakota's voice asked faintly. "What's going on, Cooper? Why are we going to Collin's home? What's this about gunshots?"

"Backup!" Wint shouted to the dispatch. "We need backup on Oglethorpe! Shots fired!"

"Copy!" another cop answered. "Heading there now."

"Stay put! We are almost there!"

I looked at Elizabeth as we stood in the street debating our next move. "How did we mess this up?"

"Stop that!" she muttered, pointing to the phone, covering it once again. "That gunshot could have just been warning shots. We don't know anything yet."

"I'm feeling useless just standing here," I said as we both paced beside her car, me with her gun in my hand. I looked at the door, but no one was standing there anymore. "Did they leave?"

"I, I don't know," she answered as she started to cross the street to get a better look.

"Elizabeth!" I softly yelled. "What are you doing?"

"Well, someone needs to find out what's going on."

"You're going to get yourself killed."

She looked back at me with a wicked grin. "I didn't see myself die in the dream."

"Didn't you say there were two deaths?"

Elizabeth stopped as her foot hit the grass.

CHAPTER 108

Stewart stood frozen as Collin darted out the door.

"Go get him!" Grant shouted. "We can't leave any witnesses."

"What's going on, Grant?" Stewart asked as his lower lip quivered. "What did you do?"

"We don't have much time." Grant motioned Stewart to step into the house with his gun.

"Grant! What's going on?" Stewart shouted as he continued to stand by the glass door looking at Gavyn lying with a gunshot wound to the side of his head.

"I had to shoot him in the head to make it look like a suicide." Grant walked over and kicked Gavyn in the side. "I think he's dead."

"You think?" Stewart didn't know what to say as he saw his world quickly crumbling around him.

Grant leaned down closer to Gavyn's head, staring at the wound. "Shit! Shit! Shit!"

"What?"

"Who shoots themselves in the back of the head?" Grant stood up, kicking Gavyn in the side one more time. "But maybe we can fix this."

"Were you planning to kill Collin and Gavyn just got in the way?"

Grant turned around and shook his head, wiping his forehead on his sleeve. "Not exactly."

"So you came here to kill Gavyn?" Stewart gasped, taking a step forward and grabbing the back of the couch to steady himself. "What did he do? Tell me? What did Gavyn do to you?"

"You want to know?" Grant billowed from across the room turning around to walk toward Stewart. "He was sleeping with Whitney!"

"Whitney and Gavyn? But why?"

"What do you mean, 'why?' My wife was apparently a whore and Gavyn was just one of the many men she slept around with."

"Are you sure?" Stewart asked looking down once again at the morbid sight as the blood had stopped oozing from his skull.

"I'm pretty sure," he nodded with a cynical grin. "Neither one denied it."

"Man." Stewart paced the living room floor scratching his head in thought. "But you didn't have to kill him."

"I kinda did," he nodded as if talking about the latest movie he had watched. He walked to the kitchen entrance and turned around, looking around at his surroundings. "Since you're here, I'm going to need your help."

"Help? What kind of help?"

"Well," Grant said. "We need to stage this scene as a murder-suicide."

"Murder-suicide?" Stewart erupted. "Collin is gone! He's not coming back, and I'm not helping you kill him!"

"You'll do what I tell you to do, or I'll tell the cops that it's your Adidas bag at Mr. Hill's house." Grant sat down on the couch allowing his words to resonate with Stewart.

"Really? You would do that?"

"I just killed Gavyn for sleeping with my wife," he laughed. "I wouldn't count anything out."

"But we've been friends for over a decade," Stewart said feebly, seeing the truth of his friend's character. "I would do anything for you. I killed for you!"

"For me?" he chuckled. "You wanted to participate. You put down Mr. Lukin's name. I didn't think he was that bad of a teacher, but you couldn't handle his snide remarks. Maybe he was right. Maybe you are a pansy."

"I did it to show you I'm not a little kid anymore that you can boss around!"

"Stu," Grant smiled as he stood up from the couch. "I'll tell you what you're going to do, and you'll do it until the day you die. Because you always do."

"Screw you!"

"Big talk for a boy who just got laid for the first time this summer."

Stewart's jaws clenched and his eyes filled with fire as he listened to the man who was once his best friend.

"What's wrong with her? There must be something off for her to fall for you."

"Leave her out of this!"

"Funny, isn't it? Who you are and who she is."

"I'm warning you, Grant! Leave her out of this!"

Grant paced around the room, holding his gun like a bottle of beer, carelessly waving it around with no worry about it going off.

Stewart's ears started to ring. He turned his head to look out the door and noticed two people standing in the street.

"People are outside watching! And you just killed Gavyn! There's no way out."

Grant grinned wickedly as he looked at Stewart. "There's always a way out."

"The cops are coming, Grant!" he said, hearing the sirens approach.

"Shit!" Grant said, punching his fist into the wall. "We can't get Whitney now!"

"Grant! Stop thinking about Whitney. You have bigger problems," Stewart said as he pointed at the dead white elephant in the room.

"Well," Grant said pursing his lips as he thought. "Yeah, Whitney's didn't look like a suicide either, so that's not going to work. Unless I hung her somewhere, but we can't get to her now."

Stewart looked toward the man who no longer looked like his friend from high school. He had changed. "Where's Whitney?"

Grant smirked at the question. "You're a good friend, but I still need a suicide." Grant raised up his gun and looked into Stewart's eyes.

"Grant! No!"

"Goodbye, Stewart."

Bang!

CHAPTER 109

His heart was pounding harder inside his chest as he looked at the bodies of two of his friends lying lifeless on the ground. He stooped down and looked into a pair of eyes gazing back up at him as if asking him a question. *How did we get here?*

He couldn't believe He heard the sirens coming closer, waking him up from this nightmare he wished he wasn't a key character in. He stood up and dashed out the door. His car was across the street where two people were standing along the grass.

They were shouting, but he couldn't hear the words. He didn't want to hear them. He just wanted to escape, and it seemed like it was going to be harder now. He ran through the grass, jumping over the rabbit hole he'd twisted his ankle in two summers ago.

He knew he was being watched, but he didn't care. He had to leave. He had to get away before the cops showed up. They didn't know who he was, but Collin knew. Collin knew everything now.

He jumped into his car and turned the ignition, ready to pull away when he saw a police car coming from up ahead. Beads of sweat started to drip down his cheek while he felt his insides tighten, as if the guilt was twisting his gut until it would snap apart.

He looked behind him, and the street was clear except for the two strangers.

"Where are you going?" the man yelled, pounding his fist on the window.

He didn't answer. He gripped his steering wheel and closed his eyes, gathering the nerve to make the next move. He moved the gearshift to Drive and started to proceed.

"Stop!" the man shouted raising a gun. "Don't make me use this!"

He wished he had picked up the gun inside the house, but he was making it look like a suicide. He looked down the barrel of the gun and then up ahead at the police cars. He felt trapped, but he had a little hope.

He ignored the man's demands and pulled out. The man looked shocked with his gun in his hand.

"Don't let him leave!" the woman shouted from behind as a fresh wave of hope crashed onto his lonesome beach. "Solo! Stop him!"

He looked ahead at the fast approaching police car and quickly made a U-turn in front of Collin's house, barely missing the cars parked along the street.

The man looked stunned as he straightened his car and continued screaming for him to stop with the gun in his hand. The woman ran across the street grabbing the gun away as he hit the gas pedal. By the look in her eyes, she wasn't afraid to use it, and that terrified him.

He heard her fire a bullet. And then another. And then another.

He heard the third bullet hit his car as he tried to keep driving away to escape into the night. He looked into his rearview mirror and saw her aim from behind. She stood in the middle of the road and took her time.

She fired another bullet. That one connected as well; he heard another pop.

He continued to drive as she fired another bullet. He didn't know how long he had before his tire would be flat, but he wasn't stopping. He saw the police car pull beside the shooting woman as she pointed in his direction. But the cop didn't follow. He parked and ran up Collin and Gavyn's yard with his gun ready.

He started to grin and hoped for the best.

Until he saw another police car with blue and red lights spinning turn onto Oglethorpe Street a block ahead. He didn't stop but hoped the police car would pass by to Collin and Gavyn's house.

The police car sped down the road and quickly blocked the street. Two police officers jumped out of their patrol car. One ran up with his gun raised while the second slowly walked up.

"Stewart!" he shouted. "Get out of the car! I'm warning you!"

"Stewart?" a woman's voice squealed in surprise.

Stewart looked up and shook his head, pounding his fist into the steering wheel at the sight of the two cops. Officer Cooper ran up, still aiming the gun at Stewart's head.

"Don't shoot!" he begged as he put his vehicle in park.

"He's getting out, Cooper!" Dakota yelled running up. "Don't shoot him!"

"Get out of the vehicle, Stewart!" Cooper demanded still aiming his gun. "I don't care who you are! Just get out!"

Stewart opened the car door, and tears streamed down his face as he looked at Dakota. "He went crazy, Dakota! He just went crazy!"

"Who went crazy?" Dakota asked rushing to his side.

"Grant! Grant killed 'em," he cried falling into Dakota's arms. "He killed 'em."

CHAPTER 110

Cooper looked up the street and saw another police car coming down Oglethorpe towards the crime scene as Elizabeth and Solo stood on the grass telling the police officers what they had seen.

"What happened?" Officer Peterson asked as Cooper listened, wondering if she was asking as a cop or his girlfriend. Cooper stood there, trying to maintain his focus. He suddenly felt a punch in the gut when he realized his partner was dating a killer.

He watched their interaction as he wondered. *Does she know?*

He shook off the question. He trusted Dakota with his life. He knew she would do anything for him. Anything. That was what partners did. He watched as Dakota grabbed Stewart's hand, rubbing it compassionately, listening to everything he was saying as another thought sprung forward.

If she would do anything for me, would she do anything for him? Even if he was a killer?

Cooper kept the question in his mind as he started listening more closely to Stewart.

"Why did you follow Grant?" Dakota asked.

"Because something was wrong and we both knew it. He's changed, Dakota. It's like he became possessed with all this anger." He looked around at the neighbors' homes who had turned on their front porch lights and were standing at their doors or in their front yards.

"So you saw him kill Gavyn McKenzie?" she asked.

He nodded his head.

"Then what?" Cooper asked.

Stewart started telling them everything that happened.

At the end of the story the three started walking towards the house.

"Do you know where Collin is?" Cooper asked as Stewart shook his head.

"He just ran."

As they approached the house, Cooper saw an officer standing behind a parked car looking in the trunk. Cooper wanted to tell Dakota to stay put, but he wasn't sure he could trust her to be alone with Stewart.

The three walked past Elizabeth's car toward the officer shaking his head.

"What?" Cooper asked. He looked into the trunk and immediately realized why. "Who's that?"

"Whitney!" Stewart screamed, looking at the body with a bloody scalp before falling into Dakota's arms. "He said he killed her too."

"Grant's wife," Dakota said filling in the gaps.

Cooper leaned into the officer's ear. "Watch these two, Pete. Okay? Don't leave them alone."

Officer Pete Robbins looked confused at the request but nodded his head at the order.

"I'll be right back," Cooper said walking across the street.

"Your partner seems to be really close to Stewart," Elizabeth commented eyeing the handholding couple. "Did you tell her about him?"

CHAPTER 111

"No," Wint answered as I nodded in understanding. It was going to take more than a five-minute conversation to detail how Stewart was a part of the group the cops didn't know about who killed a couple of people last spring. The police actually thought they had the killer since the group had used their high school enemy as a scapegoat.

"I'm sorry, Wint," I said shaking my head.

"Sorry? For what?"

"Yeah, for what?" Elizabeth snapped back.

"We didn't stop it. Not just two people died, but three. That's more than Elizabeth even dreamed." I looked around the brightly-lit street with cop cars, street lights, and portable security lights arranged around Collin's front yard.

"Grant died and he was a killer!" Elizabeth said. I could tell she wanted to shout it but had to control her rage. "I just see that as karma."

"But we didn't stop any of it."

"Bud, it's going to be okay," Wint said patting my shoulder as he turned his head to look at Stewart clutching onto Dakota. "It may work out after all."

"I hope so."

"Collin is out there running somewhere. Stewart is over there being consoled by your partner."

"His girlfriend," Wint added.

"Girlfriend!" I gasped.

"This is better than *Maury*," Elizabeth commented with raised eyebrows.

"Don't forget about Jordan," I put in. "He was one of the original four."

"See, this may be a good thing after all."

"So who are the two killers this week?" Elizabeth asked as she looked at me and Wint. I shrugged my shoulders and hoped Wint had an answer.

He looked behind him, watching Stewart as I, too, glanced back at him.

"He's taking these deaths really hard for someone who helped plan murders six months ago," Wint commented.

"Well, Collin couldn't be it. His name was on the kill list," Elizabeth reminded.

"And neither of you saw Jordan here tonight?"

"No, he was not here," I answered, growing more confused. "Your dream pointed out the kill list, and if Jordan wasn't here, then he can't be one of the two."

"But what if they are mixing it up? Each taking turns?" Wint asked. "What if they were all four doing it again?"

Elizabeth shook her head. "No, Collin isn't in this. He wouldn't ever put his own name down."

"I guess we're just going to have to go find Jordan, and you can question him and Collin." Wint smiled and took a deep breath.

"Us?" I asked.

"No, moron. Let the cops do their job now," Elizabeth quipped. "I'm exhausted and ready for a bubble bath."

I looked over at Wint who smiled with a wink. "We're going to get them," he said gripping my arm. "Criminals usually turn on one another to save their own skin."

Wint walked up to the house to look at the crime scene as the coroner parked his van up the street. I walked toward Elizabeth and caught Stewart from the corner of my eye. He looked defeated with his downcast gaze.

"That is one good actor," Elizabeth commented. "He should have picked up theater instead of killing."

"But sometimes the reviews are deadly," I grinned as I got into her car.

"That was a morbid joke, Solo." She looked shocked, but it soon faded into a grin. "I couldn't be more proud."

I laughed, and she joined in as we pulled away from a triple homicide. "Wow, some people would really think we are sick."

She looked over at me without skipping a beat.

"But we are," she said confidently. "If we told them our secret, they would probably put us away for life or do all kinds of tests on us."

I reclined the passenger seat and closed my eyes as she turned up her radio. This day had been one for the books, and it looked like it was going to go a little longer for Wint.

CHAPTER 112

Elizabeth was quiet on the drive home from Oglethorpe Street, and it didn't bother me. I was trying to mentally process the events that had just transpired. In the blink of an eye, everything went into chaos. Gun shots. Runners. Criers. Collin and Gavyn's home was something I wished to never endure again, and I didn't even see the graphic scene inside.

"Want to come in?" Elizabeth asked as she parked her car in her garage. I saw the look on her face that screamed for relaxation and alone time. So I departed and headed home. I, too, wanted to take a long shower and wash away the guilty feeling of not stopping the murders.

I pulled away from her lavish neighborhood and headed toward my apartment outside of town, making a phone call as another nagging question haunted me.

"Mrs. Nelson," I said. "How's Will doing?"

"He is doing well today," she answered with a chipper tone in her voice. "He ate some lunch and played in his room. He even sat in the living room this afternoon and watched some cartoons with us."

My heart felt fuller, hearing of Will's improvement and adaptability to the new living arrangement. We spoke for a few more minutes, but then ended our call. I drove through the nighttime streets and felt torn in many different directions just like the streets of D.C.

I felt guilt for not stopping the three deaths, but I also felt relieved in uncovering the mystery from April. I had a hopeful outlook that Wint was correct in his assumptions that the three surviving group members would turn on one another, but I also had a realistic pessimism that warned me that friends stand by one another.

Lastly, I felt joy with Will's positive change in the last twenty-four hours with the Nelsons, but I also felt my pride being dashed. A day ago, I thought I was Will's saving grace. I thought he needed me to get him through the next few weeks or months. I was patting myself on the back that I got him to eat supper last night. But truthfully, I wasn't a hero coming to his rescue. I was just a guy who helped him on the next leg of his journey.

I wasn't anything special, just a man who helped a small boy yesterday morning while I jogged. I tried to not let that thought linger in my mind, but before I knew it, I was running my water for a shower.

I stripped off my clothes and looked in the mirror. My reflection proved I wasn't anything special. I was just a man with a few scars on my leg from Jenny's attack last spring.

I stepped into the tub and felt the warm water pelting my face. I allowed the heat to wrap around my tense body, letting its steam erode the hardness and darkness I was edging toward. I closed my eyes and felt the streams of flowing water down my back, polishing my skin like a mossy rock in the riverbeds. I hoped the water would smooth out my rough edges like they do the stones along the bottom of the river.

Suddenly an image formed in my meditated state, thousands of stones under two inches of clear, tranquil flowing water. I scanned over the rocks of differing shapes and colors with their rough edges and protrusions, admiring the beauty as if hovering over a work of art. Suddenly, water started to flow faster as the water increased. The two inches quickly turned into two feet of water. The water tossed and turned, splashed and crashed onto itself. The once tranquil scene quickly ignited into a hurricane. Then as quickly as the storm started, it ceased.

The large quantities of water quickly evaporated to two inches of still flowing water once again. The stones were magnified. The rough pointy edges were turned smooth. The colors seemed brighter as if painted. The moving picture seemed more beautiful than ever.

You can't fully understand peace, Solomon, until you have fully felt the absence of it.

I opened my eyes and looked down at the drain covered in soapy water.

"What does that even mean?" I prayed, letting the water wash over me for a little while longer. "Just tell me what that means!"

CHAPTER 113

"He's not answering," Stewart said sitting on the curb across the street from Collin's home.

"Give me his number," Officer Cooper said as he quickly called and left a voicemail. "Mr. Collin Diaz, this is Officer Winston Cooper with the D.C.P.D. We need to speak with you about the events of tonight at your residence. Please call me back. We have witnesses that confirm you didn't do this tonight, but we need your statement and need to ask you some questions to move along with this investigation. Please, call me back."

"So now what?" Stewart asked.

"Now we wait," Cooper answered.

Stewart looked around the neighbors' homes and glanced down at his watch. "How much longer do you need me here? I'm getting hungry, and I don't want to stick around here anymore."

"You can go home," Peterson started before Cooper quickly refuted.

"Let's go down to the precinct, and we can get you some supper there. We have some more questions we need to ask."

"Okay," Stewart said shrugging. "Can we go now?"

"Sure thing. Just let me get one thing," Cooper said. He went back into the house and went through Grant's personal belongings, the contents in his pocket and wallet. "Is this everything?" he asked Officer Hudley who nodded. "Thanks. Did you document this?" Once again Officer Hudley nodded. "Good, I'll be taking it."

Cooper rushed out the door stopping at Grant's vehicle to look inside.

"Hey, Trent, did you look through his car?"

"Yes."

"What did you find?" Cooper asked.

306

"I did find one thing that looked interesting," he said showing Cooper a picture he took on his phone.

Cooper's eyes widened. "Can you text that to me?"

"Sure thing."

"I owe you, Trent." Cooper walked toward Stewart, who stood beside Peterson, looking at his vehicle with its flat tires. Cooper stared at the two and then looked around for an officer nearby. "Hey, Jorge, can you drive Stewart in? Our backseat is full."

"Give me a sec," Officer Jorge Ramirez shouted back finishing his conversation with Trent.

"Our backseat isn't full," Peterson said confused.

"Dakota, can you ride with me? I need to talk to you about a few things on the way."

"I thought I would ride with Stewart to keep him company."

Stewart looked up at Cooper and then turned to Dakota. "It's okay. I'll be okay."

"Okay, come on, Dakota," Cooper said as he winked at Pete standing by Stewart's vehicle.

Cooper and Dakota got into their patrol car as Jorge and Stewart weaved through the police cars lining the street. Cooper followed closely, making sure not to scratch his patrol car.

"What was that about?" Dakota asked cocking her head over to Cooper and eying him with suspicion.

"We need to talk before we get to the interrogation room."

"About what?"

"Well, first off..." Cooper took a deep breath and stared at Stewart's silhouette in the backseat of Officer Ramirez's patrol car cruising down the peaceful side of Oglethorpe Street. "Stewart isn't who you think he is."

CHAPTER 114

"What do you mean?" Dakota asked, looking at Cooper with hesitant eyes.

Cooper shook his head. He never thought he would be having this conversation with another police officer, let alone his own partner. He had been cautious all day around Dakota. He had watched her more closely than ever before and tried to read her tics and mannerisms with a fresh, new outlook and insight. At the end of the day, he didn't learn anything new.

"What do you mean, Cooper?" Dakota demanded with forcefulness behind her words.

"How well do you know his friends?"

"That's a strange question to ask." Her response was indignant as she folded her arms. "I could ask the same about you."

"Yes," Cooper nodded as he continued to drive two car lengths behind Stewart. "But my friends didn't just kill someone tonight."

Dakota shook her head and bit her lower lip. "You heard him. Grant went crazy."

Cooper looked over at her with disbelieving eyes.

"He did! Stewart wouldn't lie about that."

Cooper's phone started to ring and an unknown phone number came across his infotainment console.

"Officer Cooper," he answered.

"Hello, Officer Cooper? This is Collin. Collin Diaz."

"Collin, where are you?"

"I didn't do this! Grant killed Gavyn."

"We know, Collin. We know. Where are you?"

"I'm hiding."

"Hiding from who?"

Collin didn't answer.

"Collin, we can protect you. But first you have to tell us where you are, and someone will come and get you."

"I'm hiding on Rittenhouse Street. It's two blocks from my home."

"Collin, why are you hiding?"

"They want to kill me."

"Who? Who wants to kill you?"

"Grant. Grant and Stewart."

Dakota gasped and was about to speak when Cooper pointed at her to stay silent.

"Why do you think they want to kill you, Collin?"

There was silence on the other end of the line.

"Collin, we can't help you unless you are honest with us."

"Because Grant said, 'Get him, Stewart,' before I took off."

Dakota shook her head as she listened, taking a deep breath and huffing it out.

"Collin, did they say anything else that would imply them wanting to kill you?" Cooper asked gently, looking over at Dakota who was already building her wall to tune him out.

"They said they already killed Mr. Lukin and Mr. Hill this week, so killing me wouldn't be much more."

"Collin, we really need you to make a statement and write this out. If I get an officer to you, will you be willing to say this again at the precinct?"

"Where's Grant and Stewart?"

"They can't hurt you, Collin. You are safe. We got them."

"You got them?" he asked with excitement in his voice. "So I'm safe?"

"Let me get Officers Gusev or Robbins to come get you, and then you can give us your statement properly. Will you do that?"

"If I'm safe, I'll tell you as many times as you want to hear it."

"Okay, Collin. I'll call them now. They should be there to get you in a few minutes. Just be looking for a patrol car and they will take you in."

Cooper ended the call and quickly called Pete.

"Hey, Pete, I need another favor."

CHAPTER 115

Veronica sat her laptop aside on her chaise lounge and leaned back. She closed her eyes, and for the third time considered Gavyn's offer. She knew there were some negative aspects of having a partner who may not have the same outlook for the firm. But having a partner had many benefits that far outweighed a few measly fights about website designs and paint color.

She stood up and walked into the kitchen, pouring a glass of wine to calm her nerves. She held the goblet in her hand and swirled the merlot, allowing the fragrance to awaken and come alive.

She took a sip and allowed the smoothness to swish around her taste buds. She knew she needed to discuss this decision with Winston, but she also knew that he would affirm whatever she wanted.

She grabbed a lavender-infused candle and lit the wick. She breathed in deeply and let the sweet woodsy aroma ease the tension between her shoulders. She brought the candle with her into the living room, placing it on the end table beside her chaise. She dimmed the lighting and played a bubbling brook on her sound machine app on her cellphone.

She closed her eyes and once again considered Gavyn's offer. She breathed deeply, allowing the ambiance to relax her. She didn't know if it was the lavender or the music, but she started to smile at the idea of having Gavyn working beside her.

She picked up her phone and called him. "Hey, Gavyn, I have been seriously thinking of your offer. When you get this message, call me. I really want to pick your brain on a few other things. So, yeah, call me if you are really interested. Or call me if you're not. Just call me either way. I hate leaving voicemails as you probably can tell."

She looked over at her laptop and then down at her watch noticing she hadn't heard from Wint in the last few hours.

Just checking on you. Haven't heard from you in a while and didn't know when you'd be home. Just let me know.

She picked up her laptop and started to read the intellectual property contract she had been working on the last couple of hours. But she wasn't interested in continuing that tonight.

Instead, she logged onto the internet and did a quick search for office property for rent in the area. She was going to need more square footage than her current office had, with multiple rooms. She liked Gavyn, but they each needed their separate rooms.

CHAPTER 116

"I don't believe it!" Dakota exclaimed after Wint asked Pete to pick up Collin and bring him to the precinct. "You don't know Collin."

"So Collin lies?"

"Apparently, because he's lying now."

"How do you know?" Cooper asked trying to de-escalate the tension by speaking in a calming voice. "Were you with Stewart on Sunday or Monday?"

Dakota didn't answer. She stared out the window looking up at the streetlights overhead.

"I know this is shocking. And I'm sorry to be doing this, but when Stewart is being interrogated, I need you to stay out of the room."

She huffed, but she still said nothing.

Cooper looked over as she shook her head. He reached out his hand to touch hers, but she recoiled at his touch, hiding her hands in her lap as she stared out the window in silence.

"Do you have anything to say?" Cooper asked as they made their last turn.

"How long have you known?" She looked over and stared coldly at Cooper as if the last year together meant nothing to her.

Cooper didn't know how to answer the question because he knew more questions would come.

"Not long," he said.

"Is that why you were looking up Collin's information this morning?"

"I got a tip," he answered.

"And you couldn't tell me? You couldn't trust me?"

"If you were in my place and you were told that Veronica was caught up in something illegal, would you tell me before you were 100% sure?" Cooper knew what her honest answer would be. He just

313

needed her to answer the question, if not out loud, at least to herself. "Because I'm pretty sure you would have done the exact same thing."

They both parked their vehicles and proceeded to the precinct entrance. Stewart and Dakota walked with their elbows locked as Cooper watched, wondering if Dakota was acting or if her authenticity was truly this sickening.

"Stewart, follow me," Cooper said as Dakota let go of Stewart.

"Dakota, you coming?" Stewart asked as he turned around and saw Dakota watching from a distance.

"I'll go pick us up some supper," she smiled.

Stewart returned her smile, turned back around, and walked towards Cooper, who held the door open to the hallway. "Second door on the left." As the door closed, Cooper watched Dakota's smile fade.

She didn't look at Cooper through the glass, but shook her head and stormed through another door to watch the interrogation.

"Please have a seat, Stewart."

CHAPTER 117

"So, Stewart," Cooper started as he took a seat across the table. "First, as standard procedure, you have the right to remain silent. Anything you say can and will be used against you in a court of law. You have the right to talk to a lawyer and have him present with you while you are being questioned. If you cannot afford to hire a lawyer, one will be appointed to represent you before any questioning if you wish. You can decide at any time to exercise these rights and not answer any questions or make any statements. Do you understand these rights?"

"Yeah."

"So can you sign the waiver of your rights?" Cooper slid a piece of paper and an ink pen across the metal surface as Stewart quickly signed his name.

"Yeah, sorry about that, Stu. It's just a formality around here."

"I understand."

"Before we begin, what do you want them to get you for supper? Is a burger and fries okay?"

"Sure."

"Okay, I'll be right back." Cooper took the signed waiver and left the room. He was walking down the hall to the observation room when he noticed Pete walking up with a young nervous-looking man with dark hair and tan complexion. "Hey Pete, is this Collin?" Cooper stuck his hand out to introduce himself and then had Pete and Collin follow him down the hall to another interrogation room. "Pete, can you read him his rights?"

"My rights?" Collin's voice piqued.

"It's standard procedure," Cooper answered. "We have everyone who comes in here sign the Miranda waiver." Pete nodded in agreement.

"Oh, okay," Collin said, sounding a little more comfortable.

"So, have you eaten Collin? Want a burger and fries?"

"Sure," he grinned taking a seat in the interrogation room.

"Okay, I'll be right back." He nodded for Pete to follow him out.

"Here, read and sign this form," Pete said giving him the waiver and ink pen before following Cooper. "What'd you want?"

"Ask him to give his story."

"That's what I was going to do." Pete smiled like he hadn't done this a hundred times before.

"Yeah, but he doesn't know that we know he was involved with another killing."

"Say what?" Pete's mouth dropped as he pointed at the door. "That guy killed someone? But he's saying he didn't do it."

"He didn't kill tonight. But he did last April."

"How do you know?"

"It's a long story, but I'm sure of it. Just trust me."

"Okay," Pete said unconvinced as he scratched his head and popped his neck. "Sounds like it's going to be a long night."

"Maybe not." Cooper grinned knowing that in any other situation this may not be as clear cut, but he had a secret weapon. Elizabeth and Solo. He grabbed his phone and quickly called Elizabeth.

"Hey Wint," she yawned with her television blaring in the background.

"Do you still keep your dream journals?" he whispered.

"Yeah. Need them from April?"

"How'd you know?"

"Wint, come on. Give me a little credit. I've been wanting to get these fools for months. I'll text you the pictures now."

"You're a godsend."

"Get 'em good this time. Nail their balls to the wall."

"I'm going to try," he said with a grin. He ended his call and instantly received a text from Elizabeth with multiple handwritten notes. He opened the images as his grin widened. She had everything neatly written with names and dates, and lines drawn throughout her documents referencing one death to another. She had done her homework. He could see why she was Veronica's sister.

I thought you would be needing these. Good luck. Elizabeth texted as Wint walked back into Stewart's interrogation room and handed him a piece of paper.

"Please write down the events of the night and I'll be back shortly."

"Where's Dakota?" he asked unwaveringly.

"She's getting supper. She'll be back soon."

Cooper had already heard Stewart's side of the story. Now he wanted to hear Collin's side face to face. And maybe get him to tell about the kills in April. He walked down the quiet hallway, and Dakota popped her head out from the observation room.

"Want me to do anything?" she asked aloof, staring at the ceiling above Cooper's head.

"I'm sorry, Dakota. I wish I didn't have to do this, but…" He stopped talking when it became evident Dakota was no longer listening. She closed her eyes and went back into the observation room without another word.

Cooper dashed to Collin's room and opened the door, finding Collin already writing on the back of his sheet of paper while Pete sat silently.

"Collin, can you tell me again what happened tonight?"

CHAPTER 118

Collin held the plastic ink pen in his hand, fidgeting with it between his fingers as he watched Officer Cooper take a seat across from him.

"Sure, where do you want me to start?"

"Start from the beginning," Cooper answered with a pleasant smile, giving Collin his friendly, undivided attention.

"Well, I guess it started yesterday when Grant and I had a blow-up at lunch. He's always been a prick to me. Always talking down to me like he's better than me. And the other guys always think of him as the leader, so they listen to everything he says. I thought Grant was just being Grant and he would chill, but when he came to work this morning, he was still like he was yesterday. Cocky and rude. So I went to him and asked what his problem was and then we went to the bathroom to talk. And he threw the first punch. So, then I let him have it."

"So you fought at work and then what happened?"

"Well, Stewart came up to me before lunch and asked if I wanted to go. He started being really friendly with me and asking questions about Grant. He then started saying Grant had been treating him differently lately. So, you know, hating another person brings people together. So, we came up with a plan to follow Grant after work."

"Why?" Pete interjected. "Why follow him today?"

"Oh," Collin said shaking his head. "I forgot. Grant couldn't go to lunch with Stewart because he said he had an appointment. But his appointment lasted a long time, and then when he came back to work, Stewart said he was stranger than he had ever been. So we decided to follow him and see what was up."

Cooper glanced over at Pete who subtly nodded his head in agreement.

"So you followed him after work and you ended up at your place?" Cooper asked looking over at Pete. "Did you know he was going to your home?"

"No! That is what confused me. Because as Stewart was driving, he never seemed weirded out by driving toward my house, but I kept thinking this is really strange. Like *really* strange. I don't live near work and I kept thinking, why is Grant heading this far north?" Collin spoke quickly, seldom taking a breath, spilling out his guts as if trying to expel all his memories before he forgot something. "That is when I started thinking something was up."

"Something was up? What?" Pete asked, looking at Collin in confusion.

"Well, yesterday Grant basically said, without so many words, that I was out of the group. So I left lunch while Stewart and Jordan stayed with Grant."

"This Jordan, can you give me his number and address? We are going to need to talk to him as well," Cooper asked as he remembered the name from the previous spring.

"But Jordan wasn't with us tonight," Collin said.

"Yeah, but he saw the interactions yesterday and this morning. You know, just trying to make sure we get everything documented."

Collin pulled out his phone and gave Cooper Jordan's information, who then texted Dakota to have someone pick him up.

"Back to your story. After you got to your house, what then?" Cooper asked, leaning back and stretching his arms.

"I felt uneasy about going up to the house. Stewart and I started making assumptions about Gavyn and Grant, and I didn't want to walk in on anything."

"You thought Gavyn and Grant were seeing each other?" Pete asked wide-eyed.

"Well, I didn't think it was true, because Gavyn is a real ladies' man and Grant is married, but we knew they had both been acting differently, and we thought, maybe."

"Okay, so go on," Cooper stated.

"Yes, so, well, Stewart got out of his car and started walking up to my house, but I felt weird so I stayed back a little. Then we heard shouting."

"Shouting? What was being said?" Cooper asked.

"I can't remember, something about 'knowing what I want', but it didn't make sense. But they were both shouting at one another. Then Stewart got up to the door and opened it and walked in. I poked my head in when Gavyn screamed my name or Stewart's name. I can't remember. But Gavyn screamed out. And then Grant shot him."

"Then what?"

"Then Grant started talking to Stewart about them being partners in other killings this week."

"Other killings?" Pete asked in a controlled tone. "Who did they kill?"

"Grant said something about Mr. Lukin and Mr. Hill. They were a couple of teachers from high school."

"Okay, go on," Cooper stated.

"Then he told Stewart to get me, and he said, 'what's a third body?' So I took off and ran and kept running. I thought they were going to kill me. But I don't get it. Grant called me a third body, but they had already killed three people."

"Have you called Jordan or anyone else?"

"No! Because I was afraid Jordan was a part of their group and would come and kill me too."

"So, to get this straight, you're saying Stewart Weatherby and Grant Harper killed Ted Lukin on Sunday and Jake Hill on Monday. Correct?"

"Yes!" Collin said nodding his head. "See why I took off?"

"And do you have an alibi for Sunday or Monday evening?"

"I, uh," Collin started thinking of his week. "I should because I didn't kill anyone."

"Okay, we are going to need those names," Pete said, pulling out a pen and notepad from his shirt pocket.

"I was watching the game Sunday at home alone but then went to the gym. You can check with them that I was there. And then on Monday, yeah, I was at the gym most of the night. Then I went and grabbed some supper and headed to a bar to watch the game."

"Okay. We'll need the names of the places to corroborate your alibi," Pete said casually.

"No problem. I have nothing to hide. As I said, I didn't kill anyone." He stopped and looked at Pete. "Since I'm telling you this, are you going to keep me safe? You know, keep me protected somehow from all of them?"

"Well, Grant is dead. And Stewart is detained right now. The only one we need to find is Jordan."

That wasn't what Collin expected to hear. He looked at the two police officers who remained unfazed by the statement as he felt a mixture of emotions. He didn't know why he was feeling emotional at the news of Grant's death, but even though they weren't on the best of terms, they had been friends for half their lives. His eyes started to water when he thought of Whitney finding out that her husband was dead.

"Grant's dead?" he asked in shock. "Jesus, poor Whitney."

Cooper looked over at Pete and then back at Collin. "She's dead too." He raised up three fingers. "Gavyn, Whitney, and then you would have been the third one killed."

"Christ! Whitney was murdered? How? When? Is that why Grant was going after Gavyn?" Collin stammered his questions, letting them

321

fall off his lips like vomit as a couple of tears started to fall down his cheeks. "This can't be happening. Not Whitney. What did she do to deserve this?"

CHAPTER 119

Dakota watched from the observation room with a couple of other officers as Winston and Pete walked into Stewart's interrogation room.

"Isn't that your boyfriend?" Detective Smith Young laughed as he popped some M&M's into his mouth with his feet propped up on the table holding all the computer equipment. Dakota looked over at Young and almost made herself sick with the memory from a year ago when she thought he was attractive.

"When's your wedding, Young?" she commented with a snarl. "You've been engaged for a year and I haven't heard anything."

"We're on a break," he said, casually tossing another chocolate candy in the air to catch in his mouth.

"I heard she kicked him out," Chris, the surveillance coordinator, whispered into Dakota's ear as he adjusted the volume in Stewart's room.

"Sorry for keeping you," Cooper said as he and Pete took a seat. "We have some questions we need answered before you can leave."

Stewart nodded his head. "Okay."

"First, do you know when Whitney was murdered?"

"I, I do not."

Chris quickly pulled Dr. Santiago's preliminary findings and spoke into the microphone into Cooper's and Pete's miniscule earpieces. "Dr. Santiago estimates Whitney was murdered between 11 am and 3 pm today."

Cooper nodded at the information. "Do you think Grant could have murdered her around lunch today? Maybe instead of going to an appointment, he went home and killed his wife. Does that seem possible?"

"I guess."

Dakota leaned closer to the screen, watching Stewart's reactions. She still believed this was a mistake, and Collin was a lying scoundrel who deserved to rot in jail for false accusations.

"Now you said Collin ran off after Grant shot Gavyn. Why did he leave?"

"He was afraid."

"But why didn't *you* leave?" Pete asked. "Why weren't *you* afraid?"

"I was in shock," Stewart answered with a croak in his voice.

Dakota watched Stewart's leg start to shake and his foot tap. She knew he was nervous but didn't understand why. If he answered honestly, there would be no need to be nervous.

"Were you in shock the entire time until you left the house?"

"Yeah," he nodded. "That's about right."

"So you watched Collin run off and you stood in shock. Did you think Grant was going to kill you too because you saw him kill Gavyn?" Pete asked a little more forcefully.

"I don't know. It just happened so fast. I wasn't thinking of that."

"You know, there are two main human instincts in this type of situation, fight or flight. So, which are you?" Pete asked.

Dakota shook her head at the line of questioning. "What are they doing?"

"Looks like they are trying to corner your lover boy," Young commented.

"Cut it out, Young," Chris defended as he looked at Dakota with sympathy.

"I guess 'fight' since I didn't run," Stewart answered as he wrung his hands together.

"Did you fight Grant for the gun?" Cooper asked.

"They are trying to confuse him by tag-teaming him," Dakota let out. "Just ask the questions and move on, Cooper," she mumbled to herself as Stewart started to blink more rapidly.

"Not exactly," Stewart answered.

CHAPTER 120

"Not exactly," he answered. He looked at Officer Cooper across the table and didn't know how to answer. Would the truth cause more issues? It hadn't even been an hour, but it already seemed like a horrid dream. He closed his eyes and went back to the moment of the unraveling.

"You're a good friend, but I still need a suicide." Grant said with menacing eyes.

"Grant! No!" He shouted, stunned how quickly the proverbial knife was going to be used. But not in his back, but a bullet to his head.

"Goodbye, Stewart," Grant winked as if it was no problem to kill his best friend.

Stewart looked at the barrel pointed toward him and jumped aside. The years of being held down by Grant were over. He didn't want to fight to the death, but he wasn't going to just let Grant use him as his scapegoat either. He looked past the gun and stared Grant in the eye. If this was his last moment on earth he was going to cherish that look of shock on his friend's face.

Stewart charged toward Grant, his surprised body twisted backwards crashing to the ground. Stewart lasered in on the hand holding the gun as both of his hands wrapped around Grant's. The years of defense training from his father kicked into high gear as he tried his best to stay in control of the fight. The two men grunted, wrestling like gladiators as beads of sweat dripped from Stewart onto Grant's sweater.

Dread sprung into Stewart's mind, acknowledging his strength was no competition for Grant's. He looked down at Grant, who was starting to maliciously smile, as if chuckling at the play fight. The smile pushed Stewart over the edge.

Stewart stared at Grant's forehead and recounted all the years of playing football in England. He snapped his head forward as if headbutting the ball for a goal. He felt the pain quickly seize him, but he knew Grant was feeling it from both sides when the chain of reactions caused his head to slam into the hardwood floor.

Stewart saw his fleeting chance. He twisted Grant's hand, heard a snap and a yelp.

He pressed Grant's finger into the trigger, shooting his friend in his head.

He opened his eyes, seeing Officer Cooper staring at him. He still didn't know what story he needed to tell.

CHAPTER 121

"So, you didn't run and you didn't fight. What *did* you do?" Pete asked.

Stewart's head kept bouncing between the two police officers as if playing a game of Pong.

"I, I just talked to him," Stewart started. "Grant was screaming and acting crazy and I was trying to calm him down."

"Did you know Gavyn and Whitney were having an affair before Grant told you?" Cooper asked, looking down at the notes on his phone.

"No! I couldn't believe it. And then when he told us he killed Whitney, that's when Collin bolted."

Dakota looked at Chris for confirmation, but he told her, "Collin said he didn't know about Whitney either."

"So, that's why Collin ran off? Because Grant said he had killed Whitney and he had just watched him kill Gavyn. Is that correct?" Cooper slowly asked the question, making sure not to miss any details.

"Yeah, that's right. Grant told us Whitney was cheating on him and that he killed her, and then Collin ran."

"And you still didn't feel the need to run after finding out your friend had killed his wife and just shot and killed your other friend? I just don't understand why Collin was so afraid that he ran and you didn't run. Was anything else said? Think back. Did Grant say anything else?"

Stewart shook his head.

"So, Collin left. You stayed. And then Grant shot and killed himself. Is that right?" Pete asked matter-of-factly.

"Yes."

"Because Collin is telling us a different story."

Dakota leaned closer, almost touching the computer monitor to get a better view of Stewart's reaction.

"Collin?" his voice cracked. "You've talked to Collin?"

"Yes, Stewart, we've talked to Collin, and he's telling us another reason why he ran off." Pete stopped and looked at Cooper.

"Do you have a guess as to what Collin told us?" Cooper asked.

Stewart clenched his hands forming a fist and looking up at the ceiling, as if looking for the answer to the question.

"I, I don't know."

"Really, Stewart?" Cooper asked leaning his elbows onto the table. "You are clueless about what Collin might have told us?"

Dakota watched as Stewart twisted his neck, as if trying to ease some tension forming. He didn't answer the question.

"Do the names Ted Lukin and Jake Hill mean anything to you?" Cooper asked looking into Stewart's calloused eyes. "Because I think they do. Collin said they do."

"You can't believe everything Collin says," Stewart commented. "He gets easily confused sometimes."

"He didn't sound confused to me. Did he sound confused to you, Pete?"

Pete shook his head and looked at Stewart with disbelieving eyes. "He sounded perfectly coherent to me. That is until we told him that Whitney was dead and he broke down. He said he didn't know Grant had killed her too."

"He's lying," Stewart tried to convince them. "He's always been a liar."

"Huh, then why be friends with him all these years?" Cooper asked, cocking his head at the degrading statement. "If you two have been friends for half your life, and he is such a liar, why stay his friend?"

"Unless he's not lying," Pete answered.

"It's my word against his," Stewart said. "And that's all you have. My dad is a high military official, and his dad cleans cars for a living. Who are you going to believe?"

"Yeah, I guess you're right. Whose word should we believe when that's all we have?"

"Exactly."

The hairs on the back of Dakota's neck raised at the audacity of Stewart's statement. His attitude suddenly changed from caring and compassionate to demeaning and rotten.

"What if I tell you, Stewart, we have something else besides his word?" Cooper asked as Pete grinned.

Stewart didn't answer. Dakota watched as Stewart's shoulders went from broad to caving in, as if being deflated.

"I guess you should have told Grant to not carry his kill list with him." Cooper grabbed the sheet of paper Stewart was completing and looked at the handwriting. He pulled out his cellphone and looked at the list with two different handwritings.

"It's interesting how your handwriting is really similar to how Ted Lukin is written on this sheet of paper. It's as if you helped make the kill list and wrote some of the names yourself." Cooper showed Pete the phone and Stewart's handwritten events of the night. They were pointing out the similarities of the two writings.

Dakota watched as the two police officers continued to dissect the writing styles taking their eyes off of Stewart. She watched Stewart as he slowly lifted his hands from his lap placing them on the table. He opened his clenched fist and moved stealthily for the pen.

"Cooper!"

CHAPTER 122

"One minute." Pyotr's speech still reeked of his eastern Russian accent even after all the years of living in America. He stepped out of his son's bedroom after tucking him in for the night and walked down the hall to his home office, locking the door behind him. He had protocols to adhere to, and they had saved his life a few times. He flipped on his noise-scrambling device in case there were any bugs in the house. He had learned one could never be too careful. "What'd you want?"

"I wouldn't be calling you unless it was important," the voice answered in an American accent.

"Yes, yes, go on. You've always been very good to me."

"Gavyn McKenzie is dead."

"Dead?"

"Yes."

"How? Accident?" Pyotr asked, sitting down in his armchair as his fireplace lit up the darkened room.

"It hasn't been confirmed yet, but we are saying he was murdered in his home."

"We had nothing to do with this murder."

"No, I know. I just wanted Milo to be aware."

"Okay, I will let him know." Pyotr walked over to his window and looked out at the peacefulness of the night. He knew in life people could be deceptive, but thankfully, he had connections that helped keep him abreast of these types of matters. "Good night, Trent. I'll let Milo know you called."

"Thank you, Pyotr. Night."

Pyotr ended the call and turned off the scrambling device. He searched for breaking news stories, but they had not released the names on a triple murder-suicide. He closed his web browser and pulled out a chain from under his robe. After kissing his multi-jeweled Byzantine cross, he said a quick prayer for thanksgiving and protection.

CHAPTER 123

"Cooper!" Dakota screamed into their earpieces, causing him to look up in time to see Stewart grab the ink pen.

"No!" Cooper shouted. Pete slid over the table, trying to grab Stewart's hand to keep him from puncturing the pen into his own neck. Stewart was quick, though, and he clicked the pen in his dominate hand, raising it up at full force with his skinny arms.

Cooper jumped up, throwing his body over the table as Dakota's screams echoed inside his ear.

Pete reached out his hand, trying to catch Stewart's arm. He felt the course fabric of Stewart's long cotton sleeve rubbing against his palm as he tried to grab his forearm to stop the momentum of the pen in motion. Cooper saw Pete's reaction as his hand wrapped around his arm, but it wasn't one of relief.

Stewart's arm continued to rise despite Pete's efforts as his arm slid under the fabric. Pete held the unbuttoned sleeve, sliding it to his elbow as Stewart's fist rose to chin level.

Cooper lunged for Stewart's chest to move his trajectory of maximum damage, but missed as Stewart tilted at his waist toward the fist that was holding the pen.

Cooper looked into Stewart's eyes, but he didn't see a cold-blooded, calculated killer. He saw something scarier. He saw a caged, beaten animal with no hope. He saw a man who was but a child a few years ago, trying to appear to be something that he wasn't. Cooper looked at Pete gritting his teeth, trying to hold Stewart's hand back as he closed his eyes.

A squirt of blood splashed across Pete's face as he groaned in anguish.

"Stewart!" Dakota shrieked a painful shrill into Cooper's earpiece, causing him to wince at the deafening cry.

Stewart's draining body crashed to the ground from the weight of Pete's and Cooper's opposing forces colliding into his slight frame.

"Call the paramedics!" Cooper shouted as he applied pressure to Stewart's neck wound, his clean hands quickly turning crimson with the warm liquid.

Pete wiped the blood off of his face and looked down into Stewart's lucid eyes. The door swung open and Dakota ran into the room with a handful of rags running around the table and dropping to her knees. She covered Cooper's hands with the gray hand towel that quickly soaked up Stewart's blood like a thirsty cactus.

"Stewart!" she screamed as his eyes blinked. She squeezed his hand as large tears fell down her cheeks, dropping into the pool of blood on the marble white linoleum. "Stay with me, Stewart! Stay with me!"

His body started to shake as his lifeless eyes looked up at the ceiling tiles.

"He's going into shock!" Pete warned as Cooper continued to hold Stewart's neck.

"Come on, Stewart! Please!" Dakota moaned as she leaned over his body. Her hair fell forward as she placed her head on his chest. Her tears and running nose dripped onto his blue button-up shirt as she held onto his hand as if pulling him to safety. "Don't die on me!"

Cooper looked into Stewart's eyes. He had seen that look many times before and it never got easier. He moved one of his hands away from the wound and tried to find a pulse. He looked up at Pete's blood-splattered face and uniform like he was staring at a Jackson Pollock painting.

"He's gone," Cooper said to Dakota as he brushed her hair out of her eyes. "I'm sorry, Dakota."

She didn't respond to his sentiment as she cried, pounding her fist on Stewart's chest. Stewart laid with his glazed lifeless eyes as Cooper closed them with his blood-stained hands. Dakota raised her head up from Stewart's chest, reaching for his wrist to find a pulse. She held onto it as her groaning increased in volume.

Cooper stood up beside Pete as a few other police officers entered the interrogation room, watching a grieving woman sit beside a newly discovered killer.

"Dakota, he's gone," Cooper said, resting his hand on her shoulder.

She winced at the touch, moving her torso away from his hand. "Don't touch me," she said slowly, enunciating each throaty syllable.

"Dakota," Cooper said once again, trying to console his partner and friend.

"I said, don't touch me! Don't touch me! Don't touch me!" she demanded as her fists clenched tighter with each word. She started mumbling vicious words and threats. "You did this!" she exclaimed looking up at the police officers, turning her head until she found the one she was looking for. She looked into Cooper's eyes as if giving him a curse, squinting with pure hatred.

"But--" Cooper started as Pete pushed him back, patting his chest to leave the tense room.

"You killed him, Cooper! You killed him!"

Cooper walked out of the room looking down at his hands trying to tune out the harsh words. He looked at Pete as he continued to hear Dakota scream from behind the door as he wondered.

Did we kill him?

CHAPTER 124

Jordan Lee sat in the back of the patrol car as Officer Trent Gusev silently drove to the precinct.

"Why can't you tell me anything?" Jordan asked as he texted a few people in his contacts, trying to figure out why he needed to be questioned.

"They didn't tell me why," Officer Gusev answered as he raised the volume on the radio.

"Really? You just got a call to come and pick me up with no information or context?" Jordan stared at his phone, waiting for a message from someone to give him some insight on what was happening. He looked at Officer Gusev and got an uncomfortable feeling as the officer watched the backseat as closely as the road ahead of him. "Nice night out tonight, isn't it?"

"I guess," he answered. He proceeded through the intersection making his way through the downtown area passing a few of the Smithsonian museums as they drove.

"Who are you hoping to win the World Series?"

"I don't watch baseball," the officer answered shortly as he continued to watch Jordan as if learning his mannerisms and body language.

Jordan turned his attention back to his phone, pleading for someone to text him back. He closed his eyes and leaned back onto the headrest. This was not how he wanted to spend a Wednesday evening.

"Am I in trouble?"

"Don't know," Officer Gusev answered, once again looking at Jordan in the rearview mirror with annoyed eyes.

Jordan looked away the instant he saw Officer Gusev's eyes. He hated the feeling of being watched, but he hated watching someone watch him even more.

Grant's dead. Collin answered. *And Gavyn and Whitney.*

Jordan read the message and started typing with his thumbs as fast as they could move. *What? Dead? How?*

Jordan watched his phone, but the three blinking dots didn't appear.

Are you okay? Jordan texted Collin again and waited for a response. But there wasn't one.

"You could have told me my friend died," Jordan said as he sniffled, wiping his wet eyes and running nose with his hand. "Was that too much to ask for?"

"Who are you talking about?"

"Grant Harper," Jordan spit out. "Like you didn't know."

"Do you know the reason your boss does everything he does?" Officer Gusev asked.

"No." Jordan rolled his eyes as he stared down at his phone, eagerly waiting for some new information.

"Well, neither do I," he said as he pulled into the parking lot of the precinct.

Jordan felt a vibration as he looked down at his phone. *It's bad. Murders and suicide.*

Jordan walked into the precinct that resembled a madhouse with running men in uniforms. He headed down the hall and saw a man with blood on his hands and another one with some on his face.

"What happened?" Officer Gusev asked as they stopped in front of an interrogation room.

The officers just shook their heads and looked at Jordan. "Put him in Room 4. We'll be there in a few minutes."

"Was that blood?" Jordan asked as Officer Gusev walked him to the Interrogation Room. He didn't answer as he opened the door showing him a seat at the table. "I said, was that blood?"

Officer Gusev still didn't answer as Jordan shook his head at the complete disrespect he was experiencing. "Did something happen?" Jordan asked as Officer Gusev left the room and closed the door.

Jordan looked around the boring room with no paint or windows as his shock started to wear off from hearing about the three deaths. His grief started to show, and his eyes started to water again.

Officer Gusev returned and read Jordan his rights and asked him to sign the Miranda waiver.

"What's this for?" Jordan asked, looking down at the form suspiciously.

"Formality."

As soon as Jordan had signed the form, Officer Gusev grabbed the ink pen and paper and left Jordan to wonder in silence once again.

What in the freakin' world is going on? he thought as his mind went back to the deadly news. He reached down and pinched the loose skin on his wrist. He felt the discomfort and realized this wasn't a bad dream.

It was actually happening.

He hoped he was in the interrogation room to discuss his deceased friends. He hoped even more that it wasn't because of anything they had done together six months ago. He took a deep breath and saw the walls closing in on him from all directions. He had never been in an interrogation room, and he hoped he would soon be leaving.

He looked at the door as the knob started to turn, and the two officers he saw previously walked in. There was no blood on their faces or hands, and their formal attire had been replaced with plain white undershirts.

"Hello. I'm Officer Winston Cooper and this is Officer Pete Robbins, and I see you waived your rights, is that correct?"

"Why am I here?" Jordan asked getting straight to the point.

Cooper and Robbins looked at one another and then turned to Jordan. "We need to ask you some questions about your friends."

CHAPTER 125

"Friends?" Jordan asked standing his proverbial ground on the other side of the table. "The cop who picked me up wouldn't tell me anything. And then I found out my friends were murdered. And now you want to ask me some questions without telling me anything?"

"We were going to tell you that," Cooper said.

"When? After you asked me a hundred questions without me knowing why you were asking? You cops are really something."

Cooper looked at the man across the table releasing all of his frustrations onto him, but he, too, felt frustrated looking into the eyes of a killer. He wanted to go off and tell him what he thought, but he knew he needed to stay professional. He needed to get him to listen and tell them what he needed to hear.

He took a deep breath and counted to five, closing his eyes to find his center. He exhaled and opened his eyes. It didn't work.

"If you had given me a second we would have told you, but you didn't."

"If you say so," Jordan shrugged, rolling his brown eyes.

"Tonight, Gavyn McKenzie and Whitney and Grant Harper were found dead. I cannot go into details of their deaths just yet, but I am sorry for your loss."

Jordan didn't respond. He stared unfazed with his right elbow on the table as his hand held his cheek. He looked off into the corner of the room, staring at the blank walls. "Which one committed suicide?"

Cooper looked at Robbins as they silently agreed to tell. "Grant Harper," Robbins answered. "Mr. Harper supposedly shot himself."

Jordan hung his head, staring down at the reflective metal tabletop. "Supposedly?"

"We're still investigating," Cooper said shortly. "So, how would you describe Grant's mood lately?"

Jordan didn't look up but continued to stare at the table with both hands under his chin. "He's been off lately."

"How so?" Robbins asked.

"I don't know. He just hasn't been himself. He's been on edge. Snapping at people more than usual."

"Has he ever exhibited any suicidal thoughts?" Cooper asked with a little more compassion than a minute ago.

"Not that I know of."

Cooper and Robbins continued to ask similar questions about Grant's state of mind, his relationship with his wife, and his friendship with Gavyn. Jordan answered the questions in monotone, as if entering a hollow state of existence.

"How would you describe Collin Diaz?" Cooper asked as Robbins gave him a sideways look.

"Collin?" Jordan flinched at the different line of questioning. "What does Collin have to do with this?"

"Just covering all our bases." Cooper smiled.

"I've been friends with Collin since middle school. He's one of my best friends. He's a good guy. He doesn't always have the best, um..." He stopped and thought for a second, as if trying to phrase it correctly. "He doesn't always look ahead. Does that make sense?"

"What do you mean?" Robbins asked.

"You know, he does things without thinking of the consequences. He jumps quick and then scrambles."

"Would you say he's an honest guy?" Cooper leaned into the question.

"Honest?" Jordan smiled. "Yeah, he's pretty honest. He's a storyteller when it comes to his own life. But I don't think he wants to see the truth sometimes."

"How so?" Cooper asked.

"He always acts like he's a ladies' man. Always talking about how good-looking he is. He's one of those guys. A lot of big talk, you know what I mean?"

"I think I do," Cooper nodded. "Do you trust Collin?"

Jordan looked at Cooper and nodded his head. "I trust him."

"What about Stewart Weatherby?" Cooper asked. "Do you consider him honest?"

"Yeah, Stewart's as loyal as they come."

"So, should we believe Collin when he said Grant and Stewart killed Ted Lukin and Jake Hill earlier this week?"

"Say what?" Jordan said snapping out of his trance. His dead eyes quickly gained new life and vigor.

"Yeah, apparently they had a kill list and Grant and Stewart were killing people one by one," Cooper said.

Jordan didn't answer.

"What do you have to say about that?" Cooper asked. He watched Jordan as he was wobbling, as if trying to balance on a ball on a tightrope. He just hoped Jordan continued playing along. "Did you know about this list?"

"No. I didn't know."

"Can you think of a reason why Collin would be lying?" Cooper asked as he and Robbins once again gave a sideways look. "I mean, you said Stewart was loyal. Would he be that loyal to kill someone with Grant?"

Jordan nodded his head as if trying to wrap his head around what he'd learned in the last fifteen minutes. "If Grant asked Stewart to jump, he jumped."

"Stewart said something really bizarre a few minutes ago. He said last April, Collin tried to kill a woman." Cooper looked down at his phone, pulling up the notes Elizabeth had texted him. "Fiona Sanchez. Does that name sound familiar?"

Jordan's eyes darted around the room as if looking for a place to hide. "He said what?"

"He said, 'If I'm going down for this, I'm taking Collin down too.'" Cooper snapped his fingers in front of Jordan's face, getting his attention. "If you know something. You better tell. Because if you don't, and we find you are somehow connected to this…" He stopped and shook his head. "It won't be good."

CHAPTER 126

Robbins followed Cooper out of the interrogation room as they walked up the hall. "Cooper, what's going on here?" he asked as Chris and Detective Young came out of the observation room.

"Trying to make up lies now, Cooper?" Young asked snidely as he leaned against the wall as if posing for GQ.

"Trust me on this," Cooper said to Robbins. "I have a feeling."

"You know I have a feeling every time I piss, but that doesn't mean anything," Young laughed, popping another piece of candy in his mouth.

"That's probably the only feeling you get down there," Chris responded, catching Young off guard.

"We're going back to Collin," Cooper said to Chris. He turned to Robbins and looked him squarely in the eyes. "You don't have to say anything, okay. If this backfires, it's all on me."

Robbins nodded his head as they walked toward Collin's door and found him laying his head on the table with his eyes closed.

"Well, Collin," Cooper started as they took their seats. "Stewart saw he was caught. The cops found Grant's kill list in both of their handwritings that coincided with what Grant told you."

"Told ya!" Collin shouted, pounding his fist on the table.

"And you were right," Cooper said, taking out his copy of the kill list photo that was texted to him. He slid his phone over with the list of names in Grant's and Stewart's handwritings. "Do you recognize those names?"

Collin looked down at the phone and started reading the names. "Yeah. These were teachers from high school, a couple are professors." He stopped and looked up.

"Whose name is at the bottom?" Cooper asked.

Collin shook his head, smiling angrily as he read his name. "See, they were going to try to get me too. I knew they were up to something. I knew it!"

"Yeah, they were up to something all right." Cooper took back his phone and changed the images to Elizabeth's notes. He leaned over to Robbins and whispered, "Can you go get his signed waiver? I need it."

Robbins stood up to leave. "Can you bring the man of the hour a Coke?" Cooper asked with a beaming smile as Collin proudly grinned with his arms folded on his chest, flexing his pecs and biceps.

"It seems we will easily get Stewart for these murders thanks to you, Collin."

"Glad I could help." He leaned back spreading and stretching his legs like he was totally relaxed and not in an interrogation room.

"Yes, it is remarkable you caught on to them and ran off before you became their next victim. Without you, this night could have gone totally differently."

Collin nodded his head as Robbins entered with three cans of Coca-Cola and a signed waiver.

The three opened their cans and Cooper raised his can in a toast. "To Collin."

"To Collin," Robbins echoed as Collin raised his drink, taking in the accolades like he did the can of soda.

"We have one slight problem," Cooper started as he gave a disheartening grimace. "Once Stewart saw he was caught, he started talking about something the four of you did last April."

Collin was in mid-drink when he started choking, spitting out his mouthful of Coca-Cola. "What did he say?"

"Well," Cooper said tiptoeing delicately as if walking through a valley full of landmines. "He said you weren't man enough to kill Fiona Sanchez last April when you tried."

"Who?" he croaked. "Fiona?"

Cooper looked down at his phone. "Yeah, Fiona. I guess it was a girl from your high school you used to date or wanted to date. I don't know, he couldn't remember. He just said you were still angry with her after ten years and tried to kill her."

Collin shook his head, trying to control his rage, replacing it with nervous laughter. "He's just mad he got caught."

"Well, he bragged that he could kill the man he wanted to kill, and you fumbled like a pansy to kill yours. He said, 'He wasn't even man enough to shoot her, while I killed a man in his home. He's a wimp. A wannabe.'" Cooper could feel Robbins' eyes on him as if about to jump from a cliff as the doubting spectators watched below.

"Well, he didn't say 'pansy'," Robbins joined in looking Collin in his eyes. "If you get my drift."

Collin said the word Robbins was insinuating with a chuckle. "I'm not that."

"Well, Jordan was saying the same thing, actually," Cooper slid in feeling Collin's tension starting to rise.

"Jordan would never say that about me."

"Really? You really believe that? You think your friendship is that strong? Because bud, I'm sorry. When I showed him the handwritten list of names from the kills in April, he begged for a deal."

"A deal?" Collin's lower lip started to quiver. "Why did he get a deal? He actually killed Piper Michaelson. Fiona didn't even get hurt."

CHAPTER 127

Pete looked over at Cooper astonished. He would have never tied all of these murders together, especially that quickly.

"Look, Collin," Cooper said pointing to a nearby room. "Jordan is over there right now writing all the details he can remember."

"But," Collin said looking up with fearful eyes.

"But he hasn't signed it yet," Cooper added. "If you can write all the details and sign it before Jordan does, we may be able to offer you the deal. No promises, but if you're quicker than him, we may be able to."

"Give me some pen and paper!" Collin looked crazed as Pete and Cooper left the room.

"Cooper," Pete started, shaking his head in disbelief as they walked to another room to grab the items for Collin. "How did you know?"

Cooper looked at Pete with a cocky grin. "Do you ever just get a feeling and you have to jump on it?"

"A feeling?"

"Yeah, a feeling?"

"You have bigger balls than me, Cooper."

Winston nodded as the two walked back to Collin handing him the paper and pen. "We will be right back," Cooper said. "But write as much as you can and fast. Jordan only had a few minutes' head start."

The two walked out as Pete looked at Cooper once again in admiration. "You are really something, you know that?"

"I've been told that a time or two." Cooper laughed as he and Pete walked into the observation room as Chris turned around from behind the monitors with his mouth still open. Young didn't say a thing, but continued to lean back in his chair, watching Cooper a little more keenly than he had an hour earlier.

"Are you really going to offer Collin a deal?" Chris asked as Cooper walked over to the monitors to watch the two men in separate rooms. Collin was frantically writing, scribbling, and marking through his errors as if his life depended on it. Whereas Jordan sat with his hands behind his head, trying to stay calm with no pen and paper in the room.

Cooper shook his head no as he leaned down to look at Collin more closely. "There is no deal for Collin. I never promised a deal. I said he may get a deal, but I never promised one."

"How do you think he's going to react?" Young finally spoke as if not interested in the case.

"I don't care," Cooper answered. "He may not have killed Fiona, but he knew about the other deaths and did nothing to stop them. He is just as guilty as the others. He just missed the kill shot, and Fiona got lucky."

"I remember this case now. What was his name?" Chris asked, looking around in the files on his computer. He clicked on one and opened a video from last April of Cooper interrogating a man. "So this guy didn't kill them after all?"

Cooper shook his head. "No, but he's not getting out of jail. He raped the girls in high school, and he confessed to that."

"Was he convicted of the murders, though?" Pete asked while leaning against the wall.

"He hasn't been tried yet," Cooper said, watching the interrogation of Simon Tenney. "So I guess he was telling the truth."

"I still don't understand how you figured this out," Pete said scratching his head.

Cooper shrugged his shoulders as he looked at Pete. "I wish I could tell you."

"Well, when you get a feeling about some lottery numbers, let me know," Pete laughed. "My wife is nagging me about taking a vacation."

"I say let her go," Chris laughed. "Sounds like you need a break from her."

Pete cocked his head with a devilish smile. "I never thought of it that way. She can take a vacation to her mother's."

"I'm not sure that's going to work," Cooper chimed in.

"She never said where or if I had to go," Pete nodded, grabbing some candy from Young. "Thanks for the idea."

Cooper stretched his arms as he looked back at Pete. "Can you go check on Collin?" Pete nodded and walked out the door. "Young, can you go check on Jordan?"

"Fine." Young huffed as he stood up, stretching his body as he walked.

Cooper looked at Chris when they were the only two left in the room. "How's Dakota?"

Chris shook his head without saying a word.

"Was it my fault, Chris? You saw the tape." He looked at Chris who still didn't answer. The silence was breaking Cooper on the inside. He hadn't had much time to seriously contemplate Dakota's accusations, but he needed to. He needed to hear a third party's point of view.

Chris opened his mouth and then stopped.

"What? Just say it."

Chris rubbed his eyes and started to talk. "It happened so fast, Cooper."

"Was it my fault?"

"You didn't know he was going to do it."

"Was it my fault Stewart killed himself?"

Chris looked at the monitors and watched Young leave Jordan's interrogation room.

"Stewart killed himself, Cooper. Not you."

"But was it my fault?" Cooper asked, raising his voice as Young walked into the room.

"You gave him the pen." Young stood in the doorway with an arrogant grin on his face. "What did you expect him to do? Give you the pen and say, 'Take this, I want to kill myself now.' He knew he was caught and you left him with a deadly weapon."

Cooper looked at Young and wanted to smack the smug smile off of his spray-tanned face. Cooper didn't look at Chris as he headed out the door. He walked down the hallway to Collin's room and wondered if Young was right.

That thought sickened him. Not just because Stewart killed himself under Cooper's watch, but because Young would be right. He hated it when that guy was right, especially when Young being right meant him being wrong.

CHAPTER 128

"Are you ready to talk yet, Jordan?" Cooper asked as he and Robbins entered the interrogation room.

Jordan looked up, annoyed after sitting in the interrogation room in silence for twenty minutes. He didn't answer. He just stared at Cooper as if daring him to ask another question.

Cooper took the dare.

"So, I heard you and Piper Michaelson were something until you weren't. What happened between you two?"

Jordan's face flinched and then furrowed, his brow pressing his lips into a thin line.

"No answer?" Robbins asked.

"Well, she was murdered last April, but I'm pretty sure you know about that." Cooper rested his elbows on the table and stared into Jordan's cold, dead eyes. "I'm pretty sure you know more than you want us to know." Cooper stopped and leaned closer to Jordan as if telling him a secret. "But we already know."

Jordan smiled and crossed his arms.

"Still not talking?" Robbins laughed.

"I want my attorney."

"Okay," Cooper resigned as he leaned up from the table straightening his back. "That's fine, we can do that."

"Not sure how quickly the attorney is going to come, though," Robbins added. "It's late and you know attorneys think they are gods. They do things when they want to do them."

"Sure you don't want to tell your side of the story?" Cooper asked again.

"I want my attorney."

"Okay, we have his name and we'll make the call for you," Cooper said still seated and resting his hands on the cold table. "But how about we let you know what we know already? That way it's no surprise to your attorney why you have already been booked by the time he comes tomorrow morning." Cooper stopped and looked at Jordan with no sympathy.

"The first thing you should know is that your friend Collin is spilling his guts about the girls you all killed last April. And the funny thing is, he thinks since he didn't kill Fiona Sanchez, he is going to get off and leave the rest of you to take the heat. So he's down the hall talking faster than I have ever seen, like a backstabbed friend. He told us how Grant killed the first girl, Sabrina Latener. But you know, since Grant is dead and he was seen killing Gavyn, I'm believing Collin. If he just killed Gavyn, I bet a jury could believe he killed Sabrina.

"Then Collin told us about how you killed Piper Michaelson. And he brought up how he tried to kill Fiona, but missed. And poor Stewart, that's the interesting thing. We actually questioned him about these deaths, so you all were already kinda a suspect without us knowing. But thanks to Collin, it's an open and shut case now. I bet he can get other evidence for us besides his word. Like how you all dumped the car in a river in New York. I bet we can find some camera footage somewhere showing you all in the car. Or, how about explaining how you got home from New York that weekend?"

Cooper stopped and looked at Jordan letting him realize he was caught.

"Did I miss anything?" Cooper asked.

Jordan clenched his mouth and cocked his head. "My attorney."

"Oh, I did forget something," Cooper said as he and Robbins stood up. "Your friend Stewart? He's dead now too."

"He's what?"

"Dead," Cooper said about to leave. "I guess the guilt got to him and he killed himself when he knew he was caught."

"You're lying. Stewart would never do that."

"Didn't you say he would do whatever Grant told him to do?" Robbins pointed out from the last time they were in this room. "Seems like he was still following orders, even up to his death."

"So it's just you and Collin now. And here's another thing," Cooper grinned cunningly. "Collin is only talking because I said you were given a deal."

"You lied?"

"Let's say I misspoke about a technicality. But as you said, Collin doesn't think ahead." Cooper shrugged his shoulders as Robbins followed him out the door leaving Jordan confused and alone with only his thoughts to accompany him.

CHAPTER 129

Elizabeth rolled over on her bed, grabbing her phone as she paused her television. "Hey Wint," she answered nonchalantly.

"Wow. That's not the welcome I was expecting."

"Oh, hi Winston. How are you doing tonight?" she acted with a bubbly tone of eagerness.

"See, you can do it. Sometimes."

"Don't push it," she said snapping out of her Valley Girl persona.

"I guess I should just be happy you answered. Solo didn't even pick up."

"Hold up. You called him first? I was the one who gave you all the information, not Solo!"

"I know."

"And I'm your second choice?"

"Not second," he laughed.

"No, you called him first and then me second. That is the actual reason for saying someone is second, because Solo was in front of me."

"Third. I called you third, okay?"

"V? You called V before me?"

"She's my wife."

"Excuses. You men always have them. So why did you call me third? What is so unimportant that you needed to call me after them?"

Cooper laughed as he drove home. "Just to say we got them."

"You got them? You really got them?"

"Collin crumbled and started telling us everything. Jordan wasn't so forthcoming and asked for an attorney."

"What about Stewart?"

"Well." Cooper's attitude changed from gleeful to disheartened at the sound of his name. "He pretty much admitted to everything before killing himself."

"He killed himself? Cooper, what happened?"

Cooper shook his head and recounted all the details to Elizabeth. He expelled all his thoughts and feelings as Elizabeth was the perfect sounding board. As he spoke, he hoped people would see it his way and realize it wasn't his fault. They had the interrogation room footage to support or punish him.

"Wint, it wasn't your fault."

"You didn't see the footage. You didn't see."

"But I know you, Wint. I know you, and that means I don't need to see the footage to believe you."

Cooper pulled up to a familiar apartment building he had been to dozens of times in the last couple of months and parked his car. He sat behind the wheel frozen, looking up at the apartment on the second floor with light shining through its blinds.

"Thanks. I really needed to hear that."

"Now, I'm getting off here and catching up on my soaps I missed today. If you want to chitchat, call Solo. He's probably off saving an injured bird or rescuing a lost dog, or something idiotic like that."

"You've never been an animal person, have you?"

"I love animals. My gator skin boots. My snakeskin skirt. My fox stole. Don't tell me I'm not an animal lover. I would die if something happened to my mink coat. Just die!"

"Yeah, Cruella, remind me to never take you to the zoo."

"Oh, I would never step foot in a zoo," she huffed. "There are not enough air fresheners in the world to make that place smell good."

"Bye, Elizabeth," Cooper snickered, ending the call. He got out of the car and walked through the parking lot, making his way to the second-floor apartment. He knocked on the door and hoped this was going to go well. He heard someone fumbling around with the locks as the door swung open.

CHAPTER 130

A door opened as shouting and screaming came from down the hall. The commotion was getting louder as the overhead light flickered where one hallway intersected with another. There were about six apartments down each side of the hallway. The screaming was coming from the right with a string of shorted-out lights.

The image glided through the hallway, stopping at an orange door with off-center metal numbers 211 in flaking gold paint barely hanging on. The screaming and shouting was coming from behind the door. The image moved forward, passing through the closed door until inside the apartment.

"Please! No! Please!" a small woman begged as she stood beside a larger man. She was shaking with her black hair dangling past her neck.

"Stop screaming!" a man with tattoos on his face shouted. "Or I'll give you something to scream about!"

She slapped him. Her eyes widened in fear as he rubbed his cheek and looked at her.

"Now you did it!" His voice surged as he balled his hand into a fist, punching her in the face. She fell back onto the hardwood floor, screaming in pain. He kicked her in her side, and she quickly balled up while she moaned in agony.

"Someone help me!" she pleaded feebly as he looked down smiling at the crumbled woman. He continued to kick her until her screaming stopped. He walked away and grabbed a beer from the refrigerator. The light shined upon his face showing the details of his tattoos as if it were a mask around his blue eyes. He opened the can and chugged before walking back into the living room.

"Are you not going to get up?" he asked as he sat down in his recliner and picked up the remote control. "Suit yourself."

I woke up from the dream and wobbled from the couch to my front door. I stepped out and saw the flickering light overhead. I walked down the hallway and turned right. It was just like my dream. I watched as the numbers on the doors gradually increased until I stood in front of apartment 211. The numbers were slanted like they were in my dream. I stood in front of the orange door and touched it. There were not any screams tonight, but I knew there would be tomorrow if I didn't do something.

"Do you need something?" a voice from behind asked.

I turned to see a tall, burly man, almost twice my weight standing with flaring nostrils. I looked into the man's blue eyes surrounded by the tattoo from my dream.

"I'm sorry. I thought I heard something," I said.

"Well, I don't hear anything." He took another step forward as I stepped aside allowing him to his door. The woman from my dream stood behind him, as if in his shadow.

She had her head down, but feebly raised it. Our eyes connected. She gave me a slight smile as he unlocked the door and walked in.

"Well, are you coming in?" he impatiently huffed.

She quickly lowered her head and walked into the darkened apartment. She turned and closed the door, looking at me until the door separated us. I stood in the hallway and heard the latch of the locks behind the door.

I leaned against the hallway wall and felt a chill hit my back. I wrapped my arms around my chest and felt skin-to-skin contact. I looked down and smiled.

If anyone wanted to know what type of underwear I wore, the secret was out. I walked back to my apartment a little less bravely, hoping no one else caught me in my navy Tommy John trunks.

CHAPTER 131

"Fiona," Cooper said as he waited outside her apartment. "It's me, Officer Coo--."

She stopped him and opened the door wider, allowing him into her apartment. "I know who you are. Come on in. Why are you here?"

Cooper didn't know how to tell her, but knew he needed to. "Do you remember a man named Collin Diaz?"

She looked at Cooper skeptically as she welcomed him into her living room. "Yeah. He was just a guy from school."

"Anything else?"

"No. Why?"

"Well, he's admitted to trying to kill you tonight."

"Tonight?" she asked shocked. "No one tried to kill me tonight."

"No. No." Cooper shook his head at his wording. "Tonight, while being questioned about another matter, he said he was the one who tried to kill you last April."

"I thought--" she started as Cooper stopped her.

"Yeah, we thought it was Simon, but it appears he was framing Simon."

"So let me get this straight. Collin was the one who shot at me and Simon didn't?"

Cooper shook his head.

"What does that mean?"

"Well, Simon will still go to jail because he admitted to raping a few women. We have that confession. And now, Collin and his friend will hopefully go to jail for your attempted murder as well as the murders of others."

"Hopefully?"

Cooper wanted to be truthful that there were always chances of things going wrong. But he didn't want her to worry about that.

"Collin has admitted to everything, but Jordan is remaining quiet. But we have him."

"Jordan? Jordan Lee?" She gasped as she sat down.

Cooper nodded his head.

"Why would they want to kill me? I didn't do anything to them!"

Cooper listened to her questions and wondered why anyone would want to kill someone.

"Guys with broken hearts can do stupid things sometimes."

"Broken hearts?" she laughed. "I definitely didn't break Collin's heart. He was a player, and I didn't want to be played."

"Well, I guess even players get their feelings hurt," Cooper said as Fiona shot him a questionable look. "I'm not condoning his actions, and I'm not saying you are to be blamed. It's just guys sometimes do stupid things when they get hurt. And some guys never get over it, apparently."

"This is crazy!" Fiona got up from the couch and paced around the living room. "Are you sure I'm totally safe now?" She asked the question with a layer of attitude.

"You're safe, Fiona," Cooper said as he stood up. "This mess is finally behind us."

She looked at him confused. "I already thought it was behind me. Now I'm thinking about it all over again. Did you know Simon wasn't the real killer?"

Cooper looked into Fiona's eyes and had a hard time saying the truth to her. He wondered what would be the proper way to say it, but each statement sounded questionable. Sometimes the truth causes more harm than a lie.

"No, I didn't know, Fiona. I didn't know."

"Are you sure?" She looked at him suspiciously. "Because this may sound crazy, but I've felt like you have been following me lately."

"Following you?" Cooper laughed. "I like Mexican food, and your place has the best salsa."

She eyed him but shook it off. "I'm sorry. It's late, and all this is just making me sound crazy."

Cooper shook his head. "You're not crazy, Fiona. But you're safe now. If you ever feel unsafe, you know how to reach me."

Cooper walked out of her apartment and headed to his car. This was hopefully going to be the last time he would come to this apartment. She was right. He had been following her. After Solo said Simon wasn't the actual killer in July, Cooper had been checking in on Fiona from a distance. He'd had a routine of watching her from coffee shops near her work, sitting in her apartment parking lot in the evenings, picking up groceries at her local market. He thought he'd been pretty good at spying on her, but apparently, he needed to work on his skills.

THURSDAY

CHAPTER 132

An open white casket laid at the end of an empty room. Slowly the distance vanished, and the casket was close enough to be touched. The room suddenly filled with grieving men and women dressed in police uniforms.

"He was a good cop," a police officer at the lectern announced. "A very good cop who served this city proudly." He turned his head and looked to a woman dressed in black. "Veronica, your husband died a hero in that subway station trying to fend off those two killers. We don't know who these Carbon Monoxide Killers are yet, but we will find them, and we will bring them to justice!"

The room erupted in cheers and applause.

Slowly Wint's dead torso raised up and turned its head. "You didn't save me because you didn't have a dream. I died because you didn't have a dream."

Suddenly everyone in the room disappeared, leaving the room void except for the white casket. In the next instant, the room filled with school-age children crying, holding their parents' hands.

"Rachel Fiddelstein was too young to have experienced such a traumatic and vicious death. She had such a warm smile and a bright outlook on life. Her parents, Isaac and Amanda, loved her dearly. They will be in our thoughts and prayers for many days to come."

The room filled with moans and wails.

Slowly Rachel's dead torso raised up and turned its head. "You didn't save me because you didn't have a dream. I died because you didn't have a dream."

Once again the room emptied except for the white casket. The room spun as it went from empty to full as random people would rise out of the casket and repeat the same line. "You didn't save me

362

because you didn't have a dream. I died because you didn't have a dream." This went on and on with a different life that was spared each time.

The room dimmed as a young woman laid in her bed with an empty bottle of wine laying sideways on the floor. Pages of handwritten paper laid scattered on the floor as if carpet covered by countless tissues. She rolled over and looked into the void. "You didn't save me because you didn't have a dream. I was lost because you didn't have a dream." Elizabeth rolled onto her back and blew her nose. "Yes, I have a family and a boyfriend, but I'm not close to my family. And I am just using Jeremiah for some human contact. Without your dreams you couldn't have saved me, Solomon. Veronica and I are still distant. I'm still seeking my disgusting father's approval. I am selfish, self-centered, not helping the world in any way. And Jeremiah would be better off without me."

Elizabeth's bed dissolved like smoke as a person walking in the darkness came into view. The person was walking forward but was too far away to make out any details.

A voice in the distance started to speak. "You didn't save me because you didn't have a dream. I lived a sad existence because I didn't think I deserved any better. I was breathing, but I wasn't living. I was moving, but I wasn't going anywhere. I was smiling, but it wasn't real. I was learning, but it was purposeless. I was trying to pretend everything was okay, but I wasn't okay. I was trying to convince myself that I was whole, but I was broken. I saw people, but I wasn't truly seen." The person continued to walk until his features were clearly visible.

You can't fully understand peace, Solomon, until you have fully felt the absence of it.

"But you did save me because you did have a dream. I now live a fulfilled existence because you have dreams. I am breathing, and I am living. I am moving, and I am going places. I am smiling, and it is authentic. I am learning, and it has a divine purpose. I am no longer pretending everything is okay, because I am okay. I am finally feeling whole, and each day I am becoming a little stronger. I see people and they see the real me and love me."

The man smiled. "It's time to wake up Solomon and see. It's time to finally understand."

I woke from my dream and stared overhead recounting the moments in my dream. I leaned over and grabbed my Bible on the nightstand. I closed my eyes and opened it, pointing my finger to a random verse.

"I have said these things to you, that in me you may have peace. In the world you will have tribulation. But take heart, I have overcome the world." John 16:33

I laid my Bible aside and rolled onto my back, staring overhead as I let the words sink into my thick skull. I sorted through the memories of the last year and many of them had been hard and troubling, but I did see a common denominator in all of them. I never found peace in the saving of lives. I found excitement and fulfillment in the actions, but I rarely would say I felt peace.

But I found peace in my nighttime prayers when I bowed in reverence and thankfulness in being used. I found peace in my quick prayers as I begged for help on the subway trains going to a dream's location. I found peace when I took my eyes off of me and focused them on Him.

I rolled my eyes and saw that I was fixating on me way too much in these dreams, when it wasn't ever about me. I was just a vessel trying to be used. Without the dreams I would just be another man going through life, oblivious of the accident around the corner.

I rolled over and stared at my alarm clock and tried to recite what I told myself in my dream.

"It's time to wake up, Solomon, and see. It's time to finally understand."

These dreams did save me. They saved me just as much as they saved the person I dreamed about. I rose out of bed with a renewed outlook.

CHAPTER 133

Veronica was sleeping soundly as her phone vibrated.

"It's too early," Wint moaned. "Just ignore it."

Veronica reached out and grabbed it without looking. "Hello."

"Did I wake you?" the familiar voice asked.

She looked at her phone and saw that it was her father, with whom she hadn't spoken in a few months.

"Actually, you did."

"I guess since you aren't working for me anymore, you're able to be lazy with no ambition."

"What do you want?" she asked with disdain.

"I am just calling to warn you to never try to poach one of my employees again."

"Poach one of your employees?" she repeated in disgust as she tasted her own morning breath. "I didn't poach anyone."

"I hear you and Gavyn McKenzie were in talks of forming some type of partnership."

"I will neither deny nor confirm that statement."

"Well, sorry to break it to you, hon, but Gavyn will not be joining your measly little establishment."

She didn't answer.

"I don't even see why you would be interested in such an incapable attorney to work alongside."

"Do you need anything else?"

"Just to warn you to not come after any more of my employees or former employees."

"Former employees? Father, you can't control your employees. And you definitely can't control your former employees. They have already left and they can do and choose whatever they wish."

"You may be right, but I am sure Gavyn will not be joining you in the near future."

"Where did you get this ludicrous information?"

"I have my sources. So be careful and don't ever say I never warned you."

"Warned me?" Veronica sat up in bed irritated and furious. "Warned me? Are you threatening me with some legal action? Because there is nothing you can do if one of your attorneys wishes to terminate their employment with your firm and come work with me."

Luther laughed egotistically. "What good attorney would choose you over me?"

"I did."

"I said *good* attorney."

"Goodbye, Father."

"Ask Winston about Gavyn. He'll tell you why he won't be joining your firm."

Luther ended the call as Veronica's head turned to her sleeping husband.

"Honey," she said nudging Wint on his side.

"What'd your dad want?" Wint asked without waking up or rolling over.

"He said for me to ask you about Gavyn. Do you know something?"

Wint rolled onto his back looking up into his wife's eyes and yawned. "A man named Gavyn who works for your father was murdered last night."

"He was murdered?"

"Yeah, were you close?" he asked smacking his lips as his drowsy eyes started to close.

She looked down at her sleeping husband and then at her phone, opening her text messages from yesterday. Gavyn had never responded

367

to any of her messages, nor had he ever called her back. She opened her browser and started composing an email to a realtor she had reached out to last night.

Please disregard my last email. I will not be looking into any new properties anytime soon. Thank you.

She sent the email and laid back down. She knew nothing was agreed upon with Gavyn, and her discussion had still been in the early stages, but there was something encouraging about having someone want to come work with her.

She didn't know why she felt like life had once again pulled the rug from underneath her since she wasn't even sure he would have been interested today. He never responded after their quick three-minute conversation. But it only took three minutes for her to realize she was missing something.

She wanted a partner.

She grabbed her phone and started looking through employees at Manfield & Hyde. She had never thought of poaching one of her father's employees, but now she wanted no one else but one of his. Just to show him she could do it.

And there wasn't anything he could do to stop her.

CHAPTER 134

Jenny was sitting in the holding chambers with a guard watching her from across the room.

"You know, you don't have to stay in here. The doors lock. I don't have a key, so it's pretty secure."

The guard looked at her and rolled his eyes.

"Fine, just stand there and watch me," she said as she paced around the room. "Are you single? Because I have some time to kill."

Milo walked through the door and greeted his client as the guard exited.

"See you soon, lover," she winked as the door closed.

Milo took a seat, but Jenny continued to stand, doing a few stretches while they waited.

"Where's Gavyn?" she asked while bending and touching her toes.

"Gavyn was killed last night," Milo answered shortly.

"Killed?" she asked with a hint of sadness in her voice.

"Yes, but nothing for you to worry about."

"I know," she said in a pouting voice as her lower lip doubled in size. "He was just pretty to look at."

"I will bring you a picture. Can we move on?"

"I guess there isn't any lost love between you two."

Milo looked across the table as if disciplining a child. "He did nothing for your case. He was just a body Luther provided to sit at the adults' table as if it were Obzhynki."

"Fine." Jenny finished her stretches and took a seat at the table. "You didn't...you know?"

"I didn't what?"

"You know." Jenny closed her eyes and stuck out her tongue and drooped her head to one side.

"Today we will call the last of our witnesses, and this afternoon the jury will probably start deliberating," Milo stated ignoring Jenny's insinuation of murdering Gavyn.

"I mean, if you did, I know you probably had a reasonable explanation."

Milo once again ignored her comment and started going over the list of witnesses for the morning. It wasn't very many people, but it should be enough to sway the jury to give a not guilty by reason of insanity verdict.

"Did he suffer?" she asked.

"I do not know," he finally answered, closing his folder of notes. "He was shot in the head."

"Not the head," she huffed. "Wait. Was it the back or front? Because morticians may still be able to fix him to show him off if it was the back of the head."

"Why does it matter?" he asked cruelly. "It's not like you'll be able to attend his funeral."

"Well, that was rude, Milo."

"Jenika, I am getting tired of this attitude of yours. You tried to sexualize Gavyn, but he never once looked at you in that way. And for good reason."

"Good reason? And what is that?"

"Because you're plain, Jenika. You look plain. You act plain. You sound plain. Men like Gavyn don't go after plain girls."

Jenny crossed her arms and stared at the ceiling after that comment. She didn't respond with a cruel remark or a cunning joke. She had spent her entire life feeling inadequate compared to the cheerleaders in the hallways. She wasn't even the cutest woman on her cellblock. She knew she was plain, but hearing someone else call her that was a little too much.

But she never showed her authentic emotions when someone hurt her. She just mentally logged it into her memory.

Milo may think she was plain, but she would get even with him one day. And then she would show him how intoxicatingly extraordinary she could be when she wanted to.

There was a knock on the door, giving them warning it was time to proceed to the courtroom.

"Ready, Jenika?"

"Can you please stop calling me Jenika?" she hissed. "I'm Jenny or Jennifer."

"As you wish." He stopped and leaned into her ear. "But never, ever, tell me what to do again. Or you'll wish you had died as easily as that pretty boy lawyer."

CHAPTER 135

I stood over the kitchen sink eating a bowl of stale Raisin Bran I should have thrown in the trash a week ago when the Nelsons called.

"Hello," I said with a mouthful, trying to swallow.

"Good morning, Solomon, this is Katrina Nelson," she started as if she had never spoken to me on the telephone. "We are fostering Will."

"Yes, Katrina, how are you all doing?"

"Well, I wanted you to know that I'm not sure how much longer Will is going to be with us."

"Oh, really. Is that a good thing?"

"Well, I guess his mother has sobered up and is asking for Will back," she said in a somber tone.

"Can she do that? She put him on someone's front porch and left," I said, feeling my temperature starting to rise.

"That's the foster care system. The courts usually send the children back to their homes if the parents want them. So he'll probably be going back to his mother sometime soon."

"That is crazy," I said, dropping my cereal bowl and splattering the remnants of milk and soggy flakes across my kitchen floor. "Crap!"

"I know. It's not a perfect system. I just hope she has gotten this out of her system, but based upon what I was just told, this wasn't the first time she's done something like this."

I grabbed some paper towels and started cleaning up my mess. "So the court will just look past this type of record and give the kid back to her?"

"I don't know," Katrina sighed. "Many parents just use their kids to get the government's aid and support, and if they don't have them, then their money is taken away. I hope Will's mother isn't using him like he is just a possession to get a free handout. But it wouldn't surprise me."

"Do you know how much longer you have with him?" I asked, scooping the cereal back into the bowl.

"I do not," she said heavily. "It could be today, it could be tomorrow, it could be in a month. It just depends on how quickly child services will complete the paperwork, and if any evaluations of his parents will be given."

I threw away the wad of used paper towels and wished I could throw away the mother the same way.

"Is there anything you need from me?"

"No," she said, deflated. "I just wanted to keep you updated. I will let you know if anything happens."

"Well, just show him some extra love."

Katrina laughed at that sentiment. "Oh, we are definitely doing that."

We ended our call and I felt like the world became a little more off balance. I looked down into the drain of the sink and felt like Will's world may be going down the drain as well. He deserved to be loved, not for a paycheck, but because he was a child that needed love.

I walked away from the sink and called Elizabeth. I needed to take my mind off Will, and the best way for me to do that was talking to my partner.

"So, have any dreams last night?"

"Did I ever," she answered as she started going through her laundry list of last night's dreams.

CHAPTER 136

Cooper tried calling Dakota to check on her when he first woke up, but it went straight to her voicemail. He tried to imagine how she was feeling, but he couldn't wrap his mind around the last twelve hours. He didn't expect to see her working today, which was going to be an awkward conversation in and of itself. He wondered how a police officer would call in for bereavement for a boyfriend who'd turned out to be a murderer. He didn't want to be Human Resources on that side of the phone conversation.

He walked into the precinct and asked another officer how Jordan and Collin were doing in their holding cells.

"Jordan's attorney just got here so they are talking now," Officer Clifton answered.

"Pretty quiet then?"

Officer Clifton laughed at that question. "Quiet? Those two screamed at one another through the night."

"Jordan still not talking to us?"

"He's not talking to us, but he had plenty to say to Collin last night."

"I bet he did."

Cooper walked away and headed to his desk as Chief Johnson caught him in the hallway.

"Cooper, see me in my office."

"Yes, sir," Cooper said, following his boss down the hall. Chief Johnson was a large, burly man who was as intimidating as he looked. But he had taken the young officer under his wing a few years after seeing something different in him. Winston tried to chitchat with him, but he wasn't having any of it this morning. He sat down as Johnson closed the door.

"Tell me what happened last night, Cooper."

"We apprehended Stewart Weatherby, who was involved in the deaths earlier this week after his partner Grant Harper murdered Gavyn McKenzie and his wife, Whitney Harper. Collin Diaz fled the scene, and as we were talking to him, he let us know that Stewart and Grant killed Ted Lukins and Jake Hill earlier this week. We brought Stewart in for questioning, and I don't know what happened, but he stabbed himself with a pen. We tried to stop him."

Cooper looked at Chief Johnson who sat at his desk with his hands folded in thought under his chin. He waited for Johnson to say something, but he didn't, so he continued with his story.

"Collin said that his friend Jordan Lee was involved in some killings from last April. Then Collin started telling everything he knew. Jordan never confessed to anything but asked for an attorney."

Johnson looked at Cooper and pursed his lips. "So you're saying Stewart grabbed a pen on the table and jabbed himself in the neck as you and Robbins watched?"

"Did you watch the tape, Chief?"

"I did, Cooper. And I want to side with you, but you left the pen sitting there."

Cooper's heart froze and all the air in his lungs vanished. He felt the room spinning, but he'd had no reason to believe Stewart was going to kill himself. All he had was his word.

"But Chief, how many times do we remove all pens from the interrogation room? We keep them in there to get them to write their accounts all the time. If I thought Stewart was going to kill himself, I would have taken precautions."

Chief Johnson studied Cooper before speaking again.

"Young said--" he started before Cooper interrupted.

"Young is a--"

Chief Johnson stopped him. "Detective Young outranks you, Officer Cooper, so I would watch my tongue if I were you."

"Yes, sir," Cooper said as he took in a deep breath.

"Young said you were laughing about Stewart's death and saying it was no big deal since he was guilty."

"Chief, you know me better than that," Cooper shot out trying to keep his rage in check. "Ask Robbins or Chris, or even ask Dakota. They'll tell you the truth."

"And that is another thing, Cooper. Officer Peterson has asked to be transferred."

Cooper leaned his head back taking in another deep breath. "Chief, I understand Dakota is upset since I was the one who was going to have to arrest her boyfriend, and I can see why she would want to not be around me. She probably feels embarrassed for dating a criminal for the last six months."

"She didn't sound embarrassed," Chief added. "She was telling me about some of your antics that were borderline unethical and possibly criminal."

"Unethical? Criminal?" Cooper stammered in shock. "What did she say? Chief, I hate to sound sexist, but she is a scorned woman who isn't thinking clearly right now."

"Cooper, I don't see gender in my position. Officer Peterson is a fine member of this department who has shown some great potential partnering with you this last year. But for some reason, she is bringing up some questionable accusations that we are going to need to look into with a thorough investigation."

"Investigation?" Cooper choked out.

"Officer Cooper, effective immediately, please surrender your badge and gun until the investigation is complete."

Cooper's hands started to shake as he looked across the desk at his mentor. He stood up and handed over his gun before he looked down at the badge he had always worn proudly. He couldn't believe this was happening as he pulled it off his shirt. He held it in his hand

and looked down at his number, thinking of all it symbolized. He wanted to throw the badge across the desk, but he also wanted to remain dignified. Someone may be trying to malign his character, but he wasn't going to give them an inch in that smear campaign.

He laid the badge down on Chief Johnson's desk who reached across and slid it into his drawer.

"You are not on probation, Cooper. You can work at your desk on some cases I will give you, or you can take some time off until they finish their investigation."

Cooper looked at the ceiling and didn't know what to think. He lowered his eyes to look at the chief.

"If you were me, what would you do, Chief?"

"As your superior, I advise you to take the time off and let them do their investigation. And then when you are cleared you can come back to work."

Cooper nodded his head and was about to speak.

"But as your friend, I wouldn't give Young the satisfaction. It's easier to talk behind someone's back when they aren't nearby. If it were me, I would watch him like a hawk. Don't let him walk all over your name, Cooper. You're better than that."

Cooper held his head high and his shoulders back. "So what case do you want me to work on first?"

CHAPTER 137

Elizabeth explained her dream, which sounded vaguely familiar to mine with one slight difference.

"You said you saw a little boy?"

"Yeah, why?" Elizabeth asked.

"Because I didn't see a little boy."

"Are you saying we dreamed the same dream?"

"Abusive man with tattoos on his face?" I asked.

"Yeah."

"Apartment 211 with slanted numbers?"

"Yeah. This is really freaky. But how in the world are we going to find this apartment to save this poor woman with thousands of apartments in the area? It's like a needle in a poor man's haystack."

"Because I live in the poor man's haystack."

"What?"

"Elizabeth, the apartment is literally just around the corner from mine. I found it last night."

"Wait, it's in your building? See, Solo, I told you that you need to move."

"That's not the point."

"It may not be the point of the dream, but it supports what I have been telling you for the last year. You need to move out of that crap heap and live somewhere safer."

"I saw them." I poked my head out of my apartment and looked down the hallway seeing the sunlight shining through the windows as the hallway light continued to flicker.

"When?"

"Last night when I was checking out the apartment. I was standing in front of their place when he walked up behind me. He looked annoyed because I was standing in his way. Then I saw her behind him. But they didn't have a kid." I closed the door and walked back across my apartment and collapsed in a chair.

"In my dream there was a kid standing in a doorway."

"Okay, I have to go take some employee pictures for a job and then I'm meeting Jeremiah for lunch. Do you want to come by my place after lunch and we can go check on her together? Maybe this isn't the first time he's going to beat her and we can try to convince her to leave."

"Solo, did you see how he hit her?" Elizabeth scoffed. "This wasn't his first rodeo of beating up the defenseless clown."

"Don't call her a clown," I defended.

"That's not what I meant, and you know it."

"I'm just saying you're going to have to be extra sensitive this afternoon. And not your--"

"Not my typical self?" she asked with an attitude.

"If she's been abused for a while, your sarcasm isn't going to get through to her."

"If she's been beaten like a dog for years, your compassion isn't going to sway her either."

"Point taken," I said.

"And Solo?"

"Yeah."

"I'm serious about getting out of that rat hole."

"I know. I know," I said looking around at the dingy carpet and cracked windows. "But for once living here has been beneficial."

"Once and only once," she added before ending her call.

CHAPTER 138

The courtroom was solemn as Judge Otto announced the passing of Gavyn McKenzie. A couple of the jury members even shed a few tears over the news. Judge Otto asked if the defense needed any additional time to conclude their trial, and Milo politely declined the offer.

"No need, Your Honor. We are ready to proceed," Milo said with confidence as he called his first witness for the day.

Finn looked baffled by Milo's lack of sympathy, but based upon rumors in the attorney's circle, the lack of emotions seemed characteristically appropriate.

Jenny sat at the defense table unflinching as Milo called a proverbial revolving door of witnesses to testify about Jenny's lack of emotional stability and mental decline. For each witness, Finn would try to ask a few rebuttal questions to dismantle their claims. And then they would exit the stand and another specialist would be called.

Milo was in top form as if shaking off the memory of Gavyn's appearance at the table actually rejuvenated him to do his best.

Finn tried his best to keep up, scribbling notes and tidbits of questions to ask, but no matter what he asked or how he asked it, he never got Milo's witnesses to crack. It was as if he had coerced each of them to give their testimony.

Finn looked over at the defense table and wondered how Gavyn died. Was it a car accident? Was he murdered? Was he just a pawn in Jenny's case to gain some sympathy by the jurors? Because he could see Milo eliminating Gavyn with a simple telephone call if it bettered his case and his client's prognosis.

That assumption caused Finn to shake in his black loafers. He hoped Gavyn didn't rub Milo the wrong way and was ultimately collateral damage for saying the wrong thing or not providing enough legal knowledge to better the case. But he knew with Milo, anything was possible.

He glanced over at Jenny who sat looking drugged. He hoped that if she was mentally insane, the mental institution would be beneficial. But he hoped that if she wasn't crazy, the jury would see through the charade. He gazed at Jenny, and even though he was seeing her as a psychotic killer, he was fearful the jury would just see her as psychotic who had been dealt a rough hand.

"Mr. Garrett!" Judge Otto shouted, banging his gavel.

"Uh, yes, Your Honor," Finn said waking up from his trance.

"Do you want to ask any questions to the witness or should we move along?"

Finn looked down at his scribbles that looked more like random games of tic-tac-toe than legible words. He rose and asked the same questions he had of the previous witnesses. He learned nothing new and worse, the jury looked bored with his line of questioning as well.

CHAPTER 139

Jordan's attorney Chuck Whitmore walked out of the jail with five pages of notes from their discussion. He stood in the shade while he flipped open his tablet and started reading the notes, making sure he didn't misconstrue or misunderstand anything. But he was sure he hadn't. His client was clearly guilty.

"You have to be honest with me, Jordan," Chuck had said after a few minutes of talking. "Did you really kill Piper Michaelson?"

Jordan didn't answer. He looked away and stared into the corner of the small, white room.

"Jordan, you need to answer my questions. I can't help you if you don't answer all my questions truthfully."

"What does attorney-client privilege really mean?" Jordan asked, turning his face toward Mr. Whitmore.

"It basically means, anything you tell me, and I mean *anything*, I cannot tell anyone." Chuck looked at his client noticing a similar expression he had seen hundreds of times before.

"So, just speaking off the record like two friends, if I tell you something that is damaging towards me, you cannot go to the cops and tell them?"

"Yes, that is correct," Chuck nodded as he held his ink pen in his hand, ready to take down his notes. "So I'll ask you again, did you kill Piper Michaelson?"

"Can we start with some lighter questions first?"

"Lighter?" Chuck echoed with a grin. "Sure. It's all billable hours. We will go at whatever speed you want."

Chuck started asking questions about Jordan's childhood, how he became friends with Collin and the rest of the gang, where they went to school, and other background questions.

"Did the four of you create a kill list?"

"Yes."

"See," Chuck commended with a warm smile. "This isn't that bad."

Jordan's face twitched as if trying to smile, but Chuck never saw one.

"Did you write Piper Michaelson's name on the list?"

"Yes." Jordan answered the question with one word as if it was his last breath.

Chuck looked down at the allegations written out by the police. "Did Grant kill Sabrina Latener?"

"Yes."

He once again looked down at the allegations. "Did Collin try to kill Fiona Sanchez?"

"Yes."

"Did you kill Piper Michaelson?"

"Yes."

Chuck looked across the table at his client and laid down his pen. "Okay, I'm going to be honest with you, it doesn't look good."

"But you can get me off, right? I mean, that's what you do. I heard you got my friend Julio off on his drug charge."

Chuck smiled and shook his head. "I got your friend's charges dropped because the police didn't have any probable cause for searching his vehicle."

"So what does that mean about me? You can still get me off, right?"

Chuck stood up and shook his client's hand. "I will be back after thinking over this case."

"Wait, what do you mean, thinking over?" Jordan snapped. "You got Julio off and you can get me off. He said you were the best."

Chuck looked at his client and shook his head. "Flattery doesn't get you anywhere in here."

"But Julio said--"

Chuck waved off the statement. "I will be back this afternoon to discuss some plea agreements. Maybe by pleading guilty to the murder we can shorten the sentence. For some good news, D.C. doesn't have the death penalty, so that is one thing you don't have to worry about."

"Pleading guilty?" Jordan jumped up, slamming his fists on the table. "Why am I paying you if you're just going to make me plead guilty? I want you to get me off!"

Chuck stood up and knocked on the door to leave. "I'll be in touch."

When Chuck got to the last page of his notes and saw nothing left out after replaying the conversation in his memory, he tucked them back into his bag.

"Get him off?" He laughed at the audacity of the killer's statement as he stepped off the curb and walked through the police parking lot. "I'm not Houdini."

CHAPTER 140

I was running a little behind for lunch with Jeremiah as my morning schedule didn't go as planned. I would have rather taken school portraits for kindergarteners than for the employees of Cistotech. They were rude. They were late. They were convinced I didn't know what I was doing. As I took a few of their pictures, I knew I could ruin their year by plastering a God-awful picture on their name badge. A name badge they would have to wave around for the next 365 days. I weighed the pros and cons and decided being paid for this annual gig was better than getting even with a few of the millennials.

"Solo!" Jeremiah beamed as his face quickly frowned. "You don't look too good."

"I'm just great!" I said sarcastically with a forced smile. "I don't know how you deal with college students all day long. I just left a job and I literally wanted to smack a few of them."

Jeremiah started to laugh. "You're too young to talk like a boomer, my friend."

"I'm not a boomer," I defended.

"You don't have to be offended. I may not be old enough to be considered one, but I side more with that generation than the coming one."

I stared at him annoyed as I, too, felt old after the morning of snowflake snapshots. "Can't we come up with a cooler name than boomer?"

"But it's not supposed to be a cool thing," he added. "It's supposed to be derogatory. Of course, if you claim ownership of it, it loses its sting. Look at the slurs from the past. Some groups of people have taken ownership of the very words that used to offend them, and as a result, the words have lost their power."

"Like being call a nerd in high school."

Jeremiah smiled as he straightened his glasses. "Or still."

"Jeremiah, I wouldn't call you a nerd."

"I wasn't talking about me, you boomer nerd," he chuckled as the waitress came over and took our drink order.

"So how are you doing?" I asked. "You're more comical than normal."

He lifted his eyes from the menu. "Eugene isn't doing too well this morning."

"Not doing well?" I asked shocked. "I just saw him. He seemed to be doing fine."

"Yeah, he was good earlier this week, but something happened yesterday and," he stopped and accepted his water from the waitress. "He's not doing well."

"I'm sorry, man."

He nodded as he looked down at his menu. I watched as he read and contemplated each option, but I mostly looked at him with sympathy in not having any faith during this difficult time. I had just met Eugene last year when we struck up a quick friendship centered on faith. Whereas Eugene and Jeremiah had been friends from childhood, centered on pure friendship despite all of their differences. They hardly had a common ground between them in their thoughts. But their small island of brotherly love kept them closer than most friendships.

"How are--"

But Jeremiah cut me off before I could express my concern again. "I'm thinking of getting the chicken." He smiled, ignoring my look of condolence. "That sounds good."

I noted the change in attitude and I followed the current like a fish in the water. "Have you eaten at the chicken and waffle place up around Manor Park?"

"No, how was it?"

"Well," I grinned with a childish look, "even Elizabeth enjoyed it."

He nodded in appreciation. "I may have to check this place out."

We ordered our food and started to dive once again into our usual topics of conversation.

"You remember how I asked about possession this week?"

He nodded as I realized that was a clumsy segue to the topic I really wanted to discuss over lunch.

"Well, I asked it because I wondered if Jenny was possessed."

"What do you think?"

I considered the question and saw the ripple effects of each answer. If she was possessed, then it would be my faithful duty to help her remedy the possession through exorcism. If she wasn't possessed, then either she was truly mentally crazy and belonged in a facility instead of a prison. Or, she wasn't crazy and she was just evil and belonged in a prison for sure. But what if that, in turn, cycled back to being possessed, because could someone really be that evil?

"I see your wheels spinning," Jeremiah said. "Where are they taking you?"

"I don't know," I said shaking my head. "I really don't know. I want to believe she isn't possessed because that would help me sleep at night. Because if I'm truly honest, thinking of someone being possessed scares the bejesus out of me."

"In your faith, that would be a frightening realization to see how someone could be possessed. You could then rationalize if they could be possessed, then you could as well."

I shook my head. "No, that doesn't scare me. I don't have any fear of that because I believe I cannot be possessed."

Jeremiah listened intently as he leaned his elbows on the table. "Then why does it scare you?"

"I guess it's the whole underlying weightiness of the unseen."

"How so? Does the concept of gravity unnerve you? Because you can't see that."

"I may not see gravity, but I see the effects of it," I said as I threw a piece of bread into the air, catching it with my other hand.

"But in your belief, you see the effects of the evil forces, too, through selfish acts, murderous crimes, and corruptible governments."

I looked into space and understood his reasoning, but there was still something different. "It's just not the same."

"How so?"

"I wish I knew," I grinned. "I wish I knew."

"But you can know," he stated defiantly. "If you want to know, you should be able to figure it out. Isn't that what your faith is there for? To believe in things you cannot tangibly see? So technically speaking, you should have the upper hand over my analytical point of view."

"Faith doesn't work like that," I said flatly.

He looked at me quizzically. "Then what do you have faith in? Because if your faith is rooted in the belief in a supernatural being that was the reason for the initial introduction and will be the end all of all things, shouldn't this being also be in control of everything that happens from the beginning to the end? Even the things that scare you?"

I listened to his questions and it stung how he was pointing out the flaws in my own faith. In just a matter of minutes, he was able to break through the plastic veil and see the corruption in my heart.

"Solomon, I'm not trying to sell you on a particular thought or point you in one direction. I'm just showing you that your compass that you say is broken, really isn't broken. You're just using it wrong."

I smiled at him facetiously. "You're going to help me with my faith?"

"Why do you question that?" Jeremiah shrugged. "I may not believe in your rationalization of faith, but I can help you ask the questions that will help you find it."

I listened.

"Once again, what do you have faith in?"

CHAPTER 141

Wint sat at his desk and stewed over his probation, trying to recall anything that he should be worried about.

Are you on probation? he texted to Officer Robbins.

Probation? No. Why?

That reply was bittersweet. Wint looked around the room checking to see if he had any unknown enemies watching his every move. He didn't feel the uneasiness of someone spying on him, but he wasn't sure anymore.

Because I am.

What? Why?

He read the message and wondered if Robbins was playing him as well. Maybe he had struck a deal to keep his badge if he could infiltrate the information out of him.

Young.

Don't worry about him, man. You did nothing wrong. I was right there and we couldn't stop him. Just Young being Young.

Dakota too. Wint typed his response as he got up from his desk. He had somewhere he needed to go. He needed to find out why he was being cornered.

Your partner?

Ex-partner. He hated to type those words, but it was true. Dakota was a good partner. She was young and determined, just like he was. He thought she had his back, but it seemed like that was just an illusion.

Wint got into his car and drove to her apartment. He knew he should give her some time after they had turned her world upside down, but his world was flipping as well. And he wasn't going to sit around and let everything he had worked for collapse without a fight.

He imagined the conversation as he drove, and it seemed like the scenario changed at each intersection he crossed. In one she was livid, in another she was remorseful, in another she was apologetic, in another she was passionate, and in another she was cynical. It seemed like each scene he played out in his head was possible.

He pulled into her parking lot and found her car parked under the light. He took a few deep breaths before he got out of his car and walked with his head held high in the uniform he would die for. With each step, his confidence got stronger. His emotions were more in check. His mind was clear of all the confusion from the morning.

He knocked and waited until he heard footsteps beyond the door. But it didn't open, and Dakota didn't say a word.

"Dakota, I know you are in there. I saw your car and I heard you by the door."

Still she didn't respond.

Wint stood in an awkward position in their relationship. He was her partner, but he was also the cop who brought in her boyfriend for questioning. Questioning that ultimately caused him to kill himself. This wasn't a typical situation discussed in weekly staff meetings.

"Dakota, I know you are upset. And I'm truly sorry for your loss," he started as he wondered if he should say what he wanted to say or just let it be. "But Stewart killed those people." He couldn't let it be. It had to be said. "And their families deserved true closure for their deaths."

Still Dakota didn't say a word.

Wint didn't know if she had walked away from the door or if she was still standing inches away.

"I just wanted to check on you, Dakota. You are first and foremost my friend. A friend who is going through something horrible right now, and I just wanted you to know that I'm here for you."

Once again, Wint heard nothing.

He placed his hand on the door, feeling the hardness, wondering if her heart was just as hard. "And I'm sorry I was the one who got mixed up in all of this."

Wint longed to hear Dakota's voice. He didn't care if she didn't open the door, but he wanted to just hear her say something. Anything.

"The chief took my badge away this morning." As anger started pushing into him, he paused to fight it back down. This wasn't about him. "And he told me you didn't want to be my partner anymore." He hung his head at those words because he knew he would do anything for her. But sadly, she couldn't see that.

"I just wanted you to know that you were a superb partner, and I'm going to miss riding along with you."

Cooper stood frozen and considered apologizing, but he knew it would be a lie. He wasn't sorry for questioning Stewart on the deaths of Ted Lukin or Jake Hill. He wasn't sorry for taking him into custody under false pretenses surrounding Grant's murderous suicide. And he definitely wasn't sorry for doing his job.

He stepped back and felt at peace for saying what he wanted to say and not saying what she wanted to hear. He looked at her apartment door and knew this would probably be the last time he would stand in this spot. On the drive to her apartment he felt confused and disoriented. But standing at her door, he realized he shouldn't feel regret for her decisions.

He walked away from Dakota's apartment wondering if she had even heard what he had said. Ultimately, her attitude wasn't going to change with a few kind words. He said what he wanted to say, and he felt really good.

Cooper knew his character and integrity would shine through the investigation. He also knew he had nothing to worry about if Young was involved on the opposing side of this so-called scandal. He was pretty sure Young's lack of character and integrity would radiate through the investigation.

He would have his badge back soon.

CHAPTER 142

"Why do you ask what I have faith in? You know my faith is in Jesus," I answered unabashedly as I stared at Jeremiah with confusion.

"You say that your faith is in Jesus, but from where I'm sitting, you're holding your faith more tightly in your own belief and understanding than in the one you say you have faith in."

"What?" I shook my head in disagreement as I started to question his intent in this conversation. "I don't know what you're talking about. You know my beliefs, so how can you say that about me?"

He shrugged his shoulders and looked closely at me. "Because I'm not freaked out by the possession conundrum. It actually fascinates me."

"That is just weird." I couldn't look at Jeremiah anymore. I didn't know if he was mocking me or if he actually thought the idea of possessions were truly fascinating. But deep down, I knew he was being coy. He was seeing a part of me I wasn't able to see in myself. And that scared me.

"Why does my opinion on the matter affect you so much, Solomon?" He stopped and took a sip of his drink. "Is it because you can't even look at the topic you are fearful of? Thus calling my scholarly intrigue strange?"

I pondered his question. I couldn't answer why I was feeling so rattled with his odd fascination, but he could point out something I found awe-inspiring and consider me odd in return. I didn't want to side with him, but maybe I was misconstruing my faith in Christ for knowledge I had obtained.

"Maybe you're right. Maybe I'm struggling with the concept of possessions because I don't understand it." He eyed me approvingly as I waved it off. "But I don't know how to not struggle with it."

"Then it goes back to my fundamental question. What do you have faith in?" he asked as I started to roll my eyes. "Now hear me out, okay?"

I nodded my head and focused.

"You say your belief is in Jesus, but what if your picture of Jesus is skewed?"

"Skewed?"

"Close your eyes and picture what Jesus looks like."

I closed my eyes and let my mind drift to an image of what I thought my savior looked like.

"Do you have an image?" I nodded my head. "Now just imagine if Jesus walked into the restaurant right now. Do you think he would look like what you see in your head?"

"No," I said opening my eyes.

"Keep your eyes closed," he commanded. "So you believe the image of Jesus you have is probably not correct because you probably took the image in your mind from maybe a picture you saw at one time. A picture that was painted hundreds maybe even a thousand years after his death. You agree that your image of Jesus is not correct because no one in the last two thousand years really knew what Jesus looked like."

"Okay," I said still with my eyes closed.

"So just listen to me. Your faith is grounded on what you think you know. Not on Jesus."

My face furrowed at that comment as I still could not agree with it.

"If you know the image you concocted of Jesus isn't right, is it safe to assume there are aspects of Jesus' character that you may not have right?"

"Maybe," I winced as I continued to keep my eyes sealed shut.

"Then is your faith in Jesus based upon what you have read or heard, or is it based upon the true character of Jesus?"

"I still don't see what you're getting at, Jeremiah," I said with my eyes closed. "All I know about Jesus is what I know."

"Good. So going a step further, what if there are pieces of Jesus you don't know? Do you still have faith in that Jesus?"

"Yeah. I have faith in the whole Jesus, not just the pieces of him I know."

"Alright. Then think about this. You have a distorted image of the physical Jesus. You may have a distorted image of the character of Jesus. Therefore, would you say your faith in Jesus is not in the true Jesus, but the Jesus you want him to be?"

I opened my mouth to talk as Jeremiah continued.

"Your faith showcases Jesus' love. You see the miracles he performed. You know of his teachings. But what if your image of Jesus is skewed into an image of him you want and not the image of the real Jesus? The real Jesus who said things you may not like because it is truly hard to follow. The real Jesus that did things that may look crazy because if given a choice you probably wouldn't follow him today.

"Look closely, Solo. When you see the Jesus you follow, is he everything you want to be?"

I nodded my head. "Yeah, yeah he is."

"I'm sorry to tell you," he started in a compassionate voice. "But you're not following the real Jesus then. Because there should be things that Jesus did that you don't agree with."

"Huh?"

"You can open your eyes now," he said as I looked down and saw the waitress had slid my plate before me. "You're possessing an idol image of what you want Jesus to look like, because if you were truly honest with yourself, the real Jesus should probably scare you."

"Scare me?"

"He scared the Jews enough at the time to want him dead."

"But they were…" I started, but I couldn't finish my sentence.

"They were blinded to who Jesus was," he added. "They couldn't see the positive things because they were so focused on only seeing what they wanted to see. Just as you are so focused on only seeing what you want to see. Thus when you come face to face with some of your fears, it's not that you can't see Jesus overcoming your fears, it's just that you can't see yourself overcoming them. Thus, you have made Jesus to look like you with everything you think is good."

I looked down at my plate and wondered if Jeremiah was right.

I recalled hearing Eugene say to me, "If you agree with everything you read in the Bible, then you aren't reading it the right way. Because God's ways are higher than your ways, Solomon. And his reasoning is above yours. So if you agree with everything, then you are agreeing with your manmade image of God and not the real God."

I raised my head up as those words shot to my heart. I couldn't say anything as Jeremiah watched me from across the table. "Do you think I'm a fraud?"

Jeremiah smiled as he shook his head. "Solomon, you are no fraud. You were just a lost man holding your compass wrong."

My lips started to quiver. "I don't want to be a lost man."

Jeremiah nodded his head encouragingly. "I know, Solomon."

I stared at Jeremiah who started to cut his chicken as a wave of emotions crashed into me. "Do you feel like a lost man?"

Jeremiah looked up, chewing a piece of his chicken and swallowing before he responded. "I don't feel lost, Solomon," he said flatly. "But I also don't feel found. And if I'm truly honest, I don't know if I could tell the difference."

"I feel a little lost right now," I said pressing my lips together.

"That's a good sign, Solomon," Jeremiah nodded. "Because a lost man will ask for direction, but an indifferent man doesn't even know to ask."

"So you're indifferent?"

He nodded his head as he cut another piece of chicken. "Do you still feel a heaviness with the possession aspect of your faith?"

I smiled and started to laugh. "Possessions are the least of my worries right now."

"What's at the top?"

I let that question float in the air because I wouldn't say I was worried about finding the true Christ. Let's say, I was more determined in finding him.

Stabbing a piece of my pasta, I tasted the tanginess of the peppery marinara sauce and looked across the table. I couldn't put my finger on it, but Jeremiah had a different look.

I prayed for God to somehow use Jeremiah's own words to convict him to seek the savior. I didn't want to say, but one of my top worries was Jeremiah. Just as he said, being indifferent was a very lonely place to be.

CHAPTER 143

"Nice of you to finally show up," Elizabeth said, getting out of her vehicle in front of my apartment building.

"Why didn't you just go on in? You know where I hide my key."

She raised her right eyebrow and looked ahead at my apartment building. "How many times do I have to say this? You live in a meth addict's paradise, and I'm not ready to die."

I shook off her insult and walked towards the apartment building.

"There is a lunatic on your floor who likes to beat women." She stopped and spread her arms. "Do I look like a man?"

"Want me to answer truthfully?" I smiled as she flipped me off. We walked in silence up the stairs. "I'm seriously thinking of putting in an offer."

"Solomon! You've only looked at one house. You need to shop around. See what you like. See what fits."

"But I liked that one." I fumbled around with my keys unlocking my apartment door and holding it open for Elizabeth as she sauntered in like an heiress.

"You would have liked a slumlord's hostel if it had a front porch swing."

"It really was a nice swing," I grinned, once again ignoring her insult.

She pulled out her phone and started searching the internet as she leaned back on my sunken couch, eyeing me as she readjusted the somewhat decorative pillows and cushions. "Just please humor me and look through some homes for sale in this area."

"In *this* area?" I asked shocked as I gestured around me.

"God no. Not in this neighborhood, but you know what I mean, twerp."

"Fine."

Elizabeth pulled up a few realtor websites and showed me some pictures of homes in a comparable price range as the one in Manor Park. I scrolled through the photos as we started to devise a loose plan.

"Do you know if she works?" Elizabeth asked.

"I have no idea."

"So she could be there now?"

"Possibly."

"What about the man? Do you know if he's there?"

I shrugged my shoulders as I did my due diligence in looking through the real estate property.

"You are no good, you know that?" she huffed as she tried and failed to stand up.

"How much have you had to drink this morning?" I asked jumping up and helping her.

"Not enough to endure that botched mistake for a couch."

"It's comfortable," I laughed laying down her phone. "It molds to my body like a glove."

"Well, your couch almost assaulted me like O.J., no glove needed."

"Anyway. Want to go stake out the joint?"

"Don't ever say 'joint', Solo. It just doesn't sound right coming out of your straight-laced mouth."

"Joint. Joint. Joint." We walked out of my apartment down the hallway with the flickering light overhead.

"Oh, yeah, that really sounds much better."

"I can say it in an Irish accent if you like?"

"I'll pass," she said as we approached the end of the hall that converged into the other hallway. We both stopped and looked toward apartment 211. "Want to do the honors? I just sanitized my hands."

I rolled my eyes as I proceeded down the hall with Elizabeth close behind me. I looked at the slanting numbers and hoped this was going to turn out better than yesterday's bloodbath.

Knock. Knock. Knock.

CHAPTER 144

"Who's there?" a woman's voice asked from behind the door.

Elizabeth pushed me from behind to answer, causing me to almost hit my head on the door.

"My name is Solomon Davis and I live just around the corner. This is my friend Elizabeth Hyde."

"Why'd you give her my real name?" she hissed from behind.

I shook her off and continued. "We just wanted to come by and talk with you."

"Talk to me?" she asked still behind the locked door.

"Yes, is your husband home?" I asked.

"He's not my husband," she said weakly.

"Okay, sorry, is your boyfriend home?"

"No, he's at work."

"Well, we just wanted to check on you and your son," I said looking behind me, hoping Elizabeth's dream was correct.

She didn't answer, but I could hear the chain on the lock moving and tapping against the wood. Finally, the last lock turned. She opened the door and stood in a pair of gray sweats.

"How'd you know about my kid?"

"I've seen him come and go," I lied.

"You've seen him?" she quizzed. "You've seen him come and go?"

My eyes darted to the side, trying to see Elizabeth, but she wasn't in my periphery.

"He's not a creeper if that's what you're worried about," Elizabeth chimed in.

The woman stood cross-armed in the doorway, trying to look confident, but it was just an illusion she was trying to play. I looked into her eyes and saw a frail, scared woman. Her head jerked when she heard a sound coming from the hall.

Elizabeth tried to calm her. "It's okay, we're here to help."

She looked uncertain as she combed her fingers through her long black hair. I could see she wanted to trust us, but she didn't know if she could.

"You can trust us," I said. "We're not going to hurt you. We just want to protect you and your son from your boyfriend."

"He's a good man," she defended as she crossed her arms, rubbing them nervously.

"A good man wouldn't hurt either of you," Elizabeth added with a warm smile. "We can try to get you some help, but we can't do it without you."

She stood still, looking up and down the hall.

I turned to look at Elizabeth who shrugged her shoulders as we waited in silence in the hallway.

She finally took a step back into her apartment and welcomed us into her home.

I let Elizabeth enter first, and she leaned in and hugged the trembling woman. "You are safe with us," she said defiantly as if arming the petrified woman for battle. "We will not let anything happen to you."

We walked into the same living room I had seen in my dream as she quickly turned off the television and offered us both a seat on the couch.

"When will your son get home from school?" Elizabeth asked as she looked around at the home's meager décor.

"He doesn't go to school," she answered.

"Oh, do you home-school him?" Elizabeth asked.

"I guess you can say that," she answered, looking around her place for a spot to hide. "Why do you think I need help?"

Elizabeth looked at me to take the lead. I couldn't tell her the truth, but I had to say something.

"I've heard things about your boyfriend in the building, and I just couldn't stand by and do nothing. And then today…" I stopped and then looked around the room and saw a portrait of her and her child laying sideways on the floor partially behind the television stand. "Do you ever just get a feeling that something bad is going to happen?"

I stood up and walked over to the picture and picked it up. I turned it around. "Is this your son?"

She nodded as she continued to remain strong.

I turned around to Elizabeth and smiled and then looked once again to the unsure woman on the couch.

"Your son isn't here, correct?"

She lowered her head and shook it ashamed.

"But he'll be home today," I said. "Will's going to be home today."

"How'd you know his name?" she asked as she lifted her head.

I looked down at the picture of the child I'd found on the front porch a couple of days ago, who was now safely living in the Nelson's home. I was starting to see the full picture and realizing the idea I concocted in my head of a selfish mother leaving her child may not be the accurate image. I remembered Jeremiah's words and thought once again, I might have gotten the image wrong.

CHAPTER 145

I looked at the portrait of the mother and son. She was smiling proudly, looking at her son with warmth and love. He stared blankly into the camera, yet his eyes had a sparkle.

"I found Will a couple of days ago."

The mother started to cry as years of abuse and silence broke through her calloused shell of a body. "I was afraid he would hurt him." She crumbled on the couch as Elizabeth rushed to her side, brushing her black hair with comfort and compassion. "I didn't want to," she started as she looked up into my eyes. "I didn't know what else to do."

"Did your boyfriend threaten him?" I asked setting the picture down on the television stand.

She nodded her head as tears streamed down her cheeks.

"Does he hurt you?" I asked, stooping down beside the couch so we were at eye level. "Does he hurt you?"

Her lips quivered at the personal question. She didn't say a word as she broke away from Elizabeth's grasp.

"It's okay," Elizabeth started as she looked at me. "I don't even know your name."

The scared woman stood up and took a few steps into the middle of the living room with her back to us. She took a deep breath as she carefully raised her gray sweatshirt exposing her back with black bruises in the shape of fists.

She turned around in silence as she rolled up her sleeves, showing grip marks on her wrists. She didn't look at us, but stared at the blank wall behind the couch as she showed us the secrets hidden underneath her clothing.

"It's Kendall," she said looking away from the cracked paint in the wall and training her eyes on Elizabeth. "My name is Kendall."

"Nice to meet you, Kendall," Elizabeth said standing up and taking her hand, guiding her back to the safe confines of the couch. "You don't have to live like this."

She nodded her head as more tears flowed. She looked over at me with wide eyes. "He always apologizes."

"He doesn't mean it," Elizabeth said holding Kendall's hand like they were lifetime friends instead of two women who had just met minutes earlier.

"But he promised he won't do it again," Kendall smiled wiping away her tears. "That's why I contacted the police to get Will back."

"Has he promised to never hurt you before?" I asked.

She lowered her head. "But he means it this time."

"He doesn't mean it, Kendall," Elizabeth said rubbing her hand. "That's what they do. They hurt. Beg for forgiveness. And then hurt again. Then beg again."

"But what if it's real this time?" she asked.

I looked at Kendall and thought again of Jeremiah's words. She had the ideal image of the boyfriend she wanted. She couldn't see the reality he displayed every day.

"But what if it's not?" Elizabeth asked back. "Do you really want to put Will in that situation? He's a little boy who needs his mom to take care of him."

She caught her face in her trembling hands as tears fell through the cracks of her fingers.

"I can't leave," she cried as she raised her head up. "I don't have anywhere I can go."

"There are places you can go," Elizabeth answered as she tenderly rolled down Kendall's sleeve. "You're not alone in this."

"I don't have a job," she added as her tears flowed more heavily. "I don't have a place to live. I have no way of paying for anything."

"Don't you worry about that," I said with an optimistic smile still crouching beside the couch. "Reliance shouldn't keep you in a dangerous situation."

"But he'll find me." Her eyes widened in fear as the tears vanished. "You don't know Nolan. He will come after me like he owns me."

"Well, you are not his to own!" Elizabeth declared with feminine rage. "You are a strong, independent mother who can fend for herself like all the other single mothers out there. You are not his possession. And you are definitely not going to continue to live under his roof and depend on his money."

"Have you ever reported him to the police?" I asked as I moved from the floor to beside her on the couch. "Do they have any record of any domestic abuse?"

She shook her head no.

"Well," I said coming up with an idea. "If you are ready to leave him and take care of Will, we can help you. But we can't make this decision for you. You have to do it and follow through with it."

She looked at me with large, fearful eyes as she turned her head to look at Elizabeth. "I'm…"

"You're what?" Elizabeth asked gently. "You can say it."

"I'm not sure I can."

My heart fell as I heard those words. I hoped we were getting through to her, but a five-minute conversation wasn't going to be enough to change her world.

"But you can," Elizabeth encouraged as if talking to a sister. "I know you can. I can see it in you. You are stronger than Nolan gives you credit for."

"I wish I believed that," she said standing up to look out her window. "I just don't know if I can."

"You have to believe it," Elizabeth said getting up from the couch to stand beside her. "Look at the world out there, ready to be explored and enjoyed." She gently gripped Kendall's shoulders and twirled her around. "Now look at your world in here. This is not the world you were destined to live in. And it's definitely not the world Will deserves to grow up in."

I watched Kendall look around the living room and I hoped she saw a jail cell instead. I closed my eyes and prayed silently that Elizabeth was going to break through and show Kendall her life was more than living in these four walls.

I opened my eyes at the sound of a ringing cellphone.

"Hello," Kendall answered. "Yes, this is her." She didn't say anything else for a minute but nodded her head as she listened intently. Her eyes widened and then all the life escaped as she looked at me sitting on the couch. "Yes, I will be here. Thank you," she said ending her call as she looked at me suspiciously.

"How'd you know Will was going to be coming home today?"

CHAPTER 146

The jury watched as Finn Garrett concluded his methodological closing arguments stating Jennifer Ascot was a ruthless, cold-hearted, criminal who'd attempted to kill Elizabeth Hyde and Solomon Davis. He tried to drill into the jury's heads that Jennifer knew what she was doing when she entered Cooper and Veronica Hyde's home. He tried to paint a vivid picture where even a blind person could see the evidence and find the defendant guilty on all accounts.

Milo listened while Jennifer sat by his side. It was just the two of them at the defense table and he wondered if he could use Gavyn's untimely murder to his advantage. While he had tossed and turned through his light sleep the night before, he had tried to come up with ways of tugging on the jurors' heartstrings, but by the dawn, he had nixed the idea.

He knew he didn't need to use Gavyn's death to render the verdict he was searching for. All he had to do was lay out the evidence and witness testimony that he had purchased through various means of coercions and bribes. But the beautiful thing about his network, if anything was ever discovered, is that it would take someone with some keen intellect to trace the fraudulent testimonies back to him.

Finn took a seat as Milo rose to attention. He smiled at the jury and began his final performance of this show.

"Mr. Garrett did a great job in trying to sway you to find my client, Ms. Jennifer Ascot guilty on the attempted murder charges. But he failed to remind you that we agree with those charges. We agree she trespassed into her long-time friend's home and tied up her sister. We agree with the police officer's accounts of the events of her torturing the defenseless woman who was just at her sister's home preparing a lovely dinner. We agree with all the evidence that supports these claims.

"However, there is one major difference. She was clearly not in her right mind when she committed these crimes. We have had multiple medical professionals with almost every type of medical degree state that Jennifer Ascot was mentally unaware of these offenses. Just imagine yourself finding out your brother was supposedly one of the killers from last October's murderous tirade. How would you react? Hearing all the crimes he committed without an ounce of remorse. And then to make matters worse, the police killing him in front of your very eyes before handcuffing you, thinking you are an accomplice to these crimes. Crimes she was acquitted of, by the way. But to hear all this damning evidence about your beloved brother would cause anyone to lose a sense of themselves. Now where do you think she would turn in her hour of need, but to her best friend?

"What caused her to go ballistic? We will never know because she doesn't even know. She was shot multiple times in the chest and barely survived. Adding this trauma to her pre-existing mental instability, there is no way we will ever know what was going through Ms. Ascot's brain during these horrendous crimes. Crimes I would suspect her to be remorseful of if not in a constant state of medication to control her emotional instability."

Milo looked at the jury and spoke to each one, looking in each of their eyes and stating the names of each expert he questioned and their last remarks of Jenny's mental instability.

"But the most crucial testimony I want you to remember that Mr. Garrett failed to mention in his closing was the expert testimony of Dr. Hansel Burgg, who claimed under oath that Jennifer Ascot should not be found guilty since she was mentally insane at the time of the crimes. Mr. Garrett's own witness said these words. And yet, Mr. Garrett is still trying to persuade you to only look at the evidence he wants you to look at.

"But you can't do that. You have to look at *all* the evidence. No matter the surprises that Mr. Garrett didn't want you to remember. But thankfully, I remembered it. So when you deliberate, consider everything that has been said. Mr. Garrett wants you to find Ms. Ascot guilty with the majority of his evidence pointing in that direction. And I want you to find Ms. Ascot not guilty by reason of insanity. What if you throw out all the evidence that we gave you that supports our claim and only look at the testimonies we handpicked for you to hear that went against the verdicts we are seeking.

"That would mean there is only one testimony to fully examine. Dissect it. Take it apart. Look at the transcript with fresh eyes. Dr. Hansel Burgg is a brilliant psychologist with years of research and accolades. And he was the prosecution's witness who sided with our claim. That should tell you the truth of this case. That even Mr. Garrett's own witness couldn't support his guilty verdict."

Milo stopped and took a moment in front of the jury, lowering his head and leaning on the railings.

"In a perfect world Ms. Ascot would be locked up because she committed these crimes. But in a perfect world there wouldn't be any mental illness. You cannot convict my client for her mental handicap at the time of these crimes. That is both prejudicial and morally wrong. It seems everyone knows of someone who has had a mental breakdown or has been diagnosed with a mental illness. We ourselves may have had a mental breakdown when we have said things we didn't mean and it felt like we were having an out-of-body experience. This is just like that but on a larger scale. In good conscience you cannot convict Ms. Ascot on all these charges and send her to jail where she will not get the help she deserves. But if you find her not guilty by reason of insanity, she will get the medical help she needs to once again be a thriving member of our society.

411

"If you send her to prison, there is very little chance of her overcoming her mental instability. She needs good medical care with loving professionals to help her. Not punish her for a crime she would not have committed if she were in a better state of mind. Please, if she were your daughter, would you want her to go to prison if she was suffering? Or would you want her to get some help? I think you all know what the right answer is. And if you're not sure, just look at Ms. Ascot and consider what is best for her."

Milo walked away from the jury passing Finn while shaking his head at the prosecution table as if in pity.

Milo smiled because he knew shaking his head would not make the jury come back with the verdict he wanted any more than a fair trial would. But thankfully, Milo never played fair.

He always played to win. No matter what.

CHAPTER 147

Wint returned to the precinct with a clear conscience. He walked through the hallways with a smile on his face as he greeted his fellow police officers. Most smiled back, but a few turned their heads and whispered as he walked by. He didn't care what they were saying about him because he had the truth on his side.

He got to his desk and opened the cold case file Chief Johnson gave him to read through to see if there was anything the officer on the case had overlooked. He read the file like *The New York Times* bestseller as he quickly imagined himself at the scene of the crime in 1996. He found the crime scene picture of a husband and wife in their living room with their hands tied behind their backs and a gunshot wound to each of their heads. He was still in his trousers with a white-collared shirt and she lay with her teal dress past her knees.

He looked at the time their daughter Maddie had called the police when she came home after seeing a movie with friends and found them. 10:21 p.m.

The coroner's report stated someone had murdered them earlier in the evening, but the time frame wasn't definite. Wint shook his head, knowing how much technological advancements had helped in the last decade by narrowing times of death to within a couple of hours. In fact, based upon the old forensics of Jeff and Denise Gooding, they could have been murdered any time of the night.

Wint flipped through the pages of interviews from the neighbors and colleagues who stated that Jeff would usually leave work around 5:30 in the evening, and Denise would usually leave her job at 4:45 p.m. Wint looked through the pictures of the house, the living room, the kitchen, the bedrooms. Nothing seemed out of the ordinary.

He reviewed the medical examiner's findings including the stomach contents. He was often intrigued why stomach contents were extrapolated during cases, but he knew that even the smallest details in murder cases shouldn't be overlooked. It looked like Jeff had a turkey sandwich and Denise had a cobb salad. Wint moved past those details and examined the photographs once again.

The door didn't look like there was any forced entry, so either the Goodings knew their attacker or they were very trusting. He stared at the pictures once again and noticed a pot on the stove. He reread the file and noticed a brief sentence. "Looked like they were cooking supper when they were attacked from the pasta on the stove."

"So they were cooking," Wint said to himself as he quickly made a note that their times of death were probably earlier rather than later. He looked at the picture of the kitchen, but something didn't look right. If they were cooking pasta at six and they were not found until ten, then all the water should have been gone from the pot and the kitchen should have some smoke.

He looked through Maddie's interview but nothing was mentioned about the kitchen or supper. Only that she left for the movies around 6:15 after being picked up by her friend, Christine.

He was just getting ready to stand up and stretch when Chief Johnson walked through the door heading straight toward him. He leaned down and whispered in his ear.

"I just wanted you to know that they pled guilty."

Wint looked at Chief Johnson and then down at the cold case file. "That's strange. Who was it?"

Johnson looked at the file on Wint's desk and shook his head. "Not that. Your guys from last night."

"Collin and Jordan pleaded guilty?" Wint fist-pumped the air while Johnson didn't show any emotion.

"Good job, Cooper," he whispered once again and then turned and walked away.

Wint felt on cloud nine at that news that justice from a crime six months ago was finally righted. He grabbed his phone on his desk and saw he had a text message.

I need a favor, Solo requested.

Funny, I was going to ask you the same thing.

CHAPTER 148

"Have you ever thought about an event and hoped you dreamed about it?" I asked from my living room floor as Elizabeth sat on the couch behind me.

She looked at me like I was crazy, and that was how I felt when Wint asked me if I could try to dream tonight about a murder from years ago.

"Wint's working on a case and he needs some help."

"We're not genies," she said shaking her head as she played on her cellphone. "If we were, I would be thinking of lottery numbers every night."

"Really?" I looked back at her. "You're loaded as it is."

Elizabeth shrugged her shoulders without looking away from her phone. "You can't ever have too much money."

"Mm-hmm. Well, he's going to text us the details on the case and he wants us to read it and think about it before we fall asleep," I said as she looked up from her phone with an annoyed look. "Hey, I told him we would try. That's all I said."

"If that worked, don't you think we would have figured out some of our past recurring dreams quicker?"

"I don't know," I said not knowing what to say. "I told him we would try."

"Fine," she said rolling her eyes as she went back to scrolling.

"What are you looking at?" I asked as my phone started to ring. I looked down and saw it was Katrina Nelson. "Hey Katrina, how are you doing?"

She didn't answer immediately. "Not good." I could hear the lump in her throat commingling with her running nose. "They came by and took Will a little while ago."

Once again, I didn't know what to say. If this was yesterday, it would have sickened me that Will was returning to his unloving, selfish, drug addict mother. But today wasn't yesterday. I had seen Kendall's true character and her longing to protect her son the only way she knew how. To leave him somewhere until Nolan was in a better mood.

"I'm sorry, Katrina," I finally responded as I looked behind me and saw Elizabeth eyeing me suspiciously. "You and Phineas gave him love when he needed it the most."

"Phineas," Elizabeth snickered like a preschooler. "Who names a kid Phineas? I bet he wet his bed until he went to college."

"Elizabeth," I quietly scolded so Katrina couldn't hear.

"This is never easy, but it makes it better if you know he's going to a loving home," Katrina said as she tried to control her emotions. "I hope they know what they're doing."

I looked down and saw Will playing with some Legos on my living room floor, and I knew without a doubt child services was making a good decision.

"For some reason, I think Will is going to be okay," I smiled. Will never looked up when I said his name but continued to build using only the blue blocks as I built a multi-colored wall.

"You think?" Katrina asked as if my words were what she was needing to hear.

"Yeah," I said looking at the little boy sitting across from me. "Don't ask me why I think this, but I can see it. He's going to be safer now than ever before."

"I hope you're right," she said optimistically as I patted Elizabeth's leg showing her Will was scooting around so his crossed knee was touching my calf.

"Yeah," I smiled as I handed Will a couple of blue Legos that he eagerly took from my hand. "I'm usually right about things like this."

CHAPTER 149

Kendall sat on the couch in her living room watching the minutes on the clock slowly tick by. Nolan should be home any minute, and she was nervous. She closed her eyes and took a deep breath, hoping she wasn't making a deadly mistake.

She opened her eyes when she heard the door swing open and caught her boyfriend walking through with his blue mechanic overalls with grease stains on his chest.

"You're home." She stood up but didn't greet him with a kiss as she had been commanded to do each day.

He looked at her confused and then turned his head to see the stove empty. "Take a day off?" he gruffed as he stomped past the kitchen to his patched-up recliner. He sat down and leaned back as his feet lifted. "You've been here all day doing nothing it looks like."

"Nolan," her voice cracked as she teetered in place. "Will's coming home."

He scratched his bristly chin with his nails caked with a thin layer of grime and gave her a cunning smile as he sat up, placing his feet on the floor. "Did I say he could return?"

"Well," she feebly answered swaying uncomfortably by the television.

"Well, what?" he exploded. "Maybe you should read a magazine to learn a few things."

"But he's my son, Nolan. What did you think I was going to do?"

Nolan stood up and walked toward Kendall gritting his teeth like a wolf intimidating its prey. "I thought you were finally waking up and seeing him for what he is, but apparently you need to sleep on it a little while longer."

"Nolan, no!" she screamed as he backhanded her, throwing her to the ground. Her scream echoed through the apartment as Nolan reached down and grabbed hold of Kendall's black hair, pulling her body up from the ground. She reached up and clawed his hands as he menacingly laughed at her fragile attempts to cause him pain. With his free hand, he backslapped her once again, causing her eyes to roll back as she started to lose consciousness from his powerful blows.

"I could wring your neck and no one would care. And then," he stopped and laughed wickedly with fury in his eyes. "Then I'll do it to your dumbass son and leave you both out back for the garbage men to come pick up." He shook her stinging head, waking her up. "I want you to see this!" he shouted, almost spitting in her face. "I want you to see this and know who you chose over me! I want to see the look in your eyes as you realize you made a shitty mistake, bitch!"

"Hamburger! Hamburger!" she screamed at the top of her lungs.

"Hamburger?" he snickered as he continued to strain to lift her by her hair a few more inches off the ground.

Their bedroom door swung open and Nolan's eyes became alert as two uniforms jumped out with their guns pointed in his direction. "Let her go!" Officer Robbins shouted as he aimed his firearm at Nolan's chest. "Just back away!"

"You bitch!" he growled, looking at his chest and seeing two red dots dancing over it. He looked at the officers and yelled as he threw her down on the floor. He raised his hands in surrender, shaking his head in disgusted anger at the betrayal. Kendall fell back as tears flooded her eyes. "Whatcha going to do, bitch? How are you and your retard going to survive without me?"

Officer Robbins walked toward Nolan commanding him to shut up as Officer Clinton kept watch behind the recliner with his gun ready to shoot if Nolan tried anything.

"You believe this bitch over me?" Nolan scathed as he stared at Kendall trembling in a curled position. "You have nothing on me!"

Robbins grabbed Nolan, turning him around. "We have nothing? Man, you threatened to kill her and her kid."

"That's your word against mine! And people don't trust you guys anymore!"

"We have body cam," Robbins said flatly. "We got your word recorded." Robbins slapped the handcuffs on the disgusting, vile man and read him his rights as Officer Clinton rushed to Kendall to check on her.

"Are you okay?"

She nodded through her tears as he gripped her arm and lifted her to sit on the couch.

She watched Officer Robbins walking behind Nolan as they passed by the kitchen. She took a deep breath and watched her nightmare get led away in handcuffs.

"You're going to be okay," Officer Clinton assured her. Then he heard a scuffle outside the door as a woman shouted.

"Solo!"

CHAPTER 150

Elizabeth stood in the shadows under a darkened light as she watched Nolan being led out of his apartment by Officer Robbins.

Nolan whispered something to Robbins.

"What'd you say?" Robbins asked, leaning his head down.

"Dumbass," Nolan hissed, headbutting him on the side of his head. Robbins moaned in pain. Nolan didn't let up, throwing his body into Robbins, smashing him against the wall.

"Solo!" Elizabeth screamed as Nolan turned to see her.

"Bitch!" he hissed running around the corner with his arms still handcuffed behind his back.

Elizabeth kicked off her flats and ran behind him. "Solo!"

Solo exited his apartment and saw a stocky man running his direction with a last resort as his only hope.

"Stop!" Solo shouted as Nolan continued to run.

Solo planted his feet like a linebacker and ran toward Nolan. Elizabeth watched as it looked like a deer about to run smack into a grizzly bear.

Nolan slightly chuckled with crude slurs as he torpedoed toward Solo's skinny frame, but Solo didn't stop.

Solo continued to run, screaming like an attacking warrior.

"Watch out!" Elizabeth screamed as Nolan was within a few feet of Solo.

Solo kept his body low like a sprinter taking off, running in the middle of the hallway as Nolan played the game of chicken running head on. Elizabeth heard a pair of feet from behind her as Officer Clinton came running out of Kendall's apartment.

She watched as Solo grunted with all his might when his left shoulder collided with Nolan's chest. Solo groaned at the impact as Nolan's balance shifted. His elbows expanded like butterfly wings as

Solo hooked his right arm through Nolan's left one. Solo gritted his teeth, planting his feet firmly in the center of the hallway, using Nolan's off kilter stance against him.

Solo flung the giant around, face planting him into the wall.

Nolan moaned in pain as he lifted his face from the wall, spitting out a few pieces of paint chips.

Officer Clinton grabbed Nolan as Solo untangled his arms from the larger man's elbow.

"You okay?" Clinton asked.

"I will be." Solo winced with a shallow breath as Elizabeth came up from behind.

"Who's the pansy now?" she shouted to Nolan, but instead of that word she used the same slur Nolan had just screamed at Solo. "Pansy."

"Elizabeth," Solo chuckled.

"What? I'm not afraid of that word," she defended as she looked Nolan in the eye. "And if their body camera footage didn't pick up your vulgar threats, my phone did," she winked holding her phone up for Nolan to see. "Enjoy prison. Maybe you'll be someone's pansy there."

"Elizabeth!" I scolded. "Language."

She shrugged as Robbins came hobbling up the hallway.

"You okay?" Elizabeth asked. "He hit you good in the soft spot."

Robbins rubbed his head and tried to shake off the pain. "I'll survive."

The two officers each grabbed one of Nolan's arms and walked him toward the exit as Kendall came running down the hall.

"How are you doing?" Elizabeth asked, grabbing hold of Kendall's hand.

Kendall didn't answer, but her eyes showed the look of appreciation. "Where's Will?"

"He's safe," Solo answered, pointing her inside his apartment.

"You did a good job. I was actually impressed," Elizabeth said with a nod and a shocked expression as she patted Solo's shoulder, causing him to flinch in pain. "You need some ice and an aspirin?"

"I need an x-ray," Solo winced once again with a slight smile. "And then some ice, an aspirin, and maybe a stiff drink."

"You, a stiff drink?"

"I've never been in a hurricane before, but I think I could drink one right now."

"Hurricane Solo," she grinned. "You were like a category two with that move."

"Only a two?" he groaned. "It felt like a five."

"It may have felt like a five." She stopped and scrunched her nose. "But it only looked like a two. Try harder next time, stud."

Elizabeth walked into Solo's apartment as he coughed, still leaning against the hallway.

"I was serious about the x-ray."

"Really?" she asked with wide eyes.

Solo nodded his head. "Really."

Elizabeth ran in and grabbed her keys, giving Kendall instructions for while they were gone. "You know," she said as she closed the door and wrapped Solo's right arm around her neck. "This is becoming a common occurrence."

"Not that common," Solo huffed.

"Please. In April you had to have the paramedics take you."

"Jenny stabbed me multiple times!"

She rolled her eyes. "And then once again in July, the paramedics had to take you."

"I was in a bomb blast!"

"And then now."

"Once again, I was in a bomb blast."

"Nolan? A bomb?" She chuckled helping Solo down the stairs.

"He was almost twice my size!" Solo exploded. "Twice. My. Size."

"Really? You're going to give him that much credit? He looked like he was filled more with candy than dynamite."

"That fat still hurt when it hit me," Solo smiled as Elizabeth started to laugh.

"Sounds like a nice tagline for a t-shirt," she billowed. "Jiggle. Jiggle."

CHAPTER 151

Wint walked into his cozy home and immediately smelled his wife's favorite vanilla-lavender candle. He entered the living room and found his wife snuggled under a blanket sitting with her laptop.

"How was your day?" he asked, leaning down and kissing her on her lips.

She moved her laptop to the coffee table and offered her husband a warm seat beside her. "It was interesting."

"Interesting good or bad?"

She thought for a second and smiled. "After Dad called me, I did a little research."

"And?" Wint sat down sliding his wife's legs on top of his thighs to massage her feet.

She reclined on the couch and stared up at the ceiling. "I thought I wanted to work alone. To focus on what I wanted to practice." She sat up to look Wint in the eyes. "But after Gavyn called me yesterday, I realized I don't really enjoy working alone."

"Then hire someone."

She leaned back, combing her fingers through her hair. "Then after Dad threatened me about stealing one of his employees..." She smiled wickedly with an alluring laugh. "I called her."

"Who?"

"I really didn't work with her much since she's only been there a few years, but from what I remember, she was intelligent, tactical, hardworking, and didn't take lip from anyone."

"Well, working for your dad, she has to be."

"Yeah, that's why I called her." Veronica rose up once again jittering in excitement. "And she's actually considering it."

"Who wouldn't want to work for you?" Wint grinned his All-American boy smile as he looked longingly at his wife.

"You have to say that," she said falling back onto her pillow.

"If I didn't mean it, I wouldn't have said it."

Veronica closed her eyes and enjoyed her husband's tender touch in the ticklish regions of her feet. "So, the chief's on your side?" she asked as she started to giggle.

"What's so funny?" Wint pretended to not know as he continued to slide his fingers across the soles of her feet.

Veronica squirmed like they were back in college, kicking her feet playfully, while still wanting to be touched.

"Yeah, he's on my side," Wint nodded as his hands started to move up from her feet.

"Who cares about Young?" she asked, closing her eyes and relaxing a little more with each touch.

"Young and maybe a few others," he said not paying much attention to the conversation as he adjusted his body, moving his head towards hers. He hovered his body over hers as she opened her eyes, biting her lower lip.

"To hell with Young," she grinned wrapping her arms around his neck. "You'll always be my favorite cop."

He lowered his body onto hers and began kissing her neck. She leaned her head back, allowing him to take control of her as she ran her fingers through his hair. "I love you, Winston."

He looked up with a grin and knew no matter what happened at work, he was happier than ever at home.

CHAPTER 152

Tchaikovsky's Symphony No. 6 played quietly over the intercom speakers throughout the house, allowing the woodwinds and strings to bring a tranquil mood in the darkened den.

Milo sat at his desk with the light from a laptop illuminating his face. He sat motionless watching the screen as the music's pace started to increase as if the musicians were running a race to see who could finish the symphony first. He smiled as he looked longingly at the screen, resting his elbows on the leather-topped desk.

He opened a drawer and pulled out a cigar and lighter. A small flame appeared as he puffed on his cigar, allowing the taste to be his appetizer for the dinner that was being prepared by his chef.

He moved the mouse, clicking on another file as he wanted to replay some of the highlights of the week.

The video was like a photograph of a bookshelf in an office.

"Dr. Weaver was siding with me and then he just changed," Finn said.

"Call Dr. Hansel Burgg," Jill Stapleton said.

"Who's that?"

"A psychologist…who I am dating."

"I didn't know you were dating anyone."

"And no one needs to know. He's getting a divorce and we are trying to keep it hidden until it's finalized. Just give him a call. Tell him you know me. You have the medical records from Dr. Weaver, so send those to him. I would go back to getting her found guilty on attempted murder. Stick it to Milo and Jenny."

Milo smiled at that comment as he blew out a ring of smoke. "You couldn't stick it to me when you had a chance, Ms. Stapleton. And now you expect your little helper to do your heavy lifting?"

"You think?" Finn asked.

"So are we done here? Veronica, we're done now," Jill said as the laptop started to move.

Veronica came into view as she sat down picking up her laptop on Jill's desk. "I hope you get her."

"Aren't you supposed to be for your client?" Finn laughed as he could partially be seen exiting from the camera's view.

"Former client!" Veronica shouted. "Former!"

"Tsk tsk, Mrs. Cooper," Milo hissed as he watched the spying video Pyotr had forwarded to him earlier in the week. He smiled at the hours he had enjoyed watching various videos from Veronica's hacked laptop. He smiled even more knowing how he came to discover this little gem last July when they ransacked Mikhail's apartment and discovered his collection of spyware.

He clicked on another file sent yesterday of a conversation just an hour before Gavyn's death when he had called Veronica.

"But I was forced to take the case. My hands were tied," Veronica started as she leaned back in her chair in her office.

"And you think I chose this? You know Luther. When he assigns cases, you don't say no. You just ask when," Gavyn said.

"Gavyn, what's Milo doing this time?"

Milo smiled at the sound of his name. "Why do you think of me so often, Veronica?" He stopped as his smiled broadened. "Envious?"

"One second," Gavyn answered.

Milo watched as she disappeared from the screen as she did a few yoga stretches.

"Sorry. I didn't know if someone was standing outside the elevator and I couldn't take any chances."

"Elevator? At the courthouse?" Her voice piqued.

"No, at work."

"Gavyn! Dad has the entire office bugged. He knows everything that is going on there. Do you seriously think anywhere is safe in that

428

prison? You can't imagine how many hidden cameras he has in the bathrooms, let alone in an elevator."

Milo laughed as he watched the screen. "Veronica, if you only knew."

"Oh Veronica, I'm royally screwed now."

"Just breathe. He doesn't watch the tapes unless he suspects something."

"How about threatening to fire me? Would that warrant a reason to watch me and listen to everything I say?"

"Jeez."

"That's the reason I'm calling. Do you know of any firms that are looking to hire anyone? You talk to a lot of different people. Have you heard anything?"

"Gavyn, are you sure about this? He's not very forgiving when you walk away."

"He basically told me I was fired five minutes ago," he shouted as a car door slammed shut. "I'm just trying to beat him to the punch."

Milo shook his head watching the video. "I guess his punch wasn't what you needed to worry about, son."

"There are a few places that are hiring, but they probably can't compete with the pay or benefits," Veronica added.

"Some pay is better than none," Gavyn responded with a laugh.

"That is true."

"How's your place going? Looking for another attorney?"

"Are you wanting to get us both killed?" Veronica laughed. "Dad wouldn't have a second thought about getting Milo to whack us."

"Tsk tsk, Veronica," Milo said shaking his head and puffing on his cigar. "That is something to consider in the future. But for now, I will keep you safe."

"I'm serious. You're a good attorney. And I am too. We could do this."

"Gavyn, slow down."

"Seriously, think about it. What kind of law have you been specializing in since you left?"

"I've basically been handling business clients, trying to stay away from criminal trials. I'm finished with defending murderers and repeat offenders just because they can pay."

"Sounds like you could use someone to handle estate planning."

"Gavyn, really. You need to slow down. This is a big decision you are considering."

"Veronica, I've been thinking about this most of the week when I'm trying to fall asleep. We could do it. I can swoon the older ladies with my charm and you could get the men. I'm not opposed to using my good looks to draw up business. And I'm pretty sure you have a way of getting the men to give you a second glance. And then. Pow! We show them we have the knowledge to back it up."

Milo nodded his head eavesdropping on this little scheming plot as he saw the potential in the two. But sadly, the potential faded like his smoldering cigar.

"I don't play that card, Gavyn."

"You don't, but you should," he laughed. "We both should."

Milo nodded his head with Gavyn. "Yes, play the cards you were genetically handed, Veronica." Milo closed his eyes and listened to the dialogue as if listening to one of his favorite old Russian radio programs as a child.

"Yeah. I wish I could forget. I'm fine with letting the strings knot and strangle her. But knowing Milo, he has some magic pair of scissors that will save her from a horrendous death. Have I told you how much I hate him?" Veronica asked staring over the laptop.

"Why do you hate me so much?" Milo smiled as he leaned his elbows back onto his desk. "Tell me more, child."

"See, another reason we should partner because I hate him too. We already have something to bond over. Our number one enemy."

"Oh, dear Gavyn," Milo said shaking his head. "If only you could bond with her."

"Don't forget Luther. He's my number one."

"Your family is definitely not normal," Gavyn sighed.

"Sure you want to get closer to the drama? Because it can kinda suck you in if you don't watch out."

"I'm used to watching my back."

Milo paused the video and rewound Gavyn's last sentence and replayed it.

"I'm used to watching my back."

Milo stopped the video and grinned at those hauntingly ironic last words.

"Sir, your dinner awaits," his headmistress said after knocking on the door.

"Thank you, Ekaterina. I will be right there," Milo answered as she bowed her head and exited his room. He laid his burning cigar in his ash tray to finish later. He still had a few more videos Pyotr had forwarded for him to watch. He finished his shot of vodka and placed the glass back into his desk drawer before he stood up and stretched his aging legs. He looked out his window and saw the autumn breeze freeing some of the leaves from the trees in his backyard. He enjoyed the changing of seasons he experienced by living in Washington, D.C., but he missed the brutal winters of his homeland. They had taught him strength and determination. Without the freezing long nights of walking the dark streets of Leningrad, he wondered if he would be where he was standing today.

He turned around and closed the laptop causing the room to go black. He smiled. Even if he was raised by the beaches of Sochi, he knew he would still be where he was now. Wintry nights may have taught him some things, but his ruthlessness was what made him Milo.

CHAPTER 153

Elizabeth parted the curtain and walked into my emergency department room with two coffees in her hand, sipping one of them. "You gonna live?"

"My shoulder was dislocated," I said as she sat down with her two coffees. I reached out my good arm as she gave me a confused look.

"You don't drink coffee."

"But you got two. I thought one was for me."

She rolled her eyes as she looked down at her watch. "Solo, it's after nine o'clock. My good attitude vanished after sitting in the ER for two hours. You need me to have both of these." She sat down in the waiting room chair crossing her legs as she started to grin.

"What's so funny?" I asked, readjusting myself on the inclined bed.

"You thought you were dying," she smiled once again as she started to laugh.

"Once again, did you see how big Nolan was compared to me?"

"Oh, I see, white boy," she said glancing up and down at my shirtless torso.

"They said to wait here while they look over the x-rays."

"You could put your shirt on," she grinned. "It's not like you have something worthy of showing."

I looked down at my physique, which I didn't think was so off-putting. I reached toward the table beside my bed for my shirt when I felt an uncomfortable pull in my chest. My face winced in pain as I retrieved it.

"Oh, you're fine," she said as she continued to sit and sip her coffee flipping through the channels on the remote.

I tried to raise my arm over my head but had a little difficulty getting my arms through the holes. "Do you mind?"

"Really?" she huffed, setting the remote control down at the foot of my bed. "It's not like a car hit you."

"I think we should start referring to Nolan as Civic or Corolla."

"How about Pinto?" she laughed, helping me with my shirt. "That sounds really masculine."

"Pinto, really?" I pulled down my shirt as she went back to her chair trying to find something decent to watch while we waited. "I've been thinking."

"Jeremiah will be proud," she kidded.

"No, seriously. What if Kendall and Will move in with me?"

"Solo!" Elizabeth shook her head in amazement. "What made you think of that crazy idea?"

"Well, you heard her. She doesn't have a job, and she's going to need a place to live while she gets on her feet."

"No," she answered as she returned her attention to the television.

"But Will--"

"Solo, I know you mean well, but you just met the woman. You don't know her."

"But--"

"But nothing," she said turning to look at me. "I know you want to help every homeless dog you find on the street, but you're only one man. There are a lot of places out there for her to get help."

"But--"

"No buts. If you take her under your wing, she's never going to learn to stand on her own two feet. And that is what Will needs. A mom who will do whatever it takes to defend herself and him."

"But you don't see what I see."

"Oh, I see it," she nodded. "I see a man wanting to protect a defenseless woman. That's probably what Nolan saw at first too."

"I'm not Nolan."

"No, but she can't rebound to you for protection."

434

"I wouldn't be her rebound," I started. "It's not like that."

"No, but to her, you would be. Someone who will tell her want she can and cannot do." She stopped and folded her arms. "She doesn't need you, Solo. No matter what you think, she is strong enough to handle this on her own."

"But what if--"

"Why do men only see themselves as problem solvers and not enablers?"

"I'm not an enabler," I refuted.

She once again shook her head. "I know you don't want to see yourself in that way, but if you take them in, that's all you'll be doing." She stopped and walked over to my bed handing me the remote.

"You don't think she'd accept my invitation?"

"Oh, she'd accept it. There's no doubt. But that doesn't mean it's the right move." She sat down and sipped her coffee. "Tough love never feels good when you're being cut open, but you can't get to the infection without cutting it out sometimes. Your little bandage may make her feel warm and cozy, but eventually the gangrene of reliance will cause her life to rot."

"You're graphic tonight," I said, scrunching my nose at the gruesome picture.

"We're in an ER," she said shrugging her shoulders. "There's a man two doors down with his severed fingers in a cup of ice. Still feel like your bruised ego needs to be here?"

"It hurts," I playfully whined.

"It will hurt her more in the long run if you take her in," she said as a woman in scrubs walked through the curtain.

"Solomon Davis?" the woman asked while looking at a folder.

"Yes."

She shook her head as she pulled out the x-rays, raising them toward the light. "What hit you?"

"A Pinto," I answered as Elizabeth snickered.

"Well, you're lucky," she commented pointing at the image of my rib cage. "If it pushed a couple of your broken ribs a little more, it might have punctured your lung. And that would have been very painful."

"Broken ribs?" I asked in shock as Elizabeth rose from her chair. "What does that mean?"

"You won't need surgery, but you will need to take it easy for a couple of weeks. And if they aren't healing properly, then we may need to do something. But most of the time ribs will heal on their own."

"See, I told you I was injured," I said looking at Elizabeth who looked nervous.

Her tension passed. "Get off it. She said *if* your lung had popped it would have been painful. You just broke a rib or two. So, no more playing the superman card."

"Well, that is still painful," the doctor replied as Elizabeth hushed her.

"He doesn't need any more reason to make himself think he's a hero."

"I thought you said he got hit by a car."

Elizabeth rolled her eyes and started to tell the doctor the heroic deed I performed that night.

I just leaned back and regaled in the retelling of the events as Elizabeth used her storytelling gift to paint the crime scene with much more danger and intrigue.

"So you see, he doesn't need anyone else to tell him he's injured, because you're not the one who's going to have to wait on him tomorrow when he needs a banana peeled."

The doctor looked at me and then Elizabeth. "Did your vows not include the phrase 'in sickness and in health'?"

"Vows?" Elizabeth screeched. "We're not like that."

"Really?" the doctor asked. "You two act just like an old married couple."

"Old?" Elizabeth snapped. "Old?"

"Thank you, doctor. Can the old ball and chain take me home now?" I asked slowly getting off the bed as the doctor smiled and nodded her head.

"If you call me old one more time, I'll puncture your lung myself in your sleep. And then you'll know how it feels."

CHAPTER 154

Jenny couldn't sleep knowing this could be her last night in this jail cell. At the beginning of the trial she had hopes of Milo saving her once again from an incarcerated future behind bars, but she wasn't expecting him to give up so easily on her wish.

"Just trust me," Milo had whispered before she walked into the courtroom when it was just the two of them in the holding room.

"Trust you?" she'd asked, looking at him confused. "You're going to get me off again, right?"

"I'm going to do something even better than that." He'd smiled as he stood up to leave the room.

"What is better than my freedom?"

He'd turned around and mouthed, "Your disappearance."

Throughout the trial when she and Milo were alone, she would try to ask for some more information, but he would never tell. He would never give her a hint of his plan. She had often wondered if she had misread his lips. She had replayed the words in her head and tried different words.

Your appearance.

Your interference.

Your perseverance.

Your adherence.

Your forbearance.

She had experimented with the words many times, saying and repeating the indistinguishable phrase, putting her finger on her lips to feel the movement of the words.

Now she tossed in her uncomfortable bed with a two-inch mattress and replayed Milo's last words to her before they parted.

"You may not think this is what you want, but I know this is what will be best for you."

"You don't know what is best for me, Milo," Jenny had snapped as she'd paced around the small room until they transferred her back to her holding cell for the remainder of the jury deliberations.

Milo snapped his fingers, commanding instant respect and attention. "You have seen me in the last year showcase illusions to the jury like they were truths. Why distrust me now?"

"Because that is what illusionists do," she spit back. "They make you start to second-guess and distrust everything you know and see."

"But Jenika," he said carefully, "you're not watching the performance. You're the act, itself."

"What does that mean, Milo?" she huffed, placing her hands on her hips. "Stop talking in riddles and just answer the question."

"What question is that?" he asked standing to attention. "Why did I want to get a not guilty by reason of insanity? Why did I not try to get a not guilty verdict on all charges? Why did I get all these medical professionals to say you were crazy? It's so you can disappear."

"What does that even mean?" She stomped her foot as she clenched her fist.

"You'll see," he smiled. "And then they won't." He turned to walk out the door as he stopped. "Just trust me, Jenika. And soon the world will forget about you. And then you will see this is the best thing."

She rolled onto her other side, curling her legs up as she wrapped herself in her worn-out blanket. She didn't know if she should trust Milo, but his words gave her something to meditate on for the night.

"Will you forget about me, Milo?" she asked herself as she smiled closing her eyes as she started to drift off to sleep.

"Because if you do, you'll remember me a second too late."

CHAPTER 155

When we got back to my place, the building blocks had vanished from my living room floor. Elizabeth helped me to my bed and tried to be compassionate.

"You don't have to stay here," I smiled as she sat at the foot of my bed.

"I'm not leaving here until the sun comes up. There's no telling what's hiding in your parking lot this time of night."

I watched her as she fell backwards on the mattress. "It's been quite a day," I said, moving my pillows along my headboard.

"A day?" she said, rising on her elbows looking toward me. "This whole week has been one of the worst. I think tomorrow we should just call it a day and let whatever we dream about happen."

I cocked my head and eyed her suspiciously. "I know you better than that."

"Fine, how about we just tell Wint and let him handle everything tomorrow? Better?"

I leaned my head back, trying to find a comfortable position to recline. "Oh, I forgot to tell you. I got a text back from the realtor."

"The realtor?" she asked confused. "I didn't know you contacted a realtor."

"Well, Ruth's realtor."

"And?"

"Well, they countered a little more than I bid." I stopped as I tried to sit up. "Is it called a bid when you are buying a house?"

"An offer, Solo. It's called an offer." Elizabeth rolled from her side onto her stomach, resting her chin on her hands. "And?"

"Well, I'm not sure. What if I'm not supposed to move now that Kendall and Will are here?"

"Solo, you are not God," she huffed. "Did you like the house?"

"Yeah."

"Can you see yourself living there?"

"I really liked that porch swing," I grinned, knowing it got on her nerves.

"You and your porch swings." She shook her head frivolously. "I hope Ruth takes that porch swing when she moves or I'll burn it myself."

"No!"

"You know you can buy a freakin' porch swing. Chill."

I leaned back and started to daydream about living in that house. "I really liked it. I don't know why, but it just felt right."

"Then you know what to do," she said as she pulled one of the pillows I was propped up on, causing my body to fall back.

"Ouch."

"Oh, come on, be a man."

I leaned up and smiled. "Woman, fix me some supper."

She rose from the bed and stood up.

"I'm kidding."

She grabbed the pillow and started walking my direction. "I think I could actually smother you in your sleep." She looked down at the pillow in her hands and felt the thickness. "I wonder if anyone would hear you scream," she said before she quickly answered. "Nah, because no one came out to help this afternoon when Pinto tried to escape."

I nodded my head. "Thanks for the heads-up. I'll sleep with one eye open tonight."

She threw the pillow back at the foot of my bed and stretched and looked at her watch. "I'm starving. You hungry?"

"You don't have to cook me anything."

"Who said anything about cooking?" She pulled out her phone and looked at the nearby restaurants that delivered. "How about some Mexican? Talking about Pinto has got me hungry for a burrito."

"Sounds good to me," I said, leaning back as she looked through the website to find a menu to real aloud to me.

"Oh, pork ribs," she oohed. "I bet you'll want them tonight."

"I'll pass on the ribs," I said pursing my lips. "That's a little too close to home tonight."

"Fine, I'll order your lousy chimichanga."

The room slowly spun as the various people in the courtroom came into view. Judge Otto sat on the bench as the image revolved showing each member of the jury sitting quietly and looking straight ahead. The room slowly spun like a merry-go-round as Finn Garrett stood to attention as all eyes in the crowd behind him were wide open. The image spun to a table where Milo and Jenny were standing.

The image started to zoom in on those two as Judge Otto spoke to the jury regarding their verdict.

"Has the jury reached a unanimous verdict?"

"We have, Your Honor," a woman's voice answered.

The image continued to zoom closer to Milo and Jenny standing with their hands to their sides. They each looked solemn like a black-and-white portrait during the Civil War.

"We find the defendant not guilty by reason of insanity."

These words echoed as Milo and Jenny remained frozen except for their blinking eyes. Mile smiled before he turned to Jenny and whispered in her ear, but she never flinched. She remained transfixed, staring straight ahead, aloof and heartless.

"Trust me," Milo said in a thick Russian accent as it faded into silence.

The scene started to spin faster showing the entire courtroom once again until the image blurred in a spectrum of colors. The blended colors started to settle, forming a clear image of a family portrait on the wall with a husband, wife, and teenaged daughter.

"What's your problem?" a girl yelled in the distance.

"Our problem?" an older woman shouted. "Our problem is ever since you started seeing Dylan you have been lying to us."

"Don't blame this on Dylan," the daughter hissed.

"He's not good enough for you, Maddie," the father's voice resounded forcefully, yet lovingly.

"Not good enough for me? You don't know him like I do."

"You need to call him and tell him you are staying in tonight," the mother said as the sound of clanking pots and pans filled the background.

"No!" the daughter screamed.

"Don't shout at your mother," the father said raising his own voice.

"You can't stop me!"

"We are your parents and you have to do what we say!" the father yelled.

"I wish you were dead!" Maddie screamed stomping down the hallway, slamming her door shut. The sound of telephone buttons being pushed muffled through the crying. "Dylan, my parents say I can't go."

"You can't go? Why?"

"They want to keep me locked up and away from you," she cried.

"Oh, baby, just sneak out."

"That won't work. They'll find out. They're probably listening to me right now through the door. And then I'll be grounded for life." She continued to sob. "I wish I didn't have any parents to listen to. I wish my parents were as cool as yours."

"Do you mean that?"

"Yeah," she sniffled.

"I'll be there in fifteen minutes."

"No, Dylan! They won't listen to you!"

The phone call ended and the dial tone beeped, prompting her to hang up.

"Do you think she'll forgive us, Jeff?" the mother asked over the sound of water boiling on the stove as the image continued to show the smiling family portrait.

"She's just going through a phase."

A doorbell rang.

"Who's that?" she asked as the sound of pasta falling into the bubbling water was followed by a pair of footsteps walking away.

The sound of a door opened.

"Dylan, Maddie's not going out with you tonight," Jeff said.

"Oh, really?" Dylan said as a door closed.

"Dylan, put that down. Dylan! Stop it!"

A gun shot went off and blood splattered on the family portrait.

"Jeff?" the woman shouted followed by the sound of running feet. "Jeff!"

"Denise," Dylan said as a door creaked open.

"Maddie!" Denise screamed as another gun shot fired and more blood hit the family portrait.

"Dylan! What'd you do?" Maddie screamed as it changed to tearful cries. "What did you do?"

"You said you didn't want them anymore," he answered coolly. "Here, tie up your mom. I'll get your dad. Then we can go to the movies."

"The movies?" Maddie screamed. "You just killed my parents!"

"I love you, Maddie. I did it for you."

"How could you kill them?"

"You wanted me to."

I sat up, temporarily forgetting about my injury until I felt the tenderness in my chest. I looked at my alarm clock. 2:46 A.M. I quickly grabbed my phone and texted Wint.

You're not going to believe it, but I dreamed about your case. Dylan killed them. Maddie's boyfriend at the time killed them.

I leaned over to put my phone on my bedside table but accidentally knocked off the lamp. I looked down, assessed the pain in my ribs, and knew it could wait until the morning.

CHAPTER 157

"What are you doing in here?" Elizabeth asked, standing in the doorway.

"I was texting Wint about my dream and knocked over my lamp," Solo said as he struggled to sit upright in his bed.

"What did you dream?" Elizabeth asked. She didn't take a step forward into the room, but remained by the door.

"The boyfriend did it."

"Did what?"

"Wint's case," he grinned enthusiastically. "Before I went to sleep, I prayed for God to show me what happened. And I actually dreamed it."

"That's never happened for me before."

"Me neither, but it did tonight."

"Any other dreams?"

"Jenny is going to be found not guilty by reason of insanity."

"Hmm," she grunted. "Anything else?"

"Anything else?" he reacted. "Once again, Jenny isn't getting the punishment she deserves!"

"Life's not fair," she answered as she started to close her eyes.

"Did you dream anything?" Solo asked, looking awake and ready to talk.

"No, nothing yet," she lied. "Talk to you in the morning."

She walked away from Solo's room and went back to the couch and sat wide-eyed as she had been for the last thirty minutes reliving her vivid dream.

She wanted to pretend she didn't dream it, but she couldn't forget it. And what's worse, she couldn't ignore the feelings she had during the dream.

"I love you," she had said in her dream as she wrapped her arms around Solo's neck, kissing him on the lips.

And he kissed her back.

She sat frozen as confusion circled around her while she recalled the multiple times this week someone had commented about their romantic relationship.

"We are just good friends," she said quietly as she looked down the hall to his bedroom. "Just friends."

Suddenly images of Solo playing blocks with Will flooded her mind as she recalled sitting on the couch watching the two. That memory faded to a shirtless Solo sitting on the hospital bed, which had caused her heart to beat a little faster. She'd always kidded him about his looks because she thought of him more like a gawky brother than anything romantic. But his firm chest had seemed appealing tonight. Lastly, the image of Solo running toward Nolan to stop a man twice his size flooded her vision. His heroic deed was something any woman would want a man to do. Fight for her. And she knew Solo would fight to the death for her.

She closed her eyes as she tried to persuade herself that the dream was just a release of romantic tension and not anything specifically about Solo.

She opened her eyes and chanted her phrase like a creed.

"We are just good friends."

"We are just good friends."

"We are just good friends."

We are just good friends.